Fifty True Mysteries of The Sea

Fifty True Mysteries of The Sea

Edited by John Canning

SD

STEIN AND DAY/*Publishers*/New York

First published in the United States of America in 1980
Copyright © 1979 by Century Books, Ltd
All rights reserved
STEIN AND DAY/Publishers
Scarborough House
Briarcliff Manor, N.Y. 10510

Library of Congress Cataloging in Publication Data

Main entry under title:

Fifty true mysteries of the sea.

British ed. published in 1979 under title:
50 strange mysteries of the sea.
Bibliography: p, 461
Includes index.
1. Adventure and adventurers — Addresses,
essays, lectures. 2. Curiosities and wonders —
Addresses, essays, lectures. 3. Seafaring life
— Addresses, essays, lectures, I. Canning, John,
1920
G525.F494 1980 001.9'4'09162 80-5498
ISBN 0-8128-2734-1

Contents

Editor's Note

From earliest time men have been irresistibly drawn to the sea. It was a storehouse of food and many other precious natural products, it was the road leading to the unknown, it was the necessary pathway for trade, it was in itself an unknown and mysterious element. In its moments of repose it could be idyllic and comforting; in its periods of anger awe-inspiring and the most searching challenge.

It was both benign and cruel; the medium which had first nurtured life and the executioner which could violently take it away.

Man's destiny has always been linked with the sea, and he has taken to it in craft ranging from the simple coracle to the *Queen Elizabeth II*. He has gained much from his voyagings but he has had to pay a heavy toll: and once the enigmatic waters closed over their victims they were very reluctant to give up their secrets.

Sea mysteries exercise a continuing fascination. Partly this is due to the interest aroused by unsolved mysteries of any kind, and most of the stories in this book are of such a character. But the attraction stems also from the sea itself, whose eerie depths conceal so much which some time in the future they might be forced or persuaded to reveal.

One wonders whether one day divers will set foot on the great wreck of the *Waratah*, transformed by marine growths into an unearthly apparition, and be able to determine why she vanished on that July day in 1909 as if off the face of the earth.

Fantasy takes another turn: could treasure-seekers recover the riches of Spanish galleons sunk in the Caribbean or around the coasts of Britain as the ingenious Kip Wagner is harvesting the gold and jewels of the 1715 Plate Fleet off Florida?

Could the sea yet provide a late postscript on the fate of Commander Crabb and the passengers and crew of the *Joyita*?

But the sea is a living entity as well as a tomb. What more will its shifting patterns continue to reveal of the strange cities near the Bahamas which some observers believe to be Atlantis? Again, will it one day disgorge an antediluvian monster? Let the cynics take pause here and think of the coelacanth.

And as well as its wrecks and human victims, does the sea overlie sinister magnetic vortices such as the area which has come to be known as the Bermuda Triangle?

Some matters, such as the haunting of a U-Boat during the First World War and the alleged return briefly to his home in London of an Admiral killed that same day in the Mediterranean will never be resolved and will remain forever a source of speculation and argument. Others would be incredible if they had not actually occurred, such as the horse that "swam" to the Grand National.

Like the sea itself the mysteries connected with it have a myriad moods and I hope we have captured a fair sample of them here. Certainly it has been a task which the editor and team producing the book have greatly enjoyed. We hope that readers too, sailors and landlubbers alike, will find entertainment and diversion in its pages.

John Canning

Disappearances

WHERE IS THE *WARATAH*?

The *Waratah* ... In some families soon after the First World War this was a sinister word, along with the Huns and their Kaiser, Bolsheviks and "bolshy". Someone might say, for instance: "Sea travel is perfectly safe these days", whereupon from the head of the table would come: "Ah, but remember the *Waratah*!" Younger members would then realize that *Waratah* was a ship and something dreadful had happened to her. But what, and when? Inquiries would merely elicit silence and a change of subject. It was thought inadvisable to plant needless anxieties in the minds of children. After all, such a terrible story might never recur ...

The *Waratah* was, in fact, a ship that disappeared, entirely and completely, leaving not a stick behind, not a lifebelt, not so much as a pocket handkerchief, with all on board – 211 people. But this was not a Bermuda Triangle affair with overtones of the supernatural, or at least it doesn't seem like it. It is almost certain that she went down in a storm, capsized, rolled over with the finality of a coffin lowered into its grave, when all the hatches were battened down, all the passengers below decks, safe as they thought from wind and sea. And this was very odd, for the *Waratah* was no old lady of the ocean, creaking and rusted, but a brand-new ship of 9,340 gross registered tons on what was only her second round trip.

She had been built in 1908 for the Australia run at White-inch, Scotland, by a highly reputable and experienced firm,

Barclay Curle. Her owners, the Blue Anchor Line, already had
in service another ship, the *Geelong*, built to almost exactly the
same specifications. She was giving an excellent performance,
so when the passenger list opened for the *Waratah*'s maiden
voyage there were a great many applicants, 689 emigrants to
be exact, who were going to be accommodated in dormitories
in the holds, and 67 cabin passengers, all confident of a trust-
worthy ship. Even if they had been told – which they probably weren't – that the *Waratah* carried no wireless, they would
not have worried. Signor Marconi's invention was too recent
for that.

The maiden voyage to Adelaide, Melbourne and Sydney
was entirely uneventful. The emigrants, stowed like sardines in
the hold, no doubt longed for it to end, but in the first-class
lounge, amid the Edwardian luxury of fluted columns, ormolu,
aspidistras and plush, the other passengers felt as happy as in
London's Ritz, delighted with their "floating hotel".

The same might not have been said of the ship's captain,
Commodore Ilbery of the Blue Anchor Line. The report,
which he was almost bound to have made on the ship's performance during that first voyage, was never released by the
owners. But apart from this, it is almost certain that he was not
entirely satisfied with the *Waratah*, otherwise why – as some of
the crew noticed – should he have taken such trouble over the
balanced stowage of the cargo before the return voyage, as
though afraid it might shift and shifting even slightly endanger
the ship?

In preparation for the second round trip the liner was dry-
docked, surveyed by Lloyds and given a renewed A.1 certificate. Then, on 27 April, 1909, she sailed from London, this time
with only 193 emigrants and 22 cabin passengers. Again the
outward voyage passed without mishap and the weather was
kind, as it had been so far whenever the *Waratah* was at sea.
When the emigrants had disembarked the holds were filled
with cargo, 6,500 tons of hides, flour, wheat, oats and lead
concentrates. Only a few passengers were coming back to
England and, with the crew, they totalled 211.

The *Waratah* reached Durban safely and there one passenger
in particular, a Mr Claude G. Sawyer, got off the ship. He had
not intended to, he was booked through to London where his
wife was waiting for him, but on board he had had a dream
and the same dream, or nightmare, had repeated itself three

nights running. He dreamt he was leaning on the ship's rail, watching the sea, when suddenly from the depths arose the figure of a man in blood-stained medieval armour. In his right hand was a gleaming sword and in the left something that looked like a rag soaked in blood. As the dreamer watched the figure opened its mouth to speak. But no words came. Only the lip movements seemed to be mouthing the word "*Waratah!* . . . *Waratah!*" Then, as suddenly as it had come, it sank beneath the waves.

Was the figure a variant on the theme of Neptune, with a sword instead of the trident, and was the Sea God telling the dreamer that he meant to claim the *Waratah*? No one knows what exact interpretation Mr Sawyer placed on it, but of one thing he was certain. The dream was a warning to leave the ship and to him, convinced that something terrible was going to happen, it seemed an obvious duty to convey this to his fellow-passengers. But no one took him seriously and Sawyer with his tale of woe became almost a laughing-stock on board. "A knight in armour indeed! You've been reading too much Keats", they said, "or is it Hamlet?"

But mockery did not deter him and the evening of 26 July saw Mr Sawyer safely on shore, watching the *Waratah* with her dark hull, white upperworks and one broad blue funnel glide slowly out of Durban *en route* for Capetown, 800 miles away. As soon as she was out of sight he sent a cable to his wife, THOUGHT WARATAH TOPHEAVY LANDED DURBAN, and next day booked a passage home with the Union Castle Line.

Through the night the *Waratah* steamed steadily on, south-westwards along the South African coast through placid seas, with the sky a blaze of stars. Next morning, around six o'clock, she passed a tramp steamer, the *Clan MacIntyre*, which was heading in the same direction. The two ships identified themselves and exchanged greetings. "Pleasant voyage", signalled the tramp and the *Waratah* replied, "Thanks. Same to you. Goodbye."

That goodbye may have been the last word anyone received from her. But there is a doubt, for that same evening, around 9.30 p.m., those aboard the Union Castle boat *Guelph* spotted a liner five miles away sailing westwards in the opposite direction. Again signals were exchanged. But the other ship's lamp was so feeble that her name was not understood except possibly for the last three letters – TAH. For this reason the *Guelph*'s cap-

tain did not enter the incident in the log and it was only when
he reached Durban and heard of the latest shipping movements that he thought it might have been the *Waratah*. If it
had, it meant that the liner, with a normal cruising speed of
thirteen knots, had only covered seventy miles since she was
last sighted, in which case there must have been something
wrong with her engines.

That evening a sudden severe storm blew up and the *Clan
MacIntyre* found herself battling through mountainous seas and
gale-force winds which shredded the tops of the waves and
hurled them bodily against the ship. When at last she reached
Cape Town her captain expected to find the *Waratah* already
in harbour. But there was neither sign nor news of the larger
ship.

At this stage no one was particularly concerned. Smaller
craft had survived the storm, so why not the *Waratah*? The
Clan MacIntyre had not seen any distress rockets or wreckage
and this strongly suggested that the liner was still intact, drifting possibly after an engine breakdown or simply delayed as all
shipping had been during the last few days. She would turn up
soon, it was only a matter of waiting . . .

But a week passed and still there was no news, a situation
doubly frustrating in days before the possibility of air search or
long-range radio communication. On 4 August, one London
underwriter cautiously expressed the mounting anxiety. "Were
the *Waratah* a less fine steamer", he told the Press, "not the
same concern would be felt for her safety. But for a twin-screw
liner of over 9,000 tons, built by a first-rate firm last year and
sailing under good ownership, to be several days overdue is, of
course, an unusual event."

By now friends and relatives of the passengers were anxiously contacting the Blue Anchor Line's offices in Cape Town
and London, but the only information available was that a tug
was searching the route the *Waratah* had followed and two
naval craft would shortly be joining her, reinforced by the
cruiser *Hermes*. With this all concerned had to be content for
another five days while nautical experts propounded theories:
if the *Waratah* had broken down about half-way between
Durban and Cape Town, as seemed likely, she could have
been driven by the storm south-westwards and then east, in the
direction of the South West Indian Ocean Ridge, which was
two thousand miles away. If, however, her captain had taken

the opportunity to buy cheap coal in Durban and then stowed it on deck, as was sometimes done even in big liners, that could have unbalanced the ship and in a storm of that severity anything could have happened. If, on the other hand . . .

As on all such occasions, conjectures grew wilder as the days passed without solid news. Old men remembered other ships that for unknown reasons had vanished in the same area. A clairvoyant professed to see the *Waratah* strike a rock (where no rocks were) and go down. One newspaper ran a story of white children washed ashore in Swaziland and being cared for by natives, while, as a relief from the disaster theme, someone recalled that years previously a ship named the *Waikato* had been lost for months before turning up unconcernedly at Fremantle, Australia.

Meanwhile the searching ships had found nothing and serious anxiety began to be felt, a mood in which hope and despair could be triggered off by almost any false rumour or report. On 10 August it was said that a Blue Anchor vessel had been spotted far out to sea moving slowly towards Durban – and a ship did eventually heave in sight, but it wasn't the *Waratah*.

Next day came sensational reports from two ships sailing independently, the *Insizwa* and the *Tottenham*. Bodies had been seen floating in the water in an area roughly 350 miles southwest of Durban. One sailor aboard the second ship swore he had spotted a little girl in a red dressing gown, and his story was confirmed by the second mate who said the child, aged between ten and twelve, was wearing black stockings and a red cape complete with hood, not a dressing gown. And the captain? He did not agree. On hearing of the sighting he had put his ship about and closely inspected the objects. They were, he felt sure, the remains of sunfish or skate and that was why he had not put out a boat. Later, the seaman backed down on his story and thought that what he had seen might have been "a big roll of printing paper with a red wrapper round the middle".

As for the *Insizwa*'s report, her captain was quite sure he had seen bodies, "two clad in white, two in dark cloth", but he had not stayed to pick them up because his cargo had shifted and it might have been a dangerous operation in the heavy seas. Also, he had not wished to upset his lady passengers. His story upset quite a few people in officialdom, though, and a tug was

sent to comb the area – result, negative. Plenty of whale blubber and offal were seen, but no bodies. So then this captain,
too, began to doubt his own story and thought after all he
might have been mistaken, as some of his own officers had
claimed all along.

But soon another strange story was to break. In the afternoon of 27 July (the day when the *Waratah* had been sighted
by the *Clan MacIntyre*) another ship called the *Harlow* reported
that smoke had been seen above the horizon astern in a position where the *Waratah* might conceivably have been. Two
hours later, the masthead lights of the ship were just visible
and shortly afterwards the *Harlow*'s captain saw what he described as "two sudden flashes" in succession, the second of
which shot up a great height into the air. Yet he heard no
noise and noticed nothing more. Some of his officers thought
the flashes came from bush fires ashore, but the captain maintained they were connected with the ship.

If this was so and the ship was the *Waratah*, had she suddenly exploded and in that case why was no wreckage ever
found? Or did the flashes indeed come from ashore, or were
they simply lightning? Perhaps the stories of bodies and this
last one were merely illustrations of the psychological fact that
in stressful situations people can hypnotize themselves into
seeing things which aren't there.

By now, at any rate, wild fantasies had become positively
extravagant. Tales were bandied about of sea monsters over-
whelming the ship, of messages washed up in bottles, bits of
timber marked "SS *Waratah*", even of an attack by pirates. But
the cold fact was that after that possible sighting by the *Guelph*
on 27 July nothing of, and nobody from the *Waratah*, dead or
alive, had been positively identified.

An official inquiry was, of course, necessary, but owing to
the difficulty of tracing witnesses in Australia and Britain
whose opinion of the matter was worth hearing it took a long
time to set up and did not open before December, 1910, at the
Caxton Hall, London. Almost immediately, in the last days
before Christmas, the testimony of sailors, ship's officers,
former passengers, representatives of the shipbuilders and
owners began to concentrate on the question of the *Waratah*'s
stability.

Her late third officer, Mr Henry, was reported as saying that
on the very first trip to London after completion on the Clyde

he had been scared by her heavy rolling. Some passengers from the maiden voyage declared that Captain Ilbery, so they had heard, was definitely not satisfied with his ship and some stated she had rolled so heavily it had taken them ages even to drain out their bath water.

A sailor testified that the first officer, now presumed dead, when interviewing him for a job had warned him off the *Waratah*, saying "this ship will be a coffin for somebody", and a steward named Herbert who had also sailed in the sister-ship *Geelong* said the *Waratah* rolled much more severely, so much that a great deal of crockery had been smashed and planks on the promenade deck broke away from their bolts and moved about. An engineer who had been on the first trip had also been thoroughly alarmed. On the other hand, some witnesses said the ship had an easy roll.

That there was, nevertheless, some truth in these statements about instability and possibly a great deal was shown when a letter was produced at the inquiry from the owners to the builders. It had been sent after the maiden voyage and one sentence read: "We have consulted Captain Ilbery and he has been able to convince us that this vessel has not the same stability as the *Geelong*." Try as he might, the owner's representative at the inquiry could not explain away this remark and when questioned about a detailed report from Ilbery (which he surely must have made), he pleaded ignorance.

And there apparently the matter was allowed to rest. The stories about the floating bodies and the flashes of light, already largely discredited, were touched on and the interesting fact emerged that the *Waratah* was well equipped with lifeboats. But curiously enough, the court did not demand that the Blue Anchor Line produce its files. Perhaps it did not have the power. Equally, if it had, it is possible that the *Waratah*'s fate would no longer be so mysterious.

As it was, in February, 1911, after weeks of intermittent sessions, the court issued the somewhat lame conclusion: "The ship was lost in the gale of 28 July, 1909, which was of exceptional violence for these waters and was the first great storm she had encountered." As to the cause of the loss, not even a conjecture was added.

Somewhere, while all this was going on, and in the intervening years, the *Waratah* has lain on the sea bed, keeping her secret, perhaps for ever. Twice since those far-off Edwardian days the "Ship that Disappeared" has again hit the headlines. In the early 1950s, on a sunny day with flat-calm seas, a pilot of the South African Air Force flying near the coast saw, or thought he saw, a great ship lying wrecked beneath the water, and at once the *Waratah* came to mind. Flying back to base he reported his discovery and then returned to study the wreck again. But this time, perhaps because the sea was more disturbed, he could see nothing.

Then, in 1954, came another story, this indirectly from Jan Pretorius, a Boer who claimed to have seen the ship go down. Years before, he had told an Englishman by name Frank Price that on a day of violent storm, in July, 1909, he had been looking seawards when he saw a large ship wallowing close inshore. When he looked again it had gone. He had not told anyone at the time because he was an illicit diamond prospector and feared the publicity, and Price had kept the secret until he felt sure the old man was dead.

Both the pilot and Pretorius spoke of the ship being close to shore. Perhaps the *Waratah* really is there, waiting to be discovered, though "there" means almost anywhere along hundreds of miles of coastline. Meanwhile, her fate remains as it was pronounced seventy years ago at Lloyds of London when the Lutine bell, only sounded for a maritime disaster, was struck once, to signify that a ship had been lost, this time with all hands.

THE COMMANDER
CRABB AFFAIR

On 18 April, 1956, a Russian cruiser named the *Ordzhonikidse* accompanied by destroyers arrived at Portsmouth Harbour, bringing Marshal Bulganin, Premier of the U.S.S.R., and First Secretary Khrushchev on a courtesy visit to Britain. It was an important occasion. Anglo-Russian relations had recently been at a low ebb and the British Government under Sir Anthony Eden had strong hopes of relaxing tension.

On that same afternoon a stocky, 46-year-old ex-naval commander by the name of Lionel Crabb came down by train from London to Portsmouth and booked in at the small Sallyport Hotel in the High Street, to be joined later by someone who entered his name in the register as "Matthew Smith" but has never since been identified. It looks as though other men were already waiting for them as three days later, after a certain incident had taken place, the Chief of Portsmouth C.I.D. removed four pages from the register covering the first three weeks of April.

Crabb was an experienced frogman employed by the Admiralty Research Laboratory at Teddington and for outstanding service in the Second World War had been awarded the George Medal. He went out briefly that night with "Matthew Smith", then came back, went to bed and left early next morning, leaving behind some clothing, a swordstick which he always carried with him and his wallet. When "Smith" came down somewhat later he paid in cash for the two men and then left. Still in the early hours of that day Crabb put on his diving suit and slipped into the waters of Stokes Bay where the Russian ships were anchored. He was never seen again, at least not alive in Britain.

When friends became anxious they contacted all the sources they could think of to obtain news, but at this stage the press had no information and the Admiralty said at first no more than "he is dead". Then some newspapermen discovered about the pages taken from the hotel register and the story began to break as a nation-wide sensation.

Here was a well-known frogman, perhaps the most courageous and experienced in Britain, turning up at Portsmouth on the very day the Russian ships arrived, then diving and presumably dying in Stokes Bay where those ships were anchored. What had he been up to? Espionage, obviously. It was known that the Russian cruiser had a phenomenal turn of speed, also that she had secret devices for avoiding shoal water. Crabb had intended to examine the hull, that seemed clear, but then had been intercepted and killed, or else his oxygen supply had failed.

These conjectures were interesting, but it was the political background which made them sensational. What effect would the incident have on the Anglo-Russian talks, on the improved relationship which the Russian visit was intended to bring about? Espionage was perhaps understandable; failed espionage was quite another thing. On whose authority had Crabb made his dive, on the Admiralty's, the British Government's even? Early in May Russia sent a note to Britain asking for an explanation of the fact that a British frogman had been briefly seen on the surface near the Soviet ships and received the reply that the presence of the frogman in the vicinity of the ships, "in all appearance Commander Crabb, occurred without any permission whatever and Her Majesty's Government express their regret for the incident".

This attempt to disclaim all responsibility for the Crabb exploit was repeated in the House of Commons on the following day when, in reply to questions, Sir Anthony Eden stated: "It would not be in the public interest to disclose the circumstances in which Commander Crabb is presumed to have met his death. I think it necessary, in the special circumstances of this case, to make it clear that what was done was done without the authority or the knowledge of Her Majesty's Ministers. Appropriate disciplinary steps are being taken."

With this vague but tantalizing statement the Commons, and the public, had to be content – but for only a few days. Then rumours began to circulate, first that Crabb had been working for the American Secret Service and second, from the *Daily Telegraph*'s Bonn correspondent, quoting a West German newspaper, that Crabb was alive in Moscow's Lefortovo prison awaiting trial for espionage. Lastly, on 7 August, came a Reuter's message from Copenhagen that Russian sailors from the *Ordzhonikidse*, which was on a courtesy visit there, had been saying that on the cruiser's return voyage from England part of the ship's sick bay had been strictly cordoned off, suggesting that someone of importance was being held there, though who that person was none of them could say.

So matters rested for ten months until in June, 1957, came a sensational discovery. On a sandbank at the mouth of Chichester Harbour, twelve miles from Portsmouth, a frogman's rubber suit was washed up, and inside the suit was the headless, handless body of a man.

An inquest was opened at Chichester and postponed for a fortnight while attempts were made to identify the corpse. Mrs Margaret Crabb, his ex-wife, examined it but was unable to say definitely whether it was his or not though she did give the useful clue that he had hammer toes. A pathologist reported: "The state of the toes is not sufficiently abnormal to make any confident statement. There is no gross deformity." But the size of the feet and the height of the corpse did correspond to Crabb's and the rubber suit, with a neck seal instead of a hood, was of an unusual Italian type favoured by Crabb and sold to him in October, 1955, by a firm in Leatherhead.

At the resumed inquest further clues to identification were given by a naval friend who believed the underclothing on the body was typical of that worn by Crabb. Moreover the pathologist now referred decisively to "distorted big toes" and also to a scar on the left knee which another frogman witness claimed had originated in the war when he and Crabb had done underwater work together. Summing up, the Chichester coroner stated: "I am quite satisfied that the remains which were found in Chichester Harbour were those of Commander Crabb."

So it seemed the case was finally closed. Or was it? It had not escaped the notice of the Press and many other people that shortly before the body had been found three Russian submar-

ines had passed down-Channel on their way to Egypt. Had the
body been a plant, like the British wartime exploit of "The
Man that Never Was"? And if there had been a plant, what
did it signify and where was Crabb now?

The answer to this seemed to come, again sensationally,
when in November, 1959, what appeared to be an authentic
Russian *dossier* on Crabb reached the hands of a journalist, Mr
J. Bernard Hutton, a naturalized British subject born in
Czechoslovakia. In 1960 Mr Hutton published a book* giving the text of this file and claiming it had been smuggled
out by agents working behind the Iron Curtain. The text, of
about 30,000 words, contains a detailed record in the form of
signals and reports about Russian dealings with Crabb and
makes dramatic reading.

First on file is a report radioed by Captain Stiepanov of the
Ordzhonikidse to Moscow at 21.10 hours on 18 April, 1956, stat-
ing that a shore agent had reported Crabb's arrival at the
Sallyport Hotel. Crabb and another man who signed the hotel
register as "Smith" were under constant observation and the
Russian warships were on the alert.

A series of signals from Stiepanov to Moscow show what
happened next. At 8.24 a.m. on the 19th Crabb was spotted as
he approached the cruiser, Russian frogmen dived in after
him, captured him alive and took him on board "through the
air-lock door". When questioned Crabb refused to speak, even
to admit his identity, and Moscow then ordered him to be kept
drugged and unconscious in the sick bay. During the following
days while the Russian ships were still at Portsmouth, this rule
was relaxed and Stiepanov attempted to interrogate Crabb, to
no effect. The frogman lay or sat on his bed, refused food and
drink and said not a single word. In the end he had to be
forcibly fed.

This situation continued until after the ships left British
waters on 28 April. Then, late that night, came a surprise
signal from Moscow which read: "Helicopter will take prisoner
early 29/4/1956." In the file this is followed by a signal from
"Air Command Stettin" (100 miles N.N.E. of Berlin) and next
day by another from the helicopter itself, both giving an estimated time of arrival over the cruiser.

Early on the 29th Stiepanov reported to Moscow: "At 06.35
hours helicopter hovered over foredeck and lowered basket.

---

* *Frogman Extraordinary*, published by Neville Spearman, London.

Prisoner and his belongings were immediately transferred to this basket and hauled into hovering helicopter. At 06.36 hours, operation completed."

The helicopter is reported to have landed at Stettin at 08.03 hours – and, as we shall see, these times are significant – whereupon the still drugged and unconscious Crabb was bundled into another aircraft and flown first to Minsk and from there to a Moscow airport. At Moscow, regaining consciousness, he was taken by car to a Naval Intelligence Station where he was interrogated by "Investigation Judge Ivan Zhabotin". The file gives a transcript from the tape recording:

Zhabotin: Go on, eat, Commander Crabb. We want you to feel comfortable here. (63 seconds' silence) Don't sit here yawning and staring in front of you, Crabb. Eat, relax. (30 seconds' pause. Colonel Zhabotin orders in Russian over intercom telephone) Bring him some strong coffee to wake him up. (Continues in English) Do you admit that you are the British naval commander Crabb? (40 seconds' silence. Zhabotin continues) Now look here, we know everything –

Crabb (in a quiet voice): If you know everything, why do you ask me?

Zhabotin: Because we want to hear from you what you have to say.

Crabb: Well, I have nothing to say.

Zhabotin (in friendly voice): I would not advise you to take this attitude. We do not seek to squeeze secrets out of you. All we want is to have a friendly discussion with you so that we can re-check our facts. But if you persist in your foolish attitude I can assure you we have also ways and means of making you talk.

The interrogation continued for several more minutes with Zhabotin alternately threatening and cajoling. But all Crabb would finally admit was his identity and his attempt to examine the hull of the cruiser "out of purely personal interest" without orders from anyone.

He was then taken to the Lefortovo prison in Moscow and again interrogated in the hope of extracting an admission that he had worked for the Americans, but again with negative results. That was on 30 April. For the next eleven days attempts were made to break him down by subjecting him to a diet of stale bread and warm water with hard physical training for five hours daily, spaced at intervals – this combined with

sudden interrogations at odd hours of the day and night. Still
Crabb insisted that in Portsmouth Harbour he had acted as a
free-lance and had no connections with the U.S. Secret Service. These extracts from the transcripts are typical. A new
interrogator, Captain Nikolayev, is speaking:

Nikolayev: Are you ready to be sensible or are you determined
to continue as you have done up till now?

Crabb: I am determined to speak the truth.

Nikolayev: Will you now admit that you attempted to carry
out your underwater examination of the cruiser *Ordzhonikidse*
for United States Naval Intelligence?

Crabb: I can't admit to something which is not the truth.

And again, on 11 May, with Zhabotin as interrogator:

Zhabotin: You don't look at all well, Commander. Is there
anything I can do for you?

Crabb: No thanks. I am all right.

Zhabotin: Look here, your pride won't get you far – it won't
get you anywhere. I want to help you, if you will let me, but I
want at least some co-operation from you.

Crabb (firm voice): I'm afraid you're barking up the wrong
tree. I will never sign a false confession to save my skin.

On the same day, as threats were apparently ineffective, the
Russians decided to switch their approach and give Crabb
"favoured prisoner treatment". This included prison officers'
food and permission to partake in games on the prison play-
ground. This had some effect for on 22 May came the turning-
point in a macabre interview with "Investigation Judge Myaskov". During its course Crabb admitted that he had been
spying on the Russian cruiser, but refused to "buy his life" by
giving information about Allied naval secrets. After some spar-
ring Myaskov then suddenly came out with an offer for Crabb
to join the Red Navy as a frogman at a salary of £1,000 a year.
Crabb tried to stipulate that he would not be required to spy
on Allied ships, but Myaskov angrily rejected any provisos,
then, after threatening to have Crabb "rubbed out", said this:

"You know, Crabb, that as far as your own authorities are
concerned you are dead. In order to prove their theory we are
quite willing to let them find your body – or, to make it quite
clear to you, a body which would be accepted as yours. When
this is found, the dead Commander Crabb could be buried in
England while the live Crabb could work undetected and unsuspected in our navy."

Myaskov then ordered a stretcher to be brought in on which was a corpse. Facially it did not resemble Crabb, but the body measurements were close and if, as Myaskov explained, it was left in the sea long enough it would decompose so that no one could say it wasn't Crabb or establish the cause of death. It would be dressed, of course, in everything Crabb wore when he went out for his spying attempt. The stretcher was taken out and Myaskov repeated his offer about joining the Red Navy, with the threat that if he refused Crabb would not leave the building alive. This time, after a long pause, Crabb agreed unconditionally.

This material, greatly condensed, comprises about two-thirds of the *dossier*. The rest is concerned mainly with Crabb's training, career and supervision in the Red Navy. He was, we gather, a model pupil. First, he was transferred to a "Rehabilitation Centre" to acclimatize himself to Soviet life and given a crash course in Russian which lasted for nearly three months. Then, under his new name of Lev Lvovich Korablov, he was sent to the Naval Training Command at Kronstadt where, under the date 1 September, the commandant reported Crabb's arrival on 18 August and said that he had already promoted him "to the function of frogman instructor".

According to the *dossier* Crabb-Korablov's progress was thereafter rapid and consistent. Two months later he was promoted to petty officer and transferred to an operational command at Arkhangelsk where he earned high praise for dangerous work on the damaged rudder of an ice-breaker. By December he was a second lieutenant, in March 1957 lieutenant, first lieutenant in August, 1959, whereupon he was sent to Vladivostock, promoted in due course to commander, then to captain. By May, 1967, he was in command of the Special Task Underwater Operational Command at Sebastopol.

But what had happened meanwhile to the corpse which in May, 1956, Myaskov had produced so dramatically? In that same month we learn that the head and hands were removed to exclude all possibility of accurate identification, then the remains, dressed in Crabb's complete outfit, were anchored to the sea bed near Leningrad so that decomposition by sea water could begin. A year later they were removed and at dead of night brought alongside one of the submarines that would be passing through the English Channel on the way to Egypt. We then read this statement: "The body was secured by steel ropes round the feet and towed in the sea at a safe distance from the submarine flagship in order that it should remain continuously in the water during the journey."

Dated five days later, three days before a frogman's body was found at Chichester, the *dossier* quotes a signal from the submarine: "Cargo dispatched Stop Charts and Currents indicate that arrival can be expected in 48 hours."

So, it seems, the Crabb case is sewn up and we now need to ask no further questions. All is plain, all is clear. The Chichester body was a plant and Crabb was, perhaps still is alive in the Soviet Union.

This may be true, yet second thoughts about the *dossier* and the background to the whole affair inevitably raise questions. First, having pulled off the dramatic coup, why should the Russians have taken such trouble to conceal it? Surely, the propaganda value of capturing Crabb alive – if they had really done so – would have been immense, and a harsh warning to any future allied frogmen who attempted, on official orders or not, to examine the hulls of their vessels.

This leads to another question, connected with the origin of the dossier. The version which reached England was in German translation and this has been explained as due to the fact that a number of secret Russian files on individual cases, illustrating interrogation methods, were circulated in 1959 to the security services in satellite countries – in no less than six languages. But why, if this was done, was the Crabb file included, with the immense risks involved in a wide distribution, if the Russians were so anxious to keep his capture a secret?

We now come to the *dossier* itself. It is meticulously compiled; on the other hand there are some very curious statements. The helicopter lifting Crabb from the cruiser is said to have taken off at 6.36 a.m. and reached Stettin at 8.03 a.m., one hour and 27 minutes later. The rendezvous is said to have been in the Skagerrak north of Denmark. The cruiser might just have reached the area in time, steaming flat-out at 30 knots, but the helicopter with a maximum speed of 130 m.p.h. could not possibly have reached Stettin in the time stated, nor could it have covered the 700 miles involved in the round trip, even with extra fuel tanks. The range of the most modern Russian helicopter in use at that period was 155 miles.

And then, the dramatic speed with which Crabb learned Russian and got his post as frogman instructor! Imagine the situation in reverse. A Russian frogman is captured by the British, taught English in under three months, then posted to Teddington or H.M.S. *Vernon* where, in less than a fortnight, as an ordinary seaman, still with a thick foreign accent, still struggling with an unfamiliar technical vocabulary, he is set to teach British frogmen their job – and this at a time when his loyalty to Britain is still in doubt. To put it mildly, the situation would be grotesque. Equally astonishing is the picture of a decomposing corpse being towed in its rubber suit behind a submarine for at least a thousand miles, wherever the submarine started from in Russian-controlled territory. How much would be left of that parcel at the end of the journey, particularly if, as might well happen, the submarine were obliged to dive to avoid NATO shipping?

These are only some of the questions raised by the *dossier*, leading inevitably to another: was it a plant? One can well imagine some industrious official in Moscow being given the job of compiling it from scratch, knowing its purpose and over-reaching himself in an effort to concoct a masterpiece of Soviet efficiency and cunning with which to impress its recipients.

But suppose the *dossier* were a fake and suppose the Russians did deliberately ensure that it reached Britain. This would not mean that the whole story was false. It might still be true that Crabb was taken alive and did do service in some capacity in the Red Navy. In a further book published in 1970* Mr Hutton produced what looks like corroboration: interviews with people from the U.S.S.R. who claimed to have met Crabb, messages from him to his English fiancée, detailed reports "from underground sources" on his naval career.

But doubt is not so easily dismissed, even when, as is claimed, the former Head of M.I.5, Sir Percy Sillitoe, stated in 1961: "The dossier is genuine" – for that might have been a bluff to make the Russians believe their story was accepted.

All we do know for sure is that Crabb was an exceptionally brave man who became justly famous for his work with the Royal Navy during and after the war. Beyond that we can only hope that he eventually found peace, today perhaps, aged 69, in retirement somewhere, or long since, in July, 1957, when the headless, handless residue of a man was buried in a Portsmouth graveyard.

* *The Fake Defector*, published by Howard Baker, London. The title refers to an alleged attempt by the Russians in 1969 to persuade Crabb to state publicly that he had voluntarily defected, this for propaganda purposes.

THE *MADAGASCAR* MUTINY

Was there a mutiny? Or did she merely share the fate of so many wooden sailing ships, and sink in a storm, with the loss of all hands? No one knows, nor perhaps ever will; unless there is the unlikely event of records coming to light of another "eye-witness" account, to corroborate or in some way vary the only one we have.

It was set down some time in the 1880s – we do not know precisely when, or where, except that it was in Brazil. A widow, now herself approaching death, startled those about her by telling them she had decided to tell the truth about her life, a truth far more lurid than they had had reason to suspect of this quiet-living elderly woman, whose late husband was believed once to have been a seafaring man.

"It was in '53," she said. "I was taking ship from Australia to England. Those were in the gold days, when there was plenty of coming and going between the old country and the new. The ship was full up of passengers, and there was more gold than usual in her hold. We all knew this, because there had been a lot written about it in the Sydney and Melbourne newspapers. It worried some of us, especially the women, to think of that fortune under us. And the crew looked a nasty, shifty lot, surly and swearing, even in front of us women passengers, which was something most sailors would never do.

"The captain and officers were polite and friendly, though.

And the ship herself was said to be one of the best on the run. She was called the *Madagascar* . . ."

Madagascar: over 1,000 tons, frigate-built, square-rigged, one of the most popular of all the well-found, beautiful "Blackwallers", vessels so called because they were built in the East India Company's shipyard at Blackwall, on the Thames, home of the China tea-clippers and principal loading and discharging point in the Port of London. They were comfortable, efficient, as safe as any sailing ships could be, trusted by wealthy passengers and by merchants with consignments of exceptional value. In the minimum time possible for the long voyage, they rushed the gold from the Australian fields to the London bullion markets.

We do not know anything specific about the young woman whose dying account, some thirty years later, is all the detail we possess of the *Madagascar*'s last voyage: whether she was English-born, perhaps widowed for her first time in Australia and returning home; or perhaps the wife of one who had struck it rich, and could afford to let his homesick wife go to visit her family, while he prospected on for even greater wealth.

Or whether she was something quite different from either of these: one of those many women who had flocked to the gold towns in the wake of the rush, to sell themselves for the miners' gold, then return to England to live in style, or die in style from the diseases their trade had brought them. There is some evidence that the passengers, male and female, had been a mixed bunch. It is contained in an account written later for the *Melbourne Argus* newspaper by a man who had been a port detective there and had seen the *Madagascar* when she called *en route* from Sydney to London:

"Drunkenness, fighting, swearing, and men, women and children in a state of semi-nudity, howling like wild animals. The crew were composed of men of the most motley kind that ever signed articles. Some of the passengers were a rough lot. A pang of horror shot through me as the thought rose to my brain – should evil overtake the *Madagascar*, what would become of the young women and girls, and the better class of passengers?"

The dying woman's story tends to imply that she had been one of that "better class". Let us give her the benefit of that, at least, in view of her coming ordeal.

"It was a lovely autumn day when we sailed from

Melbourne. We hoped for a smooth passage all the way . . ."

Between that autumn day and Christmas, reports reached Lloyd's of London of the loss of many vessels, small and great: the *Annie Jane* of Liverpool, the brig *Harwood*, the screw-steamer *Marshall*, the emigrant-carrier *Tayleur*, the fine passenger ship *Dalhousie*, of the Australian White Star line. The following year, 1854, brought a further catalogue, headed by a troopship sunk with 350 rank and file of the Madras Light Infantry, and the steamship *Prince* "with 144 lives, and a cargo worth £500,000, indispensable to the army in the Crimea". But those who waited for news of the *Madagascar*, good or bad, heard nothing. She had disappeared.

"Three weeks after leaving Melbourne we were told we were rounding Cape Horn. To our relief, the dreadful weather we had been warned to expect was not met. Instead . . ."

Eight bells in the dog-watch. A sudden, unnaturally loud confusion of voices, challenging and swearing. Running feet on deck. Shots.

The passengers hurried to their cabin doors. They saw the crew running riot, fighting their officers back. Two men, unmistakably the captain and mate, lay still in their blood.

"Get back inside!" the mutineers ordered the watchers. Some of the men ran out defiantly, hoping to aid the officers. They were shot or clubbed to the deck. The rest were all bustled back into their quarters, behind locked doors. For what seemed ages they could only listen to the shots and curses as the officers' resistance was overcome, followed by the laughter and shouts of the victorious, drunken mutineers.

A naval officer among the passengers, listening more intently, was able to interpret further sounds.

"They're hauling up the gold. Running out the boats, and loading it in. This has all been well planned, and there's nothing we can do to stop it. All we can do is wait for them to leave, then take over the ship ourselves. I will undertake command, and in this sort of weather we'll have no difficulty sailing her to safety."

It seemed the best idea. So long as they had the gold, the mutinous crew would scarcely bother with the ship's passengers.

It was an optimistic conjecture, however. New sounds of heaving and hammering had an obvious meaning: the mutineers were sealing off the passengers' access to the deck.

"They're going to sink the ship!" someone cried.

"And drown us!" screamed another.

In a mass, the terrified passengers flung themselves against doors and walls, crying to be spared. The answer they got was derisive laughter and some shots. But after a little while there came the sound of hurrying feet outside the cabins. Doors were unlocked, and wild-eyed men stared in. Any attractive or reasonably comely female they saw, they grabbed, to pull them out. Husbands and other men who tried to prevent them were shot. The cabin doors were locked again, as, struggling and crying, the women were bundled away to the boats.

"Our fate was hard enough to contemplate, but at least we were spared that of our former companions. As we were rowed away from the ship we heard their screams as they felt it sinking. The men in the boats were laughing and cheering. I covered my ears and shut my eyes, to try to escape the dreadful sight and sounds. Even so, I had heard the screams – I hear them still."

"When at last I dared look, there was nothing to see of the ship but the tops of her masts vanishing, and bodies of the murdered officers bobbing in the waves."

The woman who had survived so many years to recite this narrative had evidently been luckier than most. The man who had claimed her as personal booty was comparatively mild-mannered. He quietly admitted to her that he had joined his fellow crewmen in the mutiny because to have refused would have meant being shot. He was no villain at heart, and only hoped to reach land safely, get his share-out of the plundered gold, and disappear to make an honest life.

This was what happened. The division of the spoils was much less than it might have been; the mutineers were as unskilled at handling small boats as they were heartless, and lost most of their loot when they managed to overturn two of the boats just before reaching Brazil. The narrator of their tale was glad enough to stay with her particular man and melt away with him from the rest. She was penniless and friendless otherwise, and she liked him well enough to settle for marrying him. Throughout their new life together they told no one of their connection with the *Madagascar*, or of what had occurred aboard her. But those screams went on echoing in her mind down the years, and when death was near she found some solace in telling her story.

The other version of what happened to the missing *Madaga-scar* is also tragic, but less dramatic, and certainly not bloody. An item in the *Sydney Daily Telegraph* of 10 April, 1917, said: "The mystery surrounding the loss of the old Blackwall liner *Madagascar* in 1853 has been revived in New Zealand. Those who have heard the old story of the mysterious treasure-laden ship believed to have been wrecked near Doughty Point on the west coast of Stewart Island are in doubt as to any definite details, but they are all fairly unanimous that a large vessel named *Madagascar* met her doom in the locality in the '50s. There still lives at the Bluff an old Maori who states that he saw a vessel wrecked in a storm near Doughty Bay about that period, and he maintains that she was the *Madagascar* and that not a soul escaped."

Doughty Bay and Cape Horn lie far apart. So do these two accounts of the fine vessel's loss. There is a common denom-inator, though: the story of a cut-throat seizure of the *Madaga-scar*'s gold was once current, in various forms, at a part of New Zealand's coast off which a big, well-preserved wreck could be seen at lowest tide.

The lure of gold has inspired many legends. It has also pro-voked many desperate deeds. Either, or both, could be the truth concerning the *Madagascar*.

DONALD CROWHURST
DISAPPEARS

There is an old photograph in existence of a seven-year-old boy standing against a background of lush vegetation. He wears shorts, socks and a white jersey and is laughing with wide open mouth, positively chortling with glee straight at the camera. The reason is clear. He has just been given a toy boat and he is clutching it, with hoisted sail half as long as himself, in his left hand while the right hangs firmly on to the rigging. "Look at my boat!" he seems to be saying. "My wonderful boat!" The name of the boy was Donald Crowhurst.

Thirty years after that photo was taken, on the morning of 10 July, 1969, the Royal Mail ship *Picardy*, bound from London to the Caribbean, was in mid-Atlantic when a small sailing craft was spotted, an unusual sight in that area, moving very slowly. Seeing no one on deck, the captain sent a boat with three men to investigate and when they climbed on board they found that the craft – a 40-foot trimaran in a seaworthy condition – was deserted. One sail was hoisted on the mizzen mast, the others were neatly folded on deck. The life-raft was firmly lashed in its place. There was nothing whatever to suggest that the boat had encountered severe weather and this was confirmed by an inspection of the cabin. A soldering iron was found perched on top of a tin. The sink was full of pans, cups and dirty dishes. Working tables were littered with radio spares, presumably from two receivers partly dismantled. There was enough food and fresh water on board to last for weeks.

Completely baffled, the men returned to the *Picardy*, taking with them three log books they had found in the cabin. The boat's name was *Teignmouth Electron*, which meant nothing until someone remembered a race organized by *The Sunday Times* and, fishing out an old copy of the newspaper, found some details: a single-handed, non-stopping round-the-world race – prize for the fastest time, £5,000 – another prize, "The Golden Globe", for first home – competitors to start at intervals – latest starting date, 31 October, 1968. Among nine or so entrants were Robin Knox-Johnston in *Suhaili*, Bernard Moitessier of France in *Joshua*, Commander Nigel Tetley in *Victress* and in *Teignmouth Electron*, Donald Crowhurst.

After the trimaran had been hoisted on board, the captain looked at the logs. Two books had been used for navigational records which seemed to have been kept with obsessive detail. But what struck him most was a mass of writing at the back of Log Book 2, and in particular certain phrases: "I am nostalgic as a child sensing he is about to leave 'home' for ever . . . I am what I am and I see the nature of my offence . . . It is finished. IT IS THE MERCY . . ." What did leaving "home" imply, what was "finished" and what was "the mercy"? Strange words for a sailor to use on a round-the-world race . . .

The *Picardy* and later the U.S. Air Force searched the area for Crowhurst though the last entry in the log was for 29 June and there could be little hope that he had survived. The captain then cabled his ship's owners about the strange find and that same evening two policemen called on Mrs Crowhurst in Teignmouth where she lived with her four children to break the news. For them, as for the whole of the town, it was a shattering blow for everyone had believed that Crowhurst was about to win the £5,000 prize.

Winning had in fact meant a lot to him, not least because he had told everybody he was going to win, his backers, his family, his friends and anyone who would listen. One and all were invited to recognize in him a local boy who would astonish the world.

But there was more to Donald Crowhurst than a naïve boastfulness. Even as a schoolboy in India, where his father was a railway superintendent and his mother a teacher, he had been a perfectionist, scrawling "bad", "very bad", "disgraceful" in the margin of a first-term report that had marked him never lower than "fair". In adult life he became a mathematician of considerable intelligence with a passion for electronics. At the same time he was witty, ebullient, a splendid companion for most people when on form, but subject to the phases of high elation and depression that characterize the manic-depressive.

This brilliant but unstable personality was to get him into trouble on several occasions, in the R.A.F. where he became known as a hell-raiser and later in the Army from which he was asked to resign in 1956 after a series of law-breaking pranks in his high-speed Lagonda.

In 1957 Crowhurst married an Irish girl and a few years later, after a series of jobs in electronics, founded his own firm to manufacture nautical equipment, in particular a radio direction-finding instrument, invented by himself, which he called a Navicator. The Navicator proved difficult to sell and to no one's surprise Crowhurst found he was a poor businessman, too interested in inventing gadgets to bother much about marketing them. Result: money trouble.

Then in March, '68 came *The Sunday Times* announcement and it at once caught Crowhurst's vivid imagination. Admittedly Sir Francis Chichester had recently sailed round the world, but Joshua Slocum had done that in 1898 and both had stopped at least once. Here in the non-stopping race was a chance for Crowhurst to outdo all previous sailors, revive the fortunes of his firm through the publicity and become the hero he felt he was, at any rate potentially. He had done some sailing, had a small boat of his own and so knew himself, as he wrote, "to be competent to undertake this voyage in a seamanlike manner". Moreover he would go one better. Though he had never sailed one, he had heard that multihulled boats were amazingly fast before the wind and he would therefore take a trimaran and clock up another first: first to sail a trimaran round the world.

But time was short, there were only seven months to the deadline and backers had to be found, the boat had to be built and a thousand preparations made for what was, after all, a unique test for a craft of that kind. Crowhurst flung himself into the work; he could be very persuasive when he wanted and before the end of May the money problem had been solved and two firms, one in Essex and the other in Norfolk, were building the hulls and the rest of the equipment. Even so, it was a race against the clock.

At last, on 23 September, *Teignmouth Electron* was launched
and then the maiden voyage began, right round from Norfolk
to Devon. Crowhurst was expecting to do the trip in three
days, but it took two weeks and was a near-disaster. The starboard float was damaged in a snarl-up with a chain ferry,
screws kept starting out of the self-steering gear, Crowhurst
was repeatedly violently sick, twice fell overboard during a
brief stop-over at Cowes and, worst of all, it was found that the
boat would sail no closer to the wind than sixty degrees, which
in the Channel meant endless tacks towards France, as far as
Boulogne on one occasion. But despite everything Crowhurst's
determination never flagged and a friend who sailed with him
became convinced that he really was "a man to sail round the
world". At the time Crowhurst never doubted it, or if he did
he told no one.

In the sixteen days before the deadline there was still a mass
of work to be done, in modifications to the boat, stowage of
stores and equipment, on top of press and television interviews.
Friends milled around dumping cartons of food, navigational
books and clothing while Crowhurst shopped frantically for
missing items like hacksaw blades, a blowlamp, a barometer
and a recipe for baking bread in salt water. Many people were
having serious misgivings, but whenever they mentioned them
to Crowhurst he said simply: "It's too late. I can't turn back
now."

Did he want to turn back? No one really knew. Only on
the night before he sailed has his wife seen in retrospect a
glimpse into his real feelings. They had been making a last-
minute attempt to sort out piles of equipment still littering the
trimaran's deck and did not get to bed before 2 a.m. Once
there, Crowhurst was silent for a long time. Then he said: "Dar-
ling, I'm very disappointed in the boat. She's not right. I'm
not prepared. If I leave with things in this hopeless state will
you go out of your mind with worry?" She could have said
"yes", but thinking of his wishes she asked: "If you give up
now, will you be unhappy for the rest of your life?" Crowhurst did not reply. All she heard was that he was weeping
and only later – too late – did she realize that he had been
wanting her to stop him.

At 3 p.m. on 31 October, nine hours before the deadline, he
tried to set his sails – and found they had been attached in the
wrong order. Two hours later, after this and other faults had

been rectified and a last-minute bundle of torch batteries thrown on board, he was tacking out into Lyme Bay with a motor boat escort. The boat stayed with him for a mile, then Crowhurst was alone in the cold and gathering darkness. There was a strong wind from the south and it was drizzling. It was like a death.

He had not worked out a detailed course beforehand, but he had the books to help him. All he knew in general was that the distance round the world was 30,000 miles and it would take at least eight months to cover it, sailing past the Cape of Good Hope, through the Indian Ocean, past Australia and New Zealand, across the Pacific, round Cape Horn and so back to England northwards through the Atlantic. Meanwhile, for the first few days, he was making fair progress south-westwards, past the Bay of Biscay and down towards the coast of Portugal.

But then the defects of the trimaran began to show up. Unable to sail close to the wind, he was forced to tack back and forth and in so doing found the self-steering gear coming loose again. By 5 November, near despair, he was making an inventory of everything that had gone wrong. The cockpit hatch had been taking in water and the electric generator housed beneath it was now useless. The port hull was leaking badly and as someone had forgotten to put a length of piping on board to connect to the pumps, the only cure for this was hand bailing. The sails had been incorrectly cut. Water was coming into the cabin from below. An arrangement for righting the boat if she capsized was not functioning. Summing up these and other defects, Crowhurst reckoned his chances of surviving the Horn as no more than fifty-fifty and for a married man with four children that was clearly unacceptable. Should he give up at once and sail home?

Writing his thoughts, Crowhurst considered various alternatives, but never reached a firm decision. Instead, in early December, he started almost casually to fake the log. On 10 December he sent a radio message to his press agent in Teignmouth giving distances sailed for each of the last five days, all five of them false. Example: "Sunday 243, new record single hander" (actual mileage, 170). So began a series of lying reports which eventually comprised a fake circumnavigation of the world with consequences which Crowhurst could not foresee. To feed the Press at home, for instance, besides giving

speeds the radio messages had to contain colourful material
about weather and sea conditions, problems encountered, state
of morale and so on and almost all this had to be cooked up so
as to pass checking when he got home. And there were the logs
to think of, too. They would have to contain fuller details still
of every stage in the journey – stages which in fact Crowhurst
was not covering. But how could he tell what the weather was
like off Cape Horn when he had never been there? What if he
were spotted by passing ships in a different position to the one
reported and, above all, what if he was deemed to have "won"
the race? Could he live for the rest of his life with a monu-
mental lie? In his desperation to become a hero he did not
think of this.

What he did think of, and carry out with great cunning, was
the daily task of faking, keeping a record of the imaginary and
real voyages in separate log books. For the fake he worked out
where he could and should be, given good speeds, adding an
occasional slow-up to convey authenticity and, while in fact
moving erratically towards the north-east coast of Brazil, plotted what radio stations to contact for transmission of his messages, assuming his fake position was the real one – all this
while trying to sail what he had earlier described as "this
bloody boat".

After almost touching the Brazilian coast, Crowhurst's real
route took a wide loop down towards Buenos Aires, snaked
south again to the Falkland Islands, then came up northwards
midway between South America and Africa. In other words,
he never left the Atlantic. But throughout this time, from
January to the end of April, he was sending home periodic
messages interspersed with long periods of radio silence (when
he was supposed to be in the Indian Ocean or the Pacific)
designed to suggest rapid progress round the world. He gave
no positions, but for those at home, particularly his news-
hungry agent, suggestion was more than enough. One example
is typical. In April he signalled: AFTER DEPARTING LIZARD FIRST
SIGHT LAND FALKLANDS / HOVE-TO WATCHING SUNDOWN / HAZY
AUTUMN EVENING WOODSMOKE ON WIND / THEN PELL MELL FOR
SAFETY SOUTH ATLANTIC STOP / REASONABLE WEATHER TO HORN
BUT SOUTHEASTER NEXT DAY. Who, reading this, would imagine
that "to Horn" really meant "in the direction of the Horn, but
not reaching it, from the east, the Atlantic side"?

That part of the message was cunningly deceptive, but the

first words were an outright lie. In fact Crowhurst had not only seen land, but touched it and gone ashore for repairs to his boat at a little place called Rio Salado, south of Buenos Aires. He had chosen the spot with great care as being remote and unlikely to lead to detection.

Towards the end of April it became necessary for his fake voyage to catch up with his real one, in other words for sufficient time to elapse for it to seem reasonable that, having rounded the world, he should be where he was. This involved the nautical equivalent of marking time, endless, aimless tacking to and fro in the Roaring Forties off Argentina, well out of sight of land in case he should be spotted, a highly unpleasant if not dangerous task in itself. But at last the carefully calculated day arrived, 4 May, when he could cease to deceive and sail home as fast as he could. But sail home to what?

Of the two other competitors left in the race, Robin Knox-Johnston, who had started four and a half months before Crowhurst, was now certain to win the Golden Globe for first home while Nigel Tetley, also sailing a trimaran, seemed set to win the £5,000 for the fastest time. To Crowhurst, waking at last to the implications of his deceit, this was a comforting thought: no money won by false pretences, no expert inspection of his logs, no ballyhoo on reaching home, just a quiet return after an interesting voyage, everything modestly played down, as it should be.

But then fate took a hand. Tetley's trimaran was also in bad shape, leaking badly, far worse than Crowhurst's, and on 21 May when he was pressing on regardless through a storm near the Azores – precisely because he had heard Crowhurst was on his tail – the craft broke up and he had to take to his life-raft, from which mercifully he was rescued by a passing ship.

So now Crowhurst could not possibly avoid winning the £5,000 prize – unless he stayed practically stationary for weeks on end so as to be behind Knox-Johnston even on time. But what plausible motive could he give for that? For a whole month he sailed on into the North Atlantic, at first sending cheerful messages home, writing up colourful bits about the voyage for future publication, then spending days in his tiny cabin trying to patch up his transmitter which had broken down so that he could fulfil a need to talk direct to his wife by radio telephone.

He never got through to his wife, but his agent and the

B.B.C. certainly got through to him: TEIGNMOUTH AGOG AT YOUR WONDERS/WHOLE TOWN PLANNING HUGE WELCOME . . . CONGRATULATIONS ON PROGRESS/HAVE NETWORK TELEVISION PROGRAMME FOR DAY OF RETURN. These messages made it easy to visualize what that return would be like: the crowds, the cheers, the motorcades, the interviews, the dinners – and the racking necessity to deceive and go on deceiving for the rest of his life. Was there no way out?

On Midsummer's Day, 24 June, while still sailing his boat, baling the floats, tending the sails, steering northwards ever nearer to that reception, Crowhurst began to compose a long, involved rumination headed "Philosophy". Its purpose, all 25,000 words, was to work out by mathematical logic, the method he knew best, a cosmic system in which he in his loneliness and guilt could include himself and so cease to feel an outcast. Einstein's theory of relativity came into it, concepts of God, his own theory of life as a "game", even the square root of minus one.

But this was merely a prelude. Subconsciously he was seeking a way to get out of his real-life dilemma and so his thoughts moved on – to the idea that abstract, bodiless intelligence was the greatest of all, god-like, supreme, then to the conviction that the achievement of this state was now the next step in human evolution, then to the sudden, blinding assurance that he, Crowhurst, the first of the new gods, was destined to show humanity the way.

So from disaster, triumph would emerge and he would at last find the Heroic Self he had always known was there. But there was still one matter to be settled, the "offence", his guilt. This had to be got out of the system where everything, to use one of his favourite words, had to "compute". Why had he offended? Because God had made him offend. That had been the nature of the game and of the offence. So the guilt belonged to God and he, Crowhurst, was now free of everything that still bound him to the world, free to take on bodiless intelligence.

In the depth of this madness he could still be punctilious and he jotted down his last disjointed remarks against a note of the hour, the minutes and the seconds. Between 10.30 a.m. and 11 on 1 July he wrote: "It is finished. IT IS THE MERCY". At 11.15, "It is the end of my game", and at 11.17, "I will resign the game 11–20–40. There is no reason for harmful . . ." Those were the last words he wrote.

At some time or other, perhaps in those last three minutes, he made sure, as a kind of confession, that these writings and the log books were placed conspicuously in the cabin as evidence of the fraud, evidence which most strongly suggests that he then took his life by dropping into the sea.

But of course it is not certain that he did this. There *was* another way out of the dilemma. He was in mid-Atlantic, close to shipping routes. He could have put out a distress call, waited for it to be answered, then sunk the boat and put off in the life-raft. It is not impossible that he suddenly realized this and then some time later, perhaps even days later, fell accidentally overboard – as he had done twice before on the maiden voyage. That would have been tragically ironic. But the supreme irony was this, that he was already by all normal standards a hero, having sailed for 243 days in a fragile, leaky craft, alone with the wind and sea.

THE *ADMIRAL KARPFANGER*

In the days when the only means of getting goods and people around the world was by sea, the shipping companies were flourishing concerns, taking great pride and interest in their ships. Safety, reliability, speed, comfort and appearance were the goals of the merchant marine. For generations there had been intense competition among the owners of cargo ships and among the crews themselves to bring back the sought-after spices, tea, wool and grain from the East and from Australasia as quickly as possible.

Passengers were originally a secondary consideration, being carried aboard trading ships, but as passenger traffic began to increase the competition between shipping lines extended to the liners which were built primarily for the purpose of transporting people. The whole world knew of ships like the *Mauretania*, which for twenty years held the "Blue Riband" for the fastest Atlantic crossing, the *Bremen*, the *France* and the *Queen Mary*. The *Queen Elizabeth II* almost certainly represents the last of such ships that will ever be built, and with her will pass an era in the saga of the sea comparable with that of the great tea clippers such as the *Thermopylae* and the *Cutty Sark*.

The companies which owned and operated these cargo ships and liners were household names, and intense effort went into the fitting out of the vessels and the training of their crews. In a manner rather similar to that of the world's navies, many of the merchant marine companies took on cadets at an early age and trained them to the sea. And even when sailing ships had all but disappeared from the oceans, ousted by the coming of more profitable steamships, it was considered that there was no way to learn that could compare with "sailing before the mast".

Many shipping companies, therefore, owned and operated sailing ships. Today, fortunately, there are still a number of these ships in use. Most countries own one or more sail training ships and use them partly in the training of naval cadets and partly simply as a means of broadening the experience of the youth of the country. (Britain operates two such ships, the *Sir Winston Churchill* and the *Malcolm Miller*.) Anyone who has been fortunate enough to see vessels of this type assembling perhaps for the Tall Ships Race can well appreciate their beauty. But there is another side to the picture. Working a sailing ship in even a moderate wind is hard and often frightening. The difficulty and danger of battling with flapping wet canvas on a wildly pitching ship is hard to comprehend without first-hand experience – but it is this kind of experience which, above all, teaches a sailor to know and respect the sea.

The Hamburg-Amerika Line, a leading shipping company in the early part of this century, was one of those which believed in training under sail for its officer cadets. German maritime tradition is strong, and their reputation for seamanship and discipline high. The Hamburg-Amerika Line chose its cadets from dozens of applications, all around fifteen to seventeen years old, for their potential qualities of leadership, courage and determination. Training under sail was important in building up these qualities and the company therefore looked about for a suitable ship.

They soon came upon what seemed to be an ideal choice – a four-masted barque of 2,853 tons (as a comparison, the well-known *Cutty Sark* is under 1,000 tons), built in the 1890s to sail on the grain run from Australia. Moreover she had been bought by the Belgian Navy in 1908 and completely refitted in Bremerhaven as a training ship. Among other modifications this meant that she had been fitted with a long poop deck, so that her decks were less vulnerable to the weather. She had more buoyancy and less well deck to hold heavy water and thus she could run longer and drier than the ships with a big open deck. In training ships manned largely by inexperienced boys who lacked the weight and strength of full-grown men these and other safety aids were important.

When the head of the nautical department of Hamburg-Amerika, accompanied by a nautical engineer from Germani-sche-Lloyd, went to look at the ship she was lying in Liverpool docks. The Belgian Navy had sold her to a Finnish shipowner who had both the money and the sentiment to continue to run a fleet of commercial sailing vessels, and for a number of years she had returned to the Australian grain trade. Her fastest passage was in 1936 when she sailed from Port Victoria in Australia to Falmouth in England in 105 days (clipper ships such as the *Thermopylae* and *Cutty Sark* commonly averaged under ninety days for the trip). But in the depressed years of the 1930s even a wealthy man could not continue to run many such vessels commercially and *L'Avenir*, as she was then called, was put up for sale.

She lay in Liverpool docks for only a few months before she was bought by Hamburg-Amerika and at sea again on her way to Germany for an extensive refit. Her steel hull was as sound as ever, but much of the rest of her was years out of date. She was given new auxiliary diesel engines, modern navigational aids, acoustic equipment and radio. When she was finally ready to put to sea again in the autumn of 1937, renamed the *Admiral Karpfanger*, she was as well equipped and up to date as any modern steamship – only the ancient forces of the wind remained as her motive power.

The *Admiral Karpfanger*'s first voyage as a training ship began on 16 September, 1937. Two-thirds of her crew of sixty were excited cadets looking eagerly forward to a great experience. The rest, under one of the company's most experienced captains, Walker, were proficient seamen. The ship's departure from Hamburg was accompanied by celebrations and she was seen off by dozens of the boys' relations, some tearful at the prospect of not seeing their children again for some seven or eight months.

The voyage to Port Germain in south Australia took just under four months – a creditable performance for a ship manned by such an inexperienced crew. Captain Walker was pleased with his cadets and the voyage had passed without incident while the boys, in the intervals between learning to actually handle the ship, attended classes in navigation, seamanship, maritime law and so on. At the back of the captain's mind, perhaps, was the thought that he was training the sailors who might play an important part in the war which was beginning to look inevitable. For this was the period when Hitler's Germany was actively preparing itself to be a powerful war machine, and Hitler youth was being taught to see itself as the future warrior class of a great fatherland.

German sailors, perhaps by reason of their frequent absences from their country, were never so imbued with Nazi propaganda as the other fighting services, but discipline was always strict. Captain Walker's cadets soon accustomed themselves to the dramatic change in their daily lives and adapted to the routine of a long sea voyage. But with half the crew under eighteen years of age there was always an atmosphere of high spirits aboard. Traditional crossing-the-line ceremonies were carried out with gusto, Christmas at sea was celebrated with fun and games. As the *Admiral Karpfanger* sailed southwards the weather improved, and the cadets found themselves in Australia in the middle of their second summer in six months.

During the four weeks that the ship spent in port there was still plenty of work to do. The cargo had to be unloaded, the ravages of several months at sea had to be repaired and the ship painted, cleaned and overhauled. Finally, some forty-three thousand bags of wheat were loaded for the return voyage and carefully stowed by the experienced stevedores of the port. The *Admiral Karpfanger*'s hold was fitted with "shifting boards", built strongly fore and aft and designed to prevent the cargo shifting and the ship developing a list – a further safety precaution. Last of all the ship's stores were replenished, for the long voyage home was designed to take them direct to Hamburg via Cape Horn without calling at any ports on the way. The ship was scheduled to reach Germany some time in May, and the boys looked forward to enjoying yet another summer on holiday at home with the families which they had never before left for so long a period.

The *Admiral Karpfanger* sailed up the Spender Gulf, heading for the open sea on 8 February, 1938. The captain had orders to report his position by radio every fortnight; in fact he sent his first message three days after setting sail. It was picked up by a German shore station, but the distance was so great that, although it could be identified as coming from the *Admiral Karpfanger*, the message was indecipherable. Ten days later another equally weak and indecipherable message was re-

ceived and, on 1 March, the first intelligible signal, which reported the barque as being on latitude 51 degrees South and
longitude 172 degrees East, with all well on board. The position reported by the ship is some 1,500 miles south of Wellington, New Zealand, and it can thus be seen that in the three
weeks since she set sail she had made poor progress. She was on
the traditional windjammer route and normally a ship of her
size could by that time have been expected to be closing Cape
Horn itself.

The next communication with the *Admiral Karpfanger* was on
12 March. On that day the German land station at Norddeich
radioed to inform the second mate of the birth of his first child.
The proud father radioed back his thanks and a message to his
wife. There was no hint of any problems on board the ship.

This was the last that was ever heard of the *Admiral Karpfanger*. The routine signal that was expected from the ship a
couple of days later never came, but it was not for another
week or two that some concern began to be felt. Finally, pes-
tered by anxious parents, the Hamburg-Amerika Line issued a
statement early in April to the effect that the silence was
undoubtedly due to the fact that the ship's radio had broken
down; there had been some trouble with it on the outward
voyage. If this were indeed the case, then the only knowledge
of the *Admiral Karpfanger*'s whereabouts would come from passing ships and, since the barque was on the windjammer route
and not in the usual merchant shipping lanes, this might be
slow in coming.

Despite this reassurance anxiety grew as the days and weeks
passed without any news. The Press, typically, exacerbated
forebodings of disaster and Lloyd's broadcast a request to all
shipping for any information. Hamburg-Amerika continued to
insist that the radio had most probably broken down, reminding the world that the captain had had trouble with the generators both on the outward voyage and while he was in Port
Germain. It was, nevertheless, strange that in this case she had
not attempted to close a shore station and make her position
known. By now she must have rounded the Horn and passed
Fernando Norouka, off Brazil, to which many sailing vessels
customarily reported. Moreover she should now be entering an
area covering some of the most populous shipping routes in the
world, and yet there were no reports of her having been seen.

Other ships arriving in Europe or in Australasia, which had

followed the same route, reported sighting no sailing ships. Although they could have missed her, a square-rigger – of which there were then only a dozen or so still afloat – would have been unmistakable.

May passed with still no news, and fears for the *Admiral Karpfanger* increased. Two British merchant steamers that had taken the Horn route had seen no sign of the barque. Moreover, the second ship, the SS *Durham*, had reported ice unusually far north in these seas. The *Durham*'s captain, Pilcher, said that the bergs were large and numerous, some as big as a mile long, and the pessimism aroused by this news was reflected in the reaction of the London insurance markets as brokers sought reinsurance on the ship.

During June several reports of sighting were received. Each of these reports was carefully investigated by ships or planes but, after days of anxious waiting, the sighting turned out to be of a different ship. Further hopes were raised when the harbour officials at Port Germain informed the authorities that the ship's generators were so defective that steam winches had had to be used for loading and the ship lit by paraffin lamps. It had been impossible to repair the generators in Australia, and the radio therefore could well have been rendered useless.

While such reports continued to buoy the hopes of the relatives of the *Admiral Karpfanger*'s crew, the insurance market became increasingly pessimistic, and at the end of June the reinsurance rate on the ship rose from 30 per cent to 50 per cent and continued to rise steadily. Hamburg-Amerika still refused to admit that the ship was lost, and in July ordered their freighter, *Leuna*, to leave her usual route home by Suez and take the route followed by the *Admiral Karpfanger*, keeping a careful lookout for any sign of her. At the same time the company asked the Argentine government for help and a survey ship, the *Bahia Blanca*, was immediately sent to search the southern coast and its islands. The *Bahia Blanca* carried out a minute search and, although it found many pieces of old wreckage from other ships, there was no sign of the missing barque. As August came and went it became increasingly obvious, even to those most reluctant to accept the fact, that the *Admiral Karpfanger* had disappeared.

Despite the growing threat of war in Europe, the world had had time to follow with concern the progress of the hunt for the ship and share in the hopes and fears for its safety. When,

on 5 September, 1938, the Hamburg-Amerika Line finally
accepted the inevitable and declared the ship officially lost, the
whole world was shocked. Ships of all nations flew their flags at
half-mast. Although Germany was fast becoming a symbol of
tyranny and terror, the loss of so many youthful souls on the
threshold of life engaged in an adventure to which they had
eagerly looked forward was profoundly moving. Messages of
sympathy poured into Germany from all over the world. The
fact that such a tragedy can override national barriers was well
recognized by the Hamburg-Amerika board when it wrote to
The Times stating that the paper's leading article on the loss
had been "especially gratifying" proving that "two great seafaring nations, linked by common tradition, understand each
other beyond all frontiers whenever one of them meets with the
inexorable fate of death at sea". It is ironic that, within a year,
the sailors of these two great nations were striving their utmost
to bring this "inexorable fate" upon one another.

Lloyd's of London put its official seal on the fate
of the *Admiral Karpfanger* with one peal of the famous Lutine
Bell on 21 September. But for the Hamburg-Amerika Line that
was not the end of the matter. They – and indeed the kinsmen
of those who were lost – wanted to know how and why this
strong ship, fitted with the most modern equipment, had suddenly vanished.

They could only speculate. The position at which the *Admiral Karpfanger* last reported herself had been surprisingly far
from the spot she had been expected to reach by that time, for
she was a fast ship with a large crew even if half of them were
novices. Was the captain trying to make up for lost time and
maintain the prestige of a famous shipping line, matching the
performance of other ships which had sailed on the same
route? On the outward leg of her maiden voyage as a training
ship the *Admiral Karpfanger* had made good time. In order to
improve her poor position on the return leg her captain might
have been driving her too hard. If so, and she had been carrying too much sail in the high winds which even in the summer
are common in those southern latitudes, she could have
broached to – like the *Parma* and the *Pederson*, which had survived to tell the tale. Or she could simply have been sailed
under. The absence of any wreckage pointed to some such conclusion. On the other hand, Captain Walker was a man with a
strong sense of responsibility and it was highly unlikely that he

would have endangered so many lives just for the sake of prestige.

There was also the possibility that the ship had been wrecked on one of the many reefs or islets in the area of Cape Horn. But the ship was in the charge of officers who were experienced seamen and navigators, and the ship's navigation aids were of the most modern type. It seemed highly unlikely that such a disaster could have occurred. The barque could, of course, have lost her rudder, or a mast, and had problems of control in a dangerous area of the coast. If at the same time the radio had broken down no message could have been sent. Nobody could tell, either, whether the silence from the ship after 12 March was a result of a useless radio or because she had been wrecked soon after.

The third possibility was that the ship had hit an iceberg. Other ships, as we have seen, had reported huge bergs unusually far north. It would have been only too easy for a sailing ship, going heavily in the wind and rain of a dark and squally night with visibility periodically blotted out by rain, to have been on top of one of these bergs with its murderous underwater projections before she was aware of it. In such an event the end could have come swiftly, and even if the radio were working there would have been no time to send a message.

So the search for evidence continued. The Chilean and Argentinian authorities ordered a sharp lookout to be kept for wreckage, and the former even sent out a tug, the *Galvarino*, to make a special search. During the next few months various pieces of wooden wreckage were found. On Navarin Island near the tip of Cape Horn various timbers had been washed up. They were painted white, with the inner face varnished and could have come from the *Admiral Karpfanger*. To one piece of timber was attached a length of electric cable such as was used by the Belgian Navy. A few weeks later more conclusive evidence was found by the *Galvarino* on nearby Wollaston island. Among a great amount of wreckage was a wooden door bearing a metal plate reading "Kapitän und Offiziere". This was sent to Germany, and the shipbuilders who had refitted the barque confirmed that it had come from the *Admiral Karpfanger*.

As time passed further items of wreckage were found, including a lifebuoy with an almost indecipherable name which, however, could have come from the lost ship. Since this wreckage appeared at different points and many weeks after the original search by the *Bahia Blanca*, it would seem that it had drifted some distance, supporting the theory that the ship had struck an iceberg in mid-ocean, probably soon after the last radio communication.

Despite all this evidence speculation continued. Encouraged, no doubt, by the parents who steadfastly refused to abandon hope, a large number of mediums offered their services and no less than three of them, none of whom had any communication with the others, stated that the ship had run aground on some French islands off the South American coast. Prepared to grasp at any straw the Hamburg-Amerika Line asked the French for help, but a stringent search revealed no sign of wreckage or survivors.

The mysteries of the sea invariably lead to rumour and wild surmise. The *Admiral Karpfanger* was no exception, for a fantastic rumour arose that the ship had deliberately disappeared in order to set up a submarine base somewhere in the Pacific. Despite the fact that a training ship, more than half of whose complement were barely more than children, was hardly the most suitable vessel to choose for such an exercise, this ridiculous rumour gained many adherents in a period filled with pre-war scare stories of such a type.

Nobody will ever know what actually happened to the *Admiral Karpfanger* just as nobody will ever know the fate of dozens of other ships which have mysteriously disappeared. Many perfectly seaworthy vessels with every item of up-to-date equipment have apparently been swallowed up in mid-ocean with no such hazards as rocks or ice within a hundred miles. This could have happened to the *Admiral Karpfanger*, but the state of the wreckage indicated that she had been broken up rather than been overwhelmed.

The mystery of the *Admiral Karpfanger* is so famous because, of course, the fate of her crew of boys had a special poignancy which captured the imagination of the world. But of the possible logical explanations for her disappearance, the theory that she struck an iceberg is the most likely presumption. Sadly it was perhaps these same boys – cold, sleepy, inexperienced lookouts, undecided that what they saw was really a berg and not a trick of the light – who failed to recognize the danger, and thus contributed to their own horrifying and sudden end in the icy waters of the southern seas.

THE MISSING MEMBERS

During the last week of January, 1945, Mr Winston Churchill made an urgent telephone call to Senior Army Commander, Mediterranean, in Italy, where the Anglo-American armies were steadily driving the Germans northwards. The urgency of his call, however, had nothing to do with the progress of the bitter fighting that had been going on in Italy. It was made to transmit a message to a small deputation of British members of Parliament who had gone out on a fact-finding mission.

They were in Italy to inquire into the morale and conditions of the British troops engaged on that front. Churchill's call was to ask them, as a matter of extreme urgency, to fly to Athens where a small British force had not only hurried the retreating Germans out of Greece, but had also just defeated an attempted armed takeover of that country by a large force of heavily armed communist guerillas from the mountains. What the British Prime Minister wanted the M.P.s to do was to report exactly how they found conditions in Greece and, more specifically, to report back on the attitude of the troops at having had to intervene in a bloody civil war.

The members of the mission comprised two Conservatives, Wing Commander Archibald James (Wellingborough) and Major Henry Studholme (Tavistock); two Labour M.P.s, Captain Fred Bellenger and Mr (later Lord) Jack Lawson (Chester-le-Street); the National Liberal M.P. for Bristol North, Captain Robert Bernays, and Ulster Unionist Mr J. D. Campbell. Churchill asked them to fly to Greece because, for the first time in the war, he was encountering such opposition in Parliament that there was danger of a split in the National Government which might even lead to its fall. The Prime Minister dearly wanted to keep this war-winning government together under his leadership until they finally saw the victory they had striven for since the dark days when all he could offer Britain was "blood, sweat, toil and tears".

The threatened rift in the government was being fomented by certain left-wing M.P.s. They were accusing Churchill of attempting to reinstate King George of the Hellenes on the throne of his newly liberated country with British bayonets at a time when the people really wanted a republic. The leftists claimed that the communist guerillas, whom Churchill had referred to as "murdering bandits", were indeed the true forces of national liberation. They insisted these guerillas had bravely fought the occupying Germans and Italians for three years and were now entitled to create the government that would rule Greece as a "people's democracy". Churchill had himself flown out at Christmas to Athens where, under siege conditions, he had conferred with both sides. From what he had learned and heard he was quite convinced that he was right, but the leftists in Parliament would not accept his word. So now he was sending this all-party deputation of M.P.s who happened to be so conveniently nearby.

The M.P.s were duly flown up Italy from Brindisi to Bari, travelling in ligh communication aircraft with R.A.F. pilots. James, Lawson and Studholme were in one; and Bernays, Bellenger and Campbell in the other. At Bari the planes were to refuel, then fly almost due east across the Ionian Sea to Greece; there they would follow the narrow land-locked Gulf of Corinth between the 7,000-ft mountains of the mainland and the Peloponnese to Athens aerodrome at Kalamaki.

It was presumed there was virtually no danger from enemy warplanes or from anti-aircraft fire, because by now the German armies had been driven northwards right out of Greece. It was considered unlikely that any stragglers would have remained in the mountains because this area was a bleak fastness which the Germans had virtually left to the Greek guerillas. It was even more unlikely that German gunners would still be manning any of their formidable 88-mm. anti-aircraft anti-tank guns even though a number of these weapons were still in Greece. By an agreement between the Germans and the Greek communists, these guns had been deliberately left in guerilla hands for use against the British, but it was extremely unlikely that the guerillas would be able to use them in their anti-aircraft role. Meanwhile the seas which lapped the long and rugged coastline of Greece could almost certainly be guaranteed free of any German warships capable of effective anti-aircraft fire. The Royal Navy and R.A.F. had indeed ensured this well in advance of the British forces landing in Greece.

It did therefore appear to be perfectly safe for the two light aircraft, unarmed as they were, to make the comparatively short flight across sea and mountains from Bari to Athens. As the planes were refuelled and made ready for their journey, it did not occur to the majority of the M.P.s who were to fly in them that the flight ahead might be fraught with any sort of danger. That is, with the possible exception of Captain Fred Bellenger. This Labour member who with some justification had for the past decade or more set himself up as a military expert, and in Parliament had often given his advice to the High Command, now refused point blank to fly to Greece. Whether he had a premonition of disaster or whether there were political reasons behind his decision was never to be made known.

The possible political reason, if indeed that was what prompted him to refuse to fly to Athens, was as we have seen the extreme unpopularity of the British intervention in Greece with a number of Labour members. They wanted the guerillas from the hills to take over the government of the country, even though it must be by force of arms. And in the *New Statesman*, leftist editor Kingsley Martin accused: "In Greece our troops have been manoeuvred into supporting an unpopular government which can maintain itself only by bloodshed. There is no military reason for our presence. The Prime Minister is pursuing a course which means war on a great and costly scale not against a political faction but against the Greek people . . ."

Although these allegations may have been at the back of the mind of Fred Bellenger, they did nothing to dissuade Jack Lawson from making the flight. And Jack Lawson was a true cloth-capped son of the labour movement – a Geordie miner who knew all there was to know about the hardships, the injustices and the aspirations of the working class. He was just not prepared to prejudge the situation in Greece on the say-so

of some politicians at home, whatever their political background. He intended to go out there to see what was really
happening and decide for himself the rights and the wrongs. So
Jack Lawson went in the first of the two planes to take off, with
the two Tory members as his companions. Even as they lifted
off from Bari airfield and began to climb to fly over the range
of mountains immediately ahead, they could see the other
small aircraft taxi-ing into position for take-off. The passengers
in this second plane were the two other M.P.s, Bernays and
Campbell, and Brigadier Partridge, the senior army officer
accompanying the politicians to ensure that they received all
the army co-operation they required in Athens.

As the first plane climbed higher and higher it began to lift
and drop in a sudden turbulence. The sky ahead was looming
blue black as they headed towards what was obviously a gathering thunder storm. Then up above the mountains they were
right in it. The little plane, buffeted by strong gusts of wind,
lashed by driven snow and icy rain, pitched and yawed alarmingly. But the pilot handled the aircraft competently, and soon
it was through the worst and dropping comfortably down to
the calm of a lower altitude. They continued on over the sea
without incident, until they crossed the Greek coastline. "As
we flew into Greece rebels in the hills fired at us and we could
hear the tired whine of their bullets", Sir Archibald James
recalled afterwards. But nothing hit them and the pilot took
them down to land without incident at Kalamaki airfield.

The three members were ushered into an army Nissen hut,
the nearest temporary accommodation available. They were to
wait there for the arrival of the second aircraft, expected
within a few minutes. But the minutes ticked by and it did not
arrive. Half an hour elapsed, still with no sign of it, and then a
whole hour had passed. "Give them another half hour and if
they haven't arrived by then I suggest we go off on our own,"
suggested James. And it was so agreed.

They all knew that they were being accommodated for the
night at the Grande Bretagne hotel in Athens, at the very
centre of the British position, itself a beleaguered bastion when
the city was hardest pressed by the swarming guerillas. Indeed,
during their time of utmost peril, the British had been compressed into a perimeter of only half a square mile around the
hotel. The politicians expected the rest of their deputation
would arrive there within the next few hours, whatever might

have delayed them. Meanwhile they decided to lose no time in finding out for themselves the truth of what really had been happening in Greece during the past few violent weeks.

But the next day dawned still without sight or sound of the missing plane and its politicians. So James, Lawson and Studholme went about the gruesome business of discovering whether the allegations of atrocities committed by the communist guerillas, so hotly contested by the left in the British Parliament, were true. "There was indeed ample evidence of the communist atrocities", James reported afterwards. Scores of bodies of murdered men, women and children were found in a shallow lake beside the main road to the north of Athens. Another horrible discovery was made in the garden of an elegant villa in a northern suburb. There, hastily buried side by side in rows, were people on the communists' black list and their relatives, friends or lovers. One of the very first dug up was a well-known Greek actress, Helene Papadaki, leading star of the Greek National Theatre. The expression of utmost horror frozen on her face at the moment of her brutal death shocked all those who now looked upon her naked, obscenely defiled body. The two Tory M.P.s and Labourite Jack Lawson now had no doubts that the "heroic left-wing liberators of Greece" were in fact what Winston Churchill had accused them of being – murdering bandits.

This, then, was the report that the members took back with them to England two days later. They also took their report on what they knew of the disappearance of the other aircraft carrying Robert Bernays, J. D. Campbell and Brigadier Partridge. For that plane and its occupants had indeed vanished completely. Nothing more had been seen of it since it had been observed climbing up from Bari airfield to head for the mountains and the lowering black thunder clouds. Troops in that part of Italy, among whom it might have made an emergency landing, or crashed, were asked to keep a special look-out, but it had been neither seen nor heard by any of them. Inquiries were extended among the Italian townsfolk and villagers and peasants in that area, but without result. It seemed certain it could not have come down on Italian soil.

Meanwhile a widespread search had been mounted at sea. Every available vessel, destroyers, R.A.F. air-sea rescue launches, mine-sweepers and motorized armed Greek fishing-boats used by the island-raiding special boat service, scoured the

Ionian Sea between Italy and Greece and the islands and rocky inlets of the west coast of Greece. But the result was the same. Not a trace of any wreckage. The search was carried on with equal intensity on the mainland of Greece, most particularly among the mountains flanking the narrow crooked inlet of sea that was the Gulf of Corinth. Although the British force had been everywhere victorious, and the defeated guerillas were swarming back into the mountains, General Ronald Scobie, the British commander, did not have sufficient men to send search parties out widely. But there was a widespread network of loyal Greeks in touch with his troops, even in the more remote areas, to ensure his receiving reports of anything involving British personnel. Messages were sent out to them now to report on any incident involving, or having a bearing on, a crashed aircraft, but the result was just the same. Nobody at all had seen, or heard, or heard of, a crashed aircraft or an aircraft making a forced landing.

General Scobie's efforts to discover what had, or might have, happened to the missing aircraft were the more persistent because Winston Churchill was sending him urgent messages asking that every possible endeavour should be made to find the missing politicians. Meanwhile – what could have happened to them? The most obvious answer was that lightning from the thunder cloud towards which the plane had climbed from Bari had struck it and made it crash. But had that happened it must have been seen by someone in the area or, if not, its wreckage must have been swiftly discovered.

What, then, was the likelihood of it crashing in the sea between Italy and Greece? It could, of course, have happened; but it was very unlikely to have vanished without a trace. A heavy warplane, out of control and in a dive, might conceivably plunge deep down to the sea bed without breaking up, and so vanish completely, but a light communication aircraft such as the M.P.s had been in would certainly break up on hitting the sea's surface. Some tell-tale wreckage must have been left. But what if a German warship had shot it down into the sea? In that case, of course, if it had been hit by a bursting shell from a naval anti-aircraft gun, it *might* have been so smashed up that it would be difficult to discover an identifiable floating piece. But not even a fragment that might suggest some solution to the mystery had been found at sea. And in any case, the Royal Navy was certain that it had completely eradicated from those waters any enemy warship that might have been capable of thus obliterating the missing aircraft.

There was another possibility that had to be taken into account. This was that the plane had been so badly damaged by ground fire from Greek communist guerillas still in the remote mountains that it had crash landed there. Then the guerillas could have buried the plane, taken the survivors prisoners, and marched them away northwards as potential hostages. Already the guerillas were known to have taken thousands of non-communist Greeks, men, women and children, as hostages and marched them off to Yugoslavia. There they intended to hold them against the day when they might need them as a bargaining counter. The routes of these pitiless hostage marches were remote, through mountains still dominated by the communists. When General Scobie's investigators considered this possibility they had to give it some credence, because had not Wing Commander James, passenger in the aircraft that did get through, reported that over the Greek mountains "rebels fired at us and we could hear the tired whine of bullets". But if the communists were intending to use these British politicians for bargaining, surely it must be sooner rather than later, for Scobie's terms for calling off his troops from their pursuit were even then being drawn up.

Meanwhile all through the weeks, and then months, during which the search was going on for the vanished aircraft and its occupants, Winston Churchill kept in touch with Mrs Nancy Bernays, wife of the missing member for Bristol North. He told her of each new line of investigation that was being adopted until, sadly, in due course he had to report its failure to produce any result. And finally one day he telephoned Mrs Bernays to tell her he feared she must expect the worst, and presume that her husband had died. He said he would send Sir Archibald Sinclair, the Secretary of State for Air, to Bristol to explain to her what he believed had happened. The explanation that Sir Archibald gave to Mrs Bernays was this.

As the little aircraft carrying Bernays, Campbell and Partridge climbed up towards the dark thunder clouds over the coastal mountains beyond Bari it ran into considerable turbulence. Forked lightning zigzagged around it and gusts of hot air threw it around alarmingly. The pilot decided the only thing to do was go down, so he put the nose down and flew fast towards the sea. He flattened out when just a few hundred feet above sea level, well below the storm, and headed for Greece. From then on there was no reason to suspect any danger from the enemy, for their warplanes had been swept from the skies and their ships had been blasted from the seas. But – and there was no reason at all why the pilot should anticipate danger from this quarter – there were still some German submarines in those waters lurking beneath the surface. It could only be supposed that from one of these the approaching aircraft was spotted through the periscope and the captain, recognizing an easy prey, swiftly surfaced. The very last danger the British pilot would have expected would have been an enemy submarine so that, even if he saw it, he was likely to have believed it to be British. And even if he did finally recognize it as a U-boat, who had ever heard of a U-boat shooting down a manoeuvrable light aircraft? However, the likelihood was that they were entirely surprised, otherwise the pilot must have used his radio to warn base that they had spotted a U-boat. Finally, the U-boat had opened fire with its deck-gun, had succeeded in shooting down the British plane.

Sir Archibald Sinclair stressed that although this was not a certainty, it was the only possible explanation Winston Churchill could give after unusually exhaustive inquiries. Since widespread searching on land and sea had failed to produce even one scrap of wreckage, it could only be presumed that the aircraft, plunging into the sea from not far above the surface, had gone straight down to the bottom with its occupants trapped inside. Had it been shot down from a greater height it must have broken up on the surface, so that wreckage would have been left to discover.

As the ensuing years have failed to provide any further evidence throwing light on their disappearance, the British Prime Minister's explanation must be assumed to be the likeliest one, particularly in view of one further fact. In 1943, starting in the Mediterranean where the need was greatest, the normal gun armament of U-boats had been replaced in some cases by more formidable equipment and the so-called "Flak Traps" were introduced, mounting one 37-mm. A.A. gun, four 20-mm. A.A. guns and improved machine-guns. Most of these U-boats, adapted for gun battles with aircraft, were withdrawn later that year. But some may have remained in service – and just one would have been lethal to a light aircraft that came within range.

THE LOST EXPEDITION

Until the Panama Canal was opened, in 1882, the Atlantic and Pacific regions were virtually worlds apart. From the Arctic to the Antarctic the great sprawl of the Americas lay as a barrier between them. The only way to get from one side to the other by sea was by rounding Cape Horn, that extreme tip of South America whose treacherous weather at all seasons had earned it the reputation of ship-killer.

It was not only a dangerous route; it was a very long way to travel between places nothing like so far apart as the crow flew. Many people believed – certainly hoped – that an alternative could be found: a North-West Passage. Attempts to find one were made as early as the fourteenth and fifteenth centuries, but by the time the Napoleonic Wars ended in 1815 none had succeeded, and knowledge of the region which lay between North America and the Arctic was scant.

The ending of the war brought a revival of exploration. Sir John Barrow, secretary of the Admiralty, managed to obtain a parliamentary measure in 1818 offering a prize of £20,000 for making the North-West Passage. Immediately off the mark was an expedition of four ships, sailing in pairs on differing routes. Taking the Baffin Bay approach were the *Isabella* and *Alexander*, commanded respectively by Captain John Ross and Lieutenant Edward Parry. The vessels for the Spitsbergen route were the *Dorothea* and the *Trent*, commanded by Captain D. Buchan and Lieutenant John Franklin.

Franklin at this time was in his early thirties. His life so far had had more than its share of drama. Born in Lincolnshire, he had served as a midshipman at the Battle of Copenhagen before he was quite fifteen. At sixteen he went with his uncle by marriage, Captain Matthew Flinders, to explore the Australian coast, and was shipwrecked in the *Porpoise*. He got back to England in 1803 in time to join the great *Bellerophon* as signal midshipman. This was his post when the "Billy Ruffian" went into the Battle of Trafalgar.

Once again young Franklin was lucky to stay alive. The *Bellerophon* took a fearful pounding from the French barrage. Of forty-seven men on the quarterdeck only seven survived. Franklin was one, sticking calmly to his post, carrying out orders and keeping the colours flying throughout the battle, while his messmates fell like flies about him. He was not even wounded.

He returned to England with his ship, and then transferred into the *Bedford* as an acting lieutenant. Towards the end of the French wars, when America was involved and British troops were attacking New Orleans, he was mentioned in dispatches as the first man to board one of the American gunboats. The end of the war found him a full lieutenant, eager for new excitement. The chance to explore in the Arctic suited him exactly, but that particular attempt of 1818 had to be abandoned when Buchan's vessel was seriously damaged by pack-ice.

The next year Franklin was off again, this time in command of an overland expedition from Hudson's Bay to the shores of the Arctic Ocean, with the purpose of surveying the uncharted region. The venture has been described as "one of the most daring and hazardous exploits that has ever been accomplished in the interest of geographical research". Franklin and his companions were beset by unimaginable hardships. Terrible cold, famine, even murder, did not daunt them. After nearly three hard years of it Franklin arrived back in England again, to be promoted this time to post captain.

In 1825 he went on another overland expedition to North America. In 1829 he was knighted. From 1836 to 1843 he served as lieutenant-governor of Van Diemen's Land, then the great penal settlement. When he returned to England next, in 1843, he was getting on for sixty, a time to settle down to a quiet, mellow life of writing and speaking and enjoying society with his second wife Jane.

That was not John Franklin's style, however. A renewed wave of interest in polar exploration was sweeping Britain. The North-West Passage had still not been found and a major attempt was being planned, with Sir James Ross to take command. He declined, though, and Franklin quickly thrust himself forward. Their lordships of the Admiralty demurred at his age. "No, no, my lords!" he cried. "Not sixty, but fifty-nine!" Such spirit had to win the day; besides, he had all the right experience. He was appointed.

Two former bomb-vessels, *Erebus* and *Terror*, had already proved themselves in south-polar waters under Sir James Ross. They were made ready again. They were steam-driven, which would give the expedition a great advantage over previous ones, and they would carry every up-to-date aid. With an overall complement of 129 officers and men they sailed from Greenhithe on 19 May, 1845. Sir John Franklin was in *Erebus*, with Captain James Fitzjames as his second-in-command and her captain. *Terror* was commanded by Captain F. R. M. Crozier, who had been on expeditions with Parry and Ross.

On 4 July they reached Disco Bay in Greenland and wrote cheerful letters home. Twelve days later the whaling ship *Prince of Wales* met them in Melville Bay at the mouth of Lancaster Sound. She reported back to England: "16 July, 1845. At 8 p.m. received on board ten of the chief officers of the expedition under the command of Captain Sir John Franklin, of the *Terror* and *Erebus*. Both ships' crews are all well and in remarkable spirits, expecting to finish the operation in good time. They are made fast to a large iceberg with a temporary observatory fixed upon it. They were in latitude 74° 48′ N, longitude 66° 13′ W."

In fact, they were at the entrance of the North-West Passage. Their instructions were to pass through Lancaster Sound and Barrow Strait, then turn southward to avoid the ice stream from the west. If he could pursue this sheltered course down into the channel along the Canadian coast, Franklin would be able to turn westward again and through to the Bering Strait. The passage would have been safely accomplished.

Even if the ice did catch the ships there was no urgency about getting them free. The expedition had sailed with enough provisions for three years, and they were adding to them constantly. When another whaler hailed the *Erebus*, Franklin replied through a megaphone that he now had enough food for five years, and indicated men at work on deck salting-down sea-birds.

So no one in England worried unduly when nothing more was reported of the expedition. Communications were poor in more frequented seaways than these Arctic wastes. Ater two years' silence there was the odd suggestion that something might be amiss; but it was not until the summer of 1848 that a council of naval officers, called by the Admiralty, resolved that a relief expedition should sail. Sir James Ross took the *Enterprise* and *Investigator* through Lancaster Sound and made a long sledge journey on Somerset Island, but found nothing.

The return of this expedition with nothing to report aroused considerable agitation. A major rescue operation was begun, involving a number of vessels which combed different areas. The Hudson's Bay Company joined in, sending sledge teams to search the extreme northern coastline of Canada. The years of searching led to some seven thousand miles of hitherto unexplored coastline being mapped, and to some great feats of travel; but the real purpose was to find Franklin and his men, and they seemed to have disappeared. Remains of two vessels were seen off Newfoundland, eerily encapsulated inside an iceberg. They could not be identified as the *Erebus* and *Terror*, though.

The winter quarters of 1845–46 were discovered on Beechey Island. There was some discarded equipment there, the pathetic vestiges of a small garden, and the graves of three men who had died. There was nothing to indicate the expedition's direction.

Then, in 1850, a great discovery was made by Captain Robert le Mesurier M'Clure of the *Investigator*. With six men and a sledge he had left the ship and travelled through Barrow's Strait (now known as Melville Strait). Standing on Banks Island, 600 feet above sea-level, they looked northward – and saw only sea. "The eyesight embraced a distance which precluded the possibility of any land lying in that direction between them and Melville Island. A North-West Passage was discovered." It was ironical that a ship searching for Franklin should have come accidentally upon the great object of his quest.

It was M'Clure who, some months later, had a piece of luck of a different sort. He shot a large bear, which proved to have in its stomach things indicating the proximity of civilized men.

There was surgeon's sticking-plaster, pieces of tobacco leaf, pork cut into cubes, and raisins. The party rejoiced. Surely they were on Franklin's trail at last!

Three more years passed before any more clues came to light. A Dr J. Rae had been searching for years on behalf of the Hudson's Bay Company and met a party of Esquimaux in Pelly Bay, King William's Land. They told him that some years before, one spring-time, they had seen some forty white men struggling over the ice, dragging a boat and sledges. They all looked thin and exhausted, and they managed to convey that their ship had been crushed in the ice. The Esquimaux sold them one of the seals they had just killed.

Later that same year, the Esquimaux had found thirty corpses and some graves on the mainland and five bodies on a nearby island. Beside them were some relics, which the Esquimaux had kept: a silver plate engraved "Sir John Franklin, K.C.B.", some spoons with initials and crests, and other things. Dr Rae persuaded the Esquimaux to part with these and took them back to England. It seemed conclusive evidence of the deaths of the explorer and his men. The government decided to call off the search and give Rae the £10,000 reward for determining Franklin's fate.

Lady Franklin, however, refused to give in so easily. She challenged the government: "What does all this prove? That the *Erebus* and the *Terror* had to be abandoned, perhaps, but no more. In fact, it does not even prove that. The unfortunate men to whom Dr Rae refers may well have been a reconnaissance party sent out from the ships. After that they may have lost their way and been unable to return. Only thirty-five bodies were found, but the total party consisted of 129 officers and men. Are we to believe that there was not a single survivor left alive?"

When the government refused her plea for one last effort, she herself bought a steam yacht, the *Fox*, and sent it out in July, 1857, under the command of a man who had already spent much time looking for Franklin, Captain Leopold M'Clintock. The government rather sheepishly contributed much of this latest expedition's equipment and provisions. The *Fox* was eminently suited to its task, and M'Clintock had the advantage of all the information already gathered, positive and negative.

From a warm English June the *Fox* sailed into premature winter conditions off Greenland. Changing course to avoid the clutch of the "middle ice" they came to Beechey Island, where they anchored. M'Clintock erected a marble memorial, whose inscription clearly indicated his lack of hope that the men he sought could still be alive: "To the memory of Franklin, Crozier, Fitzjames and all their valiant brother officers and men who suffered and perished in the cause of science and to the glory of their country, this tablet is erected near the spot where they spent their first Arctic winter."

In Melville Bay in August the ice closed in. For eight months the gallant little *Fox* struggled and drifted. It was not until March, 1858, that gales released her, blowing her out to sea, free again to pursue her quest. During the summer M'Clintock explored all likely territory without finding a trace. Another winter was endured. On 1 March, 1859, the *Fox* was at "about the position of the Magnetic Pole". The crew were setting up a shore camp when they met a small party of Esquimaux. Bartering began. Then one of the sailors spotted something which caused him to nudge his officer. On the coat of one of the natives there glinted a British naval button.

Careful questioning elicited the information that the button had been got from some white people who were starved on an island "where there were some salmon". Next day the entire village population arrived and M'Clintock got more news and more relics. There were six silver spoons and forks, a silver medal bearing the name of Mr McDonald, Franklin's assistant surgeon, part of a gold chain, more buttons, and bows and arrows which the natives had fashioned out of the wreck of the white men's ship.

During the weeks following more and more clues came to light. Two ships had been seen, long ago, by the natives of King William's Island. One of them had sunk in deep water and they could salvage nothing from her. The other had been forced on to the shore by ice. Her people had gone away to the large river – Back's Fish River – dragging a boat with them. They had left a dead man in their ship, a large man with long teeth; but they, too, were now no more than bones. The Esquimaux told M'Clintock where some would be found. He reached the spot on 25 May.

"I came upon a human skeleton, partly exposed, with here and there a few fragments of clothing appearing through the snow ... The dress appeared to be that of a steward or officer's servant ... We found a clothes-brush near and a pocket-comb."

An old woman told them that the survivors "fell down and died as they walked along". A trail of grim discoveries proved this true. Further on, M'Clintock found a piece of flannel marked "F. D. V., 1845", which he sadly identified as part of the clothing of the mate, Charles Des Voeux. Then, at Point Victory, about twelve miles from Cape Herschel, came written evidence. It was an Admiralty form, with a message written on it:

"28 May, 1847. H. M. ships *Erebus* and *Terror* wintered in the ice in lat. 70° 05′ N., long. 98° 23′ W.

Having wintered in 1846–7 at Beechey Island, after having ascended Wellington Channel to lat. 77° and returned by the west side of Cornwallis Island, Sir John Franklin commanding the expedition.

All well.

Party, consisting of two officers and six men, left the ships on Monday, 24 May, 1847."

The message was signed "Gm. Gore, Lieut.

Chas. F. Des Voeux, Mate."

But the hope and confidence of this was dispelled by smaller writing which filled in the margins of the paper:

"25 April, 1848. H.M. ships *Terror* and *Erebus* were deserted on 22 April, five leagues NNW of this, having been beset since 12 September, 1846. The officers and crews, consisting of 105 souls, under the command of Capt. F. R. M. Crozier, landed here in lat. 69° 37′ 42″ N., long 98° 41′ W. Sir John Franklin died on 11 June, 1847, and the total loss by deaths in the expedition has been, to this date, nine officers and fifteen men."

The signatures now were "F. R. M. Crozier, Captain and Senior Officer" and "James Fitzjames, Captain H.M.S. *Erebus*." A postscript read "And start tomorrow, 26th, for Back's Fish River."

M'Clintock followed the trail. At the western extremity of King William's Island he found a large, ruined boat. It was not empty. He and his companions gazed "transfixed with awe" at two human skeletons. "One was that of a slight young person; the other of a large, strongly made middle-aged man . . ."

Animals had ravaged the bones, but plenty of identifiable objects were left in the boat: watches, guns, furs, and some pathetic books, all of them devotional works except *The Vicar of*

Wakefield. One little volume, *Christian Melodies*, was inscribed on the title-page "G. G." – probably Lieutenant Graham Gore, who had written that earlier, optimistic message.

So the chief mystery of the Franklin expedition was solved; but there remained mysteries within it. Together with the corpses in the boat were nearly forty pounds of chocolate and some tea. Starvation could scarcely have killed them. Since that early discovery, others who have been to that place in this century have found unopened tins of meat, but also others which had been thrown away opened, their contents untouched. It suggests that the men had suspected the state of the meat, which in turn might imply that they had already eaten some and been poisoned by it.

The *Erebus* and *Terror* have never been found. Many members of the expedition remain unaccounted for. As though reluctant to relinquish this mystery of the frozen wastes, many people in England refused to believe that Franklin and his men were dead. An American explorer brought back tales of mysterious white men living among the Esquimaux. He made a hazardous journey looking for them, but found nothing.

It is generally conceded now that the "knight-errant of the northern seas", Sir John Franklin, did discover the North-West Passage; but that he and all his men perished doing it.

FLIGHT INTO LIMBO

The twenty-odd years which followed Blériot's famous flight across the English Channel in 1909 were filled with aviation milestones. New air space was conquered, new records set up, new feats of courage and endurance performed. The intrepid aviators were the heroes of the day, equivalent to this generation's astronauts, and among them were two famous women, Amelia Earhart and Amy Johnson.

Although, in concept, the achievements of today's astronauts are more frighteningly dramatic than those of the aviators of the 'twenties they are easily comparable. The flyer of that time had no banks of computers behind him, no teams of experts monitoring every moment of his flight, no high-technology equipment on which to depend. Aeroplanes were primitive, flimsy and unreliable. The aviator had to be mechanic as well as pilot, navigator as well as engineer.

At a time when woman's place was still very much in the home, the mere fact that Amy and Amelia fought their way through masculine prejudice and all kinds of difficulties to become the first women in their respective countries to obtain flying licences, was in itself an achievement. Both were attractive, feminine women yet determined and eager for adventure. Both set up world records for solo flights and both died when their planes mysteriously vanished.

Amelia Earhart was born in Kansas in 1898 and became fascinated by aeroplanes when, at the age of nineteen, she saw her first air show – a form of entertainment common in those days. Soon after her father arranged for her to have a demonstration flight and Amelia promptly decided she must learn to fly. To pay for her lessons she took a job in a telephone exchange. Eventually she became one of the first American women to be licensed as a pilot. In 1922 her family helped her to buy a light aeroplane and Amelia was set for a flying career, although at first she had only regarded it as a hobby. When she was offered the chance to be the first woman to fly across the Atlantic she jumped at it. Her sponsor was George Putnam of the publishing firm, who wanted Amelia to write her story for him and who eventually married her.

On this Atlantic flight in 1928 Amelia was only a passenger and it became her ambition to fly the Atlantic alone, as Charles Lindbergh had done in 1927. Her trip across the Atlantic brought her fame; and her husband, a great publicity seeker, made sure that she continued in the limelight.

She made a number of record-breaking flights of one kind or another, chalked up a series of "firsts", and appeared at all sorts of aeronautical occasions. In 1932 she finally achieved her great ambition, and became the first woman to fly solo across the Atlantic. After a somewhat hair-raising flight which included storms, wing-ice and a broken manifold ring, she landed in a field outside Londonderry having flown the Atlantic in 14 hours and 56 minutes.

Amelia continued to break records and make long-distance solo flights while she worked towards the achievement of her next great ambition – to fly round the world. In 1936 she bought the most advanced civil aircraft of the day, the Lockheed Electra, and had certain modifications carried out to make it more suitable for long-distance flying.

The flight was to be from east to west, starting from Oakland, California, with the first step to Honolulu. But on the take-off from Honolulu something went wrong and the plane slewed round and crashed. Nobody was hurt, but the aircraft was badly damaged. Two months passed before it could be repaired and the plans for the flight were changed; this time Amelia decided to fly from west to east. She also decided to keep with her her navigator, Fred Noonan, for the whole journey, although originally she had intended to carry out a large part of the flight alone.

On 20 May, 1937, Amelia and Fred took off from Oakland.

They flew via Tucson, New Orleans, Miami, San Juan in Puerto Rico, Caripizo in Venezuela, Paramaribo in Dutch Guiana to Portaleza in Brazil, which they reached on 4 June and where the engines were checked over by Pan-Am mechanics. From Brazil Amelia flew the 1,900 miles of ocean which separated them from Senegal in West Africa. Via Mali, Chad, the Sudan and Eritrea they came to Karachi, where once more the engines were checked over, by RAF and Imperial Airways mechanics, leaving there on 15 June for another 1,900-mile flight to Calcutta.

On 21 June Amelia and Fred reached Bandung in Java, having come via Burma and Singapore, and there they stayed for six days while a local engine specialist and crew worked on the engines and navigational instruments. At last they were able to take off for Timor and Port Darwin in Australia. On 1 July they were in Lae, New Guinea, preparing for the next and most difficult leg of the flight, 2,556 miles over open water to Howland Island, the penultimate scheduled stop on their round-the-world flight.

Howland Island is a tiny spot in the centre of the vast Pacific Ocean. It is two miles long, about half a mile wide and not more than twenty feet high. The U.S. Government had had three emergency landing strips made on the island, apparently solely for Amelia's benefit, but finding the place after such a long flight was a navigational headache. To give her all possible help a U.S. Navy ship, the *Swan*, was stationed half-way between Honolulu and Howland, the U.S.S. *Ontario* was half-way between Howland and Lae, and a coast-guard cutter *Itasca* lay alongside the island itself to act as a navigational beacon.

Amelia and Fred took off in the Electra at 10.30 a.m. without problem. Five hours later the radio station at New Guinea picked up a message from Amelia giving her position as 795 miles from Lae. She was on course, not far off the Solomon Islands, and all was well. On board the *Itasca* Captain Thompson and his crew had made all possible preparations. The Electra was expected to arrive after daylight, some 20-odd hours after it had taken off, and the ship's boilers were to start making smoke as soon as it was light, to guide the plane. But in case of a tail wind and early arrival the cutter's searchlights would go on after midnight. Boat crews were ready to go out and position themselves in case the plane overshot the runway, while other crew members tried to keep the landing strips clear of birds. Every hour and half-hour the ship's transmitter sent out weather reports and homing signals. Amelia was to transmit her call sign at a quarter past and quarter to each hour.

All night the crew of the *Itasca* waited patiently. Once or twice she contacted the *Ontario* to ask if there had been any signal. Eventually at 1.15 a.m. the *Itasca* radioed Amelia asking her to broadcast her call sign. At last the first signal, brief and distorted by static, came through at 2.45 a.m. The *Itasca* broadcast to other ships to check that her own signals were coming through clearly, and confirmed that it was the Electra's signals which were weak. One more brief message from Amelia was heard at 3.45 and the *Itasca* continued to broadcast her homing signal and weather report.

At last, at 6.15 Amelia radioed clearly and asked *Itasca* to take a bearing on her so she could check her position. At 6.45 she asked the same thing, but on both occasions was not long enough on the air to allow the *Itasca* to find her. The ship asked Amelia to signal on another frequency, but Amelia made no answer. Then half an hour later in two subsequent messages she asked for bearings again, said that she estimated they were over the island, but could not hear the *Itasca* and gas was running low. She suggested yet another frequency; the agitated captain obeyed, wondering why on earth she did not broadcast on the frequency which would allow *Itasca* to use its special gear. But then Amelia acknowledged hearing the *Itasca* for the first time. Once again she switched frequency on to the earlier range which the ship had had difficulty in finding, and again broadcast her call sign for too short a period. Thompson was now in despair. He could not understand why Amelia continued to wish to use a frequency for which his gear was not suitable, and why she did not broadcast on the frequency he requested.

Finally, at 8.45, the ship received a message to say that the plane was running north and south and that they were switching to their day-time frequency. By now the whole crew of the coastguard cutter was on deck straining to hear any sound of the plane. The funnel was belching great clouds of smoke which would be visible for miles, but to the north-west there was a massive bank of storm cloud which, if the plane were in that area, could be giving them trouble. Anxiously the radio

operator listened for any sound while the men on deck
searched the sky. Nothing.

At ten o'clock Thompson made the decision to start searching. The *Itasca* weighed anchor and set sail to the north-west,
still transmitting to the Electra, hoping that if it had come
down into the sea it might still be able to reply. But there was
silence. In the hours that followed Thompson was bombarded
with advice and suggestions and other units set out to join in
the search. President Roosevelt ordered all available ships and
planes to join in the search and during the next fortnight some
150,000 square miles of sea were searched. Amelia's husband
also contacted the Japanese consulate in San Francisco, asking
that Japanese craft should keep a lookout, but there was no
response. Towards the end of July, when all the area save that
which the Japanese controlled had been searched, the ships
came home, their colours at half mast.

Mantz, a brilliant pilot who often acted as technical adviser
on Amelia's flights and had done so on this occasion, summed
up the event as follows: "One: the navigator missed the island
and Miss Earhart flew until out of gas and, due to fatigue,
tried to land too high over the clear water which would result
in the ship falling off, causing a crash that would kill them
instantly. Two: if the sea were very rough it would be quite
hard to judge the distance properly, thus causing her to fly into
a heavy roller, having a similar result."

Despite Mantz's certainty that the plane would have broken
up there was continued uncertainty, fostered by the assevera-
tions of mediums and the reports of ham radio operators. The
death of a famous person in dramatic circumstances almost
invariably produces a rash of rumour, speculation and legend –
the assassination of President Kennedy is a typical example. In
Amelia's case, once the false hopes aroused by the efforts of
well-wishers or mischief-makers had died down, another theory
gained ground – that Amelia and Fred had been nowhere near
Howland Island, but had come down in Japanese-controlled
waters and been taken prisoners. The story gradually gained
credence, enhanced by the attitude of the U.S. Navy and State
Department, who appeared reluctant to divulge any information they had gained during the investigation. The theory
was that Amelia had undertaken a secret mission on
behalf of naval intelligence, to divert many miles off her original
course in order to fly over Japanese islands and spy on them.

In the early 'sixties the rumour still persisted and new "evidence" came to light. An American journalist, Fred Goerner, set out to investigate and searched the Pacific Islands formerly in the hands of the Japanese, on which Amelia was said to have been imprisoned and later executed. Although much of the evidence which he investigated – including two skeletons buried in a cemetery on Saipan – turned out to be false, Goerner turned up several interesting facts and came to the conclusion that Amelia did, in fact, make the flight over Japanese-held islands, got lost and ditched her plane before she could reach Howland. She was captured, he believes, and later executed with Fred Noonan by the Japanese. His conclusions are largely based on stories told by the islanders of two flyers, one a woman, who were captured by the Japanese; on the fact that he had discovered that engines of a type capable of a top speed of 220 m.p.h. had been installed on the Electra with a singular lack of publicity; and on the evasiveness of naval, military and civil bureaucrats in Washington.

Amy Johnson's death, though without the dramatic overtones of Amelia's, also became surrounded by mystery. Amy was five years younger than Amelia, whom she had first met in England just after she made her solo Atlantic flight in 1932. Amy had then held a pilot's licence for only three years but she was already a world-famous figure, for in 1930 she had made the first solo flight from Britain to Australia by a woman. Having risen overnight from obscurity to fame, she suddenly became the epitome of what every ordinary girl could do – for Amy came from a modest background – and an example of British spirit. She was fêted, lauded and idolized – and she had no publicity-minded husband to build up public interest. She took off on her lone flight almost casually, and it was only gradually that the world began to sit up and take notice as her twenty-day adventure proceeded. She failed to break the record from England to Australia, through bad weather, but she established a new record to India. By the time she reached Australia the whole world had been following her daily progress with bated breath.

Amy's life was not so happy as Amelia's. She was often in debt; she made an unsuccessful marriage to another flyer, Jim

Mollison; she sometimes drank too much; she missed the security of a settled home life and she was not physically strong. Nor was she so single-minded about flying as Amelia: although she set up another world record during a flight to South Africa, she had many other interests, hunting, sailing, gliding and writing.

For some time Amy drifted from place to place, looking for an objective in life. Various projects came to nothing, and then in June, 1939, she succeeded in getting a flying job with the Solent air ferry, which she stuck to for nine months until wartime reorganization ended it. Finally in April, 1940, she joined the Air Transport Auxiliary, whose job it was to ferry planes about to various parts of the country. At first she disliked the job; she was too much of an individualist to take kindly to regimentation and being one of a crowd. Nevertheless her reputation went with her. Whenever she arrived at an airfield she would be surrounded by airmen demanding her autograph. Gradually she found she was enjoying her work more; she was living with friends, had no money problems, and she seemed to be more contented than she had been for years.

On the afternoon of Sunday 5 January, 1941, a cold day with sleet and a biting east wind, personnel aboard ships which formed part of a convoy steaming into the Thames Estuary saw a plane flying low over them. When it was less than 200 feet up, something white fluttered out and dropped into the sea. The plane jumped up as it hit a wave, hung suspended, then turned over.

Amy had left Squire's Gate, the Blackpool airfield, at 11.49 a.m. on a flight which should have taken about an hour, in a plane which carried enough fuel for 3½–4 hours. The weather was bad, but Amy had intended to fly "over the top". It was presumed she had lost her way, run out of petrol and been obliged to abandon the plane. The nearest ship to the crashing plane altered course towards the parachutist and a seaman leaning over the rail heard the person in the water, whom he then realized was a woman, call "Hurry, please hurry". Heaving lines were thrown from the ship, but the woman made no attempt to catch them. Then, said the seaman, "the woman was now quite close in under the stern of the ship. The ship was heaving in the swell, and the stern came up and dropped on top of the woman. She did not come into view again."

Before this event, however, witnesses had seen a second person in the water, not far off. The ship's captain, Commander Fletcher, realizing nothing could be done to save the woman, leaped overboard and swam towards the second person, who seemed to be wearing a flying helmet. A lifeboat had by now been launched, and the witnesses on this boat stated that Fletcher supported the person for a short time. Then the two separated and the person disappeared. Fletcher was rescued, unconscious, and remained so until he died later in hospital.

The result of this incident was that the newspapers reported that Amy's plane had been carrying a passenger when it crashed. Wreckage and bags containing papers had been picked up by another ship some distance away, and there was no doubt that it was Amy's plane which had come down. But there was a complete denial that Amy had had a passenger. There was definitely nobody with her when she took off from Squire's Gate, and it was virtually impossible that she could have landed anywhere and picked somebody up. The second "person" in the water, declared an old friend, solicitor Sir William Crocker, who was asked to clear up the "mystery", was in fact Amy's round bag, which had been picked up among the salvaged goods. The bag could have been mistaken for a man's head, but it does not explain the fact that it disappeared when Fletcher let it go. There is a possibility that this could have been the body of an airman which had earlier fallen into the river, for there had been a raid over Canterbury that day.

Nobody will ever be able to explain for sure the mystery of the "second person" who was seen in the water. That the woman who died, presumably when the ship struck her, was Amy there can be little doubt. Her body was never found. In 1961 the bones of a woman that were washed up on the Kent coast were examined and proved not to be Amy's.

Amy and Amelia were almost the same age when they died and Amy, at least, had foreseen her end. "I know where I shall finish up – in the drink", she told a friend. "A few headlines in the newspapers and then they forget you." It was indeed often the fate of long-distance flyers, and her friend Amelia had disappeared in this way. But she was wrong about being forgotten. Both Amelia and Amy achieved fame and popularity in their day, and became the symbol of courage and freedom in their own countries and throughout the world. It is almost as if, in perpetuating the mystery which surrounds their deaths, the world is reluctant to let them go, let alone forget them.

LOST WITH ALL HANDS

Since the dawn of history all but landlubbers have known that the sea is treacherous. Ever since man first crawled out of it and developed legs it has borne him with reluctance and then only when he built for himself boats as a substitute for the dry land where he now belonged. The sea has never been man's natural element and in entrusting his life to it he has at times paid a heavy price.

Formerly this was well understood, particularly in coastal areas where seafaring people lived with their families. When a fishing fleet set out, or ships carrying goods to distant countries it had to be accepted that some might not return, wrecked perhaps on a rocky shore or lost in wind and storm. Only the skill of the sailors, the strength and suitability of their boats stood between them and the spirit of the deep which some said was ever ready to claim victims.

Now we almost believe that we have defeated the untamable sea. Radar, radio, navigation aids, detailed charts, echo-sounders, huge steel ships, powerful engines convince us that the oceans have lost their power to destroy – until a fresh calamity drives home the point that too much boldness, some unpredicted factor, some innocuous-seeming mistake can lead to disaster just as surely as they did in ancient times.

In recent years the fate of oil tankers, the *Torrey Canyon* for instance, has reminded us of this fact. But other fatalities yet more dramatic are not so well known – the case of the dis-

appearing battleship, for one. Admittedly, the circumstances
were unusual and they contributed to the disaster. All the
same, the story of the *Sao Paulo* shows once again how remorse-
lessly the sea will search out weaknesses in men and ships.

In 1910, when she was delivered from the British shipyard of
Vickers Armstrong, the *Sao Paulo* – 20,000 tons, 500 feet long,
with ten 12-inch and eight 4·7-inch guns – became the pride of
the Brazilian navy, and beyond that of the new Brazilian Republic which had been founded in 1889 after the second and
last emperor had been forced from office. In the chronically
disturbed conditions of South American politics the great
battleship also represented a warning to would-be aggressors
that Brazil would defend herself against attack by sea as well as
land. But above all, with her gleaming brasswork, formidable
armament and menacing ram bow she was a status symbol, a
reminder that Brazil was an up-and-coming country, as indeed
it was, with an unprecedented boom ahead as the world's chief
coffee supplier.

Perhaps symbols are most effective when not put to the test
of reality. At any rate, the *Sao Paulo* never fired her guns in
anger, but stayed mostly at her base in Rio de Janeiro, silent
and majestic, throughout her useful life. In the First World
War, after Brazilian ships had been sunk by German U-boats,
Brazil declared war and sent a naval squadron to European
waters to co-operate with the Allies. But the *Sao Paulo* did not
join it. Again, in the Second World War, Brazil entered hos-
tilities against Germany in 1942. But the *Sao Paulo*, already
obsolete, did not take part. By now, like many old ships that
survive into a later age, she had become something of a cult
object, to be revered for her very antiquity. No one but Brazi-
lians wanted her, and they wanted her clean and spruce like
any other monument in the beautiful surroundings of Rio. So,
in 1947, she was put into drydock, repainted and polished,
then taken back to her moorings.

But by 1951 the *Sao Paulo* had become an embarrassment. In
the last six years she had been cannibalized for many small
parts and some of her steel, the gun shields for instance of the
secondary armament. She was rapidly becoming a hulk. Yet
the remaining steel was valuable and to take her out and sink
her would have been wasteful as well as undignified. The only
alternative seemed to be to leave her where she was, but that
was no permanent solution either. So the problem remained

unsolved until in that year the old battleship was spotted by a representative of the British Iron and Steel Corporation and a contract was signed for her to be towed to Britain and broken up for scrap. The risk was not thought to be great. The Corporation had long experience of such operations and knew just where to find an expert who would prepare the ship for the journey. This was a Mr William Painter, managing director of the Ensign Rigging Company.

Painter's job was to seal the *Sao Paulo* so that she would not take in water. A ship being towed behaves differently from one moving under her own power. Lacking her own impetus to give her stability, she will tend to roll severely and wallow from one wave-crest to the next. Moreover, the *Sao Paulo*'s normal complement amounting to hundreds of men was to be replaced by a skeleton crew of eight flown out from England, too small a number to give the ship normal attention when at sea. All this called for extra care in sealing openings that the sea might penetrate: hatches, port holes, ammunition hoists, doors, skylights, ventilators. There were hundreds of them.

But at last the work was done under Painter's supervision, employing local labour, and a Brazilian surveyor was called on board to give the *Sao Paulo* a certificate of seaworthiness. After a careful scrutiny this was issued and on 20 September, 1951, ballasted with water and drawn by two powerful tugs sent from Britain – the *Bustler* (1,000 tons) and the *Dexterous* (600 tons) – the battleship began to move out from Rio de Janeiro on her final voyage.

The sea was calm, the weather fine and many people watching on shore must have felt a pang to see the old ship that by now had almost become part of their history glide slowly away towards the distant breaker's yard.

For forty-five days the weather held while the slow procession moved northwards towards the Equator, carried by the south-east trade winds. Daily, aboard the battleship, Painter reported by radio to the senior tug-master and every day the news was satisfying: no water being shipped, nothing come adrift, the ship was accepting her fate like a lamb. As for the skeleton crew, well used to these towing operations, they said they had never had such a quiet time.

Off the Cape Verde islands the *Dexterous*, a coal-burning boat, began to run low on fuel and, slipping her tow, had to put into Dakar to refill the bunkers. She was back in two days, but even that time lost, added to the slow work in Rio before the ships sailed, was now beginning to seem important. If the ships had reached their present latitude earlier in the year good weather could have been expected for most of the voyage. But now winter was coming on and the convoy would shortly enter the north-east trades where it would have to battle against contrary winds. Meanwhile the barometer was falling and a south-westerly gale was getting up. There was nothing for it, of course, but to plough on and this the ships did for several more days, dipping and swaying into the mounting seas.

Near the Azores the storm increased in fury and it became necessary to heave-to, head to wind. With the tugs pounding under full power the three ships were almost stationary, and for them this was the safest situation. But as darkness began to fall, the wind began to howl yet more fiercely, whipping up rain and spray into a curtain that swirled between the tugs and the battleship, blotting out visibility. A giant wave lifted the *Dexterous* bodily, then carried her sideways towards the *Bustler* so that the V of the towing hawsers threatened to become a single line. A minute later, they were wrenched apart again, then drawn together once more, this time not through the action of the sea but the wind: battered by the gale, the battleship with her tall superstructure was being driven astern, drawing the tugs after her.

With Mr Painter the two experienced tug-masters had worked out a drill for just such a situation as this. The *Dexterous*, being the less powerful tug, would cast off her tow and proceed independently until the storm abated – a procedure that sounded deceptively simple. But when one hawser was dropped the entire strain would, of course, come on the other one and unless it was already taut with all slack taken up it might snap. Success therefore depended on the captain of the *Dexterous* accurately judging the moment to cast off, and maybe he would have judged it perfectly if at the crucial moment a shackle holding the hawser to the tug had not broken. Instantly the hawser whipped away towards the bow of the battleship and within seconds the other one drew taut and snapped like a piece of string.

Both tugs had meanwhile received a severe battering from the wind and sea and there was now only one thing they could do: heave-to again until daylight. Then they could go to the help of the battleship. But where was she? It was dark now and the only hope was to keep in touch by radio and radar. But despite repeated calls there was no answer and nothing showed up on the radar screen. Captain Adam of the *Bustler* then flashed a searchlight in the direction where the *Sao Paulo* had last been seen drifting astern so that, if they saw it, the men aboard her would know they had not been abandoned and help would be with them next day. There was no answering light.

Once during the night Adam saw a faint glow about three miles away to the south-west and went to investigate, but it was a cargo boat hove-to in the storm and when daylight came the sea stretched on all sides blank and bare. The *Dexterous* was by now so badly storm-damaged that she had to limp off for repairs at Ponta Delgada in the Azores, and Adam radioed the British Admiralty for an aircraft search and his base at Falmouth for another tug to come out and join him.

Meanwhile the storm had at last subsided and Adam followed up a radio message from another ship that rockets had been seen twenty-five miles away to the north-east. But he found nothing. Around midday aircraft arrived from Gibraltar and began a wide sweep right round the compass, again with negative results. But Adam would not give up. Ships, even battleships, are difficult to spot from the air and the *Sao Paulo* might now be drifting in almost any direction, even north-east, caught up in the westerlies north of the Horse Latitudes. So the search was continued in ever-widening circles, reinforced after a few days by another tug, the *Turmoil* from Falmouth. But though several other ships were sighted there was no sign of the ancient battleship, not a boat, not a raft, though both were on board, no wreckage of any kind. For another ten days the two tug-masters combed the bleak North Atlantic until, on 20 November, having long since been recalled, they set a course for home, as sure as sailors can be in those vast spaces that if the *Sao Paulo* had still been afloat she would have been found.

A court of inquiry, not held until three years later, brought to light no few facts, only accusations. A cook-steward from the *Dexterous* with an obvious grudge against his officers claimed that the tow should never have been dropped. A seaman named de Vos, one of the skeleton crew who had stayed behind in Rio because of illness, swore that his mates were

thoroughly alarmed about the careless way the *Sao Paulo* had
been sealed and had even threatened to walk off the ship. Even
the tug-masters, he said, were dissatisfied. But the latter denied
this and the testimony of the two witnesses was rejected. As is
usual and fair in such cases, the court reached no firm conclusion as to the cause of the loss, declaring only that when the
battleship broke away "no doubt heavy rolling occurred. It is
highly probable that the superstructure soon received damage
and there may well have been breaching of one or more gun
ports. Large quantities of water probably entered the hull not
long after the parting."

The court might have added a regret that the towing operation did not start earlier, before the winter storms, but with
this muted requiem the *Sao Paulo*, wherever she was, had to be
content.

It is reasonably clear, nevertheless, what happened to her.
Not so with another ship that disappeared a year later.

The *Melanie Schulte* was a 6,367-ton motor cargo ship, driven
by diesel engines developing 3,350 horse power and containing
all the latest equipment to ensure safety and accurate navigation: radio, radar, an automatic steering device, an echo-soun-
der. She was owned by the Schulte and Bruns Company of
West Germany and at her launching at Emden on 9 September, 1952, a mishap occurred which was afterwards to cause
considerable discussion: her stern was already in the water
when she stuck on the slipway. Until she was released this put
a heavy strain on the hull amid-ships and after launching she
was carefully inspected for damage. It seemed to be slight, no
more than a shallow 15-inch dent in the keel, and she was
given first-class clearance by the underwriters.

There was nothing novel about her design – four sister ships
had long since been at sea doing good work – and if anything
was needed to prove she was as staunch as they were it came
on the maiden voyage in ballast to Quebec and on the return
with a cargo of grain. On both trips Force 9 gales were
encountered and heavy seas. But the *Melanie Schulte* took everything in her stride and her Captain Rohde pronounced himself
well satisfied. A rivet or two had sprung loose, there was a
dribble of water from a welded joint, but these faults were so
slight it only took two days to rectify them. Then the brand-
new ship was on her way again, this time to pick up a cargo of
iron ore at Narvik consigned to Mobile in the Gulf of Mexico.

Iron ore can shift and requires careful stowing. But Captain Rohde knew all about that, though he chose to distribute the cargo in a somewhat unorthodox fashion, putting none in hold No. 1 nearest the bow, 2,875 tons in No. 2, 3,018 tons in No. 3, 2,408 tons in No. 4 and only 1,006 tons in No. 5 at the stern. This plan put the main weight amidships, none at the bow and only a small amount at the stern. Bearing in mind that in the Atlantic a ship of even that size may at times find herself suspended between two waves with nothing beneath her, it seemed rather curious.

Still, the captain was an experienced man and of course the owners gave him full power to decide on the stowage of the cargo and also on the route he would take from Narvik to the Gulf. He chose the northerly route between Britain and Iceland as being more direct and on 17 December the *Melanie Schulte* set sail, taking a south-westerly course. Four days later she radioed her position as west of the Hebrides. At 11 p.m. that evening the ship's radio operator asked the Norddeich receiving station in Germany if there was anything more for him that night and, as there was not, he then switched to the automatic alert system and went to sleep.

Early next morning, Norddeich tried to raise the *Melanie Schulte* to pass a message to one of the crew, and got no reply. Repeated efforts were all unsuccessful, neither did the ship's routine position report come through. This was very odd as even if the radio transmitter had developed a fault, contact could still have been made with one of the lifeboats' battery-powered sets. Could have been, that was, unless . . .

Seriously alarmed, the owners sent out a call to all shipping in the area to watch out for the *Melanie Schulte*, then, four days later, when no contacts had been reported, asked the R.A.F. in Scotland to carry out a search. This proved negative except for one discovery – a huge patch of oil some three hundred miles off the west coast of Ireland. But no lifeboats were seen and no wreckage.

By early January, 1953, when the ship had failed to turn up at Mobile to unload, it was assumed she had been lost with all her thirty-five men. But how and where? Weeks passed without news until, late in February, a lifebelt inscribed MELANIE SCHULTE was washed up on Benbecula Island off the west coast of Scotland. Soon after, some broken hatch covers and other wreckage apparently from the ship's radio office were also found on the island of North Uist in the Outer Hebrides. That at least was confirmation of the ship's fate, but told nothing of what had actually happened.

A court to investigate the matter met in Hamburg on 23 April, 1953, and there was not much to go on but conjecture. No S.O.S. had been picked up from the ship, so presumably she had foundered suddenly. Had she broken her back perhaps and did that have something to do with the mishap at the launching? Hardly. A slightly dented keel would surely not be enough. Then had she by any chance struck a mine? Experts were called and were adamant that this was not possible. In the late war neither side had laid anchored mines in the area where the ship had been, moreover such mines automatically became harmless if they broke away from their moorings. Drifting mines had hardly been used except off harbour mouths and all mines after eight years would probably no longer operate. In any case, experience had shown that a sizeable ship had hardly ever been sunk by a single mine and never so rapidly as to exclude a distress call.

Satisfied apparently with these emphatic but perhaps overconfident assertions, the court moved on to discuss the question of the cargo. On her voyage south the ship had encountered very heavy weather. That was certain. On the night of 21 December other ships in the vicinity had reported waves up to 30 feet high with troughs between them of 70 to 100 yards. With the heavy weight of cargo amidships had the *Melanie Schulte* been caught between two of them and simply broken her back? Or did those pathetic remnants, the hatch covers, show that the cargo had shifted in the storm and burst through the hatches so that, like many ships of old that had foundered with their gun ports open, she had taken in a heavy sea, failed to right herself and then rolled over on to her beam ends?

The court could not decide for certain and, since nothing has been seen or heard of the *Melanie Schulte* in the intervening years, neither can we. But her fate and that of the *Sao Paulo* may well have been caused in each case by a single mistake. It seems that the battleship left Rio too late in the season and the German ship's cargo was wrongly stowed – which shows that however skilled the crews, or modern the appliances, or careful the overall plan, the sea is ever watchful to claim its victims, and seldom gives them a second chance.

Derelicts

WHATEVER HAPPENED
ON THE *JOYITA*?

Officially described as a 70-ton, twin-screw motor vessel, she was called *Joyita* and that, considering her condition in 1955, was either funny or sad, whichever way you chose to look at it. "Joyita" in Mexican means "Little Jewel".

Granted, she had good clean lines and was sturdily built, but she was twenty-five years old now and had been through many hands, many experiences – cruising off Santiago, tied up at Pearl Harbour on requisition to the U.S. Navy that day when the Japanese had attacked, carrying fish in her refrigerated hold from Canton across the South China Sea, puttering about on charter off Samoa.

She had been through a lot, and she looked it. Paint was peeling off her sides. Her hull, if anyone had bothered to inspect it, was thick with weed and barnacles. Above the original wheel-house and deck, rails and box-like shelters had been added till she looked like a contraption for carrying chickens. The engines were old, too, and the clutch on the port side was worn out. Worst of all, below the engine-room floor an iron pipe had been fitted with direct access to the sea for drawing in cooling water and unbeknown to anyone this pipe was rusting away.

But at Apia, the main anchorage in West Samoa, to her captain at least she was still the one and only *Joyita*, a ship to be cherished and loved. At sundown, when colonial officials collected in waterfront bars, conversation was bound sooner or later to turn to Lieutenant Commander "Dusty" Miller, R.N.V.R. (retired). "Funny how he dotes on that old heap of rubbish", someone would say and then, with head shakings and wise looks, people would go over, once again, the past and future prospects, if any, of old Dusty, the Welshman down on his luck.

Miller, it was agreed, was a man born out of his time. With a hint of something dangerous in his make-up, his lithe, wiry grace, his recklessness, he should have sailed with Drake in the Elizabethan age. Instead of which he had been spending years peddling fish among the islands of the Western Pacific. He had seldom made much of a profit, sometimes even a loss, and things were going no better for him in West Samoa where he had been for the last eighteen months. Latterly he had not been able to afford fishing trips at all and as no one could employ him except on a semi-charitable basis – painting chairs, for instance, at the local sailing club – he had spent weeks slouching about, hoping someone would offer him a square meal.

But now, in the summer of 1955, Miller's luck seemed about to change. The Samoa group of islands lies about 3,000 miles north-north-east of New Zealand. Due north of the Samoas, 270 miles away, are the Tokelau Islands where a zealous young man by the name of Pearless had recently been appointed District Officer. Until his arrival no one on the Tokelaus had worried much about communications with Samoa. Ships and planes called occasionally bringing in supplies and taking out copra, which was the islands' main export, but there was no regular contact. Pearless meant to change that and, having got to know Miller as an experienced seaman, he asked the West Samoa Government to charter *Joyita* for monthly trips to the Tokelaus with Miller as captain. What could be more simple?

In fact, the issue was not simple at all. *Joyita* was not Miller's property. She was owned by an American lady, a lecturer in anthropology at the University of Hawaii, whom Miller was proposing to marry, and permission would have to be obtained from Washington before the British Government in West Samoa could charter the boat. Moreover, in American-ruled East Samoa Miller had been declared *persona non grata* for failing to pay harbour dues and *Joyita*'s papers had been impounded. Consequently, if Washington inquired about the charter proposal there was liable to be – excuse the pun – a dusty answer.

Not surprisingly, in view of all this, the West Samoa Government rejected the request and the indefatigable Pearless then arranged, after some haggling, for a British firm, E. A. Coxon and Co., to charter *Joyita* for the Tokelau run.

To say the news aroused interest in Apia would be an understatement. People were both fascinated and appalled at the idea of mad Miller taking that "jewel" of his to sea again. Why, she'd been laid up for five months and it was said he was even having difficulty in starting the engines! And then, look at the numbers he was taking: twenty-four people in all – Pearless, a doctor and dispenser from Apia hospital, a bunch of Tokelau islanders including two children, and – wait for it – thirteen "crew members", more than enough for a four-masted clipper, plus two representatives of Coxon and Co., taken on as "super-cargo" – Miller's dodge, simply, to get round *Joyita*'s licence which specified no fare-paying passengers. Along the water-front opinion was virtually unanimous: "Government ought to stop him."

This possibility loomed over Miller throughout his days of preparation. But the Government did not act, and for an adequate reason. On the Tokelaus was a man with a gangrenous leg in urgent need of amputation. Food was running short there and *Joyita* was to take large quantities of flour, sugar and rice. There was also the copra to bring back which had been held up for weeks. All the same, and just in case, Miller worked frenziedly to get his engines in order and put to sea as quickly as possible.

At this time friends were making suggestions, pointing out certain facts. What with sudden, violent storms and coral reefs where ships were frequently wrecked, sailing in that part of the Pacific was a tricky business. Though some had sailed with Miller before, none of the "crew" knew the first thing about navigation. Suppose something happened to him? And where was the ship's dinghy? Surely he ought to take it with him? And finally, wouldn't it be better to postpone sailing until the port clutch was properly repaired? He might not value his own life, but what about the others?

Miller merely shrugged and laughed. "The clutch", he said, "is a simple matter. We can easily fix it. I can repair it on the way." And then with a hint of sarcasm: "I'm most grateful for

your advice, but there's one fact I've told you repeatedly and
you keep on ignoring. This ship is unsinkable. She's a refrigeration ship, remember? And there are 640 cubic feet of cork in
her hold."

It was true. But did that make *Joyita* unsinkable? One
thing was clear and perhaps it underlay the boast. Miller
would never in any circumstances abandon his "Little Jewel".
Never. Everyone was agreed on that.

But the clutch was not "a simple matter". *Joyita* was due to
sail on Sunday, 3 October, and since Thursday Miller had
been working non-stop on the engines with the help of two
men, Chuck Simpson, the American-Indian "mate", and a
young part-Samoan called Henry MacCarthy who had been
hauled in at the last moment as "second engineer". Henry was
the adopted son of a Mrs Emma MacCarthy and in due course
she was to be asked officially about his last days ashore. He
had told her that the engines were "dirty, in a terrible state"
and on the very day of departure, "there is something wrong
with the clutch". She had pleaded with him not to go, she had
heard bad things about the captain, she said, but he was determined – and so was Miller.

On Sunday morning, eighteen islanders with their bundled
possessions came on board, six Britishers and one somewhat
reluctant American, Chuck Simpson, he because regulations
required that on ships sailing under the American flag at least
one officer must be an American citizen. At noon Miller cast
off – and almost at once *Joyita* was in trouble. Those on shore
saw her pass through a gap in a coral reef at the harbour
mouth, then blue smoke started belching out of her port side.
The boat slowed up, stopped, started drifting stern-first towards the reef until an anchor was thrown out and there she
stayed, wallowing slightly in the swell, to be towed back igno-
miniously to the wharf. Soon after, while Miller stayed on
board to tinker once more with the engines, the European passengers were down at the Sailing Club, surrounded by laughing friends with "I told you so's".

Booze and badinage kept the party happy for a while, but as
hours passed with no word from Miller those waiting became
impatient, until around midnight came the message "engines
fixed, everyone embark" and at last, at 5 a.m. on Monday,
after more delays, *Joyita* finally sailed towards calm seas, in a

dawn as soft as pearl. Apia was asleep at that time, so there were no goodbyes.

Miller and the twenty-four others were never seen again, and if the boat had vanished too no doubt the whole affair would have been dismissed as one more case of "lost with all hands". In the life of the centuries foundering ships have been frequent enough. But after thirty-six days *Joyita* did turn up, listing heavily, partly waterlogged, abandoned, but still afloat some four hundred miles west of Samoa near the Fiji Islands and when she had been towed into harbour some strange facts came to light.

First the hull had to be inspected for damage and was found to be intact, but the pipe for drawing in water to the cooling system had fractured with the result that water had poured directly into the hull below the engine-room floor, then into the engine room itself and finally into the rest of the boat until it had been almost swamped. Mattresses stuffed around the engines showed that the source of the leak had never been found. The engines would have stopped, of course, the boat have become unmanageable and in a sudden storm perhaps all on board, thinking she was lost, had taken to the three life-saving Carley floats, which were missing – all, that is, but Dusty Miller who, while life was in him, would never have abandoned his "little jewel", and why should he, knowing she was unsinkable? Yet he had vanished as well.

This was odd. But odder still was the disappearance of *Joyita*'s entire cargo, stored in two holds below decks: forty-four 150-lb bags of flour, fifteen 70-lb bags of sugar, eleven 56-lb bags of rice and 460 empty copra sacks. They could not possibly have broken out of the holds, not possibly have been stacked on the Carley floats, so who had taken them? The ship must have been approached by some other vessel, either before or after becoming a derelict and if before, perhaps there had been piracy and everyone on board had been murdered, with the Carley floats thrown out as a blind. But murdered by whom? When a knife "Made in Japan" was found on deck the *Fiji Times* and other newspapers thought they had the answer: MURDERED BY JAPS.

This supposition was based on the frequent presence of Japanese fishing fleets in the area, but one knife does not spell mass murder and the story soon faded for lack of other evi-

dence, leaving the more probable theory that the ship had been
looted *after* becoming derelict. In this context it was no surprise
to discover that the chronometer was missing, the log and
£1,000 in cash known to have been on board for the purchase of
copra. But the fate of the ship's company was still mysterious
and clues were scanty. On the starboard deck and partly in the
scuppers a stethoscope was found, catgut attached to a sutur-
ing needle and several strips of bloodstained bandage. Part of
Joyita's superstructure had been damaged, in heavy seas presumably, yet some time later a temporary awning had been
fixed to it, which seemed to show that at least one storm had
been survived. Finally, in the fuel store there seemed to be
many more drums of diesel oil than was necessary for a run to
the Tokelaus and back.

In 1956 the writer Robin Maugham went to Samoa to try
and unravel the mystery, talked to many people involved, studied the Report of an Inquiry held early that year and, incidentally, ended up buying what remained of *Joyita* for his
own use. Ultimately, from a mass of material, he was able to
work out a plausible account of what might have happened
and this was published in 1962 in his book, *The Joyita Mystery*.

An hour after darkness, writes Maugham, on *Joyita*'s first
evening at sea, a terrible storm breaks with torrential rain
which, to all but Dusty Miller, seems about to sink the boat.
The English doctor, whose name is Parsons, climbs to the
bridge, reports that water is pouring in from below the engine-
room floor and begs Miller to turn back. Miller refuses, an
argument ensues, then a fight during which Miller falls heavily
backwards down the bridge ladder to the deck. Parsons, with
the dispenser from Apia hospital, rushes to him, tests his heart
with the stethoscope and finds a gaping wound in his head
which he stitches up and bandages.

Meanwhile, the storm increases in fury, giant waves smash
the superstructure, the wind howls, the ship lurches as though
about to turn-turtle. Miller lies unconscious on deck. The
others, panic-stricken, start to grope for the Carley floats but
are still undecided until Simpson, the American-Indian,
shouts "Look!", and there to the south, gleaming in the moonlight, they see a line of surf – a reef, and beyond it, land!

The floats are now launched. Some climb in, others swim
alongside, clinging on for support. Only the charterer's agent,
Mr Williams, in charge of the thousand pounds, hesitates, then

decides to abandon the money and gets down into a float. But hopes are deceptive. A strong northerly gale driving towards the reef cannot counter a yet stronger westerly current and this carries the despairing party further and further away from the reef until all are overwhelmed by the seas.

Meanwhile on *Joyita* Miller opens his eyes to find someone bending over him, a young man called Tanini, a native of the Gilbert Islands. In time past Miller befriended him and (as Maugham's researches showed) had promised to take him one day to Honolulu to be educated. As it proved impossible to get the unconscious Miller on to a float Tanini refused to be parted from his beloved benefactor and now tends him, rigging an awning to protect him from the sun, until Miller dies.

Before long a Japanese fishing vessel appears to investigate the apparently abandoned *Joyita* and sends a boarding party. Thinking the intruders are going to take away Miller's corpse, Tanini fights them and in the course of this is knocked overboard and drowns. The Japanese then slide Miller's body into the sea, transfer the cargo, the chronometer, the log and the £1,000 to their own ship and sail away.

This story cannot be faulted on factual grounds, but other accounts may be equally plausible, as Maugham himself admits, and there is one that seems to fit the facts rather better. It depends on the emphasis placed on certain incidents.

In the record of the Inquiry into the loss of *Joyita* there is, for example, a very curious passage. The efforts are being discussed of a Mr Bentham, Superintendent of Apia Radio Station, for Miller to keep in touch during the voyage. First, Bentham sent a note telling him that two times, 10 a.m. and 4 p.m., had been reserved for him to make daily contact and suggesting a test transmission. "But no word at all was received." Bentham then went down to the wharf and sent a message asking Miller if he proposed to make the test and if the arrangements were satisfactory: "he received no word". The report continues: "He waited ashore two hours but not a message was sent to him, so he went back to the Radio Station and waited there until 7 p.m. on the Sunday night, thinking that some steps would be taken for *Joyita* to make a radio test. No word was received."

Subsequently, after *Joyita* had left, the charterer's manager, a Mr von Reiche, told Bentham that Miller had agreed to call up at the times stated, but in fact he never did nor could he

have done because before leaving he had failed to test his set
which was later found to be faulty. So here is the first point. It
looks as though Miller had no intention whatever of keeping in
touch with Apia. Why?

The second strange fact is the amount of fuel found on
board. The round trip to the Tokelaus covered 540 miles. But
a Mr Plowman who lived on the waterfront told West Samoa's
Acting High Commissioner who recorded it in his diary that
Miller "insisted to von Reiche on 60 drums in place of 30".
Sixty drums was the equivalent of 2,640 gallons of diesel fuel,
enough for a voyage of 3,000 miles.

So we get this beginning of a new scenario: Miller intended
to go much further than the Tokelaus, and go surreptitiously.
But go where, and how could it be managed? There is evidence, again from the Commissioner's diary, that his fiancée in
Honolulu was desperate for him to join her and except for the
possibility of further lucrative trips to the Tokelaus it was obviously in his interest to go. Before leaving Apia he wrote a letter
to her (opened after his disappearance) and left it for someone
to post. In it he said he had no intention of going to Honolulu
until after the Tokelau trip. Optimistic as ever, he was even
hoping for future trips. But the fuel evidence shows that he was
keeping his options open.

It may well have been the false start on the Sunday, smoke
blueing from the engine, the humiliating return, that convinced him that the charter would almost certainly not be
renewed. The Samoan Government would step in and ban
future operations. Then where would he be? Unemployed,
starving again. So the time to get out was now. He would take
the party to the Tokelaus, which was *en route* to Honolulu
anyway, disembark them, then at night, with a minimum crew
including Tanini already briefed, slip quietly out to sea and
head for Hawaii.

It all depended on Tanini and the others keeping their
mouths shut. But suppose they didn't? The scenario continues:

Chuck Simpson (comes up to the bridge): What's this I hear
about Honolulu?

Miller: What do you hear?

Simpson: That you're going on there, leaving us stranded.

Miller: What do you mean, "stranded"? I said I'd take you
to the Tokelaus. That's what I said. And that's what I shall do.

Simpson: And how do you expect us to get back?

Miller: You can radio for a boat, can't you? Or you might charter a plane.

Simpson: Now look here, Miller. I'm not standing for this. If you don't stick to your contract I'm taking over this ship and I'll sail her to the islands *and back*. And there's nothing you can can do about it.

Miller: Oh, yes, there is . . .

Miller strikes the first blow, a fight ensues, then, for all we know, the story continues as Maugam wrote it – with the difference that it is only when Miller is unconscious or dead that the storm blows up.

But there may, after all, have been nothing sinister in the radio silence – just Miller being his individualistic self. And the extra fuel may have been for sale at a good profit in the islands. The field is wide open. Story-tellers galore can think up what happened on *Joyita* and no one can prove them wrong, except that, in all fairness to Miller, a brave seaman who loved his boat, we might think it unacceptable to be told that he left her while still alive.

SPITEFUL HULKS

A separate chapter in this book recounts the tragic story of Sir John Franklin's voyage in 1845 in search of a north-west passage between the Atlantic and Pacific oceans. The entire expedition perished in circumstances which remain a mystery.

Such clues as there are were discovered piecemeal during a series of search operations spanning a number of years. Not only English vessels and resources were involved, however. The American nation was stirred by the story of Lady Franklin's refusal to accept that her husband was dead without its having been definitely proved. Many Americans shared her belief that he and at least some of his men were still alive in the Arctic wastes, marooned by the loss of their ships *Erebus* and *Terror* and unable to communicate their plight to the world.

A Henry Grinnell, of New York, determined to do something practical about it, raised an expedition in 1850. He commissioned two ships, the *Advance* and *Rescue*. They got as far as Beechey Island, where the Franklin expedition had had winter quarters, but went no further and soon returned to America.

In 1853 the *Advance* went out again, this time under the direction of Dr E. K. Kane, who had been there before under Grinnell's auspices. Within a short distance of Smith Sound, the intended passage, the brig was stopped by ice. The expedition wintered there and Kane took the opportunity to explore an enormous glacier, forty-five miles long, which he named Humboldt glacier. But scurvy attacked the whole of his complement and the search for Franklin had to be abandoned. The *Advance* was left to the merciless clutch of the ice pack.

In 1860 it was the turn of the *Rescue* to try again. Fifteen years had passed since Franklin and his ships had sailed into oblivion and still no conclusive evidence had been found. Survival seemed unlikely after so long; but there were rumours of white men living among the Esquimaux. This and the persistence of the mystery was enough to whet the interest of an American journalist, formerly a blacksmith, Charles Hall, of Rochester, New Hampshire. The finding of Franklin alive would make an epic scoop, of worldwide interest. Even to discover definitive proof of his death would provide front-page copy.

Hall approached the American Geographical Society with an offer to organize and lead an expedition if enough public money were forthcoming to finance it. The society gave him its support, and the money was duly raised. His "flagship" was a whaler, the *George Henry*. In support, as store-ship, was the *Rescue*.

Some of Hall's sailors were not too pleased about this arrangement. *Rescue*'s reputation was not the best. Mortality among her crews over the years had been exceptionally high; she was dubbed unlucky. It was not overlooked that she had shared one unsuccessful expedition with the *Advance*, which herself had later been lost. But the expedition sailed and by September, 1860, had safely reached Baffin Island. In Frobisher Bay the journalist-leader had the little bonus of finding remains of a stone house built in 1578 by Sir Martin Frobisher himself on Countess of Warwick Island.

His cause for self-satisfaction was short-lived, however. A day or two later, while his vessels were still at anchor in the bay, a violent nor'-nor'-easter struck them, with heavy snow. It raged all night, and in the morning it was plain to those in *George Henry* that their sister ship was in distress. The lookout called down to Captain Hall that she was dragging her anchors. If the gale continued to blow it seemed certain that she would come adrift altogether and be smashed on the shore.

With her would go a large proportion of the expedition's equipment and provisions, but fortunately there was no risk of loss of life. Captain Hall was able to congratulate himself on his foresight. When the storm had been merely an approaching threat he had transferred all the *Rescue*'s crew into his own ship.

The anchors held, although their cables were at full stretch. There seemed hope yet that the *Rescue* might survive. Twenty-four anxious hours later she was still afloat. Then, as Hall and his crew watched, she seemed to leap in the water, heeled over, writhed convulsively like a stricken animal, and then was flung ashore. Recalling the scene some years later, Hall described her lying "among the jagged crests of the rocks that were tearing her to pieces with the raging waves breaking over her deck, a snowstorm heaped its flakes around her as though swathing her in a gigantic winding-sheet".

The simile was appropriate: the *Rescue*'s life was over. Leaving her remains, the *George Henry* sailed away, resuming the search for Franklin and perhaps to do a little whaling on the side. After wintering, she returned to anchor again in Frobisher Bay in July, 1861. The weather was good and the sea calm, so Captain Hall decided to have a boat run out and go to find out whether there might be anything worth salvaging from the remains of the lost store-ship. There was no sign of her from aboard the *George Henry*, and he assumed that she had been broken up.

What he found when he got ashore seemed to confirm this. Fragments of wood lay among those sharp-toothed rocks. Yet they were surprisingly small fragments, and there were surprisingly few of them, accounting for only a fraction of the wrecked vessel. All that could be deduced was that the bulk of the *Rescue* had been dispersed by the tides or perhaps lifted off the rocks by a high sea and sunk. The search party returned to their ship with nothing to show.

They sailed again, and a few days later were close to Whale Island, in the Hudson Strait. The lookout called down again, this time to report another vessel in sight. This was so unlikely, in that remote region, that the *George Henry*'s entire crew joined their captain to peer at the other ship, some two miles away. As they sailed closer to her it became apparent that she herself was not moving under sail. In fact, they could see that she was a derelict. With this came the uncomfortable realization that she was familiar to them all. Without doubt, they were looking at the remains of the battered *Rescue*.

It was impossible. They had seen her being pounded to bits the best part of a year ago. No vessel, all agreed, could have survived that battering to float again. Yet the fact remained, this ship *was* the *Rescue*.

And she *was* moving; not wallowing aimlessly, but steering a
course. Captain Hall felt his heart leap with excitement. He
had found the Franklin expedition! They had been on that
land all the time; had come across the wreck of the *Rescue*, and,
perhaps helped by Esquimaux, had made her seaworthy enough to attempt a passage to some place where they might
meet whalers . . .

Yet, how could the vessel be sailing a true course without
sails? The wind was not even with her. And there was no sign
of anyone aboard her. The *George Henry*'s signals were not
answered. It was uncanny. It was incredible that a ship so
wrecked could sail at all, let alone have got this far, right
round Cooper Island, from her point of disaster. If there were
no one aboard to steer her, it was stranger still.

It was more than just strange, to the *George Henry*'s crew,
mindful of the *Rescue*'s reputation. They were relieved that the
increasing presence of ice prevented their own vessel from closing with her. Come to think of it, where had the ice come from
so suddenly. One moment there had been very little of it. Then
the seeming ghost of the *Rescue* had appeared, and, with it, ice
all around them, in blocks of ever-increasing size. There was
no more time to stare at the mystery ship. Every man was put
to work fending the ice away from the ship's wooden sides. It
was the first ice trouble they had had on that voyage, and the
Rescue seemed to have brought them it.

They worked on into the night, laboriously pushing away
sharp-edged blocks which threatened to splinter their hull. As
they worked, one of the men raised his head briefly and saw
something which made him cry out in terror. The others looked.
The dreaded form of the *Rescue*, with an escort of icebergs, was
moving inexorably towards them. The *George Henry* was
stationary, unable to take avoiding action because of the ice.
If the *Rescue* continued the way she was approaching she would
ram them broadside.

Something like panic ensued. There was no escaping. To
take a small boat in this place would only bring a lingering
death instead of a swift one. Jumping overboard was out of the
question. A man would not last a minute in this frozen sea.
They begged Captain Hall to abandon ship, nevertheless. He
refused; he knew the risk. And he was justified. The approaching hulk began to veer gradually away, until she passed astern
of the *George Henry*, to recede silently into the moonlit mist

until she was no longer seen. The reprieved crew, half paralyzed with fear, babbled thanksgiving for their deliverance.

As soon as daylight came Captain Hall ordered the anchor to be raised. There was still a lot of ice about, but there seemed to be markedly less than while the *Rescue* had been near. They were able to hoist the sails and move again, thankful to get away from the spot where "the accursed thing", as Hall termed it, had been seen. A peaceful day brought relief to the men – until a sharp clatter of falling pans near the galley brought them running to find out what had happened to the cook.

He was petrified, standing rigid among his fallen pans, pointing out across the sea and ice. There they saw the derelict again. It was as if she was keeping watch on the *George Henry*, a cat waiting to pounce on a mouse.

A game of cat and mouse was, indeed, played for two more days, while the stubbornly intrepid Captain Hall insisted on making slow progress along the coast, scanning every part of it for any sign of the Franklin survivors, whom his crew would by now have happily forgotten. All the time the *Rescue* seemed to be following them at a distance.

On the night of the fifth of August they breathed relief to see their shadower turn suddenly and head resolutely away. For a sail-less, unmanned hulk it was an incredible performance, but that was not the point. It looked as though, having done all she could to unnerve the *George Henry*'s complement and take away any further heart they had for their quest, she had been summoned to make her mischief somewhere else. She was never seen again.

There is another tale of a derelict of the deep, also with icy associations, though of a different sort.

In the days of sea passages lasting months and even years, the greatest problem beside the weather was that of keeping crews supplied with food; not only fresh food, but any food at all. In Nelson's day the men were lucky to exist on rations which, in John Masefield's term, were "nearly always bad, and sometimes villainous". Ship's biscuit was made of pea-flour and bone meal, baked so hard that some men, rather than eat them, carved them into models. Softening the biscuits in water brought out weevils.

What passed for bread was full of maggots; so much so that many sailors would only eat it at night, when the darkness prevented their seeing what they were putting into their mouths. Meat, preserved in salt, sometimes for years, was equally rock-hard and almost black, also ideal for carving souvenirs, some of which survive even today. It was far less suited to eating: there were tales of the barking of dogs and the neighing of horses and donkeys coming from within the slaughterhouses where it was prepared, and every sailor knew of another who had once found a horseshoe in the rations.

Butter was edible on first putting to sea, but became putrid within weeks. Cheese was notorious for the red worms it bred.

In 1814 the canning process ("can" was derived from "canister") improved the meat situation, but it was very expensive and no one thought of spending money on sailors. Canned rations did not reach the lower deck until 1847. Meals began to improve then, and within a year or two the process of refrigerating food by pumping the heat out of an insulated chamber was being developed. The first cargo of refrigerated beef came to England from Australia in 1880. The trade was soon spreading to New Zealand, the Argentine and Europe.

The first French ship to be fitted out with refrigeration equipment was a former British mail boat, suitably re-named the *Frigorifique*. During 1884 she plied successfully between various countries, transporting frozen carcasses. Then, on a voyage home-bound for Rouen from Spain, she ran into thick fog. As she edged along, her watch heard another ship's siren in the fog. The *Frigorifique*'s own was sounded, but there came no reply for some time. When one did come it was frighteningly close. Almost immediately there loomed through the fog another ship. The collision was inescapable. She hit the *Frigorifique* amidships, splitting her open.

There was no hesitation in giving the order to abandon ship. The crew of the vessel which had rammed them worked hard to save the Frenchmen and soon they were all on board her, being fortified with a tot of rum all round. The other vessel proved to be a British collier, the *Rumney*.

She had drifted well away from the point of the collision and the sinking ship had already been swallowed by the fog. The *Rumney* altered course and steamed away. Yet, even while they were thanking their kindly hosts and congratulating each other on escaping with their lives, the rescued crew stared, to see a shape looming out of the fog. It was a familiar one. They crossed themselves.

But it seemed that the *Frigorifique*, or her ghost, had not come to take revenge on her destroyer. She disappeared, as quickly as she had been seen. Collective hallucination? The term had not been coined by then. "Ghost-ship" had, and that was what the crew of the *Frigorifique* were convinced they had seen.

They thought otherwise, minutes later, when the vision loomed up again and this time rammed the *Rumney*. Now the sinker was sinking. Boats were run out. Luckily there were enough of them to accommodate both ships' crews. As they rowed away from the *Rumney*, afraid of being dragged under with her, they could see the *Frigorifique* lurking nearby. Smoke was coming from one of her funnels and her screw was still turning.

Now satisfied that she was no ghost, some of her crew in one of the boats rowed to her and clambered aboard. The mystery was quickly solved. Water had stopped coming into her engine-room, leaving one boiler working. The way her wheel had been lashed had kept her sailing in a circle that had brought her twice across the *Rumney*'s path. On the second occasion it had proved a collision course, and the *coup de grace* for the *Frigorifique*. She was really sinking this time, to share the ocean grave of the ship she had slain.

Those notable derelicts, the *Mary Celeste* and the *Joyita*, have chapters of their own in this book. For the record, the longest drift ever by an empty ship was the 1,408 days of the *Fanny Wolston*, abandoned and set on fire in mid-Atlantic, but still being seen four years later.

THE *MARY CELESTE*

On 5 December, 1872, the British-owned brigantine *Dei Gratia* under Captain Morehouse was sailing eastwards towards Gibraltar when around 1 p.m. another ship was spotted coming westwards on a roughly parallel course. As she came closer she was seen to be a half-brig of about 200 tons with a fore-and-aft sail furled at the mainmast, one square sail set on the foremast and two jibs drawing at the bowsprit. The remaining sails, four of them, were fluttering in tatters at their spars. The ship was moving very slowly and, as Morehouse recorded later in his Log, "steering very wild" – not surprisingly for when he adjusted his telescope he saw that there was no one at the wheel.

The Log continues: "At 3 p.m. hailed her and getting no answer and seeing no one on deck got out boat and sent mate and 2 men on board, sea running high at the time." The mate (Oliver Deveau by name) and one seaman climbed up the side while the third stayed in the boat. The two men then searched the ship from stem to stern, above-deck, below-deck, the cabins, the forecastle, even the so-called lazaret aft where the provisions were stored, and found not a living soul.

Legends that grew up later claimed that a half-eaten meal was found in the captain's cabin, luke-warm cups of tea, a cat dozing on a locker, that the galley fire was still burning with a chicken simmering in a pot. But besides being pure invention these details were unnecessary, for the truth was strange enough. Apart from a stove-in binnacle and a shallow cut on one of the rails the ship seemed in perfect condition. Understandably some water had come through the hatches and the bedding in the main cabin was wet, but when Deveau took a sounding through the pumps he found less than four feet of water in the hull which meant, reckoning the distance she must have come, that the ship had been making about one inch in twenty-four hours. Nothing at all to worry about. Why then had she been abandoned?

Closer examination only deepened the mystery. The ship was well stocked with food and drinking water. There was no sign whatever of violence or disarray. The men's possessions were neatly stowed in their sea-chests. One chest, for example, contained a carpet bag, a pair of slippers, a hat, two vests, three pairs of drawers, a pair of trousers, three woollen shirts, four cotton shirts, a comforter, six pairs of cotton socks, a pocket book, two pairs of braces, a coat. All this, and over five hundred similar items found on board comprising the most valuable possessions of ordinary seamen had been left untouched by the men as though receiving a sudden call to another world. They had not even stayed to rescue their pipes and tobacco.

Having satisfied himself that the ship was staunch and sound, Deveau searched for an hour in the hope of finding clues to the mystery, and discovered a vital fact. The ship's boat was missing, not on its cradle on top of the main hatch. This seemed to show that the crew had left voluntarily, of their own accord. But again, *why?* Who in his senses would leave a sound ship for a small boat, to be tossed in the cold grey wastes of the Atlantic? Had they all gone mad?

Perhaps they had. Deveau leant over the forward hold (the hatch cover was off) and smelt alcohol. So that was the cargo! Crude commercial stuff, barrels of it, and some had obviously leaked. Had the crew got fighting drunk, killed the skipper perhaps, then put off in the boat to avoid the law? No, the idea was surely ridiculous. Crude alcohol was lethal, everyone knew that, and there were no signs of a fight on board, just the opposite, there was almost an air of domesticity. In the captain's cabin was a harmonium with sheets of music, a sewing machine, female clothing including a small child's and a box of toys. It looked as though the captain had had his wife and baby daughter on board. No doubt there had been laughter and busy activity, here as elsewhere in the ship. But now all was tantalizing silence, all seemed dead and the only sound was the wash of water passing the hull. Suddenly Deveau shouted to his companion: "Get into the boat. We're going back."

On board the *Dei Gratia* again Deveau reported to Captain Morehouse. The ship's name was *Mary Celeste* and the last entry in the Log showed that on 25 November, ten days previously, she had been 378 miles away to the west, six miles from the small island in the Azores called Santa Maria. So if she had been abandoned on that day she must have come hundreds of miles eastwards on her own and then turned west again through 180 degrees. Was that a possibility? What did the Captain think?

"Yes, no doubt", said Morehouse absently. He was thinking in fact of the derelict's master, the American Captain Briggs. He knew him well as a fine sailor, a devoted husband, a man of integrity. He also knew that Briggs was part owner of the *Mary Celeste*. They had dined together on 6 November, the night before the ship sailed from New York, a week ahead of the *Dei Gratia*. Briggs had praised his new crew, said they looked "a peaceable lot". Where were they now?

"What do you know of Santa Maria, Mr Deveau?" said Morehouse suddenly.

"I'm told it has a very dangerous coast, sir."

"Exactly. Now suppose, on the 25th, the ship was becalmed, at the same time caught in a strong inshore current. Fearful above all for his wife and child, the Master might have ordered 'abandon ship'."

"In that case, sir, how come the ship has survived?"

"Simple. The current carried her past the island, after all."

It was a possible theory and Deveau suggested another. On board the derelict he had noticed a sounding rod not in its proper place, lying beside one of the pumps, for testing the depth of water in the bilges. He had used it himself, in fact. When a seaman opened up the pump valve there could have been a gush of water which convinced him the ship was about to founder. Panic. A message to the captain and – abandon ship.

"Yes", said Morehouse doubtfully. "But that captain is an experienced sailor. I know him well. He'd hardly be taken in by a thing like that ... Still, it's a possibility." There was a pause. "But we've got more urgent things to think about, Mr Deveau. What are we going to do with that ship?"

"I'll sail her to Gibraltar, sir."

Deveau asked for two men from the *Dei Gratia*'s crew of eight, a risky proposition which Morehouse pondered long and hard. He felt he could manage with a crew of five in his own ship, but the others would each have to be on duty for sixteen hours out of the twenty-four. This at the very best. And Gibraltar was six hundred miles away . . .

"Remember there's the salvage, sir."

Yes. Probably half the value of the ship plus her cargo. A tidy sum. And Morehouse's every instinct rebelled against leaving the fine ship to her fate. Finally he shook his mate by the hand.

"All right, Mr Deveau. You're a good man, I know. And this will be your big chance."

Deveau and his men took their chance and survived, bringing the *Mary Celeste* into Gibraltar only a day later than Morehouse in his ship. It was Friday, 13 December. At once the harbour was astir with rumour tinged with hope that the captain and crew would turn up, on an island in the Azores perhaps or elsewhere, after being picked up by a passing ship. On the other hand there might have been foul play. A solid ship – she looked almost new – brought in as a derelict: who had ever heard of such a thing?

Suspicion was not confined to old salts along the water-front. Before any salvage money was granted – *if* it was granted – officialdom was determined in its slow, methodical way to get to the bottom of the matter. As a first step the *Mary Celeste* was arrested, "taken into custody" by the Master of the British Vice-Admiralty Court and a guard was placed on board. Then the Court was convened under the presidency of its Commissary Sir James Cockrane Kt. to hear the claim of "David Reed Morehouse, Master of the British brigantine *Dei Gratia* and for the owners, officers and crew of the said brigantine, claiming as salvors against the *Mary Celeste* and her cargo, proceeded against as derelict". Appearing for the Crown was a Mr Solly Flood, known as Queen's Proctor in Her Office of Admiralty and Attorney-General of Gibraltar, a resounding title stamped, as it turned out, on a gentleman of lively imagination wit a taste for melodrama.

On 23 December Solly Flood boarded the *Mary Celeste* with

the Admiralty Surveyor and spent five hours examining her minutely. The Surveyor's Report (inaccessible to the outside world for many years) seemed to demolish the theory of abandonment through fear of foundering. The ship, as Oliver Deveau had noted, was staunch in every respect, including the hull which was inspected by a diver. There were many clues to prove she had not encountered violent weather. On the other hand there were two discoveries of possible significance. On either side of the bow, two or three feet above the waterline, a long, narrow strip of wood had gone, "cut away" it seemed from the outer planks. Secondly, a sword in its scabbard had been found in the captain's cabin. "On drawing out the blade", said the Surveyor, "it appeared to me as if it had been smeared with blood and afterwards wiped."

How much significance the Surveyor attached to these finds is not known, but Solly Flood had already formed a supposition of Horror on the High Seas and they fitted it well enough. A long report from him to the London Board of Trade in January showed a mind leaping ahead of facts:

"I proceeded on the 7th inst to make a still more minute examination for marks of violence . . ." (Naval officers who accompanied him) "agreed with me in opinion that the injury to the bows had been effected intentionally by a sharp instrument . . . on examining the starboard topgallant-rail marks were discovered, apparently of blood . . . on descending through the fore hatch, a barrel, ostensibly of alcohol, appeared to have been tampered with . . . My own theory is that the crew got at the alcohol and in the fury of drunkenness murdered the Master, his wife and child, and the chief mate; that they then damaged the bows of the vessel with the view of giving it the appearance of having struck on rocks, or suffered a collision so as to induce the Master of any vessel that might pick them up, if they saw her at some distance, to think her not worth attempting to save, and that they did, some time between the 25th November and the 5th December, escape on board some vessel bound for some North or South American port . . ."

Soon further marks, "apparently of blood", had been found in various places, scraped off with a chisel and, together with the suspect sword, sent to an expert for analysis. His report (suppressed by Flood, probably because it interfered with his theory) was entirely negative. The sword marks were rust and "according to our present scientifical knowledge there is no blood in the stains observed on deck". As for the injury to the bows, men versed in shipbuilding said such splinters could easily have come off when the planks were bent to the hull.

However, in fairness to Proctor Flood it must be said that his theory, though wildly improbable, still cannot be *proved* wrong, though in sticking to it he seems to have blinded himself to other more likely explanations.

Meanwhile, the Court was taking statements from the captain and crew of the *Dei Gratia*. The men were impressive in their testimony and seemingly could not be faulted. But the mystery remained. What had happened on the *Mary Celeste*? Mate Deveau was even questioning now whether there ever had been a boat on board: a cradle for it, yes, but he had seen no tackle for hoisting it over the side. Perhaps the ship had sailed without a boat. Or perhaps . . . Captain Shufeldt of the U.S. Navy thought the ship might have creaked so badly in a gale that the crew abandoned her in panic. Others suggested Riff pirates or a conspiracy between Morehouse and Briggs to claim salvage money. Some were talking darkly of fever, yellowjack perhaps, and the men jumping overboard in delirium. As for Solly Flood, he was still saying "mutiny".

But the trouble was, almost every explanation seemed lame, even ridiculous in the light of the known facts. Violence? Panic? Storm? Why, even a small phial of sewing-machine oil had been found still upright in the captain's cabin and in the galley every pot and pan was in its place.

The Court proceedings lasted off and on for three months, deliberately prolonged perhaps in the hope that the missing crew might turn up somewhere and the mystery be solved. Moreover something occurred in February which seemed highly suspicious and directly affected the salvage claim. Without consulting the Court, Captain Morehouse allowed his mate, Oliver Deveau, to take the *Dei Gratia* out of Gibraltar and sail to Genoa, ostensibly to unload her cargo of petroleum. There might have been a valid reason for this: impatience at the delay and fear of financial loss. Or there might not. Was Morehouse, by any chance, letting Deveau slip beyond the jurisdiction of the Court before too much was said, or was there an even deeper motive? Suppose, when Deveau first boarded the "derelict" he had found her not completely abandoned. Suppose there had been two or three men who had not taken to the boat with the captain, but were now too exhausted to work the ship. Might not Morehouse, in view of the salvage possibility, have decided to transfer them to the *Dei Gratia* and keep them below decks until they could be landed surreptitiously at Genoa – with a promise, of course, of a share in the salvage money to keep their mouths shut? After all, no search had been made of the *Dei Gratia* at Gibraltar.

Some such thought perhaps crossed the mind of officialdom because Deveau was promptly hauled back to continue his examination and Morehouse's conduct was censured. At the same time, on 24 March, as there was no firm evidence and no reason to disallow the salvage claim, an award of £1,700 was announced, a miserable fifth of the value of the ship plus her cargo of alcohol.

So ended the official inquiry. But the myth of the *Mary Celeste* had barely begun. It was helped on its way by universal ignorance. The proceedings of the Court were not readily open to inspection and little or no research was done into the background and characters of Morehouse, Briggs and their crews. This enabled fiction writers to label them all as rascals. Moreover it was believed that the ship's boat was still on board when she was found and this ruled out the most probable explanations.

First in the field of fiction was Arthur Conan Doyle, then a young doctor, whose account was published in 1884 as "J. Habakuk Jephson's Statement". Jephson was described as a respected medical man who possessed a valuable talisman venerated by Africans, a black stone shaped like a human ear. His fellow-passenger on the *Marie* [*sic*] *Celeste*, one Septimus Goring, was a half-caste desperado who aimed to set up an empire in West Africa, murdered the crew with the help of accomplices, sailed the ship to the coast, then turned her adrift. Jephson was spared and given a boat from which he was picked up by a passing steamer.

In 1904, a British writer, J. L. Hornibrook, produced a sea-monster story. "There is a man stationed at the wheel. He is alone on deck, all the others having gone below to their midday meal. Suddenly a huge octopus rises from the deep, and rearing one of its terrible arms aloft encircles the helmsman. His yells bring every soul on board rushing on deck. One by one they are caught by the waving, wriggling arms and swept overboard . . ."

In the following year a Liverpool newspaper came up with the inevitable message-in-a-bottle yarn, found, in this case, on a Pacific island beside a skeleton propped against a rock. The message, suitably disjointed, told that the *Mary Celeste*'s crew had been kidnapped to replace the dead and dying crew of another ship which had finally been wrecked off South America.

Then in 1913 came "Abel Fosdyk's Story", the first "survivor's" tale, an obvious invention either by the man himself or by a preparatory school headmaster who introduced him as "an old servant, committing to my charge, on his death-bed, a quantity of papers contained in three boxes". The story told of an observation platform built round the ship's bowsprit for the amusement of the captain's daughter, now promoted to the age of seven. One winter's day the entire crew, with Mrs Briggs and the child, are standing on the patform watching the captain and the mate perform (for complicated reasons) a swimming race round the ship, both fully clothed. The platform gives way and everyone perishes, drowned or eaten by sharks.

Finally there was published in 1931 *The Great Mary Celeste Hoax* by a Mr L. J. Keating, purporting to tell the story of John Pemberton who claimed to have been the ship's cook (in fact the cook's name was Edward William Head). It was said that some men had been drafted to the ship from the *Dei Gratia* to make up her complement before leaving New York; the remainder, including the mate, were a rough lot recruited from the dockside. During the voyage Mrs Briggs was crushed to death when a piano toppled over her in a storm, her husband went mad and jumped overboard, the mate murdered a seaman and, to escape eventual arrest, put off with three other men in the ship's boat when she was nearing the Azores, leaving behind the seamen from the *Dei Gratia* and Pemberton, the only remaining member of the original crew. Morehouse now appears in his ship, sends a prize crew aboard and, so that he can claim salvage at Gibraltar, takes Pemberton aboard the *Dei Gratia*, promising to pay his fare back to Liverpool, his home town, if he will keep his mouth shut.

Of course fiction may hit by chance on elements of truth, but these and other stories can all be faulted in numerous ways, not least by the known facts concerning the condition of the ship when she was found and the characters of Briggs, his mate (whose name was Richardson) and the crew, all of them known as honest and capable seamen. What then did happen aboard the *Mary Celeste*?

There is Deveau's theory: fear of foundering. Morehouse's theory: the ship carried helplessly on to a lee shore. And there is one other theory, perhaps the most likely of all.

When the ship was finally released by the Gibraltar court she sailed on, with a fresh crew, to Genoa where her cargo, 1,701 barrels of crude alcohol, was unloaded. The barrels were made of slightly porous red oak, but all were in perfect condition except for nine which had obviously leaked. When at sea it was the usual practice to ventilate such a cargo periodically be removing the hatch cover, and perhaps this had first been done on the morning of 25 November, the last day noted in the Log. By now the leaking barrels would have produced a high concentration of gas in the hold and the moment the cover was lifted it could easily have roared up as though the entire cargo was about to explode.

Briggs may have had his doubts (such cargoes were known to "rumble" even when battened down) but with his wife and child on board he was taking no chances. Result: "abandon ship".

The boat is launched, the men pile in, a tow-line is paid out so that if nothing happens they can all return to the ship. She is not carrying much canvas, it is a calm morning with light airs. The situation seems well in hand. But then a sudden squall comes up, the ship surges forward, the tow-line snaps, and row as they may those men in the boat can never catch up. So they are left, in the howling wind, amid the spindrift and the rising waves, only six miles from Santa Maria: six miles which they will never cross.

Is this what happened?

There is one poignant detail yet to be told. Oliver Deveau found a slate on board with chalked notes for entry in the Log – and also something else, the beginning of a scribbled message from the mate, Richardson: "Fanny, my dear wife, Frances M. R. . . . ." Perhaps if he had stayed just thirty seconds longer and written two more sentences there would today be no Mystery of the *Mary Celeste*.

Sunken and Buried Treasure

THE *EGYPT*'S GOLD

Fog, at sea, is an alarming experience. The ship seems to drift languidly through a dream-like world, totally alone and yet surrounded by perils. Unseen companions sail the same ocean, and close to land invisible hazards menace. In the fog which muffles all sound the eerie clanging of the bell on a buoy tells of hidden danger: but where does that danger lie? The sound seems to come from first one direction, then another. Ears and eyes strain to locate it. And is that really the sound of waves breaking upon rocks?

At regular intervals the ship's own siren is advertising her presence and now, from far off, there is an answering signal. The ship is twenty-five miles south-west of the island of Ushant and about thirty miles off the Point du Rez on the coast of Brittany. She is steaming along the regular shipping route to-wards the Bay of Biscay and Marseilles, where she will pick up the rest of her passengers for her ultimate destination in India.

Again the strange vessel is heard, apparently on the port bow and presumably steaming along a parallel course in the shipping lanes. With her engines running dead slow the ship creeps onwards, her crew alert as the sound of their invisible companion – presumably travelling north – grows ever closer. In the dead calm, with visibility only some twenty-five yards, everyone is alert for a sight of her. It is 1922 and the magic eyes of radar have still to be invented: only that deceptive

sound – impossible to tell how close – and the vigilance of the
lookouts can keep the ship out of trouble. But it is not enough:
a shadow, then an all-too-solid shape looms from the fog. Too
late the men on the bridge can see that it is heading straight
towards them; there is a grinding, tearing crash as the other
vessel strikes a glancing blow a little aft of amidships and then,
carried on by her momentum, is swallowed up again in the
enshrouding fog.

Water pouring into her, the stricken ship shudders to a halt.
She is the *Egypt*, a P & O liner of 8,000 tons, carrying forty-four
passengers and a crew of 291, and the ship which struck her
was the *Seine*, whose bows, reinforced for ice-breaking in
northern waters, had torn through the *Egypt*'s steel sides like
paper. Within twenty minutes the *Egypt* is at the bottom of
the ocean. The *Seine* had managed to find her again before she
sank, and worked desperately to save twenty-nine passengers
and 210 members of the crew; but ninety-six people had
drowned, among them the wireless operator who, right
until the moment when the *Egypt* capsized, had continued to
send out distress signals.

The *Egypt* sank in nearly seventy fathoms of water, a depth
beyond the reach of divers in normal gear, yet a number of
people were extremely interested in reaching the wreck for she
carried a cargo of bullion valued at over £1,000,000. Lloyd's
underwriters had paid the insurance in full, and because of the
depth at which the ship lay did not consider the practicability
of salvaging her precious cargo. However two members of
Lloyd's and a British consulting engineer often discussed the
possibility of reaching the ship and, in co-operation with the
Salvage Association, plans were made to this effect. A good
deal of mechanical equipment was devised for the job including
a submersible observation chamber which could control a variety of boring tools, blasting gear, mechanical claws and so
on.

In the end this ambitious equipment was never made, for in
the latter part of the 'twenties an Italian salvage company
called Sorima had already done a good deal of commercial
work in salvage, using similar equipment, in the Mediterranean. It was obviously more sensible to make an agreement
with this company than to "reinvent the wheel". Accordingly
Sorima's salvage vessel, the *Artiglio*, which had been working
for some time on the wreck of a Belgian liner torpedoed in

1917 not far from the location of the *Egypt*, was directed in June, 1929, to set out in search of the *Egypt*.

This search was in fact one of the major problems. It is not always appreciated just how difficult it is to find a sunken ship. If the ship is within sight of land coastguards may take bearings on it; or a person on the ship may take bearings of landmarks. In the case of the *Egypt* the thick fog made such bearings impossible. However two shore stations took bearings from the broadcast of the *Egypt*'s wireless operator; the navigator of a Swedish expedition which claimed to have found the *Egypt* (after two months' search), but which did not have the equipment needed for such deep-sea diving, provided another bearing; and the captain of a British destroyer which had picked up mail bags and wreckage the day after the disaster yet another. All these bearings agreed as to longitude but differed as to latitude and thus a search of about twenty square miles of sea was involved.

Ships belonging to the Sorima company spent the whole of the summers of 1929 and 1930 in searching for the wreck of the *Egypt*. All kinds of methods were used, including the services of diviners, but the most reliable search instrument was a drag. A variety of things were found under the concealing water, including a number of other wrecks, and it was only at the end of several patient and monotonous months of sweeping back and forth across miles of ocean that the *Egypt* was finally located – when a drifting marker buoy was retrieved by the salvage ship *Artiglio*. It was found that it was held fast by something under water which had caught its anchoring weights. When it was finally dragged free it could be seen that the mooring wire had wrapped round and round a curved shaft of rusty steel which, after reference to the blueprints of the *Egypt*, was identified as part of one of the ship's davits. Down went a diver and, after an hour or so of groping around, of hide-and-seek in the gloomy depths, a positive identification was made, confirmed by the retrieval from the wreck of the captain's safe.

It was too late in the season to continue with the full-scale salvage operation involved. So the *Artiglio* moved off to another job, demolishing the wreck of a munitions ship sunk in 1917. Sadly, her crew grew careless and, during one of several sorties to blow up the dangerous cargo, remained too close and the *Artiglio* was destroyed in an enormous explosion.

The following year another *Artiglio* arrived on the scene.
The first *Artiglio* had started the work of demolition on the
Egypt, pulling off the top of the captain's cabin in order to
retrieve his safe and removing some wooden planking and rails
from the boat-deck. But there was still much to be done. The
bullion room, where the gold lay, was four decks down in the
ship, below the superstructure. It was narrow, 25 feet long, 5
feet wide and 8 feet high running athwart the ship. Carli, captain of the *Artiglio*, planned to blast his way through the various decks until he reached the bullion room which lay between
the main deck and the lower deck. When this was achieved an
automatic grab, equipped with a specially designed cage-like
structure into which it retreated once its jaws were closed – so
that loose material would not fall out between the teeth, would
scoop up the bullion.

Here at least was a treasure hunt with a difference. The
existence of the treasure itself was a certainty. The wreck had
been located without a shadow of a doubt. The only problem
which remained was a practical one, of actually retrieving the
treasure. Although the job sounded relatively simple, for everyone knew exactly where the bullion room was situated, it involved an enormous amount of patience.

The difficulties were tremendous. In 400 feet of water a man
must work from the shelter of some sort of "diving bell". The
Artiglio's method was to use a shell in which the diver could
stand in order to direct the operations; these were carried out
from the ship itself, the various tools and pieces of machinery
being lowered from above. The shell had several windows,
allowing the diver to see in all directions. To see, that is, as far
as he could, for at that depth visibility was limited to some five
or six yards. Electric lamps created a glare similar to that of
car headlamps in fog and divers found they could see better
without them. They also had to contend with the current,
which not only caused the salvage ship to strain at her moorings, but tended to push the shell itself about. Objects such as
explosive charges being lowered from the salvage ship were
also carried along by the current. Thus the work was slow and
required much patience and care as well as courage.

The divers began cutting through to the bullion room in the
middle of June, 1932. A diver would go down in the shell and
then direct the operations of the men in the ship above him as
they lowered explosive charges. Their placing had to be meti-

culously accurate according to what had been worked out using the plans of the ship and the model which they had aboard the *Artiglio*. When the explosive charges were lowered on the ends of hawsers the diver directed by telephone the men on the surface as to how to move them in order to get them in the right position. If he had had arms and been able to reach out and position them it would have been simple. As it was in the simple cylinder all he could do was watch and instruct.

Difficulties abounded. The telephone communication could be destroyed for one reason or another and the diver would be hauled up to the surface to make sure his silence was not caused by some sinister agency. Bad weather would prevent any work being done for days on end. Sometimes the charge would break loose, or fail to explode. The problems were endless and could only be overcome by continued patience.

Unlike a cargo ship, the liner is more complex in its deck construction, with many cabins and other rooms creating a honeycomb, and much stronger structure through the greater number of bulkheads incorporated in the building. It was decided to blast a crater through the middle of the ship, which would grow gradually smaller as the divers got further down. As the bulkheads collapsed, the outer walls of the hull would collapse – outwards because of the blast from the charges – which would create more problems as currents swirled across the wreck.

One by one the decks were blown into pieces. Then the grab came into operation and, its movements directed by the patient diver in the shell, began to grasp and raise to the surface the pieces of wreckage from the decks. A problem arose because the diver kept drifting away from the much heavier grab. If he was tethered to its cable he had to come to the surface with it and then waste time finding his place in the wreck again.

In the whole of July only five days' work was done because of unsettled weather; but early in August what was left of the hurricane deck was removed, the cabin bulkheads cleared off the upper deck and an opening made into the saloon, beneath the floor of which was the bullion room. Now that the gold was within reach the divers worked with less regard for weather, in fog, strong currents and bad visibility. Monotonously, patiently, the work went on; the divers spent hours in the murky waters directing the activities of those who were operating the grab. Time and again it pulled up from the depths a jawful of twisted metal and splintered wood as it gradually cleared the wreckage to make way for another charge of explosive.

And so the work went on, well beyond the end of summer until, on the last day of October, the divers found the deck-plate over one end of the bullion room turned up. One more charge of explosive and one of the deck-plates was pulled off by the grab. But the aperture it had made was not big enough – and then the weather intervened. During the whole of November only one or two more dives could be made, opening up the bullion room sufficiently for the special grab which had been designed to enter the small compartment. But now the divers found that the bad weather and the poor light of the short December days made visibility on the sea bed virtually nil. It was hopeless: full of disappointment the *Artiglio* and her crew sailed for Brest and her winter quarters.

Five months passed before the *Artiglio*, refitted and with a crew eager for the success which was now assured, sailed again for the *Egypt*. The weather was kind and now the grab began to bring to the surface all sorts of objects mixed up with broken pieces of wood and muddy slime – a bundle of spoons and forks, a broken cash box, an automatic pistol which had belonged to one of the officers, some rotted golf clubs that had been the property of the second officer, thousands of rupee notes printed in England and on their way to the state of Hyderabad, rolls of silk – but where was the bullion?

In bulk it should have occupied no more than about a third of the space of the bullion room, which the divers had otherwise expected to be empty. What were all these other things doing there? As May and June passed and more and more rupee notes and other odd debris came to the surface, the crew became increasingly impatient. Then one day, raking through the latest haul of rubbish dropped on to the deck, one of the men found a sovereign, and then another, the first drops in a sea of gold. In the afternoon the diver went down again; those on deck waited with bated breath, while slowly he manoeuvred the grab into position and sent it on its way to the surface with its fresh load.

On board the *Artiglio* during most of these months of search and discovery was a *Times* correspondent, David Scott. Nothing can better the description in his book *The Egypt's Gold* of the scene on the salvage ship as the grab was brought to the surface . . .

"The grab rises out of the sea, a stream of silvery water pouring from it. It swings high overhead, drenching heedless men to the skin. As the outer casing opens and the grab comes down we see the usual jumble of wreckage in its jaws. They open with a rattle. Among the mud and wood and paper two bright yellow bricks fall with a double thump on the deck. They lie there shining, while a great shout bursts from the men of the *Artiglio*

" 'Lingotti! Lingotti! Oro! Oro, ragazzi!'

"Now the flood gates are open. The months of waiting and striving are at an end. Pent-up hopes and patience bursts forth in a rush of emotion that sweeps us off our feet. Employer and employed, master and servant, officer and seaman, Latin and Anglo-Saxon, old and young, the man about to become rich and the man who, in spite of his bounty, will always be poor, join for a few precious moments in a frenzy of rejoicing. They throw themselves on the golden bars, laughing and crying together, scrambling to touch them, embracing one another at the sight of them. They pass them from hand to hand, stroking their cold smoothness with calloused palms, laying them against unshaven cheeks, swinging them aloft to feel their weight. They shout and dance and shout again. Four years of effort, patience, tragedy – and reward at last!"

From then on the grab brought up load after load of gold bars and coins. The representative of the Salvage Association worked furiously to record the find, put all the gold into bags and stow them in the *Artiglio*'s strong room. He need not have concerned himself, however, with safety. Not a single sovereign was pocketed by any member of the crew.

By the end of November, when the operation ended, most of the gold and silver bars and several thousand sovereigns had been raised from the wreck. The rest of the treasure was salvaged in the following year, representing 99 per cent of the *Egypt*'s precious cargo worth, in 1933, £1,200,000. Of the proceeds, by prior agreement, Sorima, the salvage company, kept 50 per cent, Loyd's received 37½ and Sandberg, the British consulting engineer who, with an associate, had first brought Sorima into the story, took the remaining 12½ per cent.

To date the recovery of the treasure from the *Egypt* has been the most successful salvage operation ever undertaken. It had, of course, the factors necessary for success: the actual existence of the treasure was well documented, the position of the wreck

was reasonably well known, the salvage operation was undertaken within a decade of the sinking. In this story of sunken
treasure there are none of the conventional elements of romance and adventure, of mysterious charts and fabulous untold
hidden jewels. Instead there is patience, determination and
courage under difficult conditions – the ingredients of the
modern treasure hunter's story.

TREASURE AT TOBERMORY

"God blew with His winds and they were scattered."

It was September, 1588. The formidable combination of God, Francis Drake and Lord Howard of Effingham had effectively disposed of the Armada, that fleet which was the hope and pride of Spain, sent to conquer England for Philip II, capture the arrogant Queen Elizabeth, bring the country under Catholic rule and end English sea power which was damaging so seriously the trade of Spain in the Americas and Indies.

The story of the Armada's defeat is an amazing one. The odds were heavy against England, yet she won through, as she had done before and was often to do again. The Invincible Armada was vanquished. When the Duke of Medina Sidonia, its commander, got back to Spain in late September he had to report to his king the loss of seventy-two ships and 10,185 men. Over twenty of those that did not return found themselves in trouble round the wild and rocky coasts of Ireland and Scotland. Reports of their movements went to London for the information of Walsingham, head of Elizabeth's secret service.

Mr Ashby, Walsingham's correspondent at the English Embassy in Scotland, wrote to him on 6 November that "a great shippe of Spain that has been for some six weeks on the West Coast is now off Mula (Mull) in Maclean's country, is unable to sail, is supplied by the Irish people with victuals, but

they are not able to possess her, for she is well furnished with
shot and men. If there bee any English shippes of war in Ireland, they might have a great prey of this shippe, for she is
thought to be *verie riche*."

Previously he had reported that this ship, which he described as being of 1,400 tons, having 800 soldiers on board
with their commander, was lying at an island called Isla (Islay)
in the west part of Scotland, there driven by weather. Guided
by a fisherman, she had arrived in Tobermory Bay in the Heb-
ridean island of Mull and there dropped anchor. She had been
lucky to find friendly natives in both her havens. Many Spaniards who came ashore from their ships or swam there from
wrecks were cruelly murdered and robbed by those to whom
they appealed for help, or, in Ireland, killed by forces of the
English Government who were afraid of their inciting the Catholic Irish to rebellion. Some were luckier, and lived to hand
down a legacy of dark eyes and curved Spanish noses.

When the tired galleon limped into the bay, Tobermory
seemed at first a heaven-sent refuge. The town of Tobermory
("Well of Mary") did not exist officially until 1788, but two
centuries before it was a fishing community living around the
shores of a natural harbour.

What was the name of this galleon, which was so "verie
riche"? Various names have been suggested. She could have
been the *San Juan di Bautista*, or the *San Juan di Sicilia*, or the
San Francisco. All ships of Spain bore resounding and holy
names, invoking the formidable saints of a Catholic heaven,
whereas the ships of England were more apt to be called the
Lion, the *Swan*, the *Rose* – suggestive of pubs rather than of prin-
cipalities and powers. The *San Francisco*'s full name was the
Galeon del Gran Duque di Florencia di Nombre San Francisco. She
had been loaned to Spain by the city of Florence, her commander was Captain Don Antonio Pereira, and around her
had grown the legend that she was the principal treasure-ship
of the Spanish fleet, with the Paymaster-General and the pay-
chest for the entire Armada aboard.

Let us examine the evidence for this report. It is, alas, very
scanty. The Paymaster and his treasure (said to be over three
million pounds in gold doubloons) were reputed to be aboard
the *San Salvador*, which was damaged in action and had to be
abandoned, her treasure then being distributed among other
ships. But which ships? Presumably the *Duque di Florencia* was

one of them. But nobody knows for certain. The seventh Earl of Argyll (the noble family whose name has for centuries been associated with the Tobermory mystery) is said to have heard the story from a descendant of Captain Pereira whom he met in Spain.

Was it, in fact, the *Florencia* which sailed into Tobermory Bay? Walsingham's agent irritatingly forebore to mention the galleon's name – an omission which would not have recommended him to M.I.5. Local tradition talks of the *Florence*, the *Florida*, the *Admiral of Florence* – but perhaps these names date from the information given by the seventh Earl. The present author was told by Rear-Admiral Patrick McLaughlin, who was in charge of the most recent attempt to locate the galleon, that the present Duke of Argyll has spoken with a direct descendant of Don Pedro de Valdes, who with his ship *El Capitana* was taken prisoner by Drake in the *Revenge*. This lady told the Duke that it has always been a tradition in the family that the Tobermory ship *was* the *Florencia*, carrying a great deal of treasure. She added that when the wreck was eventually located the emblem of a five-petalled flower would be found carved on the door of the after-cabin.

So far the evidence, though nebulous, points to the galleon being the *Florencia* rather than any other. Against this there is a story that the *Florencia* was never anywhere near Tobermory, but was captured off the west coast of England and brought as a prize into Weymouth Bay.

The mystery of the Tobermory ship sinking in the bay, from mishap or hostile intent, is almost as great as that of her name. This is what is popularly supposed to have happened.

After the galleon had anchored, the captain went ashore and approached the local chieftain, Lachlan Mor McLean of Duart, for victuals and water. To the Spaniards' relief, McLean, a far-seeing man, agreed courteously – but only on condition that the captain loaned him one hundred fighting men. It appeared that he was engaged on an intensive campaign to put down the Macdonalds, an enemy clan. The captain held no brief for the Macdonalds; he duly supplied McLean with soldiers and McLean promptly raided the islands of Rum, Egg and Muck, committing fearful slaughter.

Then, says legend, Spaniard and Scot quarrelled, perhaps over the price of victuals, perhaps over the return of the Spanish troops. Whatever the reason, the chieftain sent a young

relative, Donald Glas McLean, on board the galleon. The captain held him as hostage, so Donald, evidently a youth of fiery
temper, having heard that the ship was preparing to sail,
managed to set light to the powder-magazine and blew the
galleon and himself out of existence. Nobody called Donald
Glas McLean has been traced as living in the area at that
time, so perhaps legend got the name wrong. But a much more
likely story is that the ship was blown up by one of Walsingham's agents, a man called John Smollett, ancestor of the
author, Tobias Smollett, who was under orders to prevent the
ship leaving Tobermory.

The contemporary version of this story runs thus:

> "This day (18 November) word is come that the great ship that
> lay in the West Iles is blown in the air by the devise of John
> Smollett; most part of the men are slaine. The manner is this:
> McLean entertaining great friendship with them, desireth the bor-
> rowing of 2 cannon and 100 halberdiers . . . and delivered a foster-
> son of his as pledge for safe delivery of them again. John Smollett,
> a man that has great trust among the Spaniards, entered the ship
> and cast in the powder a piece of lint, and so departed. After a
> short time the lint took fire and burnt ship and men."

On 13 November Ashby wrote to Walsingham that the galleon had been "burnt . . . by treacherie and almost all the men
within consumed by fire. It is thought to be one of the prin-
cipall shippes, and someone of great accompt within; for he
was alwais, as they say, served in sylver."

Here the Campbells, Earls of Argyll, come into the picture.
As a reward for his father's information about the galleon
being a treasure-ship, the eighth Earl had received a Deed of
Gift from Charles I, allowing him salvage rights in the wreck.
This seriously annoyed the McLeans and they may well have
attempted a little piratical salvage of their own.

But the Earl was never able to exercise his rights, for he was
executed for treason in 1661. Poor "Gellespie Grumach", or
"the glaed-eyed marquis", so called from his squint, had
changed sides once too often. Charles II regarded the Campbells "with one auspicious and one dropping eye", like Hamlet's
step-father. The late Earl had certainly set the crown on Charles's head during his exile, but some of his other activities, such
as serving as Member for Aberdeenshire in the Commonwealth
parliament, rather weakened the king's confidence in the
Campbell loyalty to the Throne. When Archibald Campbell,

the ninth Earl, wanted to exercise the salvage rights granted to his grandfather, Charles opposed him on the grounds that they only applied to the reign of Charles I and were now extinct. An attempt at salvage had been made in 1661, in the late Earl's lifetime, by means of a diving-bell newly invented by the Swedes. The ninth Earl contested the King's decision in the courts of session in Edinburgh and won back his family's right in the wreck. The claim stands to this day.

The diving-bell went down again, manned by two Swedish divers. A cannon was retrieved, but the divers and the bell were lost, somewhere around 1677.

In 1683 a diver named Archibald Miller went down and his report can be seen in the Bodleian Library at Oxford. He described the ship as the *Florence*, of Spain, and reported her position, not more than nine fathoms deep at low water, twelve at high water, her stern pointing shorewards. He retrieved some guns and a silver bell, but though he hooked an object which he thought was a crown he was unable to get it out. He found no deck, except on the poop.

The ninth Earl of Argyll followed his father to the scaffold, also on a charge of treason, in 1685. His son joined William of Orange at an auspicious moment, retrieved the title and estates, and in 1701 was created first Duke of Argyll. His younger son, who became the third Duke, decided in 1740 to have another shot at the treasure. Like his ancestors, he was a soldier and a politician, very often in disfavour with the Crown but wise enough to keep his head on his shoulders. In 1711 he had been Ambassador and Commander-in-Chief in Spain, but was probably too busy to pick up any first-hand clues about the treasure. Under his directions an improvised diving-bell was sent down. A number of gold and silver coins were retrieved – and a greater prize, a bronze cannon wrought at Fontainebleau by the great Benvenuto Cellini. It can be seen today at the present Duke's castle of Inverary. But it bore, alas, no ship's name.

Nothing remarkable seems to have happened at Tobermory for a century and a half. One diver sent down during the nineteenth century reported that the wreck had disappeared under a mass of silt and sand. No doubt he made his explorations wearing the "close" diving suit and helmet, fitted with air inlet and regulating outlet valves, which had been invented in 1830 by the enterprising Augustus Siebe.

A Glasgow treasure syndicate was formed in 1903 after the chance discovery of a gold coin and an ancient, sea-encrusted anchor. With the Duke's permission and the promise of an equal share-out, one Captain Burns used all the resources of contemporary diving equipment to explore the bottom of the bay. He found more cannon, weapons and some coins, but not the wreck itself. Suction-pumps and steam shovels were no more effective than cruder methods had been.

Then somebody had the bright idea of employing a dowser. The sensitive, quivering hazel twig used by these gifted people can locate either hidden water or hidden metal. This particular twig correctly indicated the presence of metal which turned out to be silver, but not much of it.

A new syndicate was formed, under the leadership of an American, Colonel Kenneth Foss. It was his theory that the diver, Archibald Miller, had been misleading everybody about the wreck's position so that he could quietly cash in on it for himself. Whether this was the case or not, Foss was right in his calculations, for he found the wreck under thirty feet of silt, eighty-four yards distant from Tobermory Pier and forty-eight feet under water at low tide. He located the captain's cabin in the stern (the hold was never penetrated), and his divers brought up two small cannon, pieces of gold and pewter plate, some crystal, and fragments of arms and armour.

When war came in 1914, Foss's operations were stopped. He returned after the Armistice and found coins dated 1588. But his luck turned. He got in the way of a high-pressure hose, whose powerful jet broke his ribs and inflicted other serious injuries. He never recovered, and there were whispers in the legend-ridden Hebrides of a curse on the hidden treasure.

There were less romantic whispers that unpublicized nibbles at it had been taken by nameless persons who had suddenly begun to flourish without visible cause. It is difficult to see how this could have happened without the knowledge of interested spectators on shore.

Two more syndicates made attempts, the Anglo-Dutch Diving and Salvage Company, and an English one. But war again stopped play.

The years crept on to 1949, when the present Duke of Argyll, the eleventh to hold the title, resumed the search his ancestors had begun. The Royal Navy collaborated with him and a contract was drawn up with the Admiralty which lent

two small craft and a fishery protection vessel, the Duke
financing the costly enterprise.

On 8 May, 1950, naval divers came upon the wreck of an
oak vessel, sixty feet below the surface of the bay, buried
twenty-four feet in silt. It was in pieces, and the marks of fire
were visible. Working in spite of the strong tides and currents
that trouble the Isle of Mull, they reported that "on two occasions the probes struck substantial metal within the body of the
ship, and it appears possible that these contacts were part of
the ship's armament". Two small gold medallions of sixteenth-
century Italian design were brought to light.

In 1955 the expert team under the command of Rear-Admiral Patrick McLaughlin, by then retired from the Navy, was
joined by a man who was in the next year to be himself the
subject of a mystery which is dealt with elsewhere in this book.
He was Commander Lionel K. Crabb, the famous frogman, a
wartime diving hero. The problems of the team, operating from
the salvage ship *Reclaim*, and later the *Ardchattan*, were twofold.
They had to identify the sunken vessel, then get it up from the
silt.

First that frustrating layer had to be penetrated. A long
metal pipe was lowered from compressors in the ship to suck
up the silt at the rate of thirty-five tons an hour. Altogether it
was reckoned that there were about 12,000 tons to be removed.
As it was brought up, the silt was sieved into a hopper-ship.
The first loads produced a rusty sword blade – perhaps a
herald of greater things. But results were disappointing. More
weapons, and fragments of them, some pottery, coins – these
were all the team's reward. They retrieved no chests of gold
and silver, no jewelled crown as described by Archibald Miller
(rumoured, most improbably, to have been a gift from Pope
Sixtus V for King Philip to wear when he added the English
crown to his own); and, sad to relate, they got no glimpse of
that most attractive lady who features in one of the legends,
the statue of a golden Virgin, with eyes of sapphire. Nothing
substantial was found to add to the collection in Inverary
Castle.

The enormous cost of the enterprise meant that it had to be
abandoned when there was no prospect of quick returns. Even
when the expenses were shared between the Duke and interested financiers, they were prohibitive. "Operation Galleon"
was called off. Once again the lovely Bay of Tobermory was

left undisturbed and whatever lay at the bottom sank once more into the silt of that glacial channel.

And there the mystery rests, eternally tantalizing. The Duke of Argyll firmly believes, as do most people who know the facts, that a great Spanish ship lies there with rich treasure in her. On the other hand, the naval historian, Sir Julian Corbett, pointed out that there were two captains called Pereira commanding Armada vessels, which may have led to confusion in the stories about the *Florencia*; and also that a ship of the *Florencia*'s size would not have been able to carry the weight of troops, crew, armour and over 750 tons of coins alleged to have been aboard her. Andrew Lang, the Scottish writer and historian, worked out to his own satisfaction that the vessel was the *San Juan Bautista* of Sicily, another ship on loan to King Philip.

Soon perhaps, if the funds can be raised, another attempt will be made to plumb the cold blue waters where lie the bones of – what?

THE *LAURENTIC* AND THE *NIAGARA*

It was almost certainly careless talk which cost the lives of 200 seamen of the S.S. *Laurentic* in 1917. Talk was perhaps inevitable in view of the cargo with which she had been loaded at Liverpool docks in January, 1917, for it was no less than gold bars worth £5,000,000.

The gold represented cash payments demanded by the manufacturers in still-neutral America who had supplied Britain with arms and ammunition. Much of the latter had, indeed, been brought across the Atlantic by the *Laurentic* herself, for she had been converted from a liner, owned by the White Star Company, to an auxiliary cruiser. Her work and her appearance were no doubt well known to watchful German submarines. The one which lay in wait for her off the northern coast of Ireland, when she was less than twenty-four hours out of Liverpool and still within sight of land, made no mistake. Within minutes the *Laurentic* and her precious cargo, vital to the war effort, were lying in 22 fathoms of water.

Fortunately the comparatively shallow depth at which the *Laurentic* lay made the salvage of her cargo a practical proposition. Soon after her sinking divers went out to make sure of her position which had been fixed by radio stations and observers on shore, but salvaging the gold had to wait. The war still raged; enemy ships and submarines were everywhere and floating mines were a continual hazard. However as soon as the Armistice had been signed in August, 1918, the divers went to work.

The British Navy divers were commanded by Captain G. C. C. Damant, an expert whose report indicated that the treasure could be raised. There were, however, problems. The ship lay in a position which exposed her severely to the Atlantic currents and thus was constantly moving. Torn steel and dangling wire ropes swayed and lashed, presenting continual hazards to men below. Moreover the ship lay on her port side, at an angle of 60 degrees, while the gold had to be approached from the starboard side and the heavy boxes, each of which weighed 140 lbs, had to be manhandled up the steep slope of the deck outside the baggage compartment where the gold was stored. Reaching the gold from the baggage compartment meant working virtually head downwards, a difficult position for a diver, for the air in his suit is forced into the legs turning him upside down.

Nevertheless the first attempts to reach the cargo were highly successful. The baggage room was soon entered and cases moved out of the way to expose the door of the bullion room. When this had been opened with hammer and chisel the task of carrying out the boxes of gold began.

But nature intervened and diving was brought to an end by gales and storms. For a week the diving ship was forced to keep to port and the divers were concerned to see pieces of wreckage coming ashore which were obviously from the *Laurentic*. If the ship were beginning to break up their task could be much more difficult.

When they returned to the site the divers found their fears realized. The entry port into the baggage room which they had blasted was now 40 feet deeper than before and the ceiling of the passage to the store had collapsed. It had to be lifted and shored up before they could again reach the bullion, and when this was achieved the divers found that the floor of the bullion room had also collapsed and the boxes of gold had slid away down to port. They could no longer be reached through the entry port, with tons of dangerous and unsupported wreckage lying above their heads. It was necessary to blast a way vertically downwards through the hulk, a proceeding which entailed considerable danger as huge pieces of metal were raised and which almost – but not quite – caused serious accidents.

Further delays and difficulties were caused by the zealous efforts of British minesweepers, clearing away German mines. It was dangerous to work below when concussion from a mine exploding even as much as six miles away could harm a diver, and so the work was halted. Another pause came when the team was called away to more urgent work.

The divers' first efforts had brought up £800,000 worth of gold, and when the team returned some eighteen months later the wreck had moved but little. Salvage operations moved on apace until suddenly the "supply" came to an end. The rest of the gold had cascaded into the depths and was covered by tons of debris, while high superstructures, dangerous in the extreme, hung poised above the spot. Captain Damant allowed the men to continue while there was still gold to be found, for the removal of the superstructures would be long and tedious work.

In the event nature again took a hand. Work on the wreck had to be broken off once more, and when the divers returned in 1920 they found that the winter gales had done all that was necessary. Unfortunately nature had been over-enthusiastic; both superstructures had collapsed, but the hole where the divers had been working was now filled with twisted steel and chunks of decking. The hole was also filled with so much sand and stones that it was almost impossible to know where to begin to dig; and since the superstructure no longer existed to protect the divers from the full force of the currents, as fast as they cleared rubble so the sea brought it back again.

Captain Damant eventually devised a way of clearing the silt and debris which he described later:

"Four minutes before it is time for his predecessor to leave the wreck the order is given and the diver slides rapidly down the thin wire 'shot rope' which is put on afresh daily and leads directly to the spot where the work is being done . . . The diver has landed in the bottom of a sort of crater, the sides of which are formed by jagged shelves of plate, each one piled high with toppling masses of broken wood and indescribable junk.

"Near the bottom of the shot rope stands a large hopper or bucket, painted white so as to be conspicuous in the general gloom, and into this a diver is struggling to lift a bulging sack. It is to help him that our friend has gone down early: he stumbles across, gives a heave to the sack, and seeing it flop into the bucket with the raising of a cloud of black mud, turns his back and makes for a canvas hose close at hand. This hose terminates in a specially strong conical metal pipe about two feet long. The diver gets down flat on the sandy floor of the crater,

grips the metal pipe in his right hand and asks for the water to
be turned on from above. With a powerful jet issuing the
nozzle can be thrust deep into the caked silt and the diver's left
hand follows it up, exploring this way and that among the
pebbles, chunks of iron and other hard objects buried in the
sand. It is now absolutely pitch-dark on account of the cloud of
mud and dirt raised by the hose and if a bar comes to hand,
the diver lays it behind, in contact with his leg.

"Twelve minutes after leaving the surface he gets the order
to start bagging sand and the water is stopped. With one of the
bags he goes to work on the loosened dirt, scraping it in with his
bare hands or a bit of wood. Perhaps during the hosing period
he has located bars without being able to work them out and
he will now direct his digging towards them, bringing a knife
or a crowbar to bear and working against time for after thirteen minutes on the bag the order to 'Come up' is given from
above. He has five minutes now in which to put his bars if any,
into the bucket, lift in his heavy sack of sand and gather up
into coils the slack pipes . . ."

Naturally the divers were more interested in digging out
bars than in bagging sand, but Captain Damant cursed and
cajoled while the tedious work went on through the summers
of 1920 and 1921, during which only fifty bars of gold were
found. The following year, however, the divers found their
work much easier, with gold bars easily accessible in the silt
and metal debris; £1,500,000 worth of gold was brought up in
that year. In 1923 the haul was even better, being worth about
£2 million.

The last year of work was 1924. Then the great metal sheets
were almost cleared, but many bars had found their way
through holes and rents in the metal. Finally the whole layer of
steel was cut into pieces and removed in the search for the 154
bars which still remained to be found. Careful search found all
but twenty-five of these bars, and at that point the search was
abandoned.

The resounding, near hundred per cent success of this operation was not made public until 1926 when at last the curiosity
of those on shore, who for six years had watched the mysterious
activities of the divers, was satisfied. For in all those years of
operations the close-mouthed naval divers had never said a
word about the nature of their search in the pubs and hostel-
ries of the Irish ports they visited.

In the Second World War, before the introduction of "Lease–Lend", America again demanded "cash with order", and Britain, hard-pressed and alone in the fight for survival after the fall of France, desperately needed weapons. Britain called upon the reserves of that great gold-producing nation, South Africa, and in July, 1940, nearly eight tons of gold, worth £2,500,000, was loaded aboard S.S. *Niagara*. *En route* for Canada the *Niagara* called at Auckland, and it was when leaving this port, through the usual shipping channel quite close inshore, that the ship ran into a wholly unsuspected German minefield sewn across the narrow channel. The liner sank in just under two hours, allowing all her passengers to take to the lifeboats, from which they were soon picked up. The attack upon a ship in this part of the world so remote from the active theatre of war seemed of dubious military value. In fact Germany had struck a severe blow at Britain, for the *Niagara*'s rich cargo had sunk in 73 fathoms, far too deep for any diver to reach in ordinary diving gear.

However less than ten years had passed since an Italian company had achieved a resounding success and world-wide fame with their salvage of the gold carried by the liner *Egypt*, which had sunk at a similar depth in 1922 with a million pounds worth of gold aboard. Could the same tactics be repeated with the *Niagara*?

A local firm of salvage experts decided that it could. The problem was the shortage of materials. Even in far-off New Zealand the answer to "unreasonable" demands would always be "Don't you know there's a war on?" For the United Salvage Syndicate, which had brought in expert divers, the Johnstone brothers, the answer was to make their own. Within five months a diving cylinder had been constructed which contained fourteen windows so that the occupant could see all round him; and a dilapidated ship the *Claymore* which had been lying in the mud for years had been renovated and adapted as a diving ship.

Six months after the *Niagara* had gone to the bottom the diving syndicate was ready to set to work.

The first job was to find the wreck, for although radio fixes had been taken on her at the time the mine struck she had drifted considerably in the two hours before she sank. Moreover the *Claymore* was obliged to dodge the mines while she searched through the minefield which had brought about the *Niagara*'s

end. In fact the ship was found fairly quickly, despite Johnstone's – literal – brushes with the mooring wires of mines.

The *Niagara* had settled on an even keel but with a list of
some 70 degrees, and the strong room was located in the heart
of the ship. It took weeks to position the *Claymore* accurately
over the wreck and to moor her successfully so that there could
be no repetition of an incident when the *Claymore*'s bow mooring had parted and the swinging ship had dragged the diving
bell dangerously along the hull of the wreck, narrowly avoiding the gaping hole caused by the mine. If the bell had fallen
in the suspending wire would have been severed and John
Johnstone would have suffocated . . .

When the *Claymore* was safely positioned work could begin.
Six months' work of tedious, painstaking effort to blow a well
sixty feet long through the three decks above the strong room.
For the man in the diving bell could see and could direct the
operations of those on the surface as they lowered explosive
charges into the correct place, while those on the surface could
act but could not see. The bell had to be raised before each
charge was exploded and lowered again after the water had
cleared so that the diver could see what effect there had been.
Patience and care were the watchwords.

At length the door of the strong room was exposed but, because of the angle of the ship, when the small charges – which
had to be used for fear of damaging the walls of the room itself
and allowing the gold to fall into yet more inaccessible depths –
exploded the door fell inwards. Now there was a gap barely
nine feet by five into which the grab, similar to that used on
the *Egypt*, had to be manoeuvred.

For several hours Johnstone, directing in the depths, and
the men following his instructions on the surface, worked to
manipulate the grab through the hole. At last it went in,
opened and closed upon whatever it could grasp – just like
those tiny cranes in "penny" arcades. And Johnstone could
swear, as he directed the raising of the grab from the strong
room, that he could see a box in its grasp. Excitedly he told the
men on the surface what he had seen and they hauled him up
so that, when the box fell on the deck and broke, Johnstone too
could see that "in a mash of decaying sawdust lay two massive
ingots, so shiny they might have come hot from the mint. Each
was about 1 foot long, 4 inches broad, 1½ inches thick and 34
pounds in weight."

It was the first in a golden shower that was nevertheless only produced with a continuance of the enormous care and patience which had characterized the operation from the start. In the two months that followed that first successful haul the vast majority of the gold had been recovered. But by the end of November an average of sixty attempts were needed to collect just one ingot. Eventually the divers were fishing for just one ingot that the grab had let slip from its jaws as it came to the surface. They had then recovered 555 ingots out of 590, representing 94 per cent of the total and worth £2,379,000.

The salvage operations carried out on the *Egypt*, the *Laurentic* and the *Niagara* represent the most successful and the most valuable of all time. They lack perhaps those features associated with the traditional treasure-hunt – the mystery of its real location, the thrill of ancient legends, the special charm of antique coins. But they provide the fascination of applying science and technical skill to seemingly intractable problems and they are usually much more financially rewarding.

THE 1715 PLATE FLEET

The achievement of Kip Wagner and his syndicate of researchers and divers is the greatest story of treasure-hunting since Sir William Phips raised £200,000 from the wreck of the *Concepción*, and it far surpasses that old rascal's lucky discovery for it required intelligence and painstaking research. (*Pieces of Eight*, 1967.)

Wagner, a small building contractor, went to live in Florida at the village of Sebastian near the town of Wabasco not far from the present Cape Kennedy, at the end of the Second World War, but it was not until 1949 that he heard the legend of the great *flota*, the fleet of Spanish treasure galleons that had been lost in a hurricane on the Florida coast early in the morning of 30 July, 1715. Yet it was a famous story that had excited the dreams of several professional treasure-hunters, and was well known to the local beachcombers who from time to time picked up coins on the beaches. One of these men led Wagner to start grubbing in the sand, and he formed a small syndicate which by the end of that summer had spent £400 and found nothing. Wagner continued on his own and during several summers he collected about 100 coins, some silver and others gold, all turned black and oxidized by long immersion in sea water. On being cleaned these coins disclosed one significant fact. All had been minted in the year 1714, that preceding the famous disaster. Yet according to modern historians the eleven lost galleons had sunk either fifty miles to the north or 150

miles to the south, and they had not been lost off the mouth of
the Sebastian river.

Wagner and his friend Dr Kip Kelso, a local physician, studied the story which told that the Plate Fleet had sailed from
Havana on 24 July. It carried the most valuable cargo ever
shipped to Spain for, due to the war with England, three years
accumulated wealth, derived from the mines of Mexico and
Peru, had been piled up awaiting the formation of a convoy of
galleons. Thus, instead of sending the wealth of one year which
at that time amounted usually to about £100,000,000, the
Spaniards had entrusted the accumulated treasure to one fleet.
And as well as that the Spaniards in the New World embarked,
on the orders of the King, the fabulous collection of jewels he
had demanded for settlement upon the Duchess of Palma
whom he was about to marry. In addition the fleet had
embarked bales of silk and muslin and cases of porcelain which
had been shipped from China via the Philippines, with the
consignments of the merchants of Cartagena and Vera Cruz,
the ports where the fleet had assembled prior to sailing to Havana.

On arrival at Havana, the ships were already so heavily
laden that the Governor, Casa Torres, was forced to charter
the French ship, the *Griffin* commanded by Antoine Daré, in
which to stow his own merchandise and possessions. The fleet
was commanded by General Ubilla who, due to his inexperi-
ence at sea, deputed the navigation and the *flota*'s defence in
case of battle to General Echeverz, who despite his military
title was an experienced seaman. But even so, rigid protocol
demanded that Ubilla should lead the van in the *Hampton
Court*, a ship that had been captured from the English, and
Echeverz was forced to bring up the rear in his own galleon,
the *Nuestra Señora de Carmen y San Antonio*. Between these ships
sailed the other galleons and freighters including a chartered
Dutch vessel, all of which were under the command of Don
Antonio de Chevas who survived and wrote his account of the
greatest naval disaster that befell Spain.

From Cuba, the fleet took the usual course through the
Bahamas Passage, between those islands and the coast of Florida, intending to round the island of Bermuda to the north
before setting its course eastwards for Spain. By 1715 this had
been established as the less hazardous of the only two possible
routes from the Caribbean Sea, navigation to and from which
was dictated by the constant east wind which prevented the

galleons from returning to Spain by the way they had come, via the island chain that circles that sea. There was still time for the fleet to navigate the passage before the start of the unpredictable hurricane season which was due in a few weeks.

The fleet was well up the Bahamas Passage by 29 July when, as de Chevas describes, the ships became becalmed. The breeze dropped and the seas surged in a heavy silent swell. The accompanying flock of birds which swarmed in the ships' wake suddenly flew back to the shore that was not more than twenty miles distant. The sun shone brightly and there was not a cloud in the sky. As night fell the swell increased and the ships rolled and fell in the troughs, to the dismay and apprehension of their crews. Next day dawned hazy and cheerless and by noon the sun was observed "as through a muslin shroud". It grew dark and gusts of sudden wind came first from the south-east and then from east-north-east. The waves rose to deck height, the spray flying through the air like arrows and injuring the seamen.

By nightfall on 30 July the wind was blowing at 100 knots and the fleet was in the grip of a hurricane, a scant twenty miles from a dangerous, reef-strewn shore. There was nothing the Spaniards could do to control their heavily laden and top-heavy galleons as their sails were wrenched away and their masts toppled. Only Antoine Daré in the *Griffin* succeeded in hauling off, due to his care to give his ship more weather room than the Spaniards had allowed for.

The *Hampton Court* struck the reefs at 2.30 a.m. Ubilla and her crew of 223 men were all drowned as the vessel was torn to pieces by the jagged rocks. Echeverz's galleon suffered the same fate; he died with 124 members of his crew, and the other galleons and freighters followed. The crew of *La Holandesa* were lucky for a great wave carried the ship over the reefs and deposited her on the beach. As the hurricane screamed to its close, the survivors huddled among the wreckage, jettisoned cargo, and bodies with which the sand-dunes were strewn. More than 1,000 men had died.

Daylight brought a scene of desolation to which the senior surviving officer, Franco Salmon, sought to restore order. He despatched a boat, which had miraculously survived, to sail up the coast to the Spanish fort at St Augustine, from where succour was sent. Reaching the scene the Spanish soldiers helped the bewildered sailors to collect the treasures that had been cast on to the beach, indiscriminately shooting any sailor who was found with doubloons in his pockets. A salvage fleet was sent from Havana, its leader Don Juan Solorzano forcibly recruiting the tribe of Seminole Indians who lived near by. His method was ingenious and ruthless. Taken over the reefs in skiffs, each Indian was supplied with a cask to act as a rudimentary diving bell, from which he could replenish his air, and weighted with a stone.

Thrown into the sea to brave the sharks, barracudas and giant eels, the Indians sank to the bottom, keeping their faces within the casks, while they scoured the sea-bed. If they came up empty-handed they were thrown down again. By these means the Spaniards recovered about one quarter of the treasure that had been lost, at the cost of the entire tribe.

The gold and silver ingots and the masses of coins were collected in a makeshift fort built in the sand-dunes, and only just in time, for the pirates and freebooters of the West Indies came quickly to the scene, desperate to waylay the freighters on their return to Cuba and even to attack the fort. The English Governors of Virginia and Jamaica sent ships to share in the spoils, and before it was abandoned in 1719 the Spanish fort had been looted several times. Nevertheless the Spaniards had salvaged all the rich cargo that was possible at that time for no one could do better until modern diving equipment had been invented. Even then no serious attempt was made to salvage the galleons, or even to locate them accurately, until Kip Wagner became interested.

Unaccountably – for the galleons were stated to have been lost either far to the north, or even farther to the south – Wagner had found coins dated 1714 on the beach at Sebastian, and the conflicting statements made by historians about the place of the disaster intrigued him. One or the other must be wrong, which suggested that both opinions could be wrong. He discussed his doubts with Dr Kelso, who decided to go to Washington to consult the earliest records stocked in the Library of Congress. There he found a book published in 1775 written by the cartographer Bernard Romans and entitled *A Concise Natural History of East and West Florida*. The book contained a map of the coast and opposite the Sebastian river was remarked "Here perished the Admiral commanding the Plate Fleet of 1715", and on page 273 the author stated:

Directly opposite the mouth of the St. Sebastian river the ship wreck of the Spanish Admiral who was the northernmost wreck of 14 galleons and a hired Dutch ship, all laden with specie and plate which by of northeast winds were drove ashore and lost on this coast between this place and the bleach yard in 1715.

And Romans went on to say:

The people employed in the course of our survey while walking the strand after strong eastern gales, have repeatedly found pistareens and double pistareens, which kind of money probably yet remaining in the wrecks, are sometimes washed up by the surf in hard winds. The lagoon stretches parallel to the sea, until the latitude 27:20, where it has a outwatering or mouth; directly below this mouth, in three fathoms of water, lies the remains of the Dutch wreck.

Thus the earliest history of Florida, published within sixty years of the disaster, denied the inaccuracies of the modern historians, and it located the site of the disaster in the area in which Wagner had found coins.

On Dr Kelso's return to Florida he and Wagner floated over the reef on an inflated inner tube; gazing down through the clear water, they saw ballast stones and six cannon; stretching away fourteen miles to the south lay the wrecks of the other ships. While Wagner searched for them, Kelso organized a systematic search of the Spanish records, in Spain and Mexico, obtaining 2,000 microfilmed documents, including the cargo manifest of each ship lost. The salvage efforts of 1715–19 were fully detailed and they recorded that of the total cargo less than one quarter had been recovered. The bulk of the rich cargo still lay beneath the waves.

The task of salvage required a team of experienced divers and these were recruited from the amateur skin divers at Cape Kennedy. Financial assistance was provided by a local bank and a boat was purchased. By now it was 1958 and between then and 1964 the "Real Eight" syndicate, as they styled themselves, brought to the surface 60,000 gold and silver coins; pieces of jewellery, pottery, anchors, cannon, cannon balls, a gold chain, silver and gold ingots; a silver dinner service; a twenty-eight piece Chinese K'ang Hsi porcelain tea service, altogether worth more than one million dollars.

And this sum, believes Wagner, represents only a fraction of the treasure that still lies in the eight wrecks he and his friends have located lying a few hundred yards from the shore in a line representing approximately the formation of the fleet as it sailed up the Bahamas Passage.

Salvage work, which will continue until the last wreck has been examined, is beset by many difficulties; the opaqueness of the water, strong currents, frequent storms, and the sharks and moray eels which infest the reef but which, so far, have not molested the divers. Early in their search the syndicate negotiated an agreement with the State of Florida by which, in return for 25 per cent of the treasure recovered, it was given the sole right to search for treasure on the wrecks it had located.

Kip Wagner's discovery of the galleons wrecked in 1715 points a moral for treasure-hunters: before starting to search, check the original records. For as time goes by even the best authenticated story can become garbled, and may suffer from intentional misrepresentation.

WRECK ON THE
SILVER REEF

The galleons of Spain which carried home the fabulous treasures of the New World were fantastic vessels, more castle than ship. The depredations of the Protestant powers, whose seamen captured and looted the ships with official blessing, so alarmed the shipbuilders that they created monstrous, high-sided craft, half-merchantman, half-warship, which bristled with up to three tiers of cannon. Their high poop decks towered over the stern, creating comfortable and roomy quarters in the great cabin below for the commander, but adding to the top-heavy instability of the ship. Their design thus had the effect of rendering them more vulnerable to the wind and waves than to the assaults of the buccaneers.

The galleon *Nuestra Señora de la Concepción* was one such ship, and she formed part of the *flota* which annually sailed for Spain with the riches of the New World. It was the practice of the time for the Spanish officials of Mexico to collect the gold and silver which the Indians mined for them, and to send it to the port for embarkation only when the fleet was due to sail. In 1640 there had been no convoy to Spain due to the great hazards of the sea and so in 1641, in the weeks during which the *flota* assembled at Vera Cruz, a vast amount of treasure flowed steadily towards the port.

During the month of July the treasure steadily accumulated, augmented by the personal possessions of private individuals sending their wealth home against their own return. To the gold and silver were added chests of coin, ivory and jade from trade with China, silks from Japan and precious stones from India. The fleet of some twenty ships lay awaiting their cargo but, for some inexplicable reason, the newly appointed general of the fleet ordered that the whole of the treasure should be divided up and loaded aboard only the two largest ships. Thus the *Nuestra Señora de la Concepción*, in which the general, Don Juan de Campos, was to sail and the *Santissima Sacramento*, the admiral's ship, carried a vast fortune between them.

This decision on the part of the general caused considerable protest. The *Concepción* was in a bad way, her lead sheathing worn and her hull leaky. Admiral Villavicencio wanted to careen the ship before the fleet sailed, but de Campos would have none of it, although the *Santissima Sacramento* was in almost as bad a state. Just before the *flota*'s departure the general decided to sail in the *Santissima Sacramento*, which thus became the leading ship, while the admiral was relegated to the leaky *Concepción*.

By the time the fleet had reached Havana, thirty-six days after it had left Vera Cruz, the *Concepción* was leaking so badly that she had to be repaired. But the general would allow only the most essential work to be done, and in mid-September the fleet once more put to sea for the long crossing of the Atlantic. The departure was premature; within only a few hours the galleon was making so much water that the general reluctantly had to agree to return to Havana. The admiral fought without success for a delay to allow his ship to be properly repaired. He was equally unsuccessful in his pleas to have his cargo divided among the other ships of the fleet. Although the worst holes were repaired, the ships once more put to sea before September had ended.

They soon encountered hurricane force winds and within hours eight ships had gone to the bottom. The *Concepción* was naturally in a bad way. She had lost her mainmast and many cannon had had to be jettisoned to lighten her top-heavy weight. When the storm died away there was no sign of any other ship and only the frantic efforts of the crew kept the water in the holds at a reasonable level. It was agreed by the council which, in the Spanish custom, the admiral had to call to make decisions, that the galleon should head east and then south towards San Juan in Puerto Rico where the ship could be properly repaired.

Such a roundabout detour was necessary for the vessel was in the region of the Bahamas with its scattering of coral reefs, then largely uncharted, through which a crippled ship dared not venture. Moreover the area was a happy hunting-ground of the pirates who had their headquarters in the Tortugas. At all costs the treasure-ship must avoid risks of such nature.

So the *Concepción* sailed east, while carpenters and sail-makers strove to patch up the damage as best they could. Slowly the unwieldy ship crawled eastwards until, after some four weeks, the pilots decided it was time to bear south. The admiral protested: he had sailed these waters many times and his experience told him these young pilots were wrong. But the rules of command, the verdict of the council, overrode him. The ship turned south towards what was soon to be her grave. The admiral himself was so convinced of this that, in a Pilate-like gesture, he sent for a bowl of water and washed his hands.

Doubtless impressed by this dramatic scene, the lookouts and pilots kept careful watch. Within a few days there came the cry of warning and the jagged rocks of reefs could be seen. The galleon had no chance; crippled, she had to rely on her boats to tow her through the reefs in the wake of those sent out to find a channel. At night the ship was anchored, but rising winds caused the anchors to drift and jam among the rocks. She would scrape rocks, touch bottom, be pulled off by her boats – in a whole day she moved only three-quarters of a mile and still saw no way out of her maritime maze. Eventually the inevitable happened; during the night the anchor cables parted, the ship drifted off, brushed against the reefs, was carried against a large flat rock, recoiled and sank by the bow.

Held by the rocks, the galleon's stern lay high out of the water. Her crew, in rafts and boats, proceeded to make for safety. Some followed the instructions of the pilots and sailed east or west never to be seen again. Others, led by the admiral, sailed south and finally reached Hispaniola (Haiti). Thirty men, believing that help must soon be sent, stayed on the reef near the wreck, living on provisions from the ship. They removed some of the ship's precious cargo and piled it on to a flat rock, but as time passed they too left on rafts, only to perish. In all more than 300 members of the crew died.

As soon as the admiral had recovered he tried to organize an expedition to salve the treasure, but the red tape of the incredibly formal Spanish administration caused endless delays while lengthy inquiries were held. The admiral was exonerated from blame, the general had gone down with his ship in another gale, the pilots had vanished. But still no attempt was made to salvage the treasure. It was not until two years had passed that the admiral himself contrived to fit out a small fleet to visit the Los Abrajos reef where his vessel had foundered. But he became separated from his escort, and his ships were sunk by buccaneers.

During the years that followed various attempts were made to organize a salvage expedition, but they never so much as reached the wreck. Ships were captured by buccaneers, almost wrecked on the reefs or failed to find the ship. As the years passed the *Concepción* vanished into deep water and the bullion piled on to the rock by the men who had camped there was, so it is said, found and carried away by an English pirate, John Mors. This tale may well be true for, when Mors was later captured by the Spaniards, ingots bearing the stamp of the *Concepción* were found aboard his ship.

Forty-four years passed and then there sailed on to the scene a man named William Phips, the twenty-first child of gunsmith James Phips and his wife Mary who had emigrated from Bristol to America just before William's birth in 1650. William was ignorant, unlettered and inexperienced, but he was filled with ambition and determination. Leaving his twenty-five brothers and sisters to look after the family farm he apprenticed himself to a shipbuilder and later, by sheer effrontery and single-mindedness, persuaded a well-to-do merchant ship captain to accept him as a son-in-law. He taught himself to read and write and soon set himself up in his own shipyard in his native village. Troubles with Indians caused the hasty departure of William and most of the inhabitants, whom William put aboard his ship and took safely to Boston. There, undaunted, he set to work to rebuild his business; and on the waterfront he first heard tales of the treasures of the sunken Spanish galleons. During his travels, carrying merchandise to the Bahamas, Phips heard many more tales of the *Concepción* and the attempts to find her which had all ended in ill-luck or disaster.

Gradually the idea grew in William's mind of searching for the treasure himself. But he needed a ship and financial resources which were beyond his own means. His attempts to arouse interest in Boston failed, and he soon decided that if he was to get help he must go to England and the ever-impecunious Charles II.

Charles II, however, had already heard about the famous Spanish wreck north of Hispaniola, and at about the time that Phips arrived in England two naval ships sailed from Portsmouth harbour commissioned to discover and salvage the treasure. These were a sloop, commanded by Captain Edward Stanley, and a frigate under Captain George Churchill. They had a rough idea of where the treasure-ship lay (indeed there were believed to be many ships sunk in the area) and a description of the high flat rock on which the thirty members of the *Concepción*'s crew had attempted to survive. But for a year the ships searched in vain, alternating their efforts with various services performed at the behest of the governor of Jamaica. Discouraged, the two captains were about to give up when a sailor named Thomas Smith appeared who said that while on a cruise to New England he had been aboard a ship which had come by accident upon a reef which included a high flat rock on top of which they had seen bars of silver and gold. They had also seen the wreck of a ship wedged between two rocks. While the crew were arguing about how to salvage the treasure a gale blew up and drove them far to leeward and they had been unable to find the spot again.

Armed with the information the sailor had given him, Stanley sailed again for the Silver Reef – as it was to become known – where the *Concepción* was believed to have foundered. He searched in vain for the pinnacle of rock which, according to Smith and the survivors of the *Concepción*, marked the site of the wreck. Among the treacherous reefs he himself nearly came to grief. In the end, after three years' search, he was ordered back to England.

While the English ships were searching unsuccessfully, efforts had been made by other treasure-hunters, all without success and often ending in disaster. William Phips, meanwhile, had succeeded in his attempts to persuade Charles II to help him; in return for a quarter of the value recovered on top of the usual royalty of one half, the king had agreed to provide Phips with a ship.

Phips sailed for the New World and reached Boston in October, 1683; but he had aboard a troublesome crew, who fought and swore in the dockside taverns of Boston, and Phips himself ran foul of the authorities by attempting to insist that his ship was royal and that other ships must strike their colours as he entered harbour. None of this amused the governor, who wasted no time in reminding Phips that everyone in Boston knew about his humble origins. Nor was he very sympathetic to William's insistence that the other ships which were setting off to search for the treasure should be prevented. Altogether Phips and his crew were not popular.

Eventually he sailed off for the Hispaniola reefs, having had to replace his problem crew with another, and there he "fished" over various wrecks, observing many other vessels engaged in the same enterprise. But he failed to find the *Concepción*, and eventually decided to return to England to ask for more and better ships.

Although he had found some treasure, Phips had made a loss on the expedition and there was, moreover, a new king, James II, who lacked Charles's adventurous spirit. However he found private backers without difficulty and sailed for the Americas once more, some two months after the return of the unsuccessful naval expedition.

This time Phips had two ships, the *James and Mary* of 200 tons and the little *Henry of London*, of 50 tons, under the command of Francis Rogers, his mate on the previous expedition. These two ships reached Porto Plata in December, 1686, and, while Phips lingered on the coast, trading with the Spaniards, Rogers sailed for the area where the *Concepción* was believed to have been wrecked.

For three weeks Rogers searched the area and in the end he found the wreck – purely by chance. The crew used canoes to search among the treacherous reefs and it was from one of these that a seaman saw a particularly beautiful piece of coral which he asked a diver to fetch for him. The man obliged – and noticed great cannon lying on the sea-bed. Soon he found bars of silver, coins and plate lying about on the hull of a ship which was wedged between two rocks and which was so overgrown with coral as to be hardly recognizable. The high, flat rock on which the survivors were said to have piled bullion from the wreck had vanished, no doubt through movement of the sea-bed.

Rogers sailed back to Porto Plata where, for a while, he proceeded to tease Phips by saying nothing of his find. Phips was gloomily trying to persuade Rogers that they should give

up the search and turn to trade when he spotted a silver bar
which Rogers had left in a place where Phips would eventually
catch sight of it. "Thanks be to God! We are made", Phips
cried (according to his biographer Cotton Mather) and within
a fortnight the two ships were both back at the site of the
wreck and the great treasure-hunt began.

The wreck lay in only six or eight fathoms of water, well
within the capabilities of the Indian divers. For two months
canoes and boats plied back and forth between the wreck and
the two ships, lying safely at anchor some distance away. They
carried pieces of eight, bullion, plate, and gold worth some
£201,000 – or perhaps two millions pounds in today's value.
Finally Phips was obliged to give up because of the shortage of
supplies. He sailed for England and a hero's welcome and proceeded to share out the profits (the claim the Spanish ambassador made on hearing the news was firmly ignored). Phips
was feted and honoured, but anxious to get back to collect the
booty he had been obliged to leave.

In 1686 he arrived again at the reef, to find a number of
vessels at work and the wreck more or less picked clean. He
contrived to collect only another £12,000 worth of treasure,
which did not cover the cost of the expedition. He made every
attempt, too, to reach the treasure which still lay within the
hulk, for that which had so far been salvaged had been stored
in the upperworks of the ship, easy of access. Now the wreck
was so encrusted with coral growth that it was impossible to
break open the hatches. Phips tried gunpowder, but was
unable to devise any method of keeping the fuse alight as it led
down through the water. He and all the other treasure-seekers
were obliged to abandon the wreck while convinced that the
bulk of the treasure was still to be found.

They were not alone in their belief. Phips retired to wealth
and honours, eventually becoming Governor of Massachusetts,
and never again visited the *Nuestra Señora de la Concepción*. But
through the years other hopeful hunters have persevered. As
far as is known none has succeeded but, since the reefs do not
lie in territorial waters there is no need for treasure-hunters –
who are naturally secretive about their activities – to report to
any authority.

Some well-documented searches have been made, and have
ended in failure to find the treasure or to penetrate the ship.
But nobody knows if these attempts were actually searching

the right wreck: after 200 years locations become hazy and the sea changes many things. One of the most persistent modern hunters, Alexandre Korganoff, has made several attempts on the wreck in the belief that £50,000,000 worth of treasure still awaits discovery. Korganoff has made a life's work of researching the location of the wreck and its contents, but in spite of several expeditions has failed to reach it. His attempts have been thwarted by accidents, more or less serious, which have led to stories that an evil genie guards the sunken gold.

Where hidden treasure is concerned such tales are common. If any evil guards this looted Spanish gold it is the very real one of the treacherous reefs and hidden rocks which brought the great galleon to its grave three hundred years ago.

THE *LUTINE*

It is with extreme pain that I have to state to you the melancholy
fate of H.M.S. *Lutine*, which ship ran on the outer bank of Fly
Island passage on the night of the 9th inst. in a heavy gale of wind
from the NNW, and I am much afraid that her crew with the
exception of one man, who was saved on a part of the wreck, have
perished. This man, when taken up, was almost exhausted. He is
at present tolerably recovered, and relates that the *Lutine* left Yarmouth Roads on the morning of the 9th inst. bound for the Texel,
and that she had on board a considerable quantity of money . . .

I shall use every endeavour to save what I can from the wreck,
but from the situation she is lying in, I am afraid little will be
recovered.

This letter dated 10 October, 1799, and received by the British Admiralty on the 19th had been forwarded by Vice Admiral Mitchell, commander of the actions against the fleet of the
Batavian Republic; it was signed by Captain Portlock of
H.M.S. Sloop *Arrow*.

And there, given ordinary conditions and circumstances, the
matter would doubtless have ended. The melancholy details of
the disaster would have been entered into various archives, the
exact position of the wreck charted, the many bereaved notified
and His Majesty's frigate, *Lutine*, would have bedded down
among the treacheries of the Buitengronden Sandbanks which
had claimed her and there she would have remained undisturbed to this day.

But the *Lutine* was a bullion ship.

According to the Dutch press which reported the tragedy somewhat tardily on 13 November – and then almost as an afterthought – the stricken vessel carried a number of passengers, a hundred and forty thousand pounds in sterling for the Army at Den Helder and a considerable sum to be taken on to Hamburg "to support credit of the Trades in that town". The overall amount lost, they suggested, appeared to be in the vicinity of £500,000.

But, and here's the rub, in 1821 a Dutch government release hazards a figure which had risen to the princely proportions of £1,666,666. In 1858, John Mavor Still, Lloyd's chief agent in Amsterdam, quotes £1,200,000, while as late as 1957 a Lloyd's publication settles for £1,400,000. Still's figure incidentally apportions his amount to £900,000 in Lloyd's gold and silver bar, £160,000 for Hamburg's account and £140,000 for soldiers' pay.

To add to the confusion in April, 1869, seventy years after the disaster, the *Leeuwarder Courant* came up with the extraordinary statement that the sunken vessel had also contained the Dutch Crown Jewels which the Prince of Orange had previously sent to England to be polished and reset. These baubles, the readers were informed, were hermetically sealed in an iron chest and had been taken aboard the *Lutine* a few days before her departure. Regarding this particular item of her cargo there appears to be no further information other than the fact that the Dutch Government promised a reward of £8,000 for the recovery of the said jewels.

Whichever way one likes to look at it quite a considerable sum of money appears to be involved. With regard to that amount scheduled for Hamburg it is interesting to appreciate the necessity for its urgent dispatch. Financially this rapidly expanding city on the Elbe had far over-reached herself; her Stock Exchange was in dire straits. Her sudden growth into a great commercial centre, a direct result of the French Revolution, had been far too rapid and quite simply she lacked the facilities to cope with such a headlong increase of commerce. Instead of being virtually self-supporting as in the past, her extended business interests were now reaching out as far as America and the Indies. Too much speculation and too little money resulted in terrible stagnation. The Bank of England, not one must hasten to add in a brotherly spirit of altruism but in an effort to back British investments, offered assistance to the

Hamburg merchants to the tune of "a quantity of bullion".

Admiral Lord Duncan (North Sea Fleet) wrote: "The merchants interested in making remittances to the Continent for the supply of their credit having made an application to me for a King's ship to carry over a considerable sum of money on account of their being no Packet for that purpose I complied with their request and ordered the *Lutine* to Cuxhaven with the same, together with the mails lying here (Yarmouth Roads) for want of conveyance, directing Captain Skynner to proceed to Stromness immediately after doing so . . ." This letter was dispatched on 9 October.

The money mentioned for "soldiers' pay" appears not to have been aboard the *Lutine* at all since there is a letter in existence from the Captain of H.M.S. *Amethyst* dated 23 October stating that *his* ship had been entrusted with this particular sum and that it had been delivered in Texel on 9 October, the very day of the *Lutine* disaster. It is possible that the "Army" money had been divided between the two ships, but had that been one would have expected an echoing wail of distress from the army at the loss of half their pay. As it was there was nothing, so it may be safe to assume that the *Amethyst* delivered the entire amount intact.

The *Lutine* began life as *La Lutine*. As a ship of the French Fleet she was launched in 1779. In '93 however during the unpleasantness in France when Admiral Hood reluctantly withdrew from Toulon under the threat of a beady-eyed newcomer called Napoleon Bonaparte, he took with him, along with his own fleet, a dozen French frigates and sailed off to Gibraltar where these purloined vessels were promptly attached to the British Navy. *La Lutine* was one of them. While the British Admiralty's meticulous drawings and measurements of her tell us precisely what she looked like immediately after her capture, they do not enlighten us as to her appearance subsequent to her re-building and refitting by the British Navy. She was of course a warship and carried in the way of armaments 26 twelve-pounders, 6 twenty-four-pounder and 6 six-pounder carronades, in all a total of 38 pieces. Her crew consisted of 240 hands. The name *La Lutine* means "The Tormentress", one which during the ensuing years she was to earn in no small measure.

Steel's *Navy List* tells us that in July, 1799, the *Lutine* was lying in Yarmouth under the command of Captain Lancelott Skynner, her first lieutenant being Charles Aufrere and her ship's clerk John Strong. Walter Montgomery was the ship's doctor.

She sailed from Yarmouth on her last voyage during the small hours of Wednesday, 9 October, 1799. A report from a Mr E. B. Merriman states that she was last seen at about midnight "or later" on a clear night by the crew of a fishing vessel passing close by. They were surprised by the fact that instead of the accustomed silence and darkness of a King's ship at sea, brilliant lights were to be seen and there appeared to be a great deal of jollity going on in the State cabin. However unacceptable such behaviour might seem aboard a King's ship, there is perhaps confirmation in the statement of an anonymous writer who relates that "the Captain (of the *Lutine*) was so impressed by the important commissions he had received from the bankers that on the eve of the ill-fated voyage he invited the entire élite of Lowestoft and Yarmouth to a ball on board ship."

A further report comes from Lt. James Gardner of H.M.S. *Blonde* lying off Texel who states that the *Lutine* was seen by him at the back of the Haaks, a sandbank lying west of Texel.

Neither of these reports mention the proximity of bad weather but in those latitudes and at that time of year storms and gale-force winds could never have been far away. The Duke of York writing from his headquarters in Schagerbrug says in a letter to the Secretary of State that one of the main difficulties hindering the invasion force was the state of the weather – this on that same fateful 9 October.

The *Lutine* foundered in the Westergronden on the outer bank of the Vlieland passage at about midnight. All the passengers and the entire ship's company, with the exception of one, perished.

At two o'clock in the morning the inhabitants of Vlieland were aroused by the arrival of Captain Portlock with twenty men from the English corvette *Wolverine* reporting that rockets had been sighted and that a ship was in distress; all boats were immediately to be put to sea and make for the spot.

The sole eyewitness report, furnished as late as 1860 by eighty-year-old Jan Folkerts Visser who must have been about nineteen at the time, recounts the dismal saga of a wretched and turbulent passage with his father and six others in a pilot boat at five o'clock in the morning which resulted in the recovery, along with several items of assorted hardware, of three floating corpses, officers to judge from their "blue coats, trousers and white waistcoats: one with two epaulettes, the others each with one". It was they who picked up the solitary survivor found clinging to a piece of the upper gundeck. Returning to the waterway they plied him with wine and bread which, not surprisingly, interested him not at all, he being quite obviously half out of his mind and babbling a great deal in a language beyond their comprehension.

If one discounts this isolated eyewitness account, which in any case was not forthcoming until sixty years after the event, the odd thing which strikes one is the almost complete lack of impression which the tragedy seems to have made upon the local inhabitants. Bodies by the score were being washed up all over the place; two hundred alone were interred in a huge pit dug behind the Brandari lighthouse on Terschelling; the three dead officers brought ashore by Visser and his father were buried, under the eyes of other British officers from various vessels lying off Vlieland, in the village churchyard, and yet there remains no feeling of response from the people themselves. It is possible that to them the *Lutine* was just another shipwreck. The great pit in the dunes which contained most of the dead remained unmarked – although the name of Doodemankisten, Dead Men's Coffins, hovered around it; the interment of the three officers was unrecorded in the Island's Register of Deaths and not a monument, not a memorial plaque, not a tombstone was ever to mark the spot.

The Dutch coast has ever been a navigator's nightmare. Alongside deep channels treacherous sandbanks continually change their shapes and shift their positions. Charting becomes almost impossible and in spite of continual marking of clear passages with buoys and beacons loss to shipping has always been severe. A navigable channel of one year could be silted up the next. "The outer bank of the Fly Island passage", mentioned by Captain Portlock in his letter to Vice Admiral Mitchell, no longer exists.

One will readily appreciate that such shiftings of tons of sand on the sea-bed did nothing but frustrate any attempts at salvage operations, Admiralty instructions for which were received by Captain Portlock in a letter dated 29 October. Al-

though the wrecked ship lay maddeningly close to the surface
– a mere 25 feet or so – contrary winds and currents and
sand piling up over her made her periodically completely inaccessible.

Lloyd's agents, sent over hopefully to ascertain whether anything could be done, returned with glum faces and shaking
heads.

To increase everybody's difficulties Great Britain being at
war with the Netherlands, the Dutch promptly declared possession of the wreck as war booty.

The sheriff and Receiver of Wrecks of Terschelling, F. P.
Robbé, was instructed by the Committee for the Public Pro-
perties of Holland to do something about it all and he in his
turn, having viewed the situation, explained that the ship lying
in such an unfavourable position and the season being so far
advanced it would seem probable that the mounting of salvage
operations would have to wait. He did however ask for and
was granted the monopoly for such operations. By the New
Year he had commissioned three salvors to start work promising them a third part of the value of everything recovered on
condition that not "the smallest piece of property whatever its
nature" was to be held back.

Bad weather, ice-drift, heavy surf prevented a start being
made and it was not until August, 1800, that the wreck was
finally broached. Within a few days seven gold bars weighing
81 pounds in all and a chest of 4,606 Spanish piastres had been
brought to the surface.

The news spread like wildfire and soon poor Mr Robbé was
besieged by practically every able-bodied fisherman in the surrounding districts each demanding a chance to join in the fun,
not to mention the profits.

Trouble also came in the form of belligerent groups of fishermen from the Island of Urk in the Zuider Zee who also saw
no reason why they should not have a share in the proceeds;
indeed they made such a nuisance of themselves that Robbé
was forced to the conclusion that he would rather have them
with him than against him so he hired twenty of them on the
same conditions as his own chosen men.

Salvage at this time was simply a matter of sitting on the
surface and fishing away hopefully with hooks and tongs and
pincers and scoops, groping blindly around at a depth of about
25 feet. The disadvantages of such methods were many, not the

least being that the flimsy and waterlogged casks and chests simply fell apart at being so rudely disturbed, spilling their precious contents into the sandy sea-bed to be sucked down and lost for ever; rusted iron hoops around the casks in which the gold was packed just snapped, the casks disintegrating.

Nevertheless gold and silver was coming up. A receipt dated 15 September, 1800, declared the recovery of 29,248 Spanish piastres, 13 gold bars, 15 silver bars worth around 216,870 guilders. On 3 December, 1801, a further 301,721 guilders are noted.

But difficulties abided and tarnished somewhat the gilt on the gingerbread. "Favourable tides and clear waters," reports Robbé dejectedly, "do not coincide with favourable weather." By 1803 he was writing that it was essential to engage a good diver. "It is disheartening work . . . has caused the loss of a great deal of heavy equipment, all for nothing . . ."

Only the year 1800 appears to have been moderately successful but even so with the payment of wages, a great deal of expenditure on the equipment to say nothing of the loss of it the final accounts showed a deficit of some 3,240 guilders.

In November, 1803, storms changed the position of the wreck considerably and buried it deeper into the sand. Inevitably high costs and poor results brought Robbé's operations to an end.

And so it began and so it was to continue for another 150 years. Lying smugly in her three fathoms of water the enigmatic Tormentress lured the treasure-hunters to her watery grave and yielded up only a fraction of her purported treasure. Every known technique and method was exploited to persuade her to divulge her secrets, scoops, tongs, pincers, irons, poles with sacks on their ends, helmetted divers strutting drunkenly on the sea-bed – all to not much avail.

Every device, every machine, every engine, some invented especially for the occasion, was sailed, hauled, towed, floated and sunk over the stricken vessel; diving-bells, coal-grabs, sand-divers, towers, bucket-dredgers – all were pressed into hopeful service. 1858 turned out to be another "good" year, a further half million guilders worth of bullion being recovered, the lure of which success kept things on the boil and drove ingenious inventors back to their drawing-boards time and time again. There was even a floating saucer, 115 feet in diameter which could house 26 men, a device which though it successfully left the drawing-board never got beyond the model stage.

The *Kariwata*, a gigantic tin-dredger weighing over 4,200 tons, the biggest in the world, "a technical marvel!" appeared on the scene in 1938. The general public were invited in an advertisement in the press to view the dredging operations on the actual site, a sort of "any more for the *Skylark* – around the lighthouse and back" procedure.

The *Kariwata*'s first effort, lasting from the 9th to the 27th June, yielded copper nails and a silver coin bearing the head of Charles IV of Spain, 1789, along with various bits and pieces of previous salvage operations. A storm, blowing up on the 27th, deprived the *Kariwata* of her stern cable and tore a bollard from her deck so she was towed back to Terschelling. "A narrow escape." Her second attempt, much more successful, brought forth a gold bar weighing 7¾ pounds and worth about 7,000 guilders. It turned out to be the only one and significantly was discovered 60 feet or so from the site of the wreck. Other items brought to light consisted of gold, silver and copper coins, 330 pounds of copper, 29,000 of iron and 660 of lead, 1,000 cannon-balls of various sizes, uniform buttons, human bones and five cannon. The *Kariwata* worked over an extensive area digging down to a depth of nearly 70 feet but in July 1939 she in turn was towed away to dredge for tin in the Dutch East Indies, the job for which she was originally intended; the undertaking had cost over 442,000 guilders of which the company was able to recover less than 190,000 in insurance. Technically, it was said, a success. Economically, alas, it was a resounding failure.

The *Kariwata* was to be the last of the treasure-hunters and if she did nothing else she destroyed and certainly disintegrated what little remained of the *Lutine*. Other attempts have since been mooted but nothing has come of them. However the late late news is that in 1978 an electronic survey was made of the area of the arc of the *Lutine*'s approach to her final resting-place and should the final results of that survey prove to be as favourable as at first suspected there is every likelihood that a further attempt at recovery will be made.

On 17 July, 1858, the ship's bell was recovered bearing the date 1779 and carrying the French King's coat-of-arms and over it the words "Saint Jean". It weighs 106 pounds and is

17½ inches in diameter. This bell – the *Lutine* Bell – now hangs in Lloyd's over the rostrum in the Underwriting Room.

It is sounded only when there is important news to be announced, once for bad news, twice for good. Lord Haw-Haw, propagandist broadcaster from Nazi Germany, assured his listening public that during the war and owing to heavy British losses at sea the bell was never silent. In actual fact the bell rang only once during that time – when the German battleship *Bismarck* was sunk, and then only once; for though the sinking was good news for the British, the loss of a ship, any ship, warranted one peal only.

So, somewhere, deeply embedded in the shifting sands between Vlieland and Terschelling lies the lion's share of the *Lutine* Treasure. As late as 1956 the value of that share was estimated at no less than 42 million Dutch guilders. It is a sum which does not bear thinking about!

KIDD'S HOARD

Of all the names connected with treasure, with romantic tales of bloody pirates, buried hoards and tantalizing maps, perhaps none is better known than that of Captain William Kidd. Yet the popular picture of a bloodthirsty buccaneer who blazed a trail of murder, arson and robbery across the India seas is highly exaggerated.

It was the story of a fabulous hidden hoard which brought fame to Kidd, and this seems to have been originated by Kidd himself for, only hours before being led to the scaffold, he wrote to the Speaker of the House of Commons. He could, he said, direct an expedition to the Indies to a spot where he had "lodged goods and treasure to the value of one hundred thousand pounds". This treasure he offered to the government, adding that he expected to be fully supervised in the search for it, and that if he failed in the venture he desired "no favour but forthwith to be executed according to my sentence".

It has been suggested that Kidd was only trying to save his neck by this offer, and he certainly produced no concrete evidence of the treasure's existence. This fact has led some people to believe that the treasure was not actually concealed by Kidd – for if it had been he would have been prepared to give more details in order to save his life – but that he knew of the whereabouts of some treasure not actually hidden by himself. In any event the last-minute bid failed, and Kidd was duly hanged at Execution Dock, the Thames-side gibbet to which

pirates were customarily brought, on 23 May, 1701, and his
body then hung in chains at Tilbury.

Kidd's career as a pirate did not in fact begin until he had
reached what is usually regarded as sober middle age. He is
believed to have been born in the fishing port of Greenock, in
about 1645, and to have gone to sea at an early age. Nothing
more is known of him until, in 1689, he married a wealthy
widow in New York. He was apparently by then a man of
some social standing, carrying out a successful trading business
with the West Indies. When England and France went to war
following the accession of William of Orange, Kidd immediately offered his ship in the king's service to assist in the protection of the American colonists from the French privateers
which were cruising in American waters. He fought in two
engagements against the French and saw further service in the
West Indies. At his trial he was described as having behaved
himself very well in the face of the enemy and as being a
"mighty man". Indeed, such was his reputation that in 1691
he was rewarded by the Provincial Council of New York with
the sum of £150 "for many good services done to this Pro-
vince".

So how did this upright, middle-aged man, this pillar of
society, come to turn pirate? Well, for one thing it is perfectly
obvious that William Kidd had a taste for adventure. Many
another man of his age – and in the seventeenth century fifty
was old, rather than middle-aged – with a rich wife, a successful business and a respected position in society would have
chosen to pass the rest of his days in comfortable security. But
we know that in 1695 he brought one of his own trading sloops
across the Atlantic to London – and there made the deal which
was to bring him to Execution Dock.

Another visitor to London at that time was Robert Livingstone, an important and influential man from New York with
whom Kidd had some acquaintance. Livingstone had been
having discussions with Lord Bellomont, who had just been
appointed governor of New England, and among the subjects
under discussion was the problem of carrying out the king's
instructions to suppress the growth of piracy along the American coast.

This was no easy matter, for at this period piracy flourished.
Wars were almost always followed by piracy partly because of
the taste acquired by the privateers for freebooting and partly

because of the shortage of naval vessels for policing purposes. Moreover the American colonies actively encouraged pirates: England insisted that her colonies should trade exclusively with her – at a high price – and thus colonists were only too happy to buy smuggled or pirated goods at a cheaper price. Also, since there was no local judicial machinery for trying pirates, America provided them with a comparatively safe haven.

In addition the West Indies, right on the trade route used by the Dutch, French, Spanish and English ships, and with dozens of islands and concealed harbours in which to hide, proved a particularly happy hunting-ground. Later these pirates ventured farther afield towards the east, where they could plunder the rich ships of the Moors. (All Indians, Armenians and Muslims were then called "Moors", and Muslims were also regarded as the traditional enemy of all Christians and thus fair game.) However by the time Kidd visited London, the government was being put under pressure by the East India Company to send a man-of-war to wipe out the pirates from America and Madagascar who were preying upon the shipping of the Great Mogul. So serious had these raids become that the Company feared reprisals from the Moorish ships upon their own vessels. The government was sympathetic but it had no ships, for they were all engaged in the war with the French, and no money to spare from the Admiralty appropriation. So the king, in his instructions to Lord Bellomont, had suggested that a ship should be fitted out by means of private subscription.

The decision to employ a privateer coincided with Kidd's arrival in London and his encounter with his old acquaintance Livingstone. Kidd was obviously a thoroughly suitable man for the job, and accordingly an agreement was made between Bellomont, Livingstone and Kidd whereby Bellomont (with the assistance of friends) provided four-fifths of the sum required to fit out a ship, and Livingstone and Kidd provided the rest. Neither the seamen nor Captain Kidd would receive any pay, they and Livingstone being recompensed only be agreed shares of any prizes taken. Should they fail in the venture, however, Kidd and Livingstone stood to lose heavily, for they agreed to pay back the Earl's investment in full. For all those aboard the chosen ship, *Adventure Galley*, it was therefore important to take as many prizes as possible, and in such circumstances the dividing line between privateering and piracy is easily crossed.

By the end of January, 1696, Kidd was in possession of two commissions from the English government which authorized him to "apprehend seize and take the Ships Vessels and Goods belonging to the French King or his subjects or inhabitants within the Dominions of the said French King and such other Ships Vessels and Goods as are or shall be liable for confiscation", and also to "apprehend, seize and take into your custody" certain named pirates and also "cause to be brought such Pirates, Free-booters, and Sea Rovers, as you shall seize, to a Legal Tryal". Kidd was told that he could use force to compel them to yield, and also that he must keep an exact journal of his "Proceedings in execution of the Premises".

Kidd soon set sail in his ship of 287 tons, 34 guns and 70 men but was stopped at the Nore and held up for several days while a number of his crew were pressed for the Royal Navy. On the way to New York he took a small French ship which was sold in New York to provide the means of financing a further stock of provisions for the *Adventure Galley*. In New York Kidd also made up the strength of his crew – probaby from among men who already had piratic sympathies. In October he set sail for the Cape of Good Hope and then for Madagascar, which he reached in February, 1697.

It would seem that it was at about this point that Captain Kidd was seduced into the delights of piracy; for later it was shown that the events he recorded in his journal from this date on were highly inaccurate, and that he omitted anything which might prove to be incriminating. Since, in all this time, the *Adventure Galley* had not taken a single prize save for the small French vessel, it is likely that both Captain and crew were becoming increasingly discontented.

Soon afterwards he took a Moorish ketch, commanded by an Englishman, and another commanded by a Dutchman. He also, however, refused to give in to the insistence of his crew that he attack a Dutch ship; and later, in an argument with a seaman about this event, Kidd picked up an iron-bound bucket and, in a blind rage, swung it at the head of the seaman, killing him.

During the following months Kidd took two or three more prizes, Moorish and Portuguese, and then in January, 1698, he captured the *Quedagh Merchant*, an Armenian ship commanded by an Englishman. After seizing her goods and selling them Kidd became frightened because of the "great noise" the taking of this ship would make in England, and wanted to return her, but his crew wouldn't hear of it. So, accompanied by two prizes, he sailed for Madagascar and the part of the coast which was known to be the haunt of pirates.

In Madagascar Kidd proceeded to associate with the very men he was supposed to be apprehending and, far from bringing home the goods and prizes he obtained as he had been ordered, he divided the spoils between the crew and sold what he could. He burnt one of his prizes and, since the *Adventure Galley* had become unseaworthy, scuttled her and took over the *Quedagh Merchant*. He stayed on Madagascar for several months and eventually set sail for the West Indies. When he arrived at Anguilla he learned that he and all his crew had been proclaimed pirates.

This news caused Kidd and his men great consternation. Soon after Kidd fell in with an Antiguan merchant, Boulton, who helped him with provisions and later sold him his own ship, the *Antonia*, while the *Quedagh Merchant* was left in Boulton's charge. Many of the goods carried on the *Quedagh Merchant* had been sold, but Boulton was authorized by Kidd to sell the remainder.

Kidd sailed for New England with the intention of posing as an innocent man and handing over some of his spoils in the hope of gaining a pardon. He sent a messenger to Lord Bellomont, now installed as governor, and to Mr Livingstone. Bellomont promised to do what he could to help him and advised him to come to New York and surrender himself. Kidd sailed for Boston via Gardiner's Island where he landed a heavy chest, afterwards found to contain gold and silver, and two or three other chests, all of which were left in Mr Gardiner's care. For several days he sailed between Gardiner's Island and Block Island, landing several times. Eventually he arrived in Boston to be met by his wife and children.

But when he appeared before Bellomont and his council Kidd proved uncooperative. He denied that he had taken a Portuguese ship, although his crew had already testified that this had happened, and refused to say where he had left the *Quedagh Merchant*. Eventually, and in the face of rumours that he was planning to slip away again, Kidd was arrested. He then revealed the whereabouts of the *Quedagh Merchant*, but a captain fresh arrived from Curaçao brought the news that Boulton had removed and sold the cargo from that ship and set her on fire before sailing away.

Kidd was sent to England where feeling ran high against him. He had made a powerful enemy in the East India Company, and there were rumours that his guarantors had encouraged him to piracy. He was charged with the murder of the seaman he had hit with a bucket and with several acts of piracy. He claimed that two of the ships he had taken had shown him French "passes" (he had been flying French colours when he approached them, and since merchantmen tried to carry a number of passes from different nations this was almost certainly true), but nevertheless he knew, in fact, that they were Moorish ships. However, even if they had in reality been French, he should have treated them as prizes, bringing them to port, and not shared the proceeds with his men.

So although it has sometimes been said that Kidd was unjustly convicted because the Admiralty failed to produce these passes to the court, the court's verdict was effectively just. The trials occupied only two days and ended on 9 May, 1701, almost two years after Kidd and several of his men had been arrested. All but one of the men was reprieved and that one was hanged with Kidd at Execution Dock.

Upon Kidd's death his property and effects were forfeited to the crown and the proceeds, £6,473, given to Greenwich Hospital. Later the treasure concealed by him on Gardiner's Island, which included 200 bars of gold and silver, bags of diamonds and other precious stones, silver coin and plate, gold dust and 40 bales of silks and muslins, was recovered. But within months of Kidd's death rumours had begun to circulate, despite the statement of the captain from Curaçao, that the *Quedagh Merchant* with all its treasures was still intact and that the cargo had been taken and hidden somewhere. The story which became most popular was that the ship had been sailed up the Hudson river and wrecked.

Although the fate of the *Quedagh Merchant* is unknown, it is very unlikely that Kidd would have left in her anything other than bulky goods such as silks, muslins and grain, while he would have brought with him to Gardiner's Island all the gold and jewels with which the ship was said to have been laden. If the story of this treasure is true at all, then it must be assumed that Kidd had either taken many more prizes in the Indian Ocean than was ever known and had hidden the loot somewhere in the East or West Indies (or on Gardiner's Island), or that he knew of a hoard concealed, probably in the Indian seas.

For decades people sought to solve the mystery and various expeditions have gone out in search of the *Quedagh Merchant*. Students of the life of William Kidd are convinced that such a treasure does exist. One of these, a lawyer by the name of Hubert Palmer, collected any relics or information connected with Kidd that he could lay hands on. In 1930 he bought a chest which bore a brass plate inscribed: "Captain William Kidd, Adventure Galley, 1669" (Kidd acquired the *Adventure Galley* mentioned above in 1695, but he could have had an earlier ship of the same name: he was 24 years old in 1669 and nobody knows anything of those earlier years.) In this chest, in a secret compartment, Palmer found a map drawn on parchment showing an island with a cross in the centre and bearing the words "China Seas, W. K. 1669".

The following year he bought, from a member of the Hardy family, another chest which, it was said, Captain Hardy of the *Victory* had bought from the grandson of Kidd's bosun, to whom Kidd had given it the night before his execution. There he found another chart. In the next two or three years two more chests containing hidden charts, all apparently referring to the same island, came to light. On two of these charts there appeared to be directions pointing to a certain spot: alas, they were different.

These charts are still in existence, but so are a number of others, also said to refer to Captain Kidd's treasure. The island has been identified in many different places, and many expeditions have come to grief or been disappointed in their attempts to find the treasure.

It seems more than likely that at least some of these charts are fakes. The "treasure island" with crosses marking the spot, really do seem too good to be true and in the best tradition of romantic fiction. There is something fascinating about buried treasure and in this prosaic world a real desire for romance and adventure, which leads people to *wish* to believe. Thus myths can be and are kept alive. There is, for example, the story of the chart sent anonymously to the Japanese government in the 'thirties. This chart indicated that the treasure lay on an island south of Japan, one of the Ryukyu group. Nothing more was heard of this at the time, but the story has it that an independent investigator named Masahiro Nagashima made a study of all the available documents and years later heard of some shipwrecked fisherman who had found carved on one of the island's rock faces some strange horned animals. Kidd, it is said, used a drawing of a kid as his signature, so Nagashima investigated the spot where, in a cave, he found a heap of iron boxes from which "a flood of gold and silver coins poured out round him". Apparently Nagashima took the treasure – which was valued at £30 million! – back to Japan, and the mystery was said to be solved. However, a few months later, in September, 1952 Japanese newspapers said that the police were looking for Nagashima, who had disappeared without trace along with the treasure . . . Thus the Kidd legend is perpetuated, and the treasure has vanished once again.

Various other people also claim to "know" where the treasure lies, despite the story of the Japanese discovery, and base these claims largely on the evidence of charts which one cannot but believe are either practical jokes or deliberate forgeries made at any time during the last two hundred years. If Kidd had either had, or known of, such a treasure in his early years it seems unlikely that he would not have retrieved it long before the events which led to his death.

It is also highly unlikely that he amassed such treasure during his last fateful voyages, for he had many witnesses about him in the shape of his crew and they gave no indication that such a treasure existed. The story of Captain Kidd's hoard seems to depend on two factors: his own last-minute attempt to stave off his execution; and rumours that the *Quedagh Merchant*, with whatever cargo she carried, had not in fact been sunk but had been spirited away to an unknown location. The existence of the treasure seems to be as ill-founded in fact as is the image of William Kidd as a swashbuckling, bloodthirsty pirate.

THE GALLEASS OF PORT NA SPANIAGH

It took four centuries to prize the secrets of galleass *Girona* from the bed of the ocean, and the unravelling of the age-old mystery of her exact location is due to the twentieth-century dedication of one man – Robert Sténuit.

The *Girona* was one of four galleasses in the squadron of Naples, which was regarded as the main striking force of the most powerful expedition, the largest fleet ever seen up to that time. The Armada was launched in 1588 after twenty years of intrigue and hesitation by Philip II of Spain against Elizabeth of England "because such was the mission he had received from God".

The mystery of the *Girona* so obsessed Sténuit, a student of politics in the University of Brussels, that he gave up everything else, dropping out of university and a secure future at the age of nineteen to pursue his two great passions: deep-sea diving and historical research. He was fortunate to be supported in his ambition to seek out the *Girona* and her treasures by a giant of the present-day offshore oil industry and a team of divers equipped with the latest aids to underwater engineering and archaeology.

Why was Sténuit so obsessed with the *Girona*? Well, she was a galleass, the pride of what Philip and his Spaniards called – *before* the Armada sailed for England – "The Most Fortunate Fleet". And a galleass was something to see: a cross between a galley and a galleon, with eighteen oars on each side and a

slender hull, having two castles and a very high freeboard.
They were decked vessels about 150 feet long with three fixed
masts carrying square sails on foremast and mainmast and a
gaff-rigged lateen on the mizzen.

"The galleasses", wrote a Spanish historian, "were strikingly
beautiful and ornate, with their cabins, towers, chapels and
pulpits." There were carved figures on the castles, the prow
and the sides and large ornate lanterns above the stern. The
officers had their quarters in the aftercastle where there was
either a tent or a sumptuously decorated cabin hung inside
with velvet or tapestries and lit by stained-glass windows, with
a large lantern in the ceiling.

Pennants and banners fluttered at all points. In port dinner
was taken on board to musical accompaniment: the table
plate, candlesticks, knives and forks were gold-plated. The officers were bedecked with chains and jewels – their evening dress
was a velvet doublet and satin breeches.

But there was another reason for Sténuit's obsession: his diligent researches had established that the *Girona* was carrying
the treasures from four other ships of the Most Fortunate Fleet
– the phrase proved to be a grim irony – when they were
hurtled into oblivion by a great storm. The question exciting
Sténuit and all such treasure-seekers was: "Where?"

As Stenuit writes in *Treasures of the Armada*, his own account
of the finding of the *Girona:* "Battles, storms, five crews, the
noblest, richest, bravest men in the whole fleet, jammed with
all their treasures into one ship . . . at least 1,000 dead! This
was what tragedy was made of, what romance was made of.
This was what treasures were made of. The *Girona* had me in
her grasp."

His researches took him to Spain, Belgium, France, and
Holland, but other work held him up until he was put in
charge of the London office of an American industrial diving
and underwater engineering company. He felt confident that,
if someone back in 1588 who actually knew what had happened had noted down on some scrap of paper the exact spot
where the *Girona* was wrecked then the paper would be almost
certainly in London. So, for three evenings a week, from 6
p.m. until 9 p.m., Sténuit continued his search either in the
British Museum or in the Public Record Office. He reckons he
put in 600 hours' work on his search in eighteen months.

"I believe that everything still extant ever written in England or Ireland on the Armada or its wrecks must have passed through my hands. But where, in Heaven's name, was this ship, the *Girona?*" he asks. "It was becoming less and less clear. The more information I collected, the more contradictions I found . . ."

He decided that the time had come to call a halt to the paper work and go and take a look at the Irish coastline. This involved a team-mate, a boat, a motor, a compressor, cylinders and two cars to stow it all in. He chose as his mate the Belgian photographer, Marc Jasinski.

Sténuit found one useful clue in his long research – he discovered there was another Armada wreck, the *Nuestra Señora de la Rosa*, off the Blaskets (on the south-west tip of Ireland). And he had one piece of luck. Combing through Admiralty charts of Ireland, he and his photographer came on Chart No. 2798, the north coast of Ulster. This showed a long stretch of beach, then the coast became rocky, then came the Giant's Causeway. Still to the east the chart indicated a few bays, then cliffs. Using the 1904 Ordnance Survey map, the pair came upon Spaniard Rock, Spaniard Cove and finally Port na Spaniagh. There, too, they spotted Lacada Point.

Sténuit had studied all Armada historians and made summaries of their statements. One had written that the *Girona* "went down west of the Giant's Causeway, at Spaniard's Rock". It had also been established that 260 bodies had been washed ashore and that they had been robbed on the day after the wreck. But the chieftain, James McDonnell, who ruled north-east Ulster in those days, had probably taken the lion's share of the treasure for himself.

Then Sténuit had a brainwave . . . he remembered reading a history of the McDonnell home, Dunluce Castle, which was perched like an eagle's nest high above the beach and that, starting in 1590, the original square keep was rebuilt and greatly enlarged. Where else could the money to pay for all this have come from if not from the *Girona?* Sténuit reasoned.

The pair got down to studying all statements made by the Irish to the commission headed by the English Lord Deputy and particularly the testimony given by McDonnell. Sténuit reasoned that McDonnell would lie to send the English investigators on the wrong track: he had specified the estuary of the Bush river as the likeliest spot for the *Girona* to have struck a rock and foundered.

Sténuit dug out sixteenth-century maps of Ireland and found that the only place-names appearing on them between Portrush and Rathlin Island were Dunluce and the Bush river – so these would be the only names a civil servant would be able to quote to his superiors in the commission.

The diligent researcher discovered that there were virtually no made paths along the coast and that the cliffs were inaccessible along that stretch. So, even if the Irish had been truthful, they could not have identified the exact spot to the English. But when, in 1904, the official from Ordnance Survey asked the locals for the necessary place-names for his map, the fisherfolk had no reason to lie. So they gave him the name of Port na Spaniagh.

That, at least, was Sténuit's conclusion from all his studies – and he was prepared to set up an expedition to prove that theory. Here is his description of the spot:

"Port na Spaniagh is out of this world. An amphitheatre of 400-ft-high cliffs, sheer and terrifying. The wind howled around our ears. Beside the cliffs sea birds hovered, circling ceaselessly in one spot and their raucous cries, endlessly modulated, echoed into infinity. The rock was black, the cliffs were black with gashes of red where men have cut paths . . . mounds of fallen debris were piled up at the bottom to form a chaotic mass of boulders where the beach ought to have been. All the floating wrecks from miles around wind up here."

The pair stared down at the awesome spectacle and wondered what could be left of the *Girona* after 400 years of such elemental conditions. But when they returned to their Irish hotel after that first reconnaissance, they needed all their dedication, not to mention a sense of humour. Marc Jasinski, the photographer, bought a cheap guide-book to the Giant's Causeway. He flicked through it, then roared with laughter. He read aloud: "In 1588 . . . the galleass *Girona* was wrecked at a little cove near the Giant's Causeway, still called Port na Spaniagh."

Sténuit comments: "Easy enough to laugh then, but if I'd read it in that cheap guide like everyone else, I'd have done exactly what everyone else has done before. I'd have shrugged my shoulders and gone about finding some more serious source."

They then reconnoitred most of that coast on foot and found that, apart from Portrush, there are only small coves with little or no shelter from the open sea and to get into these the explorer has to know how to wind his way among the reefs. On their first expedition, which was mainly exploratory, they took the lightest equipment: a small inflatable dinghy with an 18-horse-power engine, four double-cylinder aqualungs and a small high-pressure air compressor. With wet suits, photographic equipment and other bits and pieces it all fitted into two cars.

First they had a good look at Dunluce ... "A fairy-tale castle, perched like an eagle's nest on a sea-swept rock promontory." They looked at some caves once lived in by early troglodyte Christians. From the windows of the castle can be seen the Western Isles – the sixteenth-century James McDonnell was well placed to organize the evacuation of Spanish survivors (at a price).

On 27 June, 1967 they put out again to the open sea in what Sténuit calls "our absurd little boat". They dropped anchor next to the reefs – "those two bared teeth in the middle of Port na Spaniagh". Sténuit dived and, guided by his compass, reached the base of the twin reefs. Following his bearings, he worked along parallel lines from north to south. Nothing. Then he moved in a hard south-westerly direction towards Lacada Point, "trying to see the sea-bed through the algae which sway ceaselessly in the swell, rather as one watches the road through moving windscreen wipers."

He stopped in a cleft in the rock and moved stones to stir up the sand. Still nothing. Suddenly he found his way barred by a cliff – the east face of Lacada Point. The cliff ran along the edge of a vast platform leading to an enormous rock. A white shape caught his eye. He went closer. A lead ingot.

"In a flash I remembered something I had read", writes Sténuit. "This was the story of a man named Boyle who discovered another Armada wreck in Donegal at the end of the eighteenth century. Apart from a few gold pieces and some bronze cannon, he found a piece of lead which he supposed to be ballast, a yard long, triangular, the sides being pointed towards the ends, getting thick in the middle. My ingot fitted the description perfectly. Arching my back, I heaved it over and there, stamped on the upper face, were five Jerusalem crosses. I had found the wreck."

He savoured a moment of intense joy, then swam on, ferreting about in a long corridor which led him directly to a large verdigris-coloured cylinder. A bronze cannon. There was nothing else around. But the diver realized that an underwater shelf inclines sharply down to Lacada Point and, if the *Girona* ran on to this, everything would have rolled down to the bottom of it. So he followed the tortuous slope all the way down. There, lying in an oblong crevice, he found another bronze cannon, but of a strange shape. Box-like, with a barrel coming out of it. A breech-loading piece. A Spanish Armada gun. "And," exults Sténuit, "there wasn't a museum in the world that had one, not even a cannon ball, not even a nail."

Lying just beside it were the powder chambers – five of them. There were lead ingots everywhere, 12 at least, and some thick rectangular plates. It all tallied with the inventory drawn up before the departure of the Armada from Lisbon.

It was 1 July before the sea was calm enough for Sténuit to dive again. This time the photographer, Marc Jasinki, went with him. While he was focusing his camera on the ingot, Sténuit picked up a flat, round, grey object. Just an ordinary pebble, he thought. Then he turned it over. There was the Jerusalem cross. Almost worn away, but it was there. It was a silver piece of eight! He found another one in the same place at the entrance to a large cave.

This was the first Armada wreck found since Boyle's success in Donegal at the close of the eighteenth century and Sténuit was determined that it would be properly excavated and scientifically studied. He decided to return fully prepared the following year, 1968. Until then they must keep the secrets of the *Girona*. Before they left the site they replaced all the odds and ends of their treasure trove, piece by piece, at the back of the great cave.

They made a long list of all the equipment needed for a full-scale expedition to recover every possible item from the wrecked galleass. Sténuit was fortunate to find a friend and patron in Henri Delauze, founder and president of COMEX (*Compagnie Maritime d'Expertises*) which has become one of the leaders in underwater engineering, employing some of the greatest experts in deep-sea diving throughout Europe. The National Geographic Society in Washington, D.C., promised a financial contribution.

By 27 April, 1968, all was ready and the well-equipped expedition made its base in Port Ballintrae. In September of that year the sea had yielded almost every item of the *Girona*'s secrets. Sténuit, summing up the entire operation, from the day he first heard of the galleass to his earliest reconnaissance in the inflatable dinghy to this full-scale exercise in marine archaeology, now knew all he wanted to know about the Armada vessel that had obsessed him for so long. He calculated that he and his team had spent 6,000 hours on the sea-bed . . .

He had found the wreckage of a ship containing Spanish cannon, coins and seals from all over the Spanish Empire, as well as Spanish lead ingots. The name of the site on which she foundered emphasizes the local tradition that she was a Spanish ship. The number of coins found from the Two Sicilies proved that the ship was connected with Naples. She sank at the close of the sixteenth century – the coins stop at Philip II and the last date on a coin is 1585. She was carrying too much shot, lead, plates and ingots to be a merchant ship. Therefore she must have been a Spanish warship – she must have come from the Armada. A great many Spanish and English documents contain accounts of the loss of the *Girona* somewhere in this area: none mentions any other Armada ship lost off Ulster.

The documents refer to jewels, gold and silver found on bodies and the remains of the ship washed ashore. Sténuit's exploration discovered 47 gold jewels, 8 chains, 1,256 coins, two insignia of knighthood and any amount of gold table plate and silver – proof that there must have been many rich men and several noblemen aboard. No other ship lost off Ireland would have contained cannon-balls corresponding exactly to the *Girona*'s.

Between the twin reefs – "the bared teeth of Lacada Point" – and the Point itself they found the remains of a smaller anchor which raised the questions: Did the *Girona*'s crew try to launch a boat and did it capsize, losing its anchor? The vessel had turned round on herself and suddenly she was being broken apart on Lacada Point: cannon-balls and lead ingots with all the kitchen equipment spilled from her gaping hull – a section of it, weighed down by the lead plates that had been nailed to it, stayed where it was; some of the cannon were left high and dry, others rolled down the underwater incline until they reached the flat. Men tumbled out to be drowned within minutes, then thrown on the cliffs or carried out to sea by the tide . . . men with bulging pockets left to the mercy of James

McConnell and his followers. The captain's cabin emptied
out its largesse, sprinkling the sea-bed with coins, gems and
a host of personal effects.

The aftercastle broke off the shattered hull and drifted eastwards. Another section of the *Girona* was carried along the
west side of Lacada Point, leaving behind a trail of perrier
balls – all found by Sténuit's team – and men, whose possessions
were also recovered by the underwater explorers. From there
the swirling currents drove the section on to a reef west of
Spaniard Cave. It ended its voyage by running into the foot of
the cave with all its cannon-balls, ballast and debris. This,
Sténuit reports, was almost certainly part of the prow, containing the crew's quarters.

This was the end of the mission for the triumphant Sténuit
and his divers. "The sea hid her secret well", he writes, "but,
with patience, we learned all her ruses, one by one, and
snatched from her all she had been keeping to herself for 400
years." Except, of course, 1,300 men, including Don Alonzo
Martinez de Leiva, the bravest captain of them all, favourite of
Philip II and commander designate of the Felicissima Armada
in the event of the death of that reluctant leader, the Duke of
Medina Sidonia. Including also sixty sons of the most noble
families in all Spain, especially entrusted to Don Alonzo and
eager to serve under none other.

Including, too, an unknown warrior – a young hidalgo who
must have spent his last night ashore with his betrothed. In the
morning, before that final farewell, she must have slipped a
ring on his finger as a keepsake, specially commissioned from a
distinguished goldsmith. But, on that most fearful night of
October, 1588, the ring was sucked from his bony finger and
rolled away into a crevice . . . where, 390 years later, beside a
two escudo piece from Toledo and a few pieces of eight, Sténuit's team found it . . .

"Out of all the treasures of the Armada", declares Sténuit,
"this is the most beautiful, the most moving. The setting is a
tiny hand holding a heart and an open belt clasp. Engraved in
the gold, I read these words: 'No tengo mas que dar te.' I
have nothing more to give you."

The legal problems thrown up by the team's discoveries
were extremely complicated. The artefacts recovered from the
wreck have no clearly defined legal status and no owner,
Robert Sténuit appears to be the only possessor of them. And

his wish was that, "rather than go under the hammer to the highest bidder", the entire collection, from the finest jewel down to the humblest cannon-ball, should remain intact in a maritime or archaeological museum where it could be on permanent display with contemporary documents and the maps, charts and photographs of his expedition which tell the story of three hard-working years. In the end Sténuit succeeded in having his wish granted – but not before years of delays and negotiations.

The Ulster Museum, part of the Northern Ireland National Museum, was officially designated to house the collection and the "Girona Rooms" were opened there on 22 June, 1972.

THE VIGO GALLEONS

Vigo Bay, on the north-west coast of Spain, provides a remarkable land-locked natural harbour. It is entered by means of an inlet from the sea which ends in a narrow neck, broadening out again to form a large lagoon-shaped bay, flanked on all sides by steep hills. Here ships could lie safely at anchor, protected by the land from the elements and by a boom and defensive forts built at the narrow opening into the bay. Here the Spanish fleet which, in 1702, had brought back fabulous riches from the New World, thought that it would be unmolested by the depradations of the impertinent English.

This fleet was one of those which sailed periodically from the coasts of South America laden with the products of the mines of Mexico and Peru. As occasionally happened the annual sailing of such fleets was postponed for one reason or another – weather, war, buccaneers or lack of suitable ships – and the fleet which sailed in 1702 was one of these. It carried three years' accumulated cargoes which, according to the documents of the *Casa de Contratación* included pearls, emeralds and amethysts; native silver in ingots and pieces of eight; native gold in doubloons; cochineal, indigo and ambergris; wood from Campeche, Nicaragua and Brazil, mahogany and redwood; cotton; tobacco in rolled leaves and powder; tanned skins and rawhide; balsam of Peru and Tolu, jalap, sarsaparilla, sassafras, bezoar, tamarind, quassia, cocoa, ginger, sugar and vanilla.

Exactly what quantities of these goods the ships carried is not known: in order to cheat the Spanish customs it was common to reveal only about half the total cargo on the ship's manifest. However when the Silver Fleet of 1702 left the Havana roadsteads it was reputed to be the richest which had ever sailed.

Philip V of Spain was urgently in need of the fleet's cargo. France and Spain were now close allies, for the grandson of Louis XIV had succeeded to the Spanish throne; but the Grand Alliance had united England, Holland, Austria, Prussia and Hanover against Louis and war was imminent. Gold was urgently needed to finance this war and the French sent warships all the way across the Atlantic to Havana, with orders that the Silver Fleet was to sail without delay, protected by its escort of French and Spanish men-of-war.

The fleet made good time, but on calling at the Azores its commanders learned that the threatened war had already broken out. British and Dutch ships were blockading Cadiz. The Spanish commander, Don Manuel de Velasco, immediately summoned a council of war on board his flagship, the *Jesus-Maria-Joseph*. The French commander, Château-renault, suggested that the fleet should make for Brest or La Rochelle, thus evading the forces which were certainly keeping watch over the coasts of England and those which were harrying Spain. But the Spaniards would have none of it. The French king was in need of money himself; and such a large treasure might prove too tempting. Their orders were to deliver it to their own king, and into a Spanish port they would go.

Vigo, on the north coast, was an obvious spot. The fleet would thus evade the English at Cadiz and also benefit from the safe anchorage. Without difficulty the "stately Spanish galleons" made their way along the fjord-like channel and through the neck into the bay where they dropped anchor off the little port of Redondela.

The fleet now felt itself safe: the precious, much-needed treasure had been brought home. But there were problems. The traders of Cadiz claimed that by virtue of a privilege they enjoyed nothing could be disembarked. Thus the tedious Spanish red tape which was so often the cause of delays and disaster resulted in the treasure staying aboard the ships until the squabbles of authority could be resolved. The commander was not particularly concerned, for the bay seemed impregnable;

but he sent for instructions from the Captain-General of
Galicia, the Prince de Barbanzon, who in turn referred to the
court in Madrid. Several days passed before the messenger
arrived with orders to unload the gold and silver destined for
the treasury; the rest of the cargo must remain in the ships
until the legal tangle could be resolved. There was no hurry:
the English had suffered a defeat at Cadiz, and had raised the
siege some five days after the Silver Fleet had sailed into Vigo.
The English had then split up, some sailing north, some south:
there was nothing to be feared.

The rest of this story is the result of a quirk of fate and a
typical example of "careless talk". One of the ships of the
English fleet put in to Lagos to take on water. The Anglican
chaplain grasped the opportunity to take a stroll ashore and
visit an inn where, in conversation with a stranger newly arrived from Cadiz, he learned that the Silver Fleet which should
have come into Cadiz had perforce diverted to Vigo. Hastily
downing his drink the chaplain returned to his ship to report
the news. The captain at once weighed anchor and contrived
to catch up with the rest of the English ships, under the command of Admiral Sir George Rook. This fleet consisted of 50
warships and 100 transports carrying 13,500 soldiers, and the
formidable force immediately turned about and sailed for
Vigo. It arrived there on 21 October, and with the calm effrontery of a strongly armed and boldly led force sailed up and
down making plans, finally anchoring outside the bay on 23
October.

The presence of the English fleet was soon known to the
Spanish. In the month which had passed since the Silver Fleet
arrived much work had been done in unloading the ships, but
the Spaniards now redoubled their efforts. Following the
orders from the court, the king's share of the treasure had at
once been disembarked. On 19 October General de Velasco,
the fleet's commander, announced that all the royal silver from
the *Capitana* and much of that from the *Almirante* had been sent
to safety. A contemporary source – the memoirs of a nobleman,
Don Goyanes Reimondez – mentions "more than three thous-
and carts, each drawn by four oxen" having been sent to Vigo
Bay; but many of them were still loading when the English
fleet launched its attack. Vigo was a small port, ill-equipped to
handle large numbers of merchant ships and the unloading
was a slow and lengthy process.

At midday on 23 October the English landed 4,000 men. Half the force assaulted the fortress on one bank, the other half the second fortress. With covering fire from the ships anchored outside the bay, they soon took the fortifications. There was still the defensive boom to overcome, not to mention the French warships assembled just inside it. The first obstacle was overcome by two heavy ships, sailing at full speed, which simply smashed bow first into the boom, sustaining some damage but destroying the obstruction. The English fleet sailed through behind them and a furious battle ensued. By evening eleven French ships had been sunk and Châteaurenault, in command of the French warships, sent word to Velasco that the battle was lost. The Intendant of the French Fleet describes the panic that ensued:

> "At every moment French soldiers and sailors were arriving at the place called Redondelle, where they managed to start a panic, saying that all was lost; and then, a few enemy frigates and galliots with bombs, having outstripped our ships and those of the Spanish fleet, and having neared the fort near the place called Redondelle, threw a few bombs. Consternation was general. The monks came out of their convents barefooted, bearing crosses and banners, uttering piteous cries and bursting into tears."

Frantic attempts had been made to unload more of the merchandise, but in the general confusion much of it was stolen. Seeing that there was no hope of saving the ships and their cargo Don Manuel de Velasco ordered the vessels to be set on fire. The English, fearful of being balked of their rich prey, leaped aboard the burning ships and desperately tried to salvage some of the treasure, many being killed in the process. The losses on both sides, in fact, were heavy. The total of dead and wounded for the British and Dutch was 1,300. The French and Spanish lost 2,000 dead and no less than 9,000 wounded, almost half their total muster.

When the noise and smoke of battle had died away the full scale of the disaster was revealed. Eleven out of the seventeen ships of the Spanish fleet were either seized afloat or grounded in shallow water: the order to scuttle them had come too late. The six that sank were in water so shallow that divers could quite easily reach their decks. The day after the battle the English and Dutch seamen set to work to plunder the sunken ships, although harassment by the Spanish guns ashore hampered their efforts considerably. Eventually the conquerors decided they could profit no further; they collected up the French and Spanish ships which were in a seaworthy condition and, with prize crews aboard, set sail for England.

It has never been established exactly how many ships were taken as prizes nor how many actually reached the shores of England. Some of the ships had to be abandoned as they grew increasingly unseaworthy and succumbed to a storm in the Bay of Biscay. One ship, described as being one of the biggest galleons, struck a rock just outside the inner harbour. The captain of the *Monmouth* which had been responsible for the prize later explained that

> the Galeon struk upon a Rock and Bulged herself so that the water came up to her lower Deck and then the things following were taken out –
>
> 1 & 2. Two bags supposed to be Dollars weight 126 pounds Haverdupois taken out of the chest of Cocao in the Main Hatchway.
>
> 3. A bag supposed to be lumps of Silver weighing 81 lbs. taken out of a chest of Cloaths.
>
> 4. A Bag supposed to be Dollars weight 64 pounds taken out of another Chest of Cloaths.
>
> Taken out of the *Oxford*'s Boats commanded by Lieut. Miles and Lieut. Harper, they having taken them out of the Galleon –
>
> 16 small parcells of Silk of several sorts
> 4 Childrens Gownes
> 2 Mens waistcoats . . .
>
> and so on.

A contemporary comment points out that the victors' gain was "much diminished" by the loss of the biggest of the galleons. Despite this, and despite the fact that it is not known how many ships were brought safely home, treasure to the value of about one and a half million pounds was deposited in the Tower of London – spoils of the Vigo raid.

While the English and Dutch rejoiced, the Spanish had reason to "deplore in silence and in tears" their "unspeakable loss" and the ignominious defeat. The inhabitants of Madrid, "not being able to recollect themselves from their consternation, have shut up their houses and shops for fear of being plundered by the common people who exclaim against the government".

The French king and his court were also plunged into "the deepest consternation", says a contemporary correspondent and "His Majesty says that not a tenth part of the money and merchandise was transferred from the fleet to the land."

This fact was borne out by three Spanish officers who had been brought back to England with the victorious fleet and who reported that the effects that were on the ships amounted to nine million sterling. The Spaniards, for want of mules to carry the plate away, "had broke the bulk of very few ships before the English forced the boom".

The fact that there was still treasure a-plenty in Vigo Bay was confirmed by the underwater salvage operations that the Spaniards immediately began. As a newspaper of December, 1702, reports, "The salvage of the precious cargo of the *Capitana* and the *Almirante* is proceeding successfully."

These successful operations did not, however, last for long. Only the most accessible goods could be reached by divers who had to descend to depths of 45 to 60 feet without any equipment save for, perhaps, a primitive diving bell. At any rate the Spanish Government seems to have abandoned the official attempt after a comparatively short time. That they knew they had failed to retrieve all the treasure is apparent from the fact that they readily granted permission to individuals who wanted to try their luck, in return for 95 per cent of the find.

In the three decades that followed numbers of people went to work on the sunken ships finding, it is said, nothing of value. (If the Spanish Government was demanding a share of 95 per cent, however, it seems more than likely that the treasure fishers would do all they could to conceal anything they found.) In 1741, after fourteen years of work, a patient Frenchman eventually succeeded in raising the whole hulk of a Spanish ship named the *Tojo*, but nothing of any value was found aboard it.

In 1766 the Spanish actually granted a concession to a member of that nation which had been responsible for putting the treasure at the bottom of the sea in the first place. William Evans used a diving bell which could be provided with fresh air by means of a pump, and with this newly sophisticated equipment he began to find several items. A number of pieces of silver plate encouraged Evans to hope that he was meeting with success; but the humiliation of Vigo at the hands of the British was still remembered by living Spaniards, whose antagonism to the work of this Englishman resulted at length in him being peremptorily told to leave.

Sixty years later, however, another Briton was permitted to try his luck. This Scotsman, Isaac Dickson, contrived to beat the Spanish Government's demand down to 80 per cent of the find, but the story has it that he got away with the lot. According to the inhabitants of the local towns of Vigo and Redondela, Isaac Dickson found a small fortune. Celebrating his good luck in the company of the Government inspectors he got them drunk, bundled them overboard, had them rowed ashore and then promptly set sail himself. Perhaps the fact that soon afterwards Dickson built himself a large house near Perth, which he named Dollar House, confirms this story.

Sadder and wiser by this experience, the Spanish posted a warship in the bay to keep an eye on the activities of the next group of treasure-hunters, an American syndicate, which also succeeded in raising one wreck, only to have it sink again at once. They were followed by a French company, which began work in 1870 with much improved equipment very like the diving gear of today. Within only a few weeks they had located a dozen wrecks (well-authenticated documents of the Vigo battle say that only six galleons sank; no doubt other wrecks beside those of the ill-fated fleet lie at the bottom of the bay). Work began but after many months of effort no treasure had been found. All kinds of goods – fragments of cannon, blocks of spermaceti, indigo, fan sticks, cedar boxes, cups and plates of pewter, copper tobacco boxes, pottery ware of all kinds, flagons, glasses and goblets – came to the surface. In the end 132 lbs. of silver was found in various locations, but this did not pay the costs of the expedition.

Undaunted, treasure-hunters continued to come to Vigo, although the Spanish Government itself obviously rated their chances as being slender: the share they demanded had gone down from the original 95 per cent to only 20. Another hulk was raised in 1907, but it contained nothing but a jumble of rubbish. Dutch and Spanish divers also tried their luck.

The invention of reliable aqualung equipment started a new wave of treasure-seekers. But by now divers had concluded that there was little left to be found at the end of the bay where the main part of the fleet had sunk. In 1955 a new expedition decided to concentrate on the *Santo Cristo de Maracaibo*, the ship which had struck a rock at the entrance to the harbour. Once more long hours of effort and a lot of money was expended. John Potter, the American leader of the expedition, was convinced that much gold remained to be found. He worked out that the value of the cargo that left Havana in 1701 was $75,000,000 and he did the following sum:

Sent to Madrid 6,500,000
Sent to Louis XIV 3,500,000
Lost in the *Maracaibo* 5,000,000
Taken to England 20,000,000
Taken to Holland 17,000,000
Left in Vigo Bay 23,000,000

Potter based his arithmetic on the assumption that far less bullion was unloaded from the ships before the English and Dutch fleet struck than was actually the case. His optimism was severely dashed by information received from Count George Khevenhuller, an Austrian who had taken part in a salvage operation in 1928. Khevenhuller stated categorically that after the exhaustive searches that had taken place among the wrecks he was sure that there was no longer any precious metals left in the bay. The *Santo Cristo de Maracaibo* presented the only hope.

In spite of this Potter set to work among the galleons. After two years he gave up and set out in search of the *Maracaibo*. There was little evidence as to the spot this ship had struck as she was being towed out of the bay, but calculations concerning the depth of the water, the draught of the ship and the likely rocks narrowed down the search. All sorts of clues led to a rock which was incorrectly marked on the charts of 1702, but a search of the sea-bed revealed nothing. A year later wreckage was found which raised high hopes, but analysis of a copper nail and inspection of the cannon-balls found indicated that the wreck was older than 1702.

The following year saw Potter casting about for further clues. This time he discovered twin rocks rising to within 15 feet of the surface in the centre of the channel which the squadron was likely to have taken as it negotiated the passages leading from Vigo Bay into the ocean. Surveys with advanced electronic instruments revealed a sandy hump on the sea-bed. Could this be the wreck of the *Santo Cristo de Maracaibo*? Unfortunately it lay in 300 feet of water, several miles from the coast and almost entirely buried in the sand and rubble of the sea-bed. To shift this sand would require extremely costly

equipment and months of work on a site which was still problematical.

No work has been carried out on this spot, the last remaining lure for the Vigo Bay hunters. John Potter may have failed
to raise treasure from the depths, but he has written a book
The Treasure Diver's Guide, which has become the bible of treasure-seekers. He lists virtually every wreck containing treasure
that is known to man, and he himself eventually came to the
conclusion that by the time the last of the salvage groups
arrived in Vigo in 1965 "there was nothing left of the ships
except scattered wooden remnants and ballast stones. The
treasure of the Vigo galleons had long since vanished."

However, he gives his account of the *Santo Cristo de Maracaibo*
three stars, which represent "the cream of the underwater treasure targets awaiting salvage". Potter's backers, unfortunately,
had run out of money, but the ship still awaits the arrival of an
expedition which can afford the search and salvage tools
needed to recover what Potter describes, with confidence, as
"her valuable artefacts and treasures".

TREASURE ISLAND

It seems strange that buried treasure is difficult to find, even when its whereabouts are reasonably well documented; but it has been established that, only ten years after a treasure has been buried, in five cases out of ten it will never be found again. After twenty-five years the odds are much higher. It is not generally appreciated to what extent the lie of the land is forgotten or changed. Trees grow and die, soil is eroded and deposited, streams change their course or dry up, and more violent events like landslides or earthquakes can change the terrain beyond recognition.

Cocos Island, that most famous hunting-ground of all treasure-seekers, is subject to just such violent hazards, and the treasures that lie there were buried generations ago. The odds against finding them are enormous after more than 150 years; nevertheless, ever since the early nineteenth century people – alone, in groups and, latterly, in well-equipped expeditions – have descended upon the island and dug and dynamited their way about it, thus altering the terrain even more.

Cocos Island belongs to the Republic of Costa Rica and lies far from the usual shipping routes off the coast of Colombia. It is about 5 miles long and 2½ miles wide. Its rocky plateau, thick with the coconut palms which gave it its name, is broken by three volcanic peaks and densely covered with trees and bushes. On its southern coasts rocky cliffs rise sheer from the sea to a height of 600 feet. Several streams empty into the two bays, where a ship can ride at anchor on the north and east of the island; and it is only along these creeks that access to the island can be gained, for an attempt to penetrate the interior involves hacking a way laboriously through thick jungle growth.

This inaccessible, uninhabited island – wrongly marked even on the charts of the day – provided a perfect bolt-hole and hiding-place for the pirates of the eighteenth and nineteenth centuries. The first record of it being used as a repository for treasure dates from the end of the seventeenth century when Edward Davis roved the Pacific, plundering many Spanish ships and cities. Before he sailed for Jamaica, there to accept the amnesty offered to pirates by James II, he buried seven boat-loads of treasure on Cocos Island. In 1702, having lived a respectable life in Virginia in the interim, Davis again sailed for Cocos Island. History does not relate what happened thereafter, but one assumes that he removed his treasure. Even so, people still seek it although no clues as to its whereabouts have ever existed.

Another pirate who buried loot on Cocos Island was known as Benito Bonito, sometimes identified as an Englishman named Bennett Graham. His presence confuses the story for he appears to have had among his crew on his ship *Relampago* (an English vessel which had been captured and renamed by Bonito) a crew member named Thompson. This man, with another member of the crew, had been given the choice between turning pirate or death, and in 1821 he was present when Bonito buried his share of pirate loot on the island. Later, when the *Relampago* was herself captured and the crew hanged to a man, Thompson and his fellow crew mate were spared and Thompson went to live in Samoa.

Another Thompson also appeared on the scene at this time. He was probably the captain of an English ship called the *Mary Dear* (although some accounts describe him merely as a member of the crew) which happened to be in the Peruvian port of Callao, close to Lima, during the period when rebel forces aiming to free Peru from the Spanish yoke were marching upon the capital.

Lima was one of the richest cities of South America. In the manner of the period her Roman Catholic churches were filled with splendid images bedecked with jewels, golden altar furniture and precious reliquaries. Her noble families possessed gold, jewellery, silver and art treasures accumulated over years of plundering the native wealth. In a panic at the threat posed by the advancing rebels this wealth, worth millions of pounds, was accumulated and loaded on to the *Mary Dear*, accompanied by a guard, and the ship sailed for a safe port.

It was too much for the crew. They turned upon the passengers and murdered them. But having turned pirate the question of what to do with the treasure and how to avoid the long arm of justice became a problem. It was impossible to sail into any port without being apprehended and some of the treasure was such that it was impossible to dispose of easily – a life-size statue of the Virgin Mary in solid gold and bedecked with jewels was one of the more notable items. So the thieves put in to Cocos Island where they buried the treasure, and made plans to return to retrieve it when the hue and cry had died down.

The accounts of the subsequent fate of the *Mary Dear* and her crew vary, but all agree in one particular – that her entire crew were hanged save Thompson and one other who contrived (various versions are extant) to escape. The second man died soon after, leaving Thompson the sole possessor of the secret.

(One must add here, for the record, that only some twenty years ago yet another story was made public. In this account the second man is named as Forbes, the mate of the *Mary Dear*. He and Thompson escaped and it was Thompson, not Forbes, who died. Later Forbes recovered some of the treasure and left the secret of its hiding-place to his descendants, who unsuccessfully searched for the treasure as recently as 1939. Here is yet another twist in the already tangled tale of Cocos Island.)

However, the traditional story maintains that Thompson eventually found his way to Newfoundland where he was befriended by a man named Keating to whom, on his death-bed, Thompson told the secret of the treasure.

Keating went to Cocos Island on one or more occasions and almost certainly brought away a substantial amount of the treasure, but was unable to remove the larger pieces and the bulk of it remained hidden. When he died in 1882 Keating passed on the secret to three people, his wife, a friend named Hackett and his servant Fitzgerald. Keating's wife and Hackett's brother made a joint attempt to find the treasure; Fitzgerald let others into the secret and they made various attempts in the ensuing years: all, however, were unsuccessful. The clues bequeathed by Keating appear to have differed, and in the course of time they have been handed from person to person and have mysteriously multiplied.

The matter was complicated still further by clues emanating from the days of Benito Bonito. Aboard this pirate ship was a man called Cabral who told his descendants that, in the days before the capture of the *Relampago*, he had helped Bonito to bury a great treasure in two separate places, on the island known as "La Palma". Cabral left the ship soon after and thus escaped the fate of the *Relampago*'s crew. In about 1880 Cabral's grandson told the story to a German seaman, Gissler, whom he met when the latter was on a voyage to Hawaii. Gissler forgot the story until some years later in Hawaii he heard a similar tale which, it seemed, could only have originated from a survivor, or someone close to a survivor, of the *Relampago*. The second tale was accompanied by a map and directions in Spanish for finding the island and the treasure. Gissler identified the place as Cocos Island and soon afterwards, in Costa Rica, he met two journalists who were armed with the information concerning the Lima treasure, which seemed to have come from the Keating source. He also met a government official who gave him a map said to have been drawn by the mate of the *Mary Dear* (Forbes?).

Armed with these various pieces of evidence which related to at least two separate treasures and which already conflicted, Gissler went off to the Cocos Islands in 1889 and lived there alone for ten months, searching without success. He came back again two years later, having in the interval done some research into navigation and other matters and adjusted his ideas accordingly. For while the differing clues were, and are, confusing enough, there are other problems to be considered.

First let us look at the clues. The most cursory research reveals seven different directions. One of the clues to the Lima treasure said to have come from Fitzgerald says: "In the north or north-east of Cocos Island there is a creek: go to the bottom of that creek and, from the high-water mark with a compass in your hand measure 25 fathoms due west, then turn to the north when you will perceive a rock rising like a cliff . . ." and so on. Another clue emanating from Keating/Fitzgerald says: "Disembark in the Bay of Hope (which is to the south of the island) between the two islets in water five fathoms deep. Walk 360 paces along the course of the stream then turn NNE for 850 yards . . ." There are references to a shadow like an eagle

cast by the setting sun at the extremity of which is a cave
marked by a cross, on the one hand, and to a hole in a cliff
face into which a lever can be inserted to move a rock on the
other. And these are only two of the Lima clues. Clues have
led to cliff faces, to under-water caves, to river banks and to
underground caverns. Various charts have appeared showing
the spot at which the treasures are hidden: all are different.

To add to these problems there is the question of interpretation. Gissler realized that both navigation and units of meas-
urement were now different from those early days. Navigational instruments were not nearly so sophisticated as they are
today, compasses pointed to a well-distinguished magnetic
north, watches were probably inaccurate. In 1820 a fathom
measured 5 ft. 2 ins., today it is 6 ft.

Then there is the question of copies and translations. Words
such as "creek" mean different things to different nationalities.
Abbreviations can be confusing: for example, in French O
stands for west (ouest) while in Dutch it stands for east (oost).
The more one considers the problem the more it appears to
become a game of wits, a grown-up "treasure-hunt" game
conducted in deadly earnest.

The most persevering of all the treasure-seekers was Gissler.
He went to the length of actually moving in to live on Cocos
Island for seventeen years from 1891. He married and brought
his wife to live there, and even established a temporary colony
there. The Costa Rican Government appointed him governor
of the island and gave him exclusive rights to search for the
treasure. It is said that after a while it was the attractions of
the simple life on the island which induced him to stay, rather
than the lure of the treasure. On the other hand later treasure-
hunters complained of suffering from the intense heat, and described the island as being infested with mosquitoes, flies and
snakes.

Gissler's sole concession, indeed, in no way deterred other
treasure-seekers who, from 1890 on, arrived at the island in a
steady stream. They each claimed to have the real clue to the
whereabouts of the treasure although by now the various stories of two separate hoards had become fused into one. And the
clues and charts, of course, all differed considerably from each
other.

The treasure-hunters came in ones and twos and in highly-
organized expeditions. One of the most notable expeditions

landed while Gissler was temporarily absent, in 1897. It was led by a British Admiral, Henry Palliser, whose ship happened to be visiting British Columbia and whose officers had encountered a man named Haffner who had been a member of the expedition organized by Hackett and Keating's wife. Haffner claimed that he knew where the treasure was, and had little trouble in interesting the officers. Nothing loth to do a little treasure-hunting to alleviate the monotony of a routine naval cruise, Admiral Palliser sailed for Cocos Island and landed 300 sailors and marines. Despite Mrs Gissler's objections the sailors proceeded to dig and blast their way round the island without any success. Palliser finally sailed away, but his activities were reported to the Costa Rican Government by Gissler and Palliser was severely reprimanded.

However Palliser's interest was now strongly aroused. He left the Navy and made plans to return as a private individual. In 1903 he and an adventurous army officer named de Montmorency, accompanied by several other treasure-seekers "all agog for the romantic exploit", as de Montmorency put it in his account of the episode, sailed for Cocos Island. The clue which they were following emanated from Fitzgerald (Keating's servant). De Montmorency considered it unsatisfactory, for although it was well established that Keating had gone to Cocos Island at least once and removed some treasure – on one occasion with a man named Bogue, who had failed to return – nobody who had ever gone to the island following Keating's clues had ever found anything, and Keating himself could never be persuaded to return.

De Montmorency guessed that either Bogue had found the treasure and Keating had killed him for it (and never knew its actual whereabouts himself), or Keating had killed Bogue in the treasure cave in order to keep all the loot for himself. However, despite the fact that these adventurers were not really convinced that their clue was genuine, they went off cheerfully enough in a spirit of adventure. They had busily analysed the clue and were well aware of the problems of interpretation (mentioned above) while de Montmorency also worked out that, if the description of the treasure buried there was correct, it would weigh some 16 tons and be about 32 or 33 cubic feet in volume. The expedition reached the spot they believed to be indicated by the clue, and found that the cliff face in which they hoped to find a cave had been covered by a succession of avalanches with tons of soil, huge boulders and fallen trees. Deterred by the problem they sailed away.

But the friend who had introduced Palliser and de Montmorency was not put off and was determined to tunnel into the forbidding cliff face. Moreover fresh information had come to hand, this time from an ex-seaman who, as a young man, had sailed with a certain Bob Flower. Flower claimed that while he was pearl fishing off Cocos Island he had found some gold coins in a cave. Flower had died during a sea battle, but he had given his friend a sketch-map showing the whereabouts of the cave.

In 1904 de Montmorency landed again on Cocos Island, accompanied by his friend Henry Gray. This time they were met by Gissler, who by now had become quite cynical about his treasure-hunting visitors, but had by no means abandoned his own hopes, he agreed to help the expedition. Once again they were disappointed, although this time they stayed on the island for many months. One of their periodic trips to the mainland for supplies brought them face to face with their old friend Palliser, who had come out with Lord Fitzwilliam on a separate expedition. De Montmorency, who had obtained permission from the Costa Rican Government, protested that only his expedition had the right to search the island, but Fitzwilliam took no notice.

De Montmorency alerted the Costa Rican Government who sent a gun-boat to the island, whither de Montmorency also repaired. But when they all got there they found that Fitzwilliam's party had left following an accident to one of their number during their attempts to dynamite the cliff previously explored by Palliser and de Montmorency. De Montmorency eventually departed for England, leaving the other members of the expedition to help Gissler continue the search for many months. But nothing was ever found.

Another notable expedition to Cocos Island was led by the famous racing motorist Sir Malcolm Campbell and Lee Guinness, another racing driver. Campbell was also armed with Fitzgerald's instructions, and like his predecessors had no luck. But the expedition received enormous publicity and encouraged a further wave of treasure-hunters. One of these expeditions was organized by a friend of Campbell, Colonel Leckie, in 1932; and although other chroniclers of the story of Cocos Island ignore the fact, one account states that they found a huge hoard of gold which they believed to be Benito Bonito's treasure. Apparently the Costa Rican Government sent soldiers to the island and the rest of the treasure was recovered. However, the news of this discovery appears to have been treated as a stunt, for it did not deter the stream of treasure-hunters.

Another expedition led by a notorious adventurer proceeded to lay claim to the island and hoist the Union Jack, which resulted in a detachment of troops being sent to Cocos Island by the Costa Rican Government and the ignominious end of the expedition. From companies financially backed by shareholders to lone explorers people continued to come to the island, finding the most unlikely spots in which the treasure could be hidden and exploring every inch of the terrain.

And in all these years there have been few finds. In the seventeen years of his occupation of the island Gissler found thirty-three gold coins, which had been minted in 1773 and in 1799. But these he found at different times and at random, and he believed they had been dropped by the depositors. Besides the somewhat suspect find of Leckie, the only other discovery is attributed to a Belgian treasure-hunter named Bergmans. Visiting the island on his own in 1929, Bergmans claimed that he had stepped upon a spot which gave way under his foot. Before him was a hole which led into a natural cave in which were piles of gold, church ornaments and chests of precious stones. He also found the skeleton of a man, and documents on which he recognized the name of Benito. Bergmans said he secreted two sacks of treasure elsewhere on the island and re-sealed the cave. But when he was taken back to the island by two members of a treasure-hunting syndicate some time later, he failed to find either the cave or the two sacks of treasure. Some accounts maintain, however, that acting on the information and experiences of a previous lone treasure-hunter, Bergmans did find a two-foot-high gold madonna (the origin of the legend of a life-size statue?) which he later sold in New York.

So, as far as one knows, the Lima treasure in all its fabulous glory still remains to be found. Expeditions and individuals armed with all kinds of equipment from dowsing rods to dynamite have searched through the vain years. But such is the psychology of treasure-hunters that it is easy to believe that they will be the lucky one. Cocos Island will lure them on, a promise of adventure in a prosaic age.

Monsters

THE SHY SERPENT OF LOCH NESS

The Loch Ness monster is too well known to need a formal introduction – in fact, from its alleged behaviour it politely declines to be introduced to anybody at all, especially homo sapiens (who would probably kill it, stuff it and put it in a museum). It (or they, should there be more than one) has been reportedly sighted, photographed and sonared over many years, and was even shown on television as recently as February, 1979. Nevertheless the "monster" is still blanketed by a very large question mark, which is roughly the shape of its long neck and head in various photographs and drawings which purport to show "Nessie", as the monster is popularly known, when surfacing the dark obscure waters of the loch.

The question mark can be split into three simple categories, namely: (1) Is there in fact a monster or serpent in Loch Ness?; (2) Is Nessie a fiction in that it is a misinterpretation of intersecting waves and boat wakes, or animals such as otters which can grow to a length of six feet?; (3) Is the whole thing a publicity stunt to attract tourists to the Scottish Highlands, particularly Inverness? In the last context it should be noted that in 1934 an American scientist asked "who ever heard of Loch Ness before the monster appeared there?"

On the other hand, an equally valid remark was made in 1972 by a tradesman at Foyers who had observed a strange area of ripples and foam he had seen on the surface of the Loch near Dores: "If that wasn't the monster then there's something queer in the loch."

That there *is* something queer in the loch cannot be denied,
and it is in no way a recent public relations operation. The
earliest reference to Nessie was in the eighth-century biography
of Saint Columba, an Irish poet, written a century after his
death by Adamnan. One chapter describes "the driving away
of a certain water monster by virtue of the prayer of the holy
man". The incident took place in the year A.D. 565. In brief, it
relates the death of "an unfortunate fellow" who had been
snatched by an aquatic monster while swimming in Loch Ness
and "viciously bitten". The corpse had been recovered by
boatmen using grappling hooks. When the victim had been
swimming in midstream the monster had, it seems, rushed
upon him with a great roar and open mouth. Saint Columba
ordered the monster to go away, which apparently it did
"more quickly than if it had been dragged on by ropes".

There were other sightings of Nessie – a much fiercer Nessie
than today's shy and bashful version – around the same era,
mainly by the Irish (if that is of any significance). The first
official reported sighting of this century took place in the early
summer of 1933. This event squeezed international and political news from the front pages of the Press all over the world,
and very soon the small town of Inverness, north of Loch Ness,
was overflowing with journalists and photographers from America to Tokyo.

Rumours ran wild. The monster was a small black hump in
the water; it was a prehistoric plesiosaur 60-feet long; it had
leaped across a main road in daylight with a sheep in its
mouth; it had seized and carried off an old woman; it was a
crocodile brought back from Africa; it was a giant seal or
whale; it was the remains of a zeppelin shot down in the First
World War – and it was even a string of sea mines laid down
by the British Navy. Newspaper editors had a wonderful "silly
season", which lasted for a few weeks then finally gave way
to the more important problem of Germany's occupation of
the Rhineland. The Second World War was only six years
away.

It is perhaps unfortunate that Nessie has always been referred to as a "monster". The *Oxford English Dictionary* defines
"monster" as (1) Mis-shapen animal or plant; imaginary
animal compounded of incongruous elements, e.g. centaur,
sphinx, griffin; inhumanly wicked person, inhuman example of
(cruelty, etc.); animal, thing, of huge size. No self-respecting

denizen of a lake or sea would wish to be associated with such a description.

More kindly is the *O.E.D.*'s definition of a sea serpent: kinds of snake living in sea, also (the sea serpent) enormous serpentine sea monster occasionally reported as seen but disbelieved in by naturalists. That, at least, sounds more like Nessie.

At this point it is necessary to take a geographical and ecological look at Loch Ness itself. It is the largest inland freshwater lake in the British Isles and the third largest in Europe. It has a very restricted outlet to the sea, but has a number of tributary streams and rivers. At about 50 feet above sea-level, it is 24 miles long and one mile wide, and is one of a chain of lochs in the Great Glen, a geological fault line cutting across Scotland. The banks of Loch Ness fall steeply into the lake to a depth at one point of nearly 1,000 feet. The water itself is obscured by peat carried down by streams and rivers from the surrounding mountains so that it has a dark reddish colour with a visibility, a few feet below the surface, of as little as twelve inches. This makes underwater photography virtually impossible.

A curious fact is that the waters of Loch Ness, though cold, never freeze. Throughout the year they vary little from an average temperature of 42 degrees Fahrenheit. The loch, with its surrounding highlands, forms a natural heat trap which has not even today been adequately explained. The abysmal underwater visibility was well confirmed in 1969 when an American, Dan Taylor, financed by a big U.S. corporation, took a mini yellow submarine (no connection with the Beatles) to Loch Ness, and because of the opaque water saw nothing and photographed nothing.

Shortly afterwards, another submarine, taking part in a Sherlock Holmes movie which involved a plastic and wire artifact monster in Loch Ness (which incidentally sank and was lost for ever), used sonar in an attempt to find the submerged pseudo-Nessie. It failed, but nevertheless revealed a previously unknown 800-feet-deep trench in the bed of the loch.

An inevitable side-effect of the rapidly growing interest in the Loch Ness monster had been the perpetration of hoaxes which, in their own small way, initially did much to destroy the "suspension of disbelief". For example, a "big game hunter" sponsored by a daily newspaper discovered large footprints of the monster on a beach. That was in 1933, the year when sightings of the monster were first reported in the Press.

On investigation by zoologists, however, the "spoor" turned out to be imprints in the sand made by the preserved and mounted foot of a hippopotamus.

That hoax was simply a bad joke, and it proved nothing because, if Nessie had come ashore from the loch, and there is evidence that she (or he) did, then there would be marks in the sand or soft soil of heavy body drag, feet or flippers, and so on – and once again there is evidence that would probably stand up in a court of law.

As is usual, when an inexplicable phenomenon demands a rational explanation (whether Nessie or UFOs), scientists generally dismissed the evidence and ignored the photographs and ciné film. It is unfortunate that of the many hundreds of pictures and ciné frames taken of sightings in the loch, none is so precisely crisp and defined as to prove incontrovertible. With modern electronic self-focusing zoom-lens cameras, however, the ultimate definitive photograph of elusive Nessie could well be taken any day. We are still waiting.

If Nessie exists, then what is it? A kind of plesiosaurus or a sea serpent adapted to fresh water? Dr Bernard Heuvelmans in his book *In the Wake of Sea Serpents* defines nine different kinds of "monsters", from marine saurians to super-otters and super-eels, some with fins, some without, some with long necks and some with short necks, and some with humps or spines and some with fins. He concludes, but not too specifically, that Nessie (and other lake monsters throughout the world) are long-necked mammals known generally as "sea horses"; in fact, the strange inhabitant(s) of Loch Ness has been traditionally known for some centuries as a "water horse".

The big breakthrough started on 11 May, 1933. A Mr Alexander Shaw and his son, standing on a high bank above the loch, saw a wake appear on the surface of the dark water about 500 yards away. A rounded black shape resembling the back of an animal surfaced but the long curved front part, presumably the neck and head, remained submerged and not clearly visible, while at the rear the water threshed as if disturbed by a tail or flippers.

During that year there were numerous sightings by various people. A Mr Thomas MacLennan saw the loch denizen several times. He described it as an animal about 30 feet long with, he thought, four flippers. His wife saw its head and neck, slender, curved and tapering, with a mane rather like a horse. On its back were humps and its tail was similar in shape to that of a fish. Another observer was Miss Nora Simpson who claimed to have seen the monster at a distance of 45 yards; she confirmed that it had humps and while surfacing appeared to be about 30 feet long.

In June of that year an aviator flying over the loch reported that he had seen below the surface of the water something which looked like an alligator about 25 feet long and 4 feet wide (he recommended that depth charges should be dropped, but happily this advice was ignored).

In July, a company director, Mr George Spicer, and his wife were driving along the road at the edge of the loch when, alarmingly, from the bushes on the hillside to their left a long neck appeared and then a huge body quickly jerked itself across the road to disappear into the bushes fringing the loch. The car was about 200 yards away. Because of a slight hill in the road they were unable to see the lower part of the animal. When they arrived at the spot, Mr Spicer stopped and looked around, but there was no further trace of the creature and it had obviously taken to the water.

The monster crossing the road was described as "dark elephant grey, of a loathsome texture, reminiscent of a snail". It had a long wavy neck rather like a scenic railway. It stood about four feet high and 25 feet long – but later the length was amended to 30 feet. This siting caused tremendous local interest, and much speculation in the area press.

That was not the first time the monster had been seen on land. In 1912 a group of schoolchildren engaged in birdnesting saw a creature resembling a camel, with humped back and long curved neck, move swiftly out of bushes and vanish in the water of the loch. A Mrs Peter Cameron recalled that when she was fifteen, while playing with other youngsters on one of the beaches of the loch, they had seen a large animal on an opposite shore, moving its head and its shoulders. Again it resembled a camel, with a long neck and a small head, but although there were two front "limbs" there was no sign of a tail. The colour was elephant grey.

Various other land sightings were made by individuals or children – Nessie lying in a glade, resting on a rock ledge, exercising on beaches, and so on. The eye-witness descriptions varied in detail, but there seemed to be general agreement about the humps, the grey skin colour and the short legs shaped like flippers. It might have been a seal, but for the long curved neck.

In retrospect it would seem that the existence of a strange creature in Loch Ness had been adequately established, although at the time (from 1933 onwards) Nessie was more of an adventure rather than an object of serious research. One must also bear in mind mass reaction to a strange phenomenon, described by the Director of London Zoo Aquarium (E. G. Boulenger) in the *Observer* of 29 October, 1933, as "a striking example of mass hallucination . . . Any person with the slightest knowledge of human nature should therefore find no difficulty in understanding how an animal, once said to have been seen by a few persons, should shortly after have revealed itself to many more". This observation could equally apply to other spheres, such as UFOs and ghosts. The important factor is corroboration of any one sighting by a number of witnesses, and a general agreement as to what was observed in appropriate detail.

In November, 1933, the monster was photographed as it surfaced briefly in the loch by Mr Hugh Gray, who had a house on the loch shore at Foyers. The creature was large, dark grey and rose two or three feet above the water; the head was underwater but there appeared to be some activity at the tail end. The photograph was taken from a cliff 30 feet high. Kodak technicians who examined the negative stated that it had not been faked or retouched in any way, and the picture was published in the *Daily Telegraph* (6 December, 1933) and also in a Norwegian newspaper (which printed it upside down!).

The photograph was not convincing enough for scientists: it could have been a picture of a seal, a whale, a shark, wreck, or a tree trunk or weeds lifted by decomposition gases which escaped at the surface, allowing the rotting matter to sink again. How a shark, whale or large seal could have entered the loch, which has a very restricted access to the sea, was not explained.

Nessie rapidly became famous, and was even the subject of discussion in the House of Commons on 12 November of that year, but the government at that time felt that the monster did not call for legislation or intervention from Westminster, and could be safely left to the scientists and the Press. This was an unsuitable combination, for the Press were in search of sensation while the scientists were not prepared to "lose face" over something which might possibly turn out to be a hoax.

Since 1933 more than 3,000 witnesses have claimed to have sighted the monster with its long neck and humped back, and the archives contain scores of books, press articles, photographs and ciné films about Nessie. Credit must be given to Mrs Constance Whyte, who meticulously researched the subject and published in 1957 a book about the Loch Ness monster entitled *More than a Legend*. In a second book she makes it clear that she considers Nessie to be a prehistoric amphibious animal, very likely a plesiosaur (which we are taught has been extinct for sixty million years – but, then, look at the coelacanth).

In 1962 the Loch Ness Phenomena Investigation Bureau was established to organize research expeditions and collect reliable evidence by means of surveys, depth sounding, constant observation and photography and setting up facilities for independent scientific investigations. In one sense the Bureau was protecting the monster, if it existed, for during preceding years Nessie had become the object of commercial interests. Bertram Mills Circus, for example, offered £20,000 to any group that could capture the monster alive; and similar rewards came from elsewhere, including £5,000 from a New York Zoo and £1,000 from a private individual. Nobody has yet collected the prize money.

The first successful ciné film of the monster in the loch, taken in the significant year of 1933, lasted for two minutes and was described in *The Times* of 3 January, 1934. Nessie had partly surfaced, and the cameraman thought he could see seven or eight humps, some of which were visible in the film. Most of the creature, including the head, was under water.

The report in *The Times* stated: "The most clearly evident movements are those of the tail or flukes. This appendage is naturally darker than the body. The photographers describe the general colour of the creature as grey, and that of the tail as black. Indeterminate movements of the water beside the monster as it swims suggests the action of something in the nature of fins or paddles."

In subsequent years other films were taken, using telephoto lenses and high-speed emulsions. In general they showed similar phenomena: there was certainly something animate active in the loch, but the definition was never quite good enough to

indicate precisely *what* was active. The Loch Ness Investigation
Bureau (whose profits, if any, go to the World Wildlife Fund)
increased its operations, so that sightings, photographs and
films increased. The habits of Nessie were analysed. Most sightings were generally in bays and at the mouths of tributary
rivers draining into the loch, where salmon and shoals of small
fish would most likely be found. Investigation was concentrated in these areas.

Liaison was established with photographic experts at the
Joint Air Reconnaissance Centre (JARIC) who meticulously
scrutinized and analysed films and photographs. In October,
1962, a party led by David James (M.P. and a founder-
member of the Investigation Bureau) patrolled the loch in
boats equipped with searchlights, on the assumption that
Nessie was nocturnal. There were two brief sightings, and on
one night a searchlight illuminated "a finger-like object six to
eight feet out of the water".

Further sightings occurred and were filmed, but on the night
of 19 October eight members of the expedition saw the back of
an animal break the surface of the loch about 200 yards from
the boat. It was moving slowly after shoals of fish, mainly
salmon and red trout which had mustered in Urquhart Bay to
catch the first rise of water up the rivers. Some 50 feet of ciné
film were taken of the semi-submerged monster as it prowled
in search of food.

The cameraman, John Luff, commented that "he had never
seen anything like it during his naval service, and if he had he
would have changed course rapidly". The visible part of the
creature was about ten feet long.

The film was sent to JARIC for examination, and the Reconnaissance Centre concluded that it was not a wave effect,
because the object appeared to be solid, was dark in tone and
glistened. The evidence was then considered by an independent panel, and their deliberations formed the basis of a television programme broadcast on 2 February, 1963. The panel
(consisting of four naturalists and scientists) reported: "We
find that there is some unidentified animate object in Loch
Ness which, if it be an animal, reptile or mollusc of any known
order, is of such a size as to be worthy of careful scientific
examination and identification. If it is not of a known order, it
is scientifically desirable to investigate it also on that
ground."

Nessie was now being taken seriously (apart from a writer in the *Financial Times* who was not yet convinced that there was a monster in Loch Ness, but was "most impressed with the evidence for David James's existence". Meanwhile, further rewards had been offered for the capture of the monster alive: £1,000 by the Scottish newspaper *Daily Record* and a fantastic £1 million by the Black & White Whisky company provided (here comes Catch 22) the British Museum accepted it as a genuine monster.

Sightings and evidence continue to mount in volume and the findings of authoritative bodies often seem quite conclusive. For example, a 16-mm ciné film taken by Tim Dinsdale in 1960 and sent to JARIC by David James in 1966 produced the response, after optical enlargement of individual frames, that the object filmed in the loch was not a boat or a motor-boat but was a black roughly triangular shape with a base of about five and a half feet and over three and a half feet high, travelling through the water at around 10 m.p.h. JARIC concluded that it was probably an animate object with some body; even if "flat bellied", normal body-rounding would suggest that at least two feet of it was under water, and a cross-section through it would be not less than six feet wide and five feet high. Tim Dinsdale was the Director of Field Operations at the Investigation Centre and was naturally encouraged by this report to extend exploration and research in the loch.

This work continues. Infra-red cameras have been used to penetrate the opacity of the loch water, and considerable use has been made of sonar and acoustic monitoring, though with no spectacular results. Sonar itself would indicate but not identify the presence of a large object, which might not necessarily be the monster.

Nessie is not unique. Monsters have been, and still are, reported in other Scottish lochs and in deep lakes throughout the world, but Loch Ness has gained most of the publicity, particularly in the Press. It is not possible in the space available here to summarize all the evidence, arguments and theories for and against Nessie. The Loch Ness Investigation Bureau no longer functions and there seems to be some doubt as to where the archives are stored. But other investigators are continuing to pursue the shy serpent, or whatever it might be.

While some day Nessie (or perhaps one of a number of Nessies) might fall into their hands, the fact remains that so far no actual monster body, living or dead, has been physically taken from the loch. Must one assume therefore that the monster(s) can live for centuries, or that if they die the carcasses never surface, despite the formation of putrefaction gas? How do they reproduce? In the summer of 1970 an attempt was made to test Nessie's sexual appetite by making an artificial monster of plastic covered with fish oil to float in the loch, but before this experiment could be completed the fake monster suddenly vanished and was never seen again! What conclusions can be drawn from that? The mind boggles!

Peter Costello, in his book *In Search of Lake Monsters*, moderates his evident enthusiasm for Nessie by quoting five simple words from the Habeas Corpus Act: "You must produce the body . . ." Until somebody does so, then Nessie will remain a continuing mystery of the waters of this planet, along with other monsters and serpents of all shapes and sizes.

DENIZENS OF THE
DEEP LAKES

Although the Loch Ness monster is undoubtedly the most famous and most publicized of the deep-lake monsters – an elusive superstar in its own right – it has many relations and friends in other Scottish lochs and in lakes throughout the world. In Scotland the lochs they inhabit are associated with the Great Glen, a geological fault line running diagonally from west to east across the Highlands. There have been many sightings recorded throughout history, and the further one goes back in time the more difficult it is to separate folklore from fact. Here we are concerned with fact, i.e. sightings that appear to be factual in fairly modern times, and taking into account the inevitable hoaxes which have at least provided some comic relief.

At the tidal mouth of the Great Glen is Loch Linnhe, and there a good sighting was made on 21 June, 1954 by a Mr Eric Robinson of Owston Ferry, Doncaster. Three humps appeared above the water, followed by considerable turbulence and churning as though of a boat's propellor. The creature was moving at around 30 m.p.h., and was in sight for two minutes. It then headed towards the entrance of Loch Leven where it had apparently been seen two weeks earlier by local fishermen.

Six years later Mr Robinson obtained another sighting, this time in Loch Lochy, where he, family and friends were caravaning. On the evening of 15 July, 1960, two "stationary waves" were seen on the water surface about two or three hundred yards from the shore, but viewed through binoculars it became obvious that the waves were a live creature. As he watched, the animal began to move, raised a massive back above the water and started to roll over and over. He and his wife saw fins on each side of the body, and the underside was lighter in colour. The back and the humps together measured 30 feet or more. The water turbulence of the monster's movements caused waves that reached the shore, and at one point it seemed as though the creature intended to land. This incident was observed by nine other witnesses.

The small Loch Oich, which lies between Ness and Lochy and is connected with Loch Ness by a river, also has a serpent or monster on record. There have been several sightings – a typical one in the summer of 1936 describes the familiar appearance of a large body surfacing, followed by humps and a "dog-like" head. It is possible that the animal often swam into tiny Loch Oich via the river from nearby Loch Ness.

Because of its small size the loch would be a suitable place for intensive investigation, but a hoax carried out in July, 1961, in which an artificial self-propelled "monster" was set afloat in the loch, then photographed and treated as a genuine sighting, only to be kidnapped by a group of students, has rather discredited Loch Oich as an area for serious study.

In Loch Eil, which is an extension of Loch Linnhe (mentioned earlier), Mrs Preston of Tadcaster, Yorkshire, saw a long head and neck rise above the water at a distance of 25 yards. It was similar in shape to those sighted in Loch Ness. Even Loch Lomond with its bonny, bonny banks has produced sightings, though only a few. One of the most recent occurred in the summer of 1964 when a large humped back was seen by a Mr Haggerty and his wife from Helensborough; and Mr Sandy Watt, train driver, and his fireman, Bob Wilson, taking a freight train to Crainlarich one afternoon emerged from a tunnel overlooking the loch and saw a huge object moving rapidly through the water "like a torpedo".

Loch Shiel and Loch Morar are centres of serpent or monster activity; they are lonely and deep lochs – Morar is, in fact, the deepest loch in Scotland and its monster is known as the Mhorag. It seems to have been sighted quite regularly and was seen ashore in 1946 by a Mr Alexander MacDonnell and a party of schoolchildren from a boat on the loch. What they saw on the northern shore was "an animal about the size of an Indian elephant, which plunged off the rocks into the water with a huge splash". The "elephant's trunk" was undoubtedly the monster's elongated neck.

Two sightings in 1969 are worth noting. In July, Bob Duff, a visitor boating on the loch, looked down through the clear water at the white sandy lake bed some 16 feet below. He was shocked to see a "monster lizard" about 20 feet long with a snake-like head, a wide mouth and slit eyes lying on the bottom looking up at him. The length of the neck was not clearly visible, but the creature had four legs with three digits each and a tail. It was grey brown in colour. Bob Duff moved his boat away fast.

In August of the same year, two men returning from a fishing trip in a motor boat saw a monster approaching them from a distance of 20 yards. It collided with the boat, possibly unintentionally. One of the men struck the creature with an oar, which snapped, and the other fired a rifle at it – at which it submerged. The animal was about 30 feet long with a snake-like head and three shallow humps on its back.

There have been many more sightings of similar creatures in other Scottish lochs, and the cumulative mass of evidence is such that even the most sceptical zoologist or naturalist must admit that intensive investigation is justified, even if nobody has yet actually captured a monster or found the remains of one.

If the Scots have their lake monsters, so have the Irish, though one hears less about them. One has to allow again for a foundation of myth and folklore, but there have been well-documented modern sightings in the Irish loughs very similar to those of the Scottish lochs.

One of the most notable occurred on the evening of 18 May, 1960 in Lough Ree, one of the three large Shannon lakes, over 100 feet deep in parts and replete with fish and eels. Three Dublin priests had gone there for fishing off Holly Point – Fathers Matthew Burke, Daniel Murray and Richard Quigley. The lake was calm and visibility good on a warm bright evening. What happened was described in a report they later submitted to the Inland Fisheries Trust. They were in a rowing boat about 50 yards off shore and watching the water for rising trout when they saw a strange object moving slowly on the surface of the water about 80 yards away.

The report states: "There were two sections above the water; a forward section of uniform girth, stretching quite straight out of the water . . . in length about 18–24 inches. The diameter of this long leaning section we would estimate to be about four inches. At its extremity, which we took to be a serpent-like head, it tapered rather abruptly to a point.

"Between the leading and following sections of this creature, there intervened about two feet of water. The second section seemed to us to be a tight, roughly semicircular loop. This portion could have been a hump or a large knob on the back of a large body under the surface that was being propelled by flippers . . . We would estimate the length of the two visible sections, measured along the surface from tip of snout to end of hump, at about six feet.

"The movement along the water was steady. There was no apparent disturbance of the surface, so that propulsion seemed to come from the well-submerged portion of the creature. There was no undulation of its body above water . . . We watched it moving along the surface for a period of two or three minutes . . . It was going towards the shore; then it submerged gradually, rather than dived, and disappeared from view completely. Another couple of minutes later it reappeared, still following the same course, where it submerged and we saw it no more . . ."

In an addendum to that report the three priests recorded a further sighting that same evening of a moving black object "about the length of a row-boat" – but this time it was three-quarters of a mile away. It was moving through the water at a steady rate and remained under observation for about ten minutes before it finally submerged. They added: "We could not help feeling that there was some link of similarity between these two strange appearances . . . We were convinced that what we saw was a living creature of a very exceptional kind and we feel that its identification poses a most interesting problem."

The story was duly published in the Irish and some English newspapers and brought forth stories of similar monsters in the Irish loughs. The Lough Ree sighting was even raised at a meeting of Westmeath County Council, where one member suggested that the monster was nothing more than "Councillor D'Arcy out for a swim". And at a meeting of the Irish Inland Waterways Association one member thought that the monster was a Russian midget submarine dropped from one of the jets that had flown over Athlone the week before. Other Irish explanations included a coelacanth, a line of hooked fish, a row of ducks or otters, a deliberate hoax and even an optical illusion. But the carefully worded evidence of three priests could hardly be dismissed so lightly, especially in Ireland.

The Lough Ree sighting is probably the most detailed of all Irish encounters. There are many others, and several of monsters ashore. For instance, on 1 May 1970, a local contractor, John Cooney, and his friend Michael McNulty were driving past Glendarry Lough in the centre of Achill Island when a creature suddenly crossed in front of the van. It was, Mr Cooney reported, "between eight and twelve feet long with a long neck like a swan only much bigger. The tail was very thick. It was moving at an angle to us and we couldn't see exactly how long it was, and it was weaving and curving. It was dark brown in colour and slimy and scaly. The eyes were glittering ... It disappeared in an instant into the thick undergrowth – and we didn't stop to make further inquiries."

The Irish lake monsters seem, in most significant respects, to be much the same as those of Scotland, and there is no point in elaborating further in the limited space available, for there are deep lakes in other parts of the world to be considered. One curious point, however, is that, apart from St George and the dragon, monsters of all kinds seem to have avoided England and Wales. One wonders why!

Sweden has a famous and rather genial monster in the great Lake Storsjö, which is the deepest lake in Scandinavia, located in the far north on the same latitude as Trondheim in Norway and frozen over during winter. The creature is grey with black spots, but greenish in front. It has large eyes in a smooth dog-like head, with big floppy ears (or fins) on either side of the head; the ears can be flipped back to lie flat against the curved long neck. When annoyed it puts its tongue out. A drawing of the monster in the official Swedish booklet on the subject (*Storsjöodjuret*) shows a long, humped serpent with a rather timid bashful expression on its face – it might have come straight out of a Walt Disney cartoon.

There seems to be no doubt that the monster exists, for it has been sighted many times by reliable observers (twenty-two times between 1820 and 1898, and most recently in 1959). Its length is said to be around 40 feet. Furthermore, special har-

poons and circular spring traps were made in an attempt to
capture it. A major effort to catch the creature was organized
in 1894 when a company was formed for that purpose, part of
the capital being contributed by King Oscar II of Sweden.
Despite a long search of the lake in a boat equipped with harpoons, large barbed hook lines and spring traps, the monster
was not even seen throughout a whole year, and the company
went bankrupt.

Sweden's monster is a fast mover – it can touch 45 m.p.h.
and make sudden sharp turns. Its method of propulsion is not
clearly known; it is said to have short thick legs, which could
be fins, and webbed hind legs. It is described as one metre
thick, with some humps, so that its overall shape is more serpentine than the Scottish or Irish monsters. Reports of sightings
go back several hundred years. The history of the monster,
with a display of photographs and drawings and actual speci-
mens of traps and harpoons devised for its capture, can be
found in a museum at Osterund on the east shore of Lake
Storsjö.

There is little point in listing the many repetitive sightings of
this peculiar lake monster, but one incident is worth mention-
ing which was reported in the Press of several countries at the
time (1893) and that was the only occasion on which the
monster showed any sign of "aggression". Two girls of Sorbyn
(aged 18 and 21) were washing clothes on the lake shore when
they saw a creature swimming towards them at some speed. It
was grey with black spots, had large eyes and floppy laid-back
"ears". It stopped near the shore and stared at them. The
girls, alarmed, began to throw stones at the animal which then
advanced closer to the beach. The girls ran off – one to the
protection of a railway while the other climbed a tree. The
monster churned up the water, dived, resurfaced and then disappeared.

The newspapers reported the event as "two girls attacked by
a sea creature" who were obliged to "run for their lives". They
did not mention that even a genial and tolerant serpent might
take exception to being stoned, and that, if anything, the aggression came from the shore rather than the water.

The Scandinavian papers, though devoting much space to
Scotland's Nessie, seldom print more than a few lines about
their own monsters. There is allegedly a monster in the Farris-
vannet, a small lake in the south of Denmark, and another was

photographed in a lake on Bear Island near the Arctic Circle. Norway also claims a few lake monsters, though at least one of these was found to be a mass of rotting sawdust and timber from a sawmill (a factor worth bearing in mind in those timber-processing countries). The emphasis, if anything, is on sea-water serpents which are said to have been sighted in many fiords of the rugged coastline – but they are the subject of another chapter.

Russia, it seems, has at least *two* "Soviet Loch Ness Monsters" in lakes in a virtually uninhabited and unexplored part of Siberia known as the Sordongnokh Plateau. A report on two separate lake monsters was broadcast by Moscow Radio in 1962. The lakes are about 1,000 metres above sea-level and were formed by the blocking of rivers when mountains were cast up in the Tertiary Age. In the summer of 1953 a geological prospecting party led by V. A. Tverdokhlebov reached the shore of Lake Vorota – it was a sunny day and the water was calm. Looking at the lake they saw an object resembling a large empty petrol drum floating some 300 metres from the shore, but soon it became apparent that the object was moving and alive – and, worse, advancing towards them. They retreated to a higher point on the cliff face and continued to watch.

When the creature was close enough it became apparent that the front part of the animal's body which showed above water, presumably the head, was about six feet wide, and there were two eyes set wide apart. On either side of the head was a whitish patch. The total length of its huge dark grey body was over 30 feet, and a kind of dorsal fin, bent backwards, stood nearly two feet high. The creature was moving in an undulating fashion, alternately surfacing and submerging. At about 100 metres from the shore it stopped, violently threshed the water, then dived and was seen no more. Lake Vorota is about seventy-five miles from the nearest inhabited place.

Among the people who live on the plateau, mainly fishermen and hunters, all the lakes have a sinister reputation, especially the biggest of them, Lake Labynkyr, which is 200 feet deep and some nine miles long. A "Devil" monster is supposed to dwell in that lake, and is reputed to eat retriever dogs when they swim in the lake to recover shot-down ducks. It also chased a raft manned by a fisherman who saw that the monster was dark grey in colour with an enormous mouth. It has

also been seen by many local inhabitants. On one occasion a
group of men saw a reindeer walk into the lake, to disappear
below the surface. Later the same thing happened to a dog.
Then a black monster rose from the lake, snorted, and submerged. One of the men who was a scholar told the group that
the monster was a dinosaur.

Lake Khaiyr (500 miles north-west of Lake Labynkir) is a
strange thermal lake which has no fish, and no ducks or geese
will alight on its surface. While quite small, nobody has yet
measured its depth. The monster there is amphibious and has
been seen on the bank, eating grass. When observed it had the
characteristic long neck with a small head and a huge black
body with an upright dorsal fin. A biologist (N. F. Gladkikh)
who saw it suggested that it might be "the last of the long
extinct Ichthiosauri".

If the Russians have lake monsters, then, of course, so must
the Americans, and these seem to survive and perhaps flourish
(in the U.S. Press, at least) in the mountain states and in the
Wisconsin and Nebraska areas. The Wisconsin lakes seem to be
the most densely populated with monsters. An interesting point
here is that any U.S. folklore or mythology must necessarily be
of Red Indian origin because of the cultural time-scale involved. The Indians regarded many lakes as haunted places.

There is no advantage in repetitiously reciting details of the
monster sightings as they all follow much the same pattern,
e.g. a sea serpent sighted in Lake Monona, Wisconsin – 30 feet
long and shaped like the bottom of a boat; a strange lake in
Wyoming inhabited by creatures which "elsewhere on the
globe are found only as fossils of a long vanished era"; a sighting of the long neck and head of a monster in Bear Lake,
Utah; a 90 feet monster with a long neck and humps; and
monsters travelling faster than cars.

There is certainly a factual substratum in the multitude of
American reports, but there are no photographs and few of the
sightings are adequately witnessed.

In Canada the most famous lake is Okanagan in British
Columbia, eighty miles long, very narrow, and deep. Its shape
makes it very suitable for sightings and research, but in the
summer the lake is full of sailboats, motorboats, water-skiers
and, latterly, windsurfers – enough activity to deter any civilized monster from surfacing during the day. Nevertheless, there
have been many sightings which would seem to be authentic.

Lake Okanagan is jocularly known as Ogopogo, which is the nickname of its monster. More than a century ago the local Indians were convinced that the lake contained a water demon, and made sacrifices when they ventured into the waters. The Indians even made carvings of the demon on stone, and immediately recognizable is the long curved neck with small angled head (with "ears" similar to those of the Swedish Storsjö monster), the large body with dorsal fins or humps, the short tail, and stumpy legs or flippers. On balance it resembles a huge serpent rather than a plesiosaur-type animal.

The Ogopogo has been observed many times. A typical sighting was made in July, 1949, by a Mr Kray and the Watson family from Montreal who together saw "a long sinuous body, 30 feet in length, consisting of about five undulations, apparently separated from each other by about a two-foot space, in which that part of the undulations could have been underwater. The length of each of the undulations that could be seen would have been about five feet. There appeared to be a forked tail, of which only one half came above the water. From time to time the whole thing submerged and came up again."

In 1960 the monster was seen by the German vice-consul in Vancouver and a friend. The vice-consul, Hans Gerade, reported "a spoil of waves with white foam, in the middle of the lake . . . It looked like the wash of a boat moving swiftly from north to south, but there was no boat." His friend said he saw "a creature about 25 feet long, with humps, which rose up and down in a mass of white foam". He added: "I never did believe in Ogopogo, but after this I certainly do."

Another group, including a Presbyterian minister and a funeral director, saw a charcoal-coloured creature, some 30 to 70 feet long with dorsal fins . . . It was a dog-faced animal with a neck the diameter of a stove pipe.

Lake Okanagan is, in effect, the Canadian Loch Ness – it receives most of the publicity and has enjoyed most of the monster sightings, though there are many other lakes throughout Canada which reputedly have their indigenous monsters, two of the most important being Manipogo (Lake Manitoba) and Igopogo (Lake Simcoe, Ontario). All the sightings are basically similar, any variations in detail probably being due to errors of human observation and reporting.

In general most of the Canadian sightings were taken up by the Press in an objective fashion with not too much tongue-in-

cheek. Any folklore foundation would inevitably be of Indian
or Eskimo origin.

Moving further south to almost the "bottom" of South
America, would the reader be prepared to accept the existence
of a fresh-water Plesiosaur in Patagonia? It may sound goonish,
but nevertheless such a beast was reported in *The Times* and
newspapers throughout the world in 1922 – eleven years before
Nessie monopolized world headlines. Large areas of South
America, in particular the Amazon basin, the Matto Grosso
and the mountains and forests of Patagonia, are still virtually
unexplored. The mysterious topography provided Arthur
Conan Doyle with a suitable environment for his famous story
The Lost World, inhabited by prehistoric monsters. The following sightings are brief, but authentic enough to include in this
short survey. In 1922, an American prospector named Martin
Sheffield who was searching for gold in the Andean foothills in
Patagonia reported to the Director of Buenos Aires zoo (Dr
Clementi Onelli): "I saw in the middle of the lake an animal
with a huge neck like a swan, and the movements made me
suppose the beast to have a body like a crocodile. Around the
lake the bushes and scrub had been crushed as if by a huge
heavy animal."

Onelli himself had, many years earlier, seen a similar creature in another lake; it had a long reptile-like neck rising high
above the water. Another virtually identical lake animal had
also been seen by an Englishman in 1913, further south near
Santa Cruz. Onelli, in 1922, set up an expedition to search for
some of these reported monsters, but it returned eight months
later having found nothing at all. Such creatures are, however,
well represented in South American Indian folklore – the
monsters, known as *cuero* (or cowhide, which describes the appearance of the skin), inhabit swamps and lakes, are enormous,
and frequently plough through the jungle, leaving crushed
undergrowth behind them.

Some years ago, Dr Bernard Heuvelmans (mentioned elsewhere in this book) wrote to Onelli seeking information about
Patagonia's prehistoric animals, only to learn that Onelli had
died. Dr Heuvelmans is known as a specialist in researching
the survival today of extinct prehistoric creatures.

In this chapter we have mainly reviewed reports of lake
monsters in the Western world, but to complete the picture a
quick look at Africa and the East is necessary, though, as one

might expect, the pattern of the tapestry is much the same – *plus ça change, plus c'est la même chose!*

There is a tradition of lake monsters in Africa, varying from the reptilian to the saurian in form. The saurians, i.e. the Loch Ness monster type, seem to be few and far between. Circumstantial evidence can be convincing – for example, it is curious that there are no hippos in Lake Bangweolo in the Congo basin. According to the local natives, this is because of the presence in the lake of the Chipekwe, also known as the Congo dragon, which though somewhat smaller than the hippos ruthlessly attacks them. Researchers, including the tireless Dr Heuvelmans, have concluded that the monster is a reptile which occurs in different forms in the basins of the Zambesi and the Nile, as well as the Congo. The evidence suggests a family of large reptiles, differing in type and habits, amphibious, with a long thin flexible neck, a small triangular head with a horn, varying in length from hippo size to 30 feet (including a powerful tail). It is not readily classifiable, but Heuvelmans concludes that the monster is probably a relic of the reptile empire that existed in the Jurassic period.

Lake Victoria is said to have a monster called the *lau* which has the more saurian form of a long curved neck and a massive body with humps; the body can be up to 100 feet long. It can also be found in the swamps of the Upper Nile. Leaving aside a rather dubious "sea serpent" seen in Lake Nyasa (it may have been a large python swimming with its head above the surface), we come to the Orange River where Mr Fred Cornell reported in 1922 that he had seen a monster "black, huge and sinuous" near Great Falls. Witnesses in his party included two men from Cape Town and three Bantu. The creature had "a huge head and a neck 10 feet long 'like a bending tree'." The Bantu said it had attacked their cattle and pulled them under water. Similar sightings of this animal were made elsewhere, and one made in 1950 in the Ingruenfisi River was reported in the South African Press.

Armenian and Persian mythology has its quota of dragons and lake or river monsters, in particular the famous Dragon of Ishtar Gate in the ruins of Babylon, uncovered in 1902 by Robert Koldewey, the German archaeologist. According to author Peter Costello, if large unknown animals survive anywhere, the Tigris marshes are a likely place to find them – and they may reveal the true dragon of Ishtar Gate. In this chapter, however, we are concerned with fact, or what may be fact, rather than legend or myth.

Going further east, we find that the Orient is almost knee-deep in dragons of one kind or another, especially in China, where the dragon was the god of rain to which the Chinese made sacrifices in periods of drought. It is generally pictured as a kind of huge lizard with a flat long head with horns, a long mane, and short feet with nailed claws, although in other parts of the East it is said to have "the head of a camel, the scales of a carp . . . the neck of a snake" – which is nearer to the lake monsters of the West.

Central Malaya seems to be a good spot for lake monsters, especially Tasek Bera, a swamp enclosed by jungle and fed by weed-choked rivers. The denizens of the lake are called *nagas*, apparently related to the Chinese dragon. In the early 1950s a Malayan senior police officer reported a strange animal in the swampy lake. It took the form of a head and long neck rising some 15 feet above the weeds; behind the head two grey humps curved above the water. There were two small horns on the head. The local Semelai people considered them harmless as they fed on water plants. None of them knew the total length of the animals (for there were several of them in the lake) because the size and weight of their bodies were such that they could not emerge from the water on to land.

Australia's best-known lake and river monster is the bunyip, which has been sighted on many occasions. It is said to be brown in colour, with a long neck, shaggy mane and a head like a kangaroo. Encounters with creatures in other lakes in Australia were probably with freshwater seals, which can grow up to 15 feet in length, or sea lions; both are commonplace and can be found in river water and lakes up to 900 miles inland. The bunyip, however, seems to correspond more closely to the familiar saurian pattern associated with "Nessie" and most lake monsters although, according to Gilbert Whiteley, a naturalist, the bunyip has been thought to have been "an extinct marsupial otterlike animal, rumours of whose existence have been handed down in aboriginal legends, the latter confused and corrupted with crocodiles in the north of Australia and seals in the south".

And so the case rests. Are the lake monsters descendants of prehistoric animals such as the plesiosaurus, or are they merely massive variants of familiar creatures such as seals, sea lions, eels and the like? What is significant is that no monster has, as yet, been captured and put on the dissecting table.

It is also true that a sensational report of one alleged monster may trigger off a mass psychological reaction among people resulting in many reports of further monsters. It could well be that in the long term lake monsters will prove to be the domain of the psychologist rather than the zoologist. Perhaps the mind of man needs concepts of monsters, ghosts, yeti, vampires, werewolves and the like to support the need for faith in a supreme being, force or deity representing security and safety.

It is curious that in this new space age the two basic psychological drives have achieved an uneasy blend in the form of UFOs, not one of which, like the lake and sea monsters, has ever been captured and examined in a scientific laboratory. Nevertheless, Nessie and its world-wide relatives are doubtless here to stay.

SEA MONSTERS AND USOs

If water monsters are to exist and thrive anywhere, the vast and salt seas of the world must offer a safer and more nourishing environment than fresh-water inland lakes. There is evidence that this is so. Sightings are fewer, but that is hardly surprising, for the chances of encounter in the wide expanses of the oceans are statistically more remote, and the chances of satisfactory identification are far more difficult because of the longer distances involved in most alleged sightings. Thus, a remote object seen surfacing on ocean or sea which cannot readily be defined is, in the jargon of today, referred to as a USO – Unidentified Submarine Object – i.e., the "inner space" version of "outer space" UFOs.

Large sea serpents, generically known as the Great Sea Serpent, have been seen by mariners throughout the world for centuries. They appear to have been more commonly sighted in the days of the sailing ships, which made little noise, compared with the throbbing engines of modern powered ocean-going ships. Nevertheless, recent eyewitness reports of encounters are also impressive. Whether the creatures observed were truly enormous snake-like serpents without fins or limbs, or other strange animals (USOs) from the deep, is only too often a matter for speculation. Once more, as in the case of lake monsters, no such animals have ever been captured for scientific examination. One must form a judgement by evaluating the steady accumulation of evidence.

The following incidents appear to be authentic and all make particular reference to a very long neck. Even so, such sea monsters that have been recorded tend to fall into one of two types: reptile and saurian, the first having a smooth and finless body and the other the classic humped body not unlike that of the Loch Ness monster. Both, however, are generally of a much larger size than inland lake monsters.

On 7 December, 1905, some distance off the coast of Brazil and just below the Equator, the steam yacht *Valhalla* was engaged in a series of zoological exploration of little-known islands in three oceans. In the morning of that day Mr Michael John Nicoll, a naturalist, and Mr E. G. B. Meade-Waldo saw "a most extraordinary creature about 100 yards from the ship and moving in the same direction but very much slower . . ." At first only a dorsal fin was visible – projecting about two feet above the water and about four feet long; it was a brown-black colour and resembled "a gigantic piece of ribbon seaweed".

Under the water they could see a massive brownish-black patch, but were not able to make out the shape of the creature. The fin kept dipping below water level. Suddenly an "eel-like neck, about six feet long and the thickness of a man's thigh, having a head shaped like that of a turtle" emerged in front of the fin. The head and neck threshed the water with a wriggling movement, after which the creature fell so far astern that it could no longer be clearly seen.

On the following morning at 2 a.m. a great commotion nearly 150 yards from the yacht was observed. The moonlight was bright enough for the crew to see something moving slightly faster than the ship, but there was so much turbulent wash that they could not see the creature itself. It looked as if "a submarine was going along just below the surface". They agreed it could not be a whale. After a few minutes it disappeared. The creature was, they decided, the Great Sea Serpent, but "it was not a reptile that we saw but a mammal" (because of the soft rubberlike fin).

In his book *The Leviathans*, Tim Dinsdale, of Loch Ness monster fame, remarks that the Great Sea Serpent may in fact be a type of gigantic long-necked seal (or Pinniped), and the head, described "like that of a a turtle" should be noted. A full report of the incident was given to the British Zoological Society and published in its Proceedings on 10 October, 1906.

The reference to a submarine is of interest, and one wonders how many submarine periscopes, with the bulk of the craft submerged, may have been misinterpreted as the rearing head of a sea serpent or monster. To be on the safe side the *Valhalla* encounter should perhaps come under the heading of "USO".

While on the subject of submarines, the story of H.M.S. *Hilary* is worth listing. This was an armed merchant cruiser of 6,000 tons sunk by a German submarine in the Atlantic on 25 May, 1917. A full account of the incident, written by her commander, Captain F. W. Dean, R.N., was published in *Herbert Strang's Annual* in 1920.

The *Hilary* was in Icelandic waters one calm morning in May, 1917, when the lookout reported "something large on the surface". A submarine was suspected, but from the bridge the captain saw that it was a living creature, though not a whale. It was nevertheless a suitable subject for anti-submarine gun practice, and he called up three of his six-pounder gun crews – then, on second thoughts, held fire and decided to move in and take a closer look at the unidentified creature.

At a range of 30 yards he observed that "the head was about the shape of but somewhat larger than that of a cow, though with no visible protrusions such as horns or ears, and was black, except for the front of the face which could clearly be seen to have a strip of whitish flesh very like a cow has between its nostrils." As the ship passed, the head raised itself two or three times, but seemed unperturbed. Apart from the head and dorsal fin, no part of the animal showed above water, but the top edge of the neck was level with the surface, and its "snake-like" movements could be clearly seen – "it curved to almost a semicircle as the creature moved its head round to follow us with its eyes". The dorsal fin, about four feet high, was "thin and flabby".

Later the navigator estimated the full length of the animal's neck at not less than 20 feet, and the total length of the creature at some 60 feet. Having completed observation, the captain took the *Hilary* to a range of 1,200 yards, turned the ship about, and opened fire. The creature remained passive as the first two shells straddled their target, but the third shell was a direct hit. There was a tremendous commotion and lashing of water for several seconds, and then the creature sank. As gun practice it may have been effective, but ironically the *Hilary* was torpedoed by a German submarine two days later. The crew managed to take to the lifeboats.

The first lieutenant, despite the sudden and unexpected German attack, had already packed his personal belongings in a small brown bag. When questioned about this he admitted to a belief in the old sailors' superstitions about sea serpents and was certain that after the killing of the unfortunate creature the *Hilary* would never reach port again, so he had packed his valuables in preparation for the inevitable disaster. The ship's log-book was lost at the time of sinking.

A genuine sea serpent or a USO? That, on balance, is a matter for conjecture.

A more direct contact was made with a monster in the waters of the Great Barrier Reef of Australia, a coral formation 1,250 miles long and up to 300 miles wide. It is a favourite location for underwater photographers and skin-divers. The following incident, centred on a French travel-photographer, Robert le Serrec, and a young Sydney skin-diver, Henk de Jong, was reported in *Everybody's Magazine*, Sydney, on 31 March, 1965. While crossing the bay to Hayman Island in an 18-foot motor-launch in December, 1964, they observed a huge dark shape, rather like a tree, lying in the shallow water. Coming closer they saw a large head at one end of a body about 70 feet long.

The creature lay motionless as, with considerable trepidation, they circled it quietly in the boat, the engine cut back to idling speed. There was a large white patch on its body which looked like a wound. Moving in closer, they saw two white eyes in the head of what appeared to be a giant snake. Henk took to the dinghy while Serrec filmed him circling above the monster, which still did not move. The two men then decided to go underwater with one ciné camera to examine and film the monster. The big wound in its side indicated that it might be dead.

In the water their enthusiasm waned somewhat, but pride would not permit retreat. They advanced smoothly with their flippers to within 20 feet of the serpent. The head was about four feet high with jaws about four feet wide. The white eyes were in fact pale green, and the creature's skin dark brown, without scales. There were neither fins nor spines. The inside

of the mouth was whitish and the teeth rather small. The body
was about two and a half feet thick over a length of about 25
feet, then slowly tapering to a narrow tail.

Serrec later wrote: "I started the camera, and the head rose
from the sand. The mouth opened menacingly several times.
Moving with effort, the front of the great creature began to
turn towards us . . . and after filming for a short while longer, I
made for the surface with Henk by my side. We swam frantically towards the boat . . ."

Back on the boat they searched the area for the monster, but
it had disappeared into deep water. The large wound in its
side was about five feet long and looked as if the flesh had been
torn out by teeth almost to the spine. The men concluded that
the creature had been struck by a ship and then constantly
plagued by fish and sharks tearing flesh from the open wound.
It probably sought shelter in the shallow water of the bay.

A more conventional sea-serpent story appeared in *Everybody's Magazine* a few months later. Mr Boyd Lee, a well-
known Barrier Reef fisherman, and a friend watched a giant
turtle floating idly on the surface of the lagoon. The turtle was
moving its flippers and looking down into the water rather
expectantly, as if something were about to happen. It was not
disappointed.

In the words of Boyd Lee: "Seconds later something did
happen. A mighty head that resembled a giant snake came out
of the water and struck once, but only once, at the turtle. Then
the turtle and the vast head that had engulfed it disappeared.
That turtle must have weighed 500 pounds . . . We didn't
investigate. We made off at the double – that darn thing was
capable of picking any of us off the deck on the boat."

Nearer home, a sea serpent was observed off the coast of
Suffolk by a Mrs Sibyl Armstrong who had rented a bungalow
at Thorpness for one month in the summer of 1961. In the
early evening, Mrs Armstrong, the governess and the cook
were eating supper in a room with french doors overlooking
the beach and sea when she saw what appeared to be the head
of a man swimming, but it was moving at great speed and was
too big to be a man's head. Going outside for a better view she
was surprised to see a long length of snake-like body behind
the head. She was joined by the other women, and they ran
along the cliff-top to keep pace with the strange creature. At the
end of the beach was a large sandbank on to which the mon-

ster pulled itself; it now had its back to them. The front part went over the sandbank, where it beat the water violently with fins or flippers, while the rear part was still in the water on the beach side, and then the beating ceased and the whole body slid into the water on the far side of the bank.

It all happened so quickly that Mrs Armstrong could not recall seeing the tail end of the creature, but the body, which looked black in the water, was a tawny sandy colour on the sandbank. The length of the monster was about the same as five fishermen's rowing boats in line. Mrs Armstrong later remarked: "It was a marvellous sight . . . and the agility with which the monster crossed the sandbank makes me realize they are not completely helpless on land."

One of the most dedicated researchers into sea serpents is Dr Bernard Heuvelmans of Belgium. His book, *In the Wake of the Sea Serpents*, published in 1969, contains nearly 600 reports of sightings and encounters. Of these about forty-eight cases can be regarded as positive sightings, and thirty or so as probabilities; the remainder are open to speculation or alternative interpretation. The following examples are of interest in that they hardly diverge from the usual pattern of long-necked single creature sightings which is today familiar enough to become almost a cliché.

There have been very few encounters reported in the Mediterranean, but in 1889 the captain of a British ship passing between Gibraltar and Algeria saw what he thought were two masts sticking out of the water, probably from a wrecked vessel. Inspection through a telescope, however, revealed two animals, partly surfaced, between 25 and 30 feet long. Both had long necks, and the head of one projected some five feet above the sea level, while the other was raised about one foot. They were dark brown to grey in colour.

In 1893 a sea serpent was observed by another British ship, the *Umfuli*, near the Mauritanian coast. This incident was recorded in the ship's log, which is seldom done because of a maritime superstition that encounters with sea serpents should not be mentioned for fear of subsequent disaster to the vessel. This creature was 80 feet long with three humps and smooth brown skin; it looked like "a hundred-ton gun partly submerged". Toothed jaws could be discerned. One passenger had a camera with him but was "too excited to use it" (cameras in those days were big, took a lot of setting up and required long exposures, so he would hardly have had time to use it anyway, as the serpent was moving at around 10 knots). Once again it had a long 15-foot neck.

In the South Atlantic in 1910, the first officer of the *Potsdam* saw an enormous sea serpent at least 120 feet long and moving fast. It was black (but whitish underneath) and occasionally would raise its head up to 10 feet above water level. When it dived he saw a flat wide tail with a forked end.

Two detailed reports of sightings are of particular interest in that they demonstrate a high degree of physical correlation from opposite sides of the world. The first occurred in Tasmania in April, 1913, was reported to the Tasmanian Secretary of Mines, and later appeared in a London newspaper. A Mr Oscar Davies, a prospector, and a friend were walking along a lonely beach near Macquarie one late evening when they noticed a dark shape under the sand-dunes. As they approached a large animal arose, looked at them, sped down to the sea and dived out of sight. It was described thus:

> Fifteen feet long . . . very small head, only about the size of a kangaroo dog. It had a thick arched neck, passing gradually into the barrel of the body. It had no definite tail and fins. It was furred . . . resembling that of a horse of chestnut colour. It had four distinct legs (and) travelled by bounding – that is, by arching its back and gathering up its body so that the footprints of the forefeet were level with those of the hind feet. These showed circular impressions with a diameter (measured) of nine inches, and the marks of claws, about seven inches long, extending outwards from the body. There was no evidence for or against webbing . . . The creature travelled very fast. Its height, standing on four legs, would be from three feet six inches to four feet.

The other incident took place in August, 1919, in the Orkney Islands where a Scottish lawyer, Mr J. Mackintosh Bell, was holidaying as crew member of a fishing boat. Near Hoy, according to Bell: "About 20 to 30 yards from the boat a long neck as thick as an elephant's foreleg, all rough looking like an elephant's hide, was sticking up. On top of this was the head, which was much smaller in proportion, but of the same colour. The head was like that of a dog, coming sharp to the nose. The eyes were black and small, and the whiskers were black. The neck stuck about five to six feet, possibly more, out of the water.

"The animal was very shy, and kept pushing its head up

then pulling it down, but never going quite out of sight ... Then it disappeared, and I said 'If it comes up again I'll take a snapshot of it.' Sure enough it did come up and I took as I thought a snap of it, but on looking at the camera shutter I found it had not closed owing to its being swollen, so I did not get the photo. I then said 'I'll shoot it' (with my .303 rifle) but the skipper would not hear of it in case I wounded it, and it might attack us."

A point of interest is the number of photographers who fail to photograph these monsters, and the numbers of photographs which, when taken, are obscure and ill-defined (rather like pictures of UFOs). Equally interesting is the evidential fact that the first reaction of so many human observers when confronted with such an enormous creature (which appears to be quite harmless and diffident) is to shoot it. But such are the ways of photographers and homo sapiens (leaving aside the genuine and humane researchers who pursue scientific integrity).

Mr Bell added to his report some physical details of the sea serpent. Its neck was six to seven feet long, and the body could not be seen when the neck was straight up but was covered by water. One could detect the "paddles" causing the water to ripple. When swimming, the creature's body to the end of the tail flippers was about 12 feet in length, and if the neck were extended to eight feet the overall length would reach some 20 feet. The neck was roughly one foot in diameter and the head, "very like a black retriever", some six by four inches broad, with short black whiskers. The circumference of the body was about eleven feet.

Reports of sea-monster encounters over the centuries, as with inland lake monsters, run into three figures, if not four. Some are more spectacular and dramatic than others in the particular circumstances of encounter, but the important point is the monsters themselves. With or without humps, whether small or large, nearly all seem to have long swanlike necks with small heads set approximately at a right-angle to the vertically extended neck. Not all have massive bodies. There is little positive evidence that they are savage and aggressive – at least so far as humans are concerned. Nevertheless, they do form a hard foundation for maritime superstitions.

On the evidence (but it is largely hearsay and circumstantial evidence) one has to accept the existence of sea serpents. They are less strange to human eyes that the squid or the octopus or the giant Japanese marine spider crabs. On the other hand, squids, octopuses and giant crabs can be captured, dissected, analysed and even eaten – which no sea serpent ever has been. In effect, therefore, we are still dealing with a creature which may well be a particular outsize version of one of several marine animals familiar to us all. It is necessary also to make due allowance for what one might term the "angler's catch" syndrome – in which the fish hooked in the river by the enthusiastic angler grows bigger and bigger every time he retells his story.

The trouble is that the vast majority of monster sightings have been made by just one or a few people, and what is lacking is mass corroboration. Would the eye-witness accounts stand up in a court of law under stringent cross-examination? If there were a thousand witnesses to any one sighting then a barrister would be a happy man, but such is not the case.

In the famous instruction of Mrs Beeton, "First take one dozen eggs . . ." At present we have not taken even one monster, let alone a dozen; to mix metaphors, "a bird in the hand is worth . . ." etc.

Sea serpents and monsters, and lake monsters, are none the less a valid mystery. That they exist can hardly be doubted; the mystery lies in their true zoological identification. They may indeed be surviving relics of the prehistoric saurians – on the other hand they may not. One day, perhaps tomorrow, we shall finally acquire the true facts and comprehend the reality.

THE DAY OF THE ICE MAN

Ever since Darwin published his works on evolution and the variation of species, anthropologists, zoologists and scientists have been seeking the "Missing Link", the hypothetical ape-man that allegedly bridged the gap between monkeys and humans in the complex evolutionary tree. Remains of Neanderthal man have been discovered, the earliest and perhaps most important of which were at Neanderthal, Germany, in 1856 (a male skeleton) and at Gibraltar (female skull) in 1848. Other skulls and parts of skeletons have been found in Europe, Asia Minor, and the East.

The nearest approach to a missing link seems to be the fossiled remains of *Pithecanthropus erectus*, discovered in Java in 1891, though whether this was in fact the ape-like ancestor common to both the modern great apes (Pongids) and modern man (Hominids) is still a matter of debate. All remains generally are dated as Upper Pleistocene, late Early and early Middle Paleolithic form, and some, on carbon dating, go back as far as one and a half million years.

True, the skull and skeletal structures of the Pongids and the Hominids are basically similar, although there is considerable diversity in the proportions of skull and limbs. Nevertheless, there is today a growing tendency to regard Hominid man as a separate creation from the Pongid ape. The famous "Piltdown man" might have provided an acceptable link, but that turned out to be a clever fraud – there was no such man.

All arguments and theories to date have been based on bone
– whether skulls or skeletal. The chances of finding a mum-
mified "missing link", complete with dehydrated flesh, skin,
and hair, are nil. Yet in 1969 a most astonishing report was
published in the U.S. magazine *Argosy* – a complete and well-
preserved body of a "missing link" had been discovered embedded in a block of ice!

The article in question was written by Ivan T. Sanderson,
Argosy's Science Editor, and published in the May, 1969, issue
of the journal. It was luridly illustrated by large photographs
of the ape-man taken through the transparent ice block in
which the body was entombed. Sanderson made this spectacular claim: "He's the greatest anthropological find in history –
and he was alive less than five years ago!" The dead creature
was nicknamed "Bozo".

The news of Bozo's existence came to Sanderson via a telephone call to his office in January, 1969. The caller was a
Minneapolis man, not named, who described himself as a
zoologist engaged in the business of importing and export-
ing reptiles. Sanderson considered him authentic.

The caller said he had just returned from the well-known
annual Chicago Stock Fair, and while there had seen a remarkable side-show which featured just one large glass-en-
closed coffin containing a massive ice block. Areas of the ice
surfaces were smooth and clear and other parts frosted and
somewhat opaque, but under the bright display lights the six-
foot hairy thing frozen into the ice was impressively visible.
The carcass of the dead thing was unmistakably an ape-man or
a man-ape. The body was strongly built and covered in dark
hair about three inches long.

The Minneapolis caller suggested that Sanderson should go
and examine it because he, the caller, was a student of "ABS-
Mery", i.e. Abominable Snowman Related Information, and
was convinced that this was the real thing, although the side-
show billed the exhibit as a "mystery".

Sanderson himself had a keen interest in research into oddities such as monsters, yeti, the missing link and similar im-
ponderables. In addition, in his role as Science Editor, he
frequently received letters and calls on these matters, nearly all
of which were from cranks perpetrating hoaxes or fraud, or just
seeking spurious publicity. His attitude was therefore necessarily cynical, but he too had once collected animals professio-

nally for zoos and museums, and something about that Minneapolis call struck him as genuine – or at least having a foundation in fact.

Coincidentally (and there is much coincidence in this
strange story) in another room in the same building was Dr
Bernard Heuvelmans D.Sc., of the Royal Institute of Natural
Sciences, Belgium; Fellow of the Zoological Society, London;
plus various other academic qualifications in Belgium and
Rome; and author of the books *On the Track of Unknown Animals* (1962) and *In the Wake of Sea Serpents* (1969). The work of
Dr Heuvelmans is referred to in other chapters of this volume
dealing with the Loch Ness monster, lake monsters in general,
and sea serpents – matters in which he is recognized as an
expert by a number of scientists.

Precisely what Dr Heuvelmans was doing in January, 1969,
in the *Argosy* organization is not explained, but it was
undoubtedly connected with his twenty years of work in the
strange field of the animate anomalies of the living world.
Apparently he agreed to accompany Sanderson on a visit to
view, inspect, measure and photograph the thing in the ice
block in the glass coffin.

The *Argosy* report does not disclose precisely where they
went in the station wagon which had been packed with jour-
nalistic and recording equipment, but it was "west of the Mississippi". Possibly Sanderson suspected that it might be a side-
show publicity trick, although the reason he gives for main-
taining secrecy is "because I know only too well what publicity
can do, so I respect the plea of the gentleman in whose care
this exhibit is stored during the winter season – especially because it is on his private property."

After a stopover in a motel, the two men eventually arrived
"by backtracking and using a compass" at a ranch-type house
with a snow-covered garden edged by a grove of conifer trees.
Near the house was a big trailer containing the "thing". They
were invited to stay by their gentlemanly host as house guests,
and very soon "tottered out to the trailer to look at the thing".

And so we come to Bozo himself, who, according to Sanderson, had been alive within the previous five years. The body,
visible through the ice, was that of a six-foot tall male
"human", covered in stiff dark hair between two and four
inches in length, apart from the face, palms of hands, soles of
feet and pubis. All fingers and toes had nails, not claws.

Bozo's build was sturdy, with wide shoulders tapering to narrow hips. He had virtually no neck, so that his head seemed to have grown out of the top of his broad chest. His legs were of normal length for a tall man, but his arms were longer than usual. The hands were perhaps the most striking feature of the corpse – very large Humanid hands but with a long slender thumb (almost as long as the index finger). In the case of the toes ("stubby and chubby") it was the little toe that was almost as big as the others. The big toe was not opposed to the others, as is the case with apes (or Pongids) which suggests that Bozo was Humanid. The width of each foot across the toes was more than ten inches.

As for Bozo's face, it was, according to Sanderson, "gruesome". Both eyeballs had been "blown out of their sockets", and this was "enhanced" [sic] by a large quantity of blood frozen into the ice around the face. Dr Heuvelmans's view was that Bozo had been shot through the right eye, and the impact had shattered the back of his skull and forced the left eye out of its socket. Apparently the left eyeball was just visible "to some, at least" in the bloodstained ice.

The two men were, however, carrying out a morphological rather than a pathological study of the corpse. The most outstanding feature of the face was the large pug nose, bulldog rather than gorilla-like (the gorilla does not have a nose as generally understood). The circular nostrils, quite large, pointed straight forward, which was considered odd. The mouth was a little wide with no clear sign of lips, and on one side which was partly open two small teeth could be seen, presumably the upper canine and the first premolar. Folds and wrinkles of the skin around the mouth below the cheeks were of the kind commonly seen in an old, heavy-jowled human.

All this, plus the stench of rotting flesh escaping from some faulty insulation of the coffin, was enough to convince Sanderson and his colleague that here was the "genuine article" – the "missing link".

Photographs were taken from all angles on the first day, and on the next day the two men, using suitable rules and instruments, made careful measurements of the corpse. Bozo's left arm, incidentally, was seen to be badly broken and there were indications of another bullet wound in his chest, but it must be stressed that these were visual observations made through glass

and ice and it was not possible to examine the body physically.

Many might consider it significant that although Bozo's
body in its ice coffin had been publicly exhibited for nearly
two years in various states in the U.S. at no time did it attract
the attention of scientists, zoologists, anthropologists or even
doctors. No attempt was ever made to penetrate the ice block
to obtain even minute samples of flesh or blood for microscopic
and genetic examination. True, the exhibit was in the form of
a fairground side-show, but even so one would think that some
serious professional interest would have been aroused during
that time. Sanderson's explanation is that practically nobody
in those scientific categories attended the exhibit. One wonders
how he could possibly know that, just as one wonders how and
why the anonymous man from Minneapolis was apparently
the first to realize the sensational nature of missing link Bozo,
and why he chose to telephone *Argosy* instead of the daily newspapers and periodicals such as *Time* and *Newsweek*.

Even more obscure is the matter of Bozo's origin. The care-
taker of the corpse "west of the Mississippi" reportedly said
that it was bought by an American in Hong Kong where the
block of ice (containing Bozo), wrapped in a large plastic sheet
or bag, was being stored in a commercial deep-freeze unit. The
bag and its contents weighed over two and a half tons, and this
was presumably shipped back to the U.S., no doubt under
continuing refrigeration.

But how did Bozo get into a Hong Kong deep-freezer in the
first place? Here we run into a variety of different stories, all
apparently related by the Hong Kong salesman to the American buyer. Only two are quoted by Sanderson, though other
versions are referred to.

One tale is that Bozo was found, in his block of ice, floating
in international waters in the Bering Sea by a Russian ship.
The block was recovered and stored in the ship's hold, but in
an unnamed Chinese port the authorities found the specimen
and took it away into Communist China. Some months later
Bozo, still in his ice block, turned up in Hong Kong. In another story the ice block was discovered by a Japanese whaling
vessel in the sea of Kamchatka, taken to Japan and then sold
to the deep-freezer man in Hong Kong.

It seems odd that neither the Chinese nor the Japanese took
the trouble to open the ice block in order to examine the fan-

tastic ape-man inside. Sanderson points out that the names of the Russian and Japanese ships involved were never divulged and that "nothing further is known".

In America, however, experts were said to have inspected the astonishing freight when it arrived in the country – the whole thing still weighing over two and a half tons. They reportedly took hair and blood samples (perhaps by drilling a narrow hole through the ice) and discovered that the blood contained both red and white corpuscles, which is hardly surprising, while the hair was similar to that of Mongolian Humanids rather than any other known man or animal, which probably *is* surprising to Mongolians.

No samples of either hair or blood were (in 1969) available, nor were any copies of scientific reports on Bozo which must have been made by the examining experts. Bozo, it seems, was "owned" by somebody who preferred to remain anonymous, and who wished to exhibit him for another year before donating him to a learned institution, probably still decomposing in his block of ice. So far as is known, there is no record that this was ever done, and Bozo's whereabouts today are an enigma.

Sanderson mentions that despite "furious resistance" to any attempt to publicize the discovery of the ape-man, he was in fact shown reports of it in trade magazines, though he does not name them. Bozo's owner, it seems, did not want to fool the public; he even cynically thought that Bozo in ice was some kind of Oriental fakery, and therefore, with commendable honesty, billed the exhibit as a mystery. Nobody could quarrel with that sentiment.

According to Sanderson, the technical reports on the ice man already amounted to a sizeable volume, although they had not yet then been published, but he had no doubt that they would indeed appear in due course in technical journals. At that time he did not wish to burden his readers with all the details. He did, however, stress that Bozo was no "phony Chinese trick" or "art" work. The smell of rotting flesh alone proved that. Finally, he expressed the hope that one day Bozo would be given "the homage which he, of all Hominids ever born, manifestly deserves".

The *Argosy* report ends with the comments of a number of prominent anthropologists and primatologists, who based their opinions on the preliminary reports submitted by Ivan Sanderson and Dr Bernard Heuvelmans, and inspection of photographs and drawings.

Dr Carleton S. Coon (Professor of Anthropology, Harvard) thought Bozo was a whole corpse and not some composite or model, and was a Hominid "though displaying a number of most unexpected anatomical features". Dr John R. Napier (Primate Biologist, Smithsonian University) wrote: "Assuming its validity, it is quite clear (to me) that the specimen belongs to neither family (Pongid or Hominid)." He would prefer to create a new family which might be called "Parahumans" evolved from a common hominoid stock.

Professor W. C. Osman-Hill (Yerkes Regional Primate Centre, Emory University, Atlanta) was more cautious and objective: "I really do not know what to make of this one except that with the limited data available it strikes me as more Pongid than Hominid, but be that as it may no pains should be spared to obtain this (for proper examination) before it becomes irrecoverable for one reason or another."

Professor George A. Agogino (Paleo-Indian Institute, Eastern New Mexico University, Portales, New Mexico) decided that the visible parts of the body in the photographs suggested a "Homo" male of unknown time period. He added: "While it is impossible to rule out fraud, the structure of the ice and the complexity of making a composite animal with scientific continuity makes this unlikely." He considered that while the body seemed to exhibit both Humanid and Pongid features, the human factors predominated – "It is possible we are dealing with a modern human anomaly, although absolute determination must wait until the body can undergo chemical and physical analysis under laboratory conditions."

Finally, one must consider some of the positive points made by Dr Bernard Heuvelmans himself in a long comment which began: "For the first time in history, a fresh corpse of Neanderthal-like man has been found. It means that this form of Hominid, thought to be extinct since prehistoric times, is still living today.

"The long search for rumoured live 'ape-men' or missing links has at last been successful. This was not accomplished by expeditions to far away places and at great expense, but by the accidental discovery, in this country, of a corpse preserved in ice."

Dr Heuvelmans lists the main physical characteristics of

Bozo, which have been previously described in this chapter, and states that they agree with what is known of classical Neanderthalers. He then categorically pronounces: "It has been established that: (1) It cannot be an artificial, entirely manufactured object (it is actually decomposing); (2) It cannot be a composite, produced by assembling anatomical parts taken from living beings of different species (if the face looks merely unusual, both hands and feet are unknown in any zoological form); (3) It cannot be a normal individual belonging to any of the known races of modern man . . . (4) It cannot be an abnormal individual or freak (because of the nature of the growth of hair in certain parts of the body); (5) The specimen cannot have been preserved in ice for centuries or millennia – this is physically impossible."

One could, perhaps, challenge that final statement in certain respects, but Dr Heuvelmans then makes a further positive statement, not mentioned previously in Sanderson's report, which casts a new light on the entire mystery, namely: "The peculiar structure of the ice and the presence of a pool of blood around the head show that, immediately after death, the corpse was placed in a freezer tank filled with water and artificially frozen." He does not suggest, however, that this was done in Hong Kong, nor does he mention the Russian and Japanese ships, one of which allegedly hauled aboard Bozo in his ice coffin.

He sums up thus: "This specimen is a contemporary representative of an unknown form of Hominid, most probably a relic of the Neanderthal type. The belief, based on strong testimonial evidence, that small, scattered populations of Neanderthals survive, has been held for years by some scientists, mostly Russian and Mongolian.

"A full scientific report of the present finding, with a description of this form of living Hominid under the name of *Homo pongoides* (i.e. Apelike Man) has been published in the *Bulletin of the Royal Institute of Natural Sciences of Belgium* (Vol. 45, No. 4)."

And that, more or less, is the story of the coming and the going of the ice man, though where he truly came from and where he is now remain a mystery – and, in part, a mystery of the sea. Was he an artefact, with thick hair glued on to assembled anatomical body parts to conceal the joints, and then frozen in ice to prevent detailed physical examination, or was he truly a

relic of a prehistoric missing link still surviving today somewhere in the world in limited numbers, like the legendary but
unproven yeti, or for that matter the Loch Ness monster(s)?
The "expert reports" written when Bozo arrived in the U.S.
have never been published as Sanderson hoped, so far as can
be ascertained, and if his body was ever presented to an institution or university as was promised then there has been a
remarkable silence and a dearth of further information.

Spectres
of the Sea

SEA PHANTOMS

It would have been better for Cornelius Vanderdecken to have prayed to God, instead of cursing Him. Unfortunately for him and his crew, he had a reputation for godlessness and blasphemy to maintain. So, instead of praying, he cursed; and they say he has been doing so ever since.

Vanderdecken was a seventeenth-century Dutch sea captain, of the toughest school. He was merciless to his ship, his crew and himself. Where a more rational skipper would have run for shelter, or hove-to, or at least trimmed sail in the face of storm, Vanderdecken pushed on regardless of hazard. As he faced into the tempest he shouted his challenges to it, taunting it with its inability to overwhelm his vessel.

By the law of averages, a master of that period, in so relatively frail a craft, should soon have been overpowered by the elements he scorned, and dashed to a watery grave. But by all accounts, Cornelius Vanderdecken holds the record for longevity of voyage; for there are those who say he sails still, and will do so for ever.

It was during a voyage from Batavia to Holland that he sealed his unique fate. The headwinds which were the bane of sailing vessels increased in force as he neared the Cape of Good Hope, at length halting his progress entirely. For nine weeks he tacked and tacked about, determined to find some freak air that would sneak him round. He found none, and at last his patience left him completely. He dropped to his knees on deck

and accused God of obstructing his ship's passage from personal malevolence. He swore that he would not be outdone,
though. He would round the Cape, if it took him until Judgment Day to achieve it.

Then he sprang up and shook his fists towards the heavens
and burst into blasphemous song. At once, from the blackness
of the night, a brilliant light shone down, as if directed by
unseen powers. Down its beams there seemed to float a daz-
zling being, coming to rest on the ship's poop deck. The sailors
were convinced it was the Holy Ghost, or at the very least an
angel. They knelt down and prayed for forgiveness. Captain
Vanderdecken did not join them. He did not even remove his
hat, but stood where he was, regaling the celestial visitor with a
selection of a very earthly oaths and curses. It displayed no
shock, but made him a graceful, gentle salutation. Exasperated
beyond his small limit, Vanderdecken dragged his pistol from
his belt. As the crew stared with new horror he ordered the
being to get off his ship. He fired as he spoke.

The being was untouched. It spoke quietly: "Captain Vanderdecken, you have taken an oath to sail until Judgment Day.
So be it. For your blasphemies, you shall do so. You shall neither eat, drink, nor sleep, nor ever see your home port again.
You shall continue to sail the Seven Seas, a portent of disaster
to all who see you. God is not mocked, Captain Vanderdecken!"

And that is the supposed origin of the world's best-known
ghost, the *Flying Dutchman.* In Wagner's operatic version of the
legend he was permitted to go on land every seven years, and
would be redeemed if he should meet a woman capable of
giving him her love, which is what the village maiden Senta
proves to be. In German legend he is named von Falkenberg
and sails eternally in northern waters, alone in his crewless
ship, casting dice against the Devil for his soul.

Sir Walter Scott's explanation of the phenomenon is more
prosaic. It suggests that the original ship was a bullion carrier
whose crew mutinied and took her over. But plague broke out
among them, and they were turned away from every port they
approached, thus having to sail on until all died.

It is an often-repeated fact that sailormen have always been
the most superstitious of humans. It is easy to understand why.
Even today they are more affected by the mighty elements of
air and sea than any others. In the "old days" of not so long

ago they were isolated for months at a time from the commonplace things of shore life, displacing reality from their minds. The sea has its own natural phenomena: the ghostly fluorescence of the bow-wake in certain waters, the freak effects of electrical storms, the uncanny sobs and cries of wind in rigging, the tricks the moon can play through a swirling vapour of mist, the crackle and glow of St Elmo's Fire at the mast tops in certain sorts of rough weather.

Sailors' yarns were a prime means of relieving monotony during a voyage, and a good spinner of them was rewarded by his mess mates. There was reward, too, in the form of ale and tobacco, for Jack when he came ashore and passed on the stories to avid hearers, claiming offhandedly that they had been his own experiences, and enlarging and embroidering them for as long as his mug would be replenished.

And if there are real ghosts, the case for them persisting at sea is perhaps stronger than on land. It is widely held that the decline of the visible ghost has been due to, or hastened by, the glare of electric light, which their frail outlines could not survive. There is plenty of electric light in most ships today; but they move like bright torches through great wastes of darkness, in which who knows what is lurking.

Consider this first-hand description of the *Flying Dutchman*, and then the blunt, no-nonsense nature of the man who recorded it in a ship's log:

"The *Flying Dutchman* crossed our bows. A strange red light, as of a phantom ship all aglow, in the midst of which light the masts, spars and sails of a brig two hundred yards distant stood up in strong relief... On arriving there, no vestige nor any sign whatever of any material ship was to be seen either near or right away to the horizon, the night being clear and the sea calm. Thirteen persons altogether saw her."

The writer in the log of the *Bacchante*, sailing from Melbourne to Sydney in 1881, would in due course become King George the Fifth of England, a sailor king not noted for fanciful ideas. If he said he saw the *Flying Dutchman*, along with twelve shipmates, we may take it that he did, or that the illusion was a very convincing one indeed. The first of the thirteen to have spotted the ghost ship fell from the fore topmast crosstrees to his death on the deck; and the admiral aboard the

Bacchante at the time became fatally ill when they reached port. One wonders.

The future king described her as a brig, but other accounts of her have made her a sloop and a schooner. However she has appeared, sailors have shuddered and crossed themselves. One of her most frightening manifestations was in 1911, to the crew of the whaler *Orkney Belle* off Reykjavik. She rose from the waves, sails swelling in a non-existent breeze, and bore down on their vessel, seeming certain to ram her. Just in time, three bells sounded within her. She heeled sharply to starboard, and drifted silently away.

Perhaps, in the blackness of the sea night, Captain Vanderdecken sometimes finds himself being hailed by a compatriot and contemporary, Captain Bernard Fokke, a brilliant navigator with a bad reputation, of whom it was said he had a close relationship with the Devil, who ordered him to sail on for ever. The notion of two ghost ships converging briefly for a blasphemous exchange between their damned masters could have been done stirring justice by Wagner, if only it had occurred to him. But perhaps he was among those who believe that the legends of Vanderdecken and Fokke, together with a similar one concerning the two Waleran brothers of Falkenberg Castle in Lower Lorraine, are one and the same.

The Dutch, for all their respectable reputation, seem to have made their corner in ghost ships with brutal captains. Another such one was the master of the trading vessel *Palatine*, which sailed from Holland in 1752 with a load of emigrants bound for New England. He and his ruffianly crew seem to have been more preoccupied with drinking and terrorizing their passengers than looking to their seamanship, for the ship grounded on Block Island, the headquarters of wrecking gangs, who may have lured her to disaster with false lights.

The wreckers proved even worse than the sailors. They surged aboard, to knife or throw over the side any man who dared oppose them, robbing and beating the others and raping the women. Then they set the vessel on fire and left her to drift away back into the Atlantic. As she went, a woman's screams were heard coming from her. A girl – some accounts say she was a young mother with a baby – had hidden below from the violence and now was trapped aboard the blazing ship. The masts crumpled, the deck caved in, and she was seen to fall to her death, still shrieking for help. It is maintained by those who reject explanations involving natural phosphorescence that the so-called "Palatine Fire" which sometimes bathes Block Island in eerie light is rightly named.

Further north, in the Gulf of St. Lawrence, between Quebec and Newfoundland, there is said to be a colourful once-yearly spectacle of a ghost warship, originally one of those sent out by Queen Anne to fight the French. She sank under the cliffs of Cap de'Espoir, in Gaspe Bay. Each anniversary of the disaster is alleged to be marked by her reappearance, decks crowded with red-coated soldiers in mitre hats, her ports ablaze with light. In the bow stands an officer pointing landwards, his other arm round the waist of a pretty girl. The lights quickly fade, the vessel gives a heave, capsizes and vanishes.

The Gulf of St. Lawrence is also the haunting-place of a burning ship. The *Packet Light* was wrecked in those waters, too, and reappears in the form of a ball of fire.

There are ghost vessels in English waters, notably the Solway Firth, which begins the border with Scotland. The dragon-prowed galleys of Danish raiders, long ago the terror of these coasts, have been seen at nights. Two of them which had sunk at their moorings with all hands are reputedly those which reappear, manned by spectral crews. A venturesome little boat went out to investigate a sighting at about the turn of the eighteenth century. The galleys sank again as it approached and the whirl of water almost capsized the inquisitive vessel. The visitants have been left alone since.

Another Solway ghost is of a shallop which had been bearing a young bridegroom and bride across a bay, together with their attendants. A boatman, rival to its owner, caused it to sink. When it reappears it is he, in skeletal form, who is aboard, not the ghosts of those whose happiness he abruptly ended.

A sight of this manifestation, like that of the *Flying Dutchman*, is held to portend misfortune, and the same is said of some other sea ghosts. Not all, however, as Captain Rogers, of the *Society*, was lucky enough to discover in 1664 during an apparently trouble-free passage along the east coast of America, Virginia-bound. Satisfied with the weather outlook and the correctness of his course, he turned in for a night's sleep. He was awakened some time later by a cold touch on his shoulder and a voice saying, "Turn out, Captain, and look about you".

It had seemed too real to have been a dream, so he obeyed

and went on deck. Nothing appeared to be wrong, though. The *Society* was ploughing placidly on her way in a calm sea. Captain Rogers returned to his cot and his interrupted deep sleep.

But a second chilly summons came. Once more he investigated. Once more he found nothing amiss. He retired again.

The third warning was more urgent. This time the voice ordered, "Go on deck and cast the lead." There was something in the way this was spoken that made him hurry up on deck yet again. He ordered a watchman to cast the lead. To his horror, it registered only seven fathoms, instead of the deep water he had expected. Hurriedly he gave orders to anchor.

When dawn came it was seen that the *Society* lay close inshore, under the Capes of Virginia, far off the course which should have kept her out at sea. The ghostly visitor had saved her from certain destruction.

A remarkable case of spectral benevolence was recorded by the famous circumnavigator Joshua Slocum. He was a master mariner who had worked his way up from deckhand to owner of a small barque. A setback to his progress was his little craft's wrecking, reducing him to working as a hand in a Boston shipyard. After two years of this, in 1892, the kindly captain of a whaler made him a present of a beached and battered old sloop named the *Spray*. Although she had been lying abandoned for seven years, Slocum vowed that he would make her seaworthy and undertake a great voyage in her.

He personally felled a great oak tree from which to fashion for her a new keel and ribs. It took him thirteen months to build his new *Spray*, but he had made her better than new. He took aboard equipment and provisions, and, on 1 July, 1895, set sail alone in her from Yarmouth, Massachusetts, to voyage round the world.

His sturdy spirit overcame the loneliness. He took to conversing with an imaginary crewman, asking him how things were going. "All well, sir; all well," he would answer himself comfortingly. But he was glad of the real human contact which occasional landfalls brought him. The most notable of these, perhaps, was a young woman on the island of Fayal, in the Azores. For a nominal wage, she proposed, she would undertake the rest of the voyage with him as "domestic staff". Slocum politely declined, settling for the company of his imaginary crewman, whom he could summon up and dismiss as the fancy took him.

What he did accept from the generous-minded people of Fayal was an enormous white cheese and a great deal of fruit. When he was back at sea, heading for Gibraltar and settled into his solitary routine, he decided to sample the cheese. It was delicious. He nibbled and nibbled at it throughout an entire day, alternating mouthfuls of it with delicious, juicy plums. Not surprisingly, after weeks of austere dieting the combination of richnesses began to affect him. The stomach cramps turned agonizing. He realized his foolhardiness, but it was too late. The sea was getting up rough. It took him all his strength to reef his sails. He just managed to lash the helm before collapsing. Somehow he reached his cabin, and then fainted.

When he came to he could feel the *Spray* tossing about like a cork. She would need steering in the storm. It took Slocum all the effort he could muster to crawl back up on deck. And there, he saw something incredible.

The helm was already manned, by a tall man in clothing unfamiliar to Slocum. The stranger smiled and swept off his headdress, as casually as if greeting a friend in the street. Then he spoke. He was, he said, the captain of one of the fleet which Columbus had commanded on the historic voyage from Spain to the New World in 1492, *four hundred years* before Slocum had put to sea. It would be as well, he added, if Slocum were to return to his cabin and get back his strength. His little vessel would be in safe hands meanwhile. Indigestion being the better part of valour, the lone sailor accepted gratefully and asked his ancient helmsman if he would stay with him until next day. There came cheerful agreement, together with a jocular warning that cheese and plums were not an ideal mixture, and that white cheese was better not eaten at all unless its origins were precisely known.

As history records, Joshua Slocum reached Gibraltar safely, alone.

A father and son, also engaged upon a daring small-boat adventure, had a similar experience in 1900. Captain Johansen and his fourteen-year-old boy were sailing from Gibraltar to America in the *Lotta*, with no other crew. The weather was treating them most kindly. The first eight days brought nothing but calm airs and sunshine. One morning like all the others they lay basking on deck, the boy fast asleep. Suddenly Captain Johansen heard a voice speak out clearly something he did not catch. He looked at his son. He was sleeping on, not having stirred.

Then the voice spoke again, and another, and then even more, until it became a regular chatter. It was in a language foreign to the incredulous sailor. He woke his son, and must have been rather relieved to find that he, too, could hear the voices, which went on for some time.

Two days later, young Johansen was at the helm when a gale quickly blew up. "Let go the jib-sheet!" ordered the father. The boy leaped to obey, but left hold of the tiller in order to do so. The sea at once snatched at the boat and swung it beam-on. Disaster could have followed within moments, had not the helm been grasped and swung to bring the *Lotta*'s bows to face into the waves. But it was neither of the Johansens who had acted just in time. It was a shadowy figure of a stranger, wearing rough, primitive clothing, and with an iron prop where his left leg should have been. With him there had materialized three companions. They chattered continuously among themselves, occasionally turning to the staring father and son, smiling and reassuring, but addressing them in a tongue they could not understand.

Their presence so comforted the Johansens that they both slept that night. The phantom crew were not to be seen when they woke at sunrise; but they returned with nightfall, seeming to signal to other craft which the Johansens could not see. At last the boy ventured forward to try to speak to them. They vanished instantly, and were never seen again.

Captain Johansen, a sober, sceptical man, reported these occurrences of 30 and 31 August, 1900, as solid fact.

During the First World War, one of the British submarines which failed to return to base from a routine patrol off the Dutch coastal shoals was commanded by a popular officer named Ryan – at least, that is the name used for him by the officer who recorded the story after the war. When three weeks, a month, then two months had passed, with no sign of the vessel's return, it was assumed at its base in south-east England that it had been sunk, either by accident or by the Germans.

Another submarine took up the same patrol, moving on the surface of the sea by night and submerged by day. One sunny morning her commander brought her up close to the surface and ordered the periscope raised for observation. The second officer, on periscope duty, scanned the sea around them for some moments before exclaiming suddenly: "By Jove! There's jolly old Ryan! He's waving like mad to us from the water."

The submarine was immediately surfaced. The conning-tower hatch was flung open and crewmen scrambled out, seizing lifelines to throw to the officer who had seemingly miraculously survived drowning. He was not to be seen, though.

Perhaps he had gone under in the few minutes it had taken to make ready to rescue him. But the officer who had seen him insisted that he had appeared to be in no distress in the calm sea; just his old cheerful self, his identity unmistakable. It was not wishful thinking, either, he insisted. His mind had not been on Ryan at all beforehand.

The submarine circled slowly. There was nothing to be seen, and the threat of observation from the air was too great to allow further time on the surface. They began to make way again, on the same course as earlier, preparing to dive. Suddenly, though, a dark object was spotted dead ahead. There proved to be two; and they were mines, which the submarine would certainly have struck, had not Ryan – or his spirit – brought her up to search for him, just in time to see them.

The red-bearded, one-eyed paymaster of the U.S. Navy corvette *Monongahela* was also a popular figure during the First World War. His spirit's return to the messmates with whom he had spent so many convivial hours, however, was less than welcome in its manner.

The drink, which had been largely responsible for his geniality, exacted its price at last. As he lay dying on board ship he told his brother officers, "Dear boys, you've been good to me. I love you for it, and I've loved the old ship, too. I can't bear to think of leaving you all for good, so I'll come back, if I can. You'll find me in my old cabin, No. 2 on the port side."

Out of deference to his memory – or was it superstition? – that cabin was left unoccupied for three cruises. Then it was allocated to a young new Assistant-Paymaster, who settled in comfortably for a cruise to South American waters. The mission proved peaceful, and they were homeward bound one April night, when screams brought everyone running towards Cabin 2. On the deck outside it they found the young man lying unconscious.

When he was brought round he was able to explain: "A corpse – in my berth! One eye and a red beard."

He had awakened to find himself strangely cold. In the bed with him was something chilly and wet. He pulled back the sheets to reveal the awful dead thing, with seaweed entangled in the straggling beard. The other officers crowded inside to see for themselves. There was no corpse – but the berth was still wet and contained a few strands of barnacled seaweed.

It is strange that there are not legends, engendered by the nervous fear of approaching battle, of spirits of the great naval commanders of the past appearing to urge on the sailors of more recent times to victory and glory. Nelson's shade, we are told, used to be seen walking briskly across the quadrangle of Somerset House in London, to disappear into the former Admiralty office. If so, it was probably concerned with some of that querulous business which the fretful Nelson was always urging upon his unenterprising masters. Sir Francis Drake's drum is expected to sound in warning of disaster to England; but, for all that has happened in recent years, it has not been heard lately.

And now that the traditional rum ration of the Royal Navy has been abolished, and no sea-cook would be likely to serve white cheese and plums as a dessert, the materials from which some of the ghost yarns of the sea have been concocted have been diminished.

THE HAUNTED U-BOAT

Life in a submarine is at all times uncomfortable and in war can be horrific. At best it is unnatural for human beings – thirty or forty of them – to be shut up in a steel tube beneath the sea for hours, possibly days on end in conditions so cramped that one man is practically breathing in another's face, amid a universal fug laced with reeks from the bilges, diesel oil and unwashed bodies.

The submarine (or the "steamer", as the men of the German U-boats used to call it) is in constant motion, too, slight in deep water but more and more noticeable as it reaches the surface until in heavy seas the boat pitches and shudders like a horse trying to throw its rider. Watery cascades pour down the conning tower hatch and slice over the bridge so that the men on watch have to lash themselves to supports for fear of being swept overboard. Sleep for everyone is about half the normal adult requirement.

In war of course the submariner's life is even more unpleasant. Now he has the enemy as well as the sea to cope with. The pressure hull – all that stands between him and a miserable end – is packed with delicate machinery which a depth charge, bomb, torpedo or shell can wreck beyond repair. Extreme alertness is necessary, especially when attacking or being attacked, by the captain at the periscope, the hydrophone operator listening for enemy propellor noises, the planesmen putting on the angle for diving, the men at the wheel valves blowing or flooding the tanks. Everyone knows that one small mistake on anyone's part can spell disaster, but also that when one crisis has been surmounted another may loom within hours, minutes or even seconds.

In the two world wars some men broke down under the strain and had to be discharged from the service. But most managed to shake down eventually and found the life tolerable. After all, the dangers, the discomfort were part of normal submarine life and after a patrol or two they almost became part of routine. But what if conditions were thoroughly abnormal, if events occurred that could not be ascribed to Acts of God, or accident, or the treachery of the sea, or the cunning of the enemy? What then? The men of U-boat 65 could have told us.

The term U-boat derives from the German *Unterseeboot*. At the outbreak of the First World War Germany had thirty-three of these craft with another twenty-eight building, mostly large, ocean-going submarines of 550 to 850 tons displacement, capable of intercepting Allied shipping on the high seas and wreaking havoc with Britain's supply lines. But the possibility of rich prizes off the British and Irish coasts, particularly in the Channel and the entrances to the Irish Sea, was not neglected and the construction of smaller boats with a surface speed of 13 knots, manned by 3 officers and 31 men, was going ahead. In early 1916, 24 of these, an entire flotilla, were launched at Bruges and one of them was the U-65.

Sailors were and still are to some extent superstitious, so with the U-65 it was felt proper to observe certain precautions. During construction no woman was allowed on board (at the sight of women, so an old story went, the sea grows angry), no flowers (as wreaths are made of them) and no one, for some reason, carrying a black bag, presumably a token of disaster. And of course the usual bottle had to be broken over the bows at the launching, as a libation to the gods.

All this seemed doubly necessary because suspicions about that particular boat had already been aroused. She had not yet been completed when one day at the shipyard a heavy steel girder being lowered into place slipped sideways out of its sling and crashed to the ground, killing one workman outright and pinning another, until after an hour he was released and rushed dying to hospital. Then, a few weeks later, when final adjustments were being made to the diesels, yells were heard coming from the engine room and when help arrived the sliding door in the bulkhead was found to be jammed. Ultimately, when the rescuers got through they found three men dead on the floor amid lethal, choking fumes. Strangely, an inquiry failed to establish what had happened. What sort of fumes? Carbon monoxide from the diesels? But they had not been running. Chlorine from sea water getting into the batteries? But the boat had been in dry-dock . . .

The new captain of the U-65 heard about all this, of course, and he clamped down strenuously on idle talk about "jinxes" or "hoodoos". Such chatter could easily get out of hand. But chatter feeds on facts – and there were plenty more to come.

After launching, the U-65 sailed for her trials off the Schelde Estuary in good conditions: light airs, sea Force 3, excellent visibility, just the occasional squall, the odd sea sweeping over the deck – nothing to worry about. But a submarine's first dive is always an anxious moment and before giving the signal the captain sent a rating to check something on the upper deck, perhaps to see that the breech of the gun was closed. The bridge watch later maintained that the man deliberately walked overboard, others said a sea must have caught him. Anyway, he went without a sound, apparently without effort to save himself and despite a search was never seen again.

There was only one thing for the captain to do, dive as soon as possible and help the crew to clock up a success. Then perhaps those anxious looks, the muttered words would cease. The order was given. The watchmen clattered down the conning tower, the heavy hatch cover was closed and slowly, while water poured into the tanks to remove positive buoyancy, the U-boat angled down to the sea-bed – and there she stuck, refusing to budge when compressed air was blown into the tanks to clear them. It is said that water was coming in through the pressure hull, but if there had been enough to keep the boat down it would also have drowned the crew. More likely there was a series of faults which had to be dealt with one by one. At any rate, it took the crew twelve hours to cure the trouble, by which time they were staggering about like drunkards, literally fainting for lack of oxygen. Then at last the wretched boat surfaced and they could gulp in great lungfuls of fresh air, remembering perhaps that twelve hours was considered the very maximum for which a U-boat could stay submerged. They had only just survived.

Still, this was war-time and the German people were not fighting ghosts. Jinx or no jinx the U-65 had to put to sea again and sink ships. So she returned to Bruges to load supplies for her first patrol: food, ammunition, spares, torpedoes – and when the last "tin fish" was being lowered down the forward hatch the warhead exploded. Result: five dead men, some outside, some inside the boat and others severely wounded.

While the boat, herself badly damaged, was put into dry-dock for repairs the dead were taken to Wilhelmshaven for burial, among them the second officer, known to the crew as *der Schwarze* because of his dark complexion. His real name has not come down to us, so let's call him Erich Forster.

The men were given leave while the boat was in dock, then, one evening some days later, they were coming up the gang-plank with their kit-bags to be mustered for the delayed patrol. A petty officer was counting them – 28, 29, 30, 31, yes, all correct, including new men drafted to make up the complement. But then another man appeared, thirty-two . . .

Seconds later, the P.O. was stumbling into the wardroom (a small space abaft the conning tower) where the officers were discussing plans.

"Permission to speak, sir, please!"

The captain looked up, astonished. The man was trembling and deathly pale. "What is it?"

"Sir, I've been on deck counting the men in. There should be thirty-one."

"Well . . .?"

"There aren't, sir. There's thirty-two. And the last one, sir, was . . . he was Lieutenant Forster."

The petty officer wasn't drunk, that much was obvious, and the captain already knew him as one of the steadiest men in the boat. In those dreadful twelve hours when she'd refused to surface he had gone methodically about his work, checking faults, telling the younger men that a U-boat was designed to surface and surface she surely would, in time for them all to see daylight again. A valuable man, so now the captain was going to treat him with care.

"Now come on, Brinkmann. You know perfectly well, Forster's dead."

The P.O. tried hard to recapture his reasonable self. For him this sort of behaviour was right out of character. "I know that, sir. And believe me, sir, I wasn't in a fanciful frame of

mind, or anything like that. I wasn't dwelling on the troubles
we've had in the boat. I was just counting the men when suddenly, at the end of the queue, so help me, was Lieutenant
Forster. I recognized him clearly."

"Yes, yes, I'm sure you believe this, Brinkmann. But the mind
can play funny tricks, you know, quite unexpectedly. The
strain we've all been under . . ."

"I'm sure that's true, sir. But I'm not the only one. Petersen
who was with me, he saw the lieutenant as well."

The captain sighed. "All right then. I'll talk to Petersen.
Fetch him down here."

"I doubt if he'll come, sir, not in the state he's in. I left him
crouching behind the conning tower."

"Then I'll go and see him. You stay here, Brinkmann, and
sit down. Meanwhile, keep your mouth shut, understand?
Give him a drink, someone."

The captain and the first lieutenant climbed up to the deck
and there, sure enough, was able seaman Petersen, far from
able at this moment, trying to roll himself into a ball in the
shadow of the bridge. He looked up, white-faced, as the captain approached, only too glad to talk. Yes, he'd seen Lieutenant Forster come aboard, no, not prompted by Brinkmann but
independently. Yes, it was definitely Forster, he'd never mistake that face. The officer had moved slowly along the deck
towards the bow, then turned . . .

"He turned, sir, very still and slow, and crossed his arms
over his chest and looked at me from those dark eyes of his,
and at that moment I just couldn't stand it, I took shelter here.
And when I looked again, he'd gone."

Two days later, just before the U-65 was due to sail, Petersen vanished, deserting the craft he had told everyone was a
"death boat", and the captain, who could not afford to believe
in the ghost, managed to convince himself, despite negative
inquiries, that some joker from ashore had played the dangerous trick.

This theory seemed to be confirmed when, out of touch with
land, on the first patrol down-Channel and others later
nothing in the least unusual occurred in the U-65. She sank
some ships and she certainly eluded pursuit – surely a chance for
the jinx to operate, if there was one. This fact did not escape the
crew and morale slowly improved until, after eighteen months,
by the beginning of 1918, even the petty officer concerned was

calling his vision a trick of the mind and other men frankly
disbelieved the whole story.

The captain may have felt a twinge of anxiety when, for ten
days in early January, the U-boat's gang-plank was touching
the dock-side at Zeebrugge, but nothing happened there either
and she sailed once more for patrol with orders to seek out
shipping off Portland. On the evening of the 21st, as it was
getting dark, the captain surfaced to recharge the batteries.
The weather was stormy with low cloud scudding across the
moon and as the boat was near an enemy naval base there
were three men on the bridge keeping a specially sharp lookout, the first lieutenant and two ratings, these back to back
covering segments to port and starboard. So it was the lieutenant who saw the figure first, showered with spray, standing on
deck near the bow, feet straddling the plates as the boat
lurched and pitched in the seas.

The lieutenant cupped his hands. "You there, whoever you
are, what the hell do you think you're doing? Get below or
you'll be overboard!"

Then the figure turned, and it was Forster.

Electrified, the officer called the captain and both of them
then, with the lookouts, stared in numbed horror as the ghost
of the dead lieutenant folded its arms and stared back, silent
and, as it seemed, accusingly until, after nearly a minute, it
was suddenly there no more.

The captain's first thought was for his crew. If they got to
hear of that encounter, morale would be finally shattered and
he swore the three men on the bridge to silence. As for himself,
he felt doubly cautious now and filled with nameless apprehension. In the following days he managed to torpedo a supply
ship heading for Plymouth and cripple another by gunfire. He
could have sunk it easily, but refrained. Somehow it would
have seemed like tempting fate, inviting retribution. But, as it
happened, a different fate was reserved for him. *He* was not to
die at sea but on land, by what looked like one chance in a
million.

Some weeks later, when the U-65 was tied up again at
Bruges, he went ashore to visit the officers' club. On the way
he heard the air-raid siren followed by ack-ack fire and falling
bombs. He decided to go back and almost as soon as he had
turned a splinter from a shell or a bomb neatly sliced his head
from his body.

When a new captain arrived, a tough, well-seasoned sub-mariner, he found the crew in a state of shock. As he had not witnessed any of the sinister incidents it was easy for him to deride them as "a bunch of hysterical women" and threaten anyone who as much as mentioned the word "ghost". But everyone knew this was a bluff. There are no detention cells in a submarine and the worst a captain can do is to dock a man's pay or make him sleep on the bare lower deck – no cure for the jitters. In any case, punishment was not the answer, but re-cognition that the men's fears were reasonable. Eventually the new captain seemed to realize this and instituted an inquiry into all that had happened. High-ranking officers came on board, listened carefully to what each man had to say, drafted those most demoralized to other duties ashore or afloat, filled the gap with a fresh draft – and then did something really stupid. They called in a priest to exorcize the boat, drive out the evil spirit in the name of God.

Comments in the seamen's mess can easily be imagined. "Ah! So there was a devil all along, you see. Now they've admitted it! . . ." "Yes, they've made it official . . ." "Question is, have the parson's prayers driven it out? We'll be the ones to know about that, won't we? Parson's all right, he's gone back ashore! . . ." And from one of the newcomers: "Nobody told us about this when they signed us on, nobody said a word about devils then. Well, I'm not standing for it. I'm applying for transfer . . ."

Understandably, morale in the U-65 never recovered and it is astonishing to hear she was still kept in service. The only reason we might think of, apart from the demands of war, is that to decommission her on the grounds of diabolic possession would have set a precedent dangerous indeed. And what other grounds were there?

So it was – as we hear from an account written by one of her petty officers who survived – that in May, 1918, the wretched crew, thoroughly demoralized, set out for yet another patrol, under yet another commanding officer, this time in the Bay of Biscay. It was a terrible trip: high seas, poor success against enemy shipping, in other words the sort of patrol most U-boats experienced from time to time. But it was terrible for other reasons. After two days at sea a torpedoman named Eberhard went raving mad and had to be given morphia. When he came round he was sent to the upper deck to get some air, accompanied by another seaman. Once there, Eberhard went berserk again and before the other man could stop him, took a running jump overboard. He made no attempt to swim.

More was to come. Off Ushant, when the boat was rolling heavily, the chief engineer slipped and broke a leg. Soon after, when the gun's crew was closed up, firing at a British tramp steamer, one of them was washed overboard and drowned.

Twenty-nine men left. How many more to go? Everyone on board now felt that a malevolent fate had the U-65 in its grip and would never relent. Why attack enemy shipping when any such attempt might hasten the end that all were sure would come? The captain tried to counter this by quoting the German proverb, "Better a terrible end than terror without end", but the men noticed that he, too, was losing his aggressive spirit.

There was one inevitable trial yet to come, the passage of the Straits of Dover on the way home. Three U-boats had recently been destroyed there and, sure enough, in the narrows the U-65 was picked up by enemy hydrophones when submerged and depth-charged on and off for a good half-hour. The men thought their last moment had come, but the jinx held its hand till the captain was able to surface. Then, as Coxswain Lohmann was taking up the watchmen, before he had even reached the bridge, an enemy shell splinter came humming through the conning tower and severed his jugular.

A battered U-65 reached Zeebrugge at last and an exhausted petty officer wrote the account already mentioned. By that time, he was in hospital with acute rheumatism and thankful to be there, confident he would never see the accursed boat again. He had served in her right from the start.

"The U-65", he remembered, "was never a happy ship, though we were always fortunate in our officers. I am convinced myself that she was haunted. One night at sea I saw an officer standing on deck. He was not one of us. I only caught a glimpse of him, but a shipmate swore he recognized our former second officer. Several of the bluejackets saw the ghost quite often. Our last captain but one would never admit the existence of anything supernatural, but once or twice, when coming on deck, I saw him very agitated and was told by the men that the ghost had been walking on deck. Later I heard from a steward at the officers' shore mess that our captain openly declared his ship to be haunted by devils."

On the eve of the U-65 sailing once more for patrol one of her officers, Wernicke by name, visited the sick man in hospital with some personal belongings which he asked to be sent on to his wife if –. But the "if" really meant "when", both men understood that.

On 31 July, 1918, German naval headquarters reported that the U-65 was missing, presumed lost, and but for an extraordinary chance that brief announcement would have been the end of this story. But three weeks previously an American submarine off Cape Clear on the west coast of Ireland had spotted from periscope depth a surfaced U-boat and read the number on the conning tower, U-65. The American was manoeuvring for attack, the outer torpedo doors were already open, when, as her captain later told his friends: "Right in front of my eyes that U-boat just blew up, sky-high, with a roar you could have heard in Arizona. Impatient to go, I reckon. Couldn't be bothered to wait . . ."

Had another warhead exploded? Had another U-boat attacked in error, then made off undetected? Or was it sabotage, by an unhinged crewman perhaps, wanting only one thing: peace and an end to fear? We shall never know.

Nor can we pass final judgement on the haunting of the U-65. After the war a German psychologist, Professor Hecht, made a careful study, followed in 1932 by the English naval historian, Hector C. Bywater. Understandably, neither reached any firm conclusions. It may be that the ghostly sightings were hallucinatory, generated in a terror-stricken crew. We notice that the ghost was first seen after five frightening incidents had occurred – fertile soil for fantasies of the supernatural. On the other hand – and who can deny it? – the ghost may have been genuine. In either case, the apparition, real or imaginary, is the central factor in the story. Take away that and all the other incidents, horrifying though they were, assume a different complexion.

So we are left with conjecture. But something can be said for sure: once belief in the haunting had established itself among the crew, panic was inevitable, and from that much else may have flowed. For it is one thing for a man to visit a haunted house, knowing he can leave, but quite another to be shut up with an evil spirit in a steel cigar, fathoms beneath the sea, amid the perils of world war.

A SAILOR HOME FROM SEA

Besides the usual means of communication between people, visual or verbal, there are others which make use of neither sight nor sound, telepathy for instance. But how this faculty operates and how often is still largely a mystery. It may be that it functions quite often, but so unobtrusively that we do not usually recognize it. What is it, for instance, that produces our passing moods, is it purely something subjective or are we affected subconsciously, without the use of the senses, by other minds, even by events?

Certainly, when a major disaster occurs people often become aware of it in this way, or something strange occurs that suggests paranormal faculties at work. Was it just a coincidence, for example, that in the early afternoon of 22 June, 1893, after lunch at the Whitehead torpedo works at Weymouth the stem of a wine glass suddenly shattered of its own accord and one of the officers present said jokingly: "That should mean a big naval disaster"? And what was it, that same afternoon, that drew vast crowds to the dockyard gates in Malta even before the telegraph had hammered out the terrible news? And why, that night in London, where nothing untoward was yet known, at a reception given by a lady in Eaton Square were the shadows seen to stir at the top of the big staircase and her husband, Sir George Tryon, K.C.B., came slowly down in his Vice-Admiral's uniform, to be greeted by some of the guests – though his body at that moment was lying at the bottom of the Mediterranean?

Curiously, Lady Tryon herself did not see the tall bulky figure of Sir George or even sense his powerful presence and she felt increasingly annoyed to be confronted time and again during the evening by other people's apparent certainty that they *had* seen him. "You must be so pleased to have your husband back, Lady Tryon." "What a surprise to see Sir George again, Lady Tryon." "My dear, you must have hauled him away from those ships of his especially for tonight's reception!" What were they talking about? Was it some kind of joke? Endlessly she kept on repeating: "But George can't be here. He's in the Mediterranean." And so he was.

It was not until the next morning that, breakfasting in bed, Lady Tryon received the fatal news. As Commander-in-Chief, Mediterranean Fleet, her husband had been supervising manoeuvres off the coast of Syria when a collision had occurred between his flagship *Victoria* and another battleship, *Camperdown*. Within fifteen minutes *Victoria* has capsized and sunk, taking the Admiral and hundreds of others with her.

In the days and weeks that followed a picture began to emerge of what had happened, though an air of mystery and confusion continued to hang over an incident that has remained one of the most tragic in naval history.

However, the background at least is now clear. In an age when the Royal Navy had fought no major engagement since the Napoleonic Wars its role had become largely representative, shadowing forth the might of the greatest empire the world had ever seen. A squadron (stronger in itself than any other nation's entire navy) might be sent to overawe the Russians or the Turks, or support British policy in Egypt; but there was hardly any difference between this role and the purely ceremonial occasion when a fleet was dressed overall, brasswork was polished, decks were scrubbed and dignitaries from every part of the world were piped aboard to be welcomed by white-gloved officers.

At all this the Navy was supremely competent, and at hoisting signals that only a few specialists in an entire fleet could read, according to a complicated system that had not changed since the days of Nelson. But was it fit for war? Vice-Admiral Tryon thought not. Fast-moving fleet actions would require something less cumbersome than strings of coloured flags – easily obscured anyway in the smoke of battle – that had to be repeated and replied to with yet more flags of different

shapes and sizes, and in due course that something came –
wireless telegraphy. But that, for the navy, lay six years
ahead.

Meanwhile Tryon was developing a loose and, according to
naval diehards, a dangerous system which he called "T.A.".
This used a mixture of the established signals with straightforward follow-my-leader tactics, at the same time leaving considerable scope for independent initiative to subordinate commanders. When he took over the Mediterranean Fleet in September, 1891, this system was immediately introduced. At the
same time the Admiral explained its purpose to his ships' captains in a memorandum which began: "I have long been
impressed with the importance of exercising a fleet from
the point where the drill books leave off . . ." Anxious about
what was to come, particularly as Tryon was known to be
a man of dominating personality who tested subordinates
to the utmost, some of them resolved there and then to
follow his orders, understood or not, to the letter and so
keep out of trouble. One of these was Rear-Admiral Albert
Markham, an anxiously conscientious officer who joined
the Fleet in January, 1892, as second in command.

But for over a year all went well. Interspersed with ceremonial obligations – the Prince and Princess Ferdinand of
Bulgaria to be entertained, Queen Victoria to be escorted
on a visit to Florence, "showing the flag", courtesy visits to
foreign ports – there were torpedo trials, night exercises,
manoeuvres, many of them highly unorthodox, after
which Tryon would collect his captains and rear-admiral
in the big stern cabin of the *Victoria* and, like some awesome
father-figure, explain just where they had gone wrong, then
challenge them to a discussion. For many, including Markham, it was a nerve-racking experience.

So came the summer of '93, and the best word to describe it
was "torpid". Day after day the sun glared from a cloudless
sky, only an occasional breeze stirred a flat-calm sea and over
Tryon's fleet – 8 battleships, 3 armoured cruisers, 2 light cruisers – the heat hung like a suffocating blanket. But as ever
Tryon himself was alert and determined to keep his men on
their toes. In mid-June the fleet had anchored off Beirut in two
lines parallel to the shore and on the morning of the 22nd
Tryon ordered it to sea again, not simply by turning to port in
line ahead, so clearing the anchorage, but with a difficult

manoeuvre whereby the inner line would pass at an angle through the outer and then wait for the latter to form up abreast on a wing. In every ship, from the captain on the bridge to the engine-room staff answering telegraphs, a sigh of relief must have gone up when it was successfully completed.

But more was to come. The next port of call, the Syrian Tripoli, lay sixty miles away to the north-east and glancing at their charts the captains probably hoped that Tryon would simply swing to starboard through ninety degrees towards the open anchorage and drop the hook. There would be plenty of room. A simple manoeuvre, then down with the anchor, off jackets and feet up in the wardroom while half the crews went to "make and mend", which meant darning socks, sleeping, letter writing – universal peace. But this was not what Tryon had in mind. From the master-choreographer another intricate ballet movement was on the way. First, from line abreast he ordered the ships to form line ahead in two parallel columns, six cables (i.e. 1,200 yards) apart, the first division to starboard headed by himself in *Victoria* (11,000 tons) and the second to port by Markham in *Camperdown* (10,600 tons). When this was completed the ships would still be sailing eastwards at right-angles to the anchorage. How would Tryon bring them in? Just after 2 p.m. he told Captain Bourke of the *Victoria* the first part of this operation: "I shall reverse the course by turning inwards."

At this moment the horror of that afternoon began to unfold. "Reversing the course" meant that, having been sailing east the columns would end up sailing west and presumably Tryon intended to achieve this by each turning inwards towards the other. Afterwards they would have to turn south towards the anchorage, but that was irrelevant. What mattered was the distance between the columns and the turning circles of the ships. *Victoria*'s was 800 yards, *Camperdown*'s practically the same, so that a minimum of 1,600 yards (8 cables) was necessary between the columns if a collision was to be avoided. But Tryon had said "six".

"It will require at least eight cables for that, sir", said one of his officers, Commander Hawkins-Smith, as soon as Tryon had spoken to Bourke, and Tryon replied somewhat abstractly: "Yes, it shall be eight cables." Immediately after this Tryon sent for his flag-lieutenant and told him to hoist the signal to the fleet for the line-ahead formation, adding: "Make the columns six cables apart." And at six, despite anxious reminders from Bourke and the flag-lieutenant, it stayed.

Over an hour passed during which the fleet moved majestically eastward in the two columns: 100,000 tons of steel, black hulls, white upperworks gleaming, and 6,000 men all blissfully unaware of the danger impending except for Bourke, Lord Gillford, the flag-lieutenant, and Hawkins-Smith, yet all three feeling it impossible, within the bounds of naval discipline, to challenge the vice-admiral further.

So at 3.25 p.m., on Tryon's instruction, the signal was hoisted for each line of ships to alter course through 180 degrees — at six cables distance. And still Bourke, the *Victoria*'s captain, said nothing. Perhaps he was hoping that Tryon, whom he often referred to as "a master mind" had some trick up his sleeve that would make all well, and apparently the other captains had the same hope, for one after another they replied that the signal had been both received and understood, on the pretext presumably that all they had to do was to follow their respective leaders in the two columns, regardless of consequences.

"Mine not to reason why" was an accepted principle in Tryon's fleet and this applied to Markham, too, with, this time, a slight difference. As leader of the second column with a heavy responsibility he started to query the signal. But this merely drew the sharp rejoinder, "What are you waiting for?", whereupon Markham suddenly thought he had the clue to the riddle: the First Division (Tryon's) would circle round and outside the Second Division. That was what would happen, that was the C-in-C's trick! Confident that he now had the answer, Markham quickly hoisted "understood" and put *Camperdown*'s helm hard over so that his ship started circling to starboard almost at the same time as *Victoria* began turning to port. Soon the two ships, 21,000 tons of steel, were converging on one another across twelve hundred yards of water at a combined speed of 17 knots.

Markham watched *Victoria*, hoping desperately she would turn wider, while Tryon, incredibly, was not looking towards *Camperdown* at all but aft at the ships following in his own line. At last Captain Bourke spoke, urgently, pointing out *Camperdown*: "We had better do something, sir, we shall be too close to that ship." No reply. Bourke then told a midshipman to take the distance between the two ships. Back came the answer: "three-and-a-quarter cables, sir" – 650 yards.

If a collision was to be avoided the next thirty seconds were crucial. Again Bourke appealed in almost the same words. Again, no reply. "May I go astern with the port screw, sir? . . . We must go astern, sir, *at once!*" At last the admiral turned and for the first time saw *Camperdown* bearing down slantwise on *Victoria*, terrifyingly close. "Yes, go astern!"

Bourke shouted an order. *Victoria*'s huge propellers began to turn in reverse. But it was too late.

Meanwhile in *Camperdown* Markham was intent only on carrying out his orders and these were, in his opinion, to circle inwards towards *Victoria* at maximum helm, while still hoping that Tryon would take the initiative to avoid a collision. So, like some fearful scene in a Roman arena when gladiators pounced on one another, the two ships drew closer and closer – 400 yards, 300 yards, 200 yards. At the last moment Tryon shouted across to Markham: "Go astern – go astern!" But the order had already been given – again, too late.

At exactly 3.34 p.m. *Camperdown*'s bow, reinforced with a steel ram, sliced at an acute angle into *Victoria*'s forecastle, forward of the main turret with its colossal 111-ton guns, smashing through bulkheads and tearing up the deck to a depth of nine feet. If the ships had stayed locked together there could have been time to close the watertight doors in *Victoria* and the blow might not have been fatal. But in less than a minute, still going astern, *Camperdown* backed slowly out of the wedge she had driven and then the water began to pour in.

Standing calmly on his bridge, Tryon at first intended to steer *Victoria* for the shore only four miles away and beach her. But the flood could not be stopped. Within five minutes the bow was fifteen feet underwater and minutes later the stern was so high that the propellers, still revolving, were clear of the water. Tryon said: "I think she's going", and then to his flag-lieutenant: "Make a signal to send boats immediately." Almost at that moment the ship gave a sudden lurch to starboard.

The speed at which *Victoria* took in water caught everyone by surprise and now, when she was on the point of capsizing, it was too late to fetch up the men on watch below in the boiler and engine rooms. Only those sailors, midshipmen and officers already near the deck, some 600 of them, were mustered, four deep, facing inwards, perfectly controlled and disciplined, as though on parade. An officer gave an order, the master-at-arms repeated it: "About turn!" And the men turned, facing the sea. Still no one broke ranks until, with a final sickening lurch, *Victoria* rolled over and there were shouts of "Jump!"

Tryon was still on the bridge and with hundreds of others went down with his ship. In those last few agonizing minutes he had remained calm and, in the circumstances, tantalizingly reticent. He never told Bourke or anyone else how he had intended the fatal order to be carried out, why he had issued it or what, in his opinion, had gone wrong. All he was heard to say – to no one in particular – was: "It was all my fault, entirely my fault."

When the ship went down a vast amount of wreckage shot to the surface with giant air bubbles from the interior, turning the sea for yards around into a lethal cauldron in which many men struggling in the water were killed. Others simply drowned. Some, jumping from the stern, were caught in the still revolving propellers. In all, of the 600, 355 were never seen again.

Of course there had to be a court martial and, according to naval law, it had to be on Captain Bourke, one of the survivors, because it was his ship that had been lost. He was officially the "accused" – and was eventually acquitted of endangering his ship – but it was Tryon and Markham who were really in the dock.

The court, presided over by Vice-Admiral Sir Michael Culme-Seymour, Tryon's successor as C-in-C, Mediterranean, had to proceed carefully in order not to inflame public anxiety at home. The collision between two of Britain's newest ironclads in broad daylight, clear weather and calm seas under the command of an admiral uniquely prestigious in the Royal Navy had been deeply humiliating and disturbing. Moreover the speed at which *Victoria* had capsized raised doubts about the soundness of naval architecture. How would such ships behave in war?

All this had to be gone into discreetly with the help of technical reports. But the main interest was on the human element. Bourke, testifying in his defence, and Markham, called at a later stage as a witness, spoke several times of Tryon's power and influence in the fleet: "We had complete confidence in him" – "His was the master mind" – "We had never questioned an order." Personal loyalty came in as well. Bourke spoke of him as "my chief and my kindest friend". Time after time they had carried out manoeuvres under Tryon's command without knowing their purpose until it was explained to them afterwards.

No doubt this accounted for Bourke's obedience to orders right up to the moment of collision and, for the sake of naval discipline, the court could not bring itself to disapprove. But it left open the question of Tryon's original intention and this became even more problematical when Bourke declared he had specifically reminded Tryon that *Victoria*'s turning circle was 800 yards, and still received the answer: "Keep it at six cables."

Possible light was thrown on the mystery during Markham's examination when he was asked if he had been aware on 22 June "of a memorandum which had been previously issued by Sir George Tryon on the subject of discretion in obeying orders". Parts of this document read: "When the literal obedience to any order, however given, would entail a collision with a friend . . . paramount orders direct that the danger is to be avoided, while the object of the order should be attained, if possible. Risks that are not only justifiable, but are demanded during war are not justifiable during peace."

Having confirmed that he knew the memorandum Markham was then asked why he had not acted on it and turned away from *Victoria* in time to avoid the collision. Because, he said weakly, that would have meant passing her starboard to starboard, so infringing the "rule of the road" which prescribed port to port. The fact was then pointed out to him, which he should have known perfectly well, that the rule did not apply during manoeuvres.

It was not the court's duty to try the dead but the living, so this clue to Tryon's intention was not followed up. But it suggested that, in issuing the controversial order, he may have simply intended to test Markham's initiative. Several facts supported this theory: the memorandum only recently issued – the impossible distance of six cables – "rule of the road" not operative during manoeuvres – the prodding signal, "What are you waiting for?" All this pointed to a solution which Markham never even considered, namely that he with his column of ships was meant to circle outside Tryon's. Was Tryon's remark, "It was entirely my fault" one of grief that he had put too much trust in his subordinate?

There was one other supporting fact. In issuing the original signal to turn, Tryon had specified "preserving the order of the fleet". The order, *before* the turn, had been Tryon's column to starboard, Markham's to port. If they had turned inwards towards each other, assuming there had been space for the manoeuvre, they would have ended up with Markham to starboard and Tryon to port. On the other hand, if either column had circled outside the other, the order would have been preserved because in both cases Tryon would have ended up to starboard. Beside the need to avoid a collision, then, someone had to circle outside the other. But who? According to this theory Tryon meant it to be Markham, while Markham thought, or in his timidity chose to think, that it would be Tryon.

This could be the solution to the mystery. Yet doubt remains. Preserving the order of the fleet may have had another meaning for Tryon and it seems incredible that a man of such experience could have risked everything on a subordinate's initiative, particularly one like Markham. So perhaps Tryon was ill on that fatal day, more sick than anyone knew, and perhaps took the radius of the turning-circle to be the diameter. Perhaps, at the crucial moment, he suffered a blackout. And perhaps, on the night of 22 June, his spirit returned to his home in Eaton Square, restlessly hoping to tell someone what really happened, what his real intention had been, but then, realizing it was impossible, withdrew for ever to the shades – while Markham, eased into retirement, lived on, a broken man, for another twenty-five years.

THE VOICE FROM
THE *PRESIDENT*

There are many reasons why those who are interested in mysterious occurrences at sea are unlikely to forget the strange story of the steam-packet, the *President*.

The inexplicable disappearance of what was, in 1841, a veritable giant of a vessel was bound to have a considerable impact. After all, a steam-ship 120 metres in length, weighing 2,350 tons, and equipped with the latest fittings and machinery does not just vanish without trace. And even if the engines had unaccountably failed, the *President* would not have been without alternative means of propulsion. Apart from her two enormous paddle-wheels, the ship also had three masts and a bowsprit and sails. Her crew included not only engineers; there were several topmen or riggers aboard. It is therefore not surprising that the loss of such a vessel gave rise to alarm and despondency on both sides of the Atlantic.

Another circumstance puts the loss of the *President* in a special category. The voice of one of its passengers was heard in England before it was known that the ship was even in danger.

But let us first consider briefly a few facts relevant to what eventually happened to the doomed vessel.

The *President* was one of the earliest steam-packet boats on the transatlantic run. As recently as 23 April, 1838, the first two steam-ships to cross the Atlantic, the *Sirius* and the *Great Western*, had arrived at New York and had been given a tremendous welcome by the quayside idlers and others who were present for various reasons. The *President*'s sister ship was the *British Queen* and both vessels were owned by the British and American Steam Navigation Company.

Launched in December, 1839, the *President* had made three successful transatlantic runs by 1841, but not everybody was happy about her seaworthiness. One writer in *The Times*, for instance, had this to say: "Before the *President* had her keel laid I ventured to prognosticate from her dimensions that she would not prove a fast goer, and before she was launched I expressed a strong opinion that she would be very subject to lose her rudder." Her own captain referred to her as a "coffin-ship", while many knowledgeable seafaring men were disturbed by her great length and feared she might broach to or founder on the Newfoundland banks in a severe gale.

Although report had it that she presented "a very handsome appearance to the superficial beholder", experts were not impressed by the *President*'s lines and said bluntly that the ship would not break any records. She had shown herself to be slower than the *British Queen* and the *Great Western* when in August, 1840, she took sixteen and a half days to complete the voyage from Liverpool to New York.

Captain Roberts of the *President* had already established himself as something of an uncompromising disciplinarian. Three years previously, when in command of the *Sirius*, he had dealt summarily with a mutinous crew. In a situation that might have turned ugly, he had threatened the trouble-makers with his revolver and the potential rising had fizzled out. That he was evidently a man who could make bold decisions was borne out when on another occasion he chopped up part of the bridge to provide fuel for the ship's boilers as the coal-bunkers were empty. Clearly Captain Roberts was a "hard" man who would never admit defeat.

Such was the ship and such was her captain when the *President* set sail from New York, destination Liverpool, on 11 March, 1841. But what about the others who were to embark on this ill-fated voyage? The crew, of course, was more or less the same, but some of the passengers were of interest.

There was, for example, the Chaplain to the United States Senate, the Reverend G. G. Cookman, whose father had been the Mayor of Hull. Leaving his wife and family in America, he was making the voyage in order to visit his relatives and friends in Yorkshire.

Another noteworthy passenger was Lord Fitzroy Lennox who had been serving with an infantry regiment stationed in Canada but had recently applied successfully for a transfer to the 13th Dragoons back in England and was on his way to join his new outfit. His father, the Duke of Richmond whose residence was at Goodwood, was looking forward eagerly to his son's arrival.

But perhaps the most interesting passenger, especially in view of what happened later, was a celebrated British actor who had been touring the larger American cities. The same name was destined to become famous again almost a century later when it was familiar to cinema goers everywhere.

Tyrone Power . . .

Together with his servant, Mr Power sailed on the *President* bound for England on that fateful date, 11 March, 1841. Moreover, his American tour had proved doubly successful. In addition to his earnings as an actor, he had also speculated wisely in land in Texas and had with him £30,000 in specie, a considerable fortune in those days.

When the *President* steamed slowly past the Battery, weather conditions were far from propitious. The sky was grey, sullen and menacing, while the massed black clouds on the horizon were messengers of the storm that was about to break. The passengers, however, putting their trust in Captain Roberts' reputation and seamanship, retired to the narrow confines of their cabins.

On the following day the threatened storm was raging in all its fury and the situation grew steadily worse. Sharing the same tempestuous waters with the *President*, other vessels, three-masters and steam-packets, were rolling heavily at the mercy of the gale-force winds somewhere off the coast east of Nova Scotia. To the north lay small islands that did not figure on any map. More dangerous still were the huge icebergs, sources of many a wreck, that had detached themselves from the ice pack during the spring weather. In spite of churning seas and lashing winds, these other ships eventually weathered the storm and came safely to port. One vessel alone had at last to be listed as missing.

The *President*.

What happened to the *President* after her departure from New York is, and will always remain, a matter for conjecture. In the old days of sail, if a ship failed to observe its expected time of arrival, nobody worried over much. Adverse weather conditions could bring about delays that might run into weeks. With the advent of the steamship the whole situation was changed. The average time for the transatlantic crossing was cut down to twelve or thirteen days. It was generally believed that nothing could go wrong with a vessel powered by steam. Consequently, as far as a steamship was concerned, any delay immediately gave rise to concern.

The first warning that all was not well with the *President* came in an unusual and private manner, conjured up apparently by the same storm that was battering Atlantic shipping on 12 and 13 March. At any rate a fury of wind and rain was rattling the doors and windows of the buildings in Blackheath, a residential area of London. Now, living in that particular district was a wealthy friend of Tyrone Power – a director of the Haymarket Theatre. His name was Benjamin Webster.

The storm increased in violence and eventually this – and another – noise awakened Mr Webster's butler whose bedroom was on the second floor. The butler sat up in bed and listened for a while; then he rose, crossed over to the window and peered into the darkness. He could make out nothing in the murk, but he could hear heavy thuds, as if somebody was hurling himself again and again at the front door. At the same instant an agonized voice kept pleading for admittance.

The butler lit an oil lamp and hurried to his master's room. Shaking Mr Webster awake, he excitedly described the strange sounds he had heard, identifying the voice as that of his master's theatrical friend, Tyrone Power.

Webster, who was under the impression that Tyrone Power was still in America, at first reacted testily to being thus rudely awakened. The butler insisted that the person outside was calling to Mr Webster for help and kept crying over and over again that he was "drowned in the rain".

Yielding at length to his butler's entreaties, Webster made his way to the front door. With nervous fingers he unlocked it, drew back the bolts and lit the porch light. He flung open the door. Outside were squally gusts and beating rain, but that was all.

The butler remained adamant that he had heard the voice of Power. Worried and uncertain for the moment what to think – the servant, after all, knew Tyrone Power's distinctive voice as well as he himself did – the theatrical manager returned to bed.

A short while later, when it became known that the *President* was overdue and that his friend was indeed a passenger, a cold sense of foreboding gripped at his heart. He tried to find reassurance in the fact that the delay could easily be attributed to the appalling weather conditions.

On 2 and 3 April three steam-packets *did* arrive – the *Orpheus*, the *Virginia* and the *Britannia*. The captains, when interrogated, described the crossing as unpleasant in the extreme but not really dangerous. They were surprised to hear that the *President* was missing. All three of them expected that she would have reached Liverpool at least a week before. Despite the bad weather it had taken the *Virginia* only fifteen days to make the crossing.

An early "report" (7 April) stated that the *President* had been seen making for Fayal. This uncorroborated announcement was closely followed by another one saying that a large steamer, believed to be the *President*, had been seen a good distance from Cork moving up the Channel. The *President* was actually mentioned by name in the Cork shipping list.

On 14 April Her Majesty, Queen Victoria, set out from Buckingham Palace to spend some time at Windsor. She left strict instructions that as soon as news of the *President*'s safe arrival reached London, a special messenger should carry the good tidings immediately to Windsor. Unfortunately an unconfirmed reference to the ship's successful docking at Liverpool was accepted as the truth and the Queen was duly informed. To their subsequent embarrassment both Victoria and Prince Albert "expressed the highest satisfaction at the gratifying communication".

In *The Times* dated 16 April a letter signed "Observer" dealt with the various possibilities in detail. Although his optimism turned out to be ill-founded, his conjectures and reasoning are convincing and worth quoting in so far as his views were shared by many others.

After giving an assurance that he had studied all that the American papers had said about the *President*, "Observer" wrote: "It is certain that the first storm commenced on Friday night, 12 March, and probably the *President*'s speed had previously been much impeded by the heavy sea from the eastward, which usually precedes a gale from that quarter, so that she was not eastward of the meridian of New Bedford when she met the gale. The wind was from the north-east and continued with violence all of Saturday the 13th. As the next gale commenced on the 16th, and is reported to have lasted three days, probably the head sea continued; so that when she encountered the second gale on Wednesday the 17th, in all probability she was not eastward of where, with usually moderate weather, or a fair wind, she would have been in three days of a common passage."

The writer then went on to point out that the continuing gale and the need for re-fuelling would have prompted a prudent captain to make for a port where he could replenish his coals and put right any damage the ship might have sustained. Driven south-east by the gales, the captain of the *President* was most likely to steer a course for Bermuda.

Dismissing as "idle" all notions that the *President* had broached to in the first gale or had fallen foul of icebergs, "Observer" continued: "I should be unwilling to encourage unwarranted hopes, but it appears to me there is nothing to fear above the ordinary danger to a good strong ship lying to in a heavy gale, excepting so far as her machinery, or her being improperly loaded, might have increased that danger. An unlucky sea in a heavy tempest, it is true, may start a wood end, and send a ship to the bottom; but all seamen agree that there is no position of less danger during such a gale than lying to, and it is very seldom that any heavy accident happens in such a position. If the steam could be used it would enable her to keep to the sea more steadily, and thus be more safe than a sailing ship. The great length of time that had elapsed since the *President* sailed is certainly rather discouraging, but I should by no means despair until after receiving dates to the 28th from Bermuda and the West India Islands."

In a follow-up letter to *The Times* the same writer stresses the fact that other ships (the *Caroline* for one) had safely weathered the storms. Although acknowledging the possibilities of fire or collision or being struck by a particularly heavy sea, he concluded that all such dangers "are known to be very small to a well-appointed vessel".

As the weeks dragged by and there was still no reliable information about the *President*, guesses as to her fate grew wilder and rumours more rife. The vessel "had been seen lying off Liverpool, her masts gone and taking in water". A ship on the Liverpool to Halifax run had passed a steamship steering east by south. Some swore it was the *President*; others (obviously unaware that the *Britannia* had already docked) reckoned it was the *Britannia* off its usual course to avoid icebergs.

Towards the end of May, when most people had abandoned any hope that the *President* would ever again be heard of, the name of Tyrone Power figured once more in the headlines. The actor's wife received a letter which purported to come from her husband, who appeared to be in Madeira. The gist of the message was that the *President* had been badly damaged by the storms, was undergoing repair and would soon be heading for Liverpool. Both Mrs Power and Benjamin Webster, to whom she showed the letter, declared it to be a forgery.

Then again, a message in a bottle was picked up on the Irish coast at about the same time and that, too, could have been the work of a heartless practical joker. It said simply: "The *President* is sinking. May God help us! Tyrone Power." Most people could not believe that the bottle had traversed the great distance of the Atlantic in such a short time impelled only by the currents.

As he followed the speculation and counter-speculation about the fate of the *President*, and hopes for its safety gradually diminished to vanishing point, Benjamin Webster's mind returned again and again to the strange visitation in the early hours of that March morning. He became convinced that the spirit of his old friend had tried to speak to him at the moment of death.

Webster did not make the matter public, and it remained a family secret until recently. His high integrity and the fact that Power was an old and close friend makes it difficult to believe the story was a fabrication. The frantic banging at the door and the voice crying out that he was drowned in the rain must be assumed to have happened.

Does this mean that the *President* went down on the night of 12–13 March?

The mysterious disappearance of the *President* was never satisfactorily explained. Perhaps her engines failed and left her a helpless victim of the elements. Perhaps a collision with an iceberg or a derelict was responsible for the tragedy. There are plenty of theories, but no real evidence to support any of them. All we know for certain is that there were no survivors and no wreckage. The sea, unfathomable, all-powerful, ruthless, had triumphed over puny man. The waters had closed over the *President* as they were to close over many another famous vessel.

THE GHOST CAPTAIN

As a living paradox, there could be no equal to the skipper of the tall, elegant three-masted bark moored on the water front one cold, bleak morning of 1899.

Between voyages, he spent his time like other folk, going about his daily business. He was an ordinary, middle-aged, unimposing man, with lean face and steady blue eyes expressing not the least hint of emotion, a type one sees often on the streets.

But afloat he conflicted with every conceivable notion of what was reasonable or possible; once aboard his ship, he had the cut of a legendary figure, able to achieve what is beyond the strength of ordinary mortals. Slight of build, he wore a short, greying beard that gave him the appearance of a buccaneer. One could imagine he kept a flintlock in his cabin and used it to blast strangers off his ship or repel raiders; he might well have been equally at home in a Viking longboat or on the quarter-deck of a modern cruiser. Nothing ever convinced him of the existence of haunted ships, though he would freely admit the possibility of haunted houses, spectral shapes lurking in dim corners ashore; nothing, that is, until this voyage to Indian ports.

No one with an expert eye for ships would have said that this three-master of his, which he had commanded for upward of fifteen years, was a speedster, yet in her time she made some fine runs, notably London–Calcutta in eighty-one days. For a while she went trooping, but when de Lesseps put the finishing touches to his magnificent canal, and steam-driven ships seemed to be pushing tall sailing vessels off the world's ocean routes, her owners tried her on the long haul to Australian ports, where she produced reasonable dividends, then they returned her to the Indian ports service to end her days usefully. At her masthead she wore the house flag of one of the oldest companies in the business. Square-rigged on all but her mizzen, which was fore-and-aft rigged, she was a picture-book ship; and when she took the bit between her teeth every so often, she went like a Kentucky Derby winner.

They eased her from her water-front moorings in the London River that cold midwinter morning of 1899, let her thread her own leisurely passage among a varied collection of ships and, as always when passing steamships with their noisy thump-thump of triple-expansion engines, like a woman turning up her nose at a displeasing odour, she lifted her stem and went her way.

She swung downriver, past the Old Stairs of Wapping, past Limehouse Reach with its bow-windowed water-front houses, past the Isle of Dogs, so named because an English king once maintained royal kennels thereabouts. Then she took the wide sweep off Blackwall Reach where, not so many years before, gibbets bore the bodies of river pirates hanging in creaking chains. To her, to her captain, all this was home; and it would be many months before she returned. She was bidding farewell to all these well-known landmarks, as she had so often done in the past.

The wintry sunlight glinted momentarily on her gleaming brasswork and moved fleeting across her black-and-white deck-houses; then she was gone in the haze. She dropped her hook at sundown, a ponderous lump of metal with a vast stock and even vaster rings on the purchase of the cathead, and came to rest swinging leisurely on the tide as her crew began to shake down. Sixty-eight officers and seamen, with four apprentices, were her tally, but now she was short four ordinary seamen. Meantime, the remainder stowed their sea chests and ditty bags, each man jealous of his own spike, his own set of sailmaking needles, great three-sided affairs with points well worn, and his own horn of grease.

Her four apprentices, all from good homes, had been indentured by their parents to the owners, and a bond paid against their deserting the ship before completing their apprenticeship; that bond, a substantial amount, wasn't easy to find when a boy was one of a large family. After four years of hard work and theoretical examinations had been passed, the boy qualified as second mate, usually when he was about eighteen. Thereafter he had the chance of obtaining a master's deep-sea ticket before he reached the ripe old age of twenty-five. So there was nothing at all unusual for an eighteen-year-old second mate to rule the toughest bunch of seamen anywhere afloat.

By sunset, the passengers filed aboard and the decks were crowded with seasoned planters and merchants returning from a spell in England rubbing shoulders with side-whiskered young men making their first voyage to India. Among them went the second mate, cursing the world in general as he superintended stowage of passengers' belongings in the main hatch.

An hour later, with some semblance of order on deck, a rowboat put out from the water front and spilled its sorry-looking passengers aboard – four listless seamen rounded up at the last moment by a crimp to whom they owed debts; he was glad to have them off his hands, money or no money. The first mate looked them over, muttering unprintable comments well known to men of the sea.

The night hours slipped by and, by dawn, her blue peter aloft, she was ready to go. A pale sun climbed into the eastern sky as her capstan was manned; the pilot took a last look around her decks, nodded to the skipper, and her anchor cable came slowly aboard. She was on her way, feeling the bite of a freshening wind in her sails. Her house flag dipped as she rounded Barking Creek and headed for the open sea. Later she rolled through the short Channel seas, heading into the west. In his cabin the skipper prepared to sign on the four last-minute ordinary seamen; at his side stood the senior apprentice, due to become second mate.

The skipper had carried out this necessary bit of paperwork so many times in the past, he could have recited the ship's articles from memory. But it had to be done. The second mate pushed open the door. The four ordinary seamen filed in and the captain looked them over. A poor lot, he decided, but maybe they could be licked into shape; he took a seat at his desk and intoned the words:

... hereby engaged to serve as sailors and agree to work aboard the said ship in the several capacities set against our names on voyage from London to Bombay. And we do agree to conduct ourselves in an orderly, honest and sober manner, and to be at all times diligent in our respective duties, and to be obedient to the lawful commands of the said Master ...

The captain's voice droned on to the end; then he sighed, waited as the four men scrawled signatures to the document, and dismissed them. From now on they would be the mates' headaches. To the senior apprentice he said:

"That's how we do it, my son. Never forget, a seaman has his rights equally with those of his master. You get along to the galley and find some hot coffee." He shivered. It was a bleak, inhospitable day.

The apprentice had taken a seat on an upturned bucket in a dark corner of the cook's domain when the four newly signed seamen ambled in, seeking hot coffee also. Craggy-jawed character that he was, the cook, in the light of his galley fire, appeared a bare-chested mountain of a man whose steel-blue eyes plainly showed that he would just as soon fling a cleaver at unwelcome visitors like these as dish out their chow. Long ago, on the Indian run, the cook had slept on deck one stifling night and had, it was said, been moonstruck, which accounted for his twisted mouth and cruel expression. Actually, he was almost as mild-mannered as the skipper, but his fearsome-looking face paid dividends.

He shoved four cans of coffee across the top of his galley stove, looked across at the senior apprentice and deliberately winked an eye; then he addressed himself to his four visitors.

"Ain't seen anything the likes of you since I come up screamin' from a nightmare when I was a kid." He paused, allowing his preamble to sink in, and continued: "Tired o' living, are you? You don't bear no resemblance to seamen, but who cares? We ain't callin' no place till Bombay, so you got to go through with it." He contrived a twisted leer, lowered his voice as if about to impart a fearful warning. "I reckon it won't be long before th' Old Man breaks your perishin' 'earts; that is, if he don't bust your heads in first. Why else d'you think he got the name Haunted Cap'n?

"I'll tell you," he went on, "and what I'm tellin' you is truth. We was beatin' north at the time, along the Bay o' Bengal, and the Old Man a-drivin' her like no man in his

senses ought. He gets the notion the helmsman ain't on his
mark, so he grabs a belayin' pin, meanin' to put the fear o'
God into the poor devil, when along comes an ugly sea, climbs
the weather rail, takes the skipper's legs from under him. As he
goes down, the helmsman does the same, only with a busted
skull.

"We buried 'im that same day. We dassn't take a peek at
the Old Man as he reads the committal service, an' when it's
over somebody calls him the Haunted Cap'n, an' the name
sticks. 'Cause why, you ask? 'Cause we know the ghost of the
dead helmsman'll come back aboard soon as it's decent. That
same night, in dirt, the watch was doin' their best to shorten
sail which is comin' adrift from the bolt ropes, when one of 'em
lets out a yell which can be heard at Cape Stiff, sayin' as how
he's seen a ghost. Then he passes out an' would've fell clear to
the deck if a mate hadn't grabbed him.

"They get him down on deck, carry him to the skipper's
cabin. The Old Man looks him over an' swigs a tot o' rum
between the poor devil's teeth. When he comes to, the seaman
says he's seen a ghost. 'Yes,' says th' Old Man, sceptical, but
always ready to humour a loony, 'an' what did this here ghost
look like, tell me that?' 'Why, it was th' helmsman!' cries the
seaman, half out of his wits. 'It comes edgin' towards me in the
yards, looks me clear in the eye, but it ain't got no eyes – only
empty sockets!' Then he gets up, bolts for the door, yellin' 'You
murdered him! Now it's come back to haunt you and the
ship!'

"That's all he got to say before he was out on deck and over
the weather rail, an' we never saw him again." The cook drew
a breath that whistled between his teeth. "You fellers take my
tip. Don't never cross paths with the Old Man, not unless you
ain't got no more interest in life."

The four men shuffled out of the galley, muttering; it was a
story the cook had told a dozen times before to newcomers he
disliked on sight. It was always the same, highlighting the skipper as a fiend in captain's rig.

And right now, that same "human fiend" was welcoming
into his cabin a favoured passenger, an elderly planter making
his last voyage to India. The skipper poured a generous measure of whisky for his guest, helped himself to a glass of neat
unsweetened lime juice, for he had been a strict teetotaller
since he first went to sea. They toasted each other. Then the

guest asked whether the cook still told that old fantastic yarn of his, and how did it feel to be a haunted captain? The skipper grinned.

"There was one occasion," he said, "when I was nearly convinced we had a real ghost aboard. We were homeward bound from Melbourne at the time and made good running as far as Cape Town, when the weather broke and we were forced to heave-to. We lay waiting for the wind to ease and, as it did, the ship seemed curiously quiet. Then a seaman came running, scared out of his wits, and said he had heard a 'fearful sound' in the fo'c'sle, like a dying man would make – the death rattle. It seemed two or three other hands had heard it, so I decided the only thing to do was organize a search party and scour the ship from stem to stern, if only to prevent panic.

"With the second mate, I took charge of one party, the first and third mate starting from the stern; we proceeded in the direction of the fo'c'sle and there, to our astonishment and, I suspect, to the men's utter dismay, we saw a white-clad figure, its arms raised to the skies, with long, fair hair down to its shoulders. It uttered a fearful cry, and the men in our party fell to their knees, covered their eyes or prayed as if the last day was upon them and they were coming up for judgment. It was a tense moment. And then the second mate stepped forward and took that 'ghost' in his arms and carried it to my cabin. It was one of our passengers, a young woman suffering from some mental disturbance. She recovered soon enough. We had no more hauntings after that, and this ship never will. Take my word on it."

"But that death rattle?" the skipper's guest asked.

"Quite simple," said the skipper. "Just a loose guy rope rattling in the wind against the fo'c'sle door. No sir, in thirty-odd years I've spent at sea I've yet to find anything genuine in any of the stories of the supernatural."

With a favourable following wind, in good weather and calm seas, the bark pushed ahead and made the running in elegant style. She rounded the Cape of Good Hope, stuck her forefoot into cross-seas and headed into the 4,600-mile run to Bombay. Six days later the course was set for the final leg of her voyage, due north-east. But then the glass fell rapidly and within a matter of hours the wind reached full gale force with monstrous seas cracking over the weather rail.

Poultry coops were stove in and washed adrift; cabins were
flooded as cataracts of water poured over luckless passengers.
The galley was cleared by a mountain of water and reduced to
chaos. Sails were torn adrift from gaskets and hung in shreds.
On the orders of the captain, oil bags were hauled out of the
main hatch, hung out to windward and punctured so that
their contents would smooth the water. For a whole day the
crew fought like demons to save themselves and the ship. With
a lull in the gale fury, they cleaned up much of the wreckage,
got one of the galley stoves going, and the cook prepared a
meal. Then it blew again, though now with less venom.

In the middle watch, a day later, gripping the wheel spokes
until the knuckles of both hands showed white, the helmsman
gulped his coffee and spoke grimly to the senior apprentice.

"You seen more'n your share of real dirt these last few days,
I reckon? God knows, we'd never have come through without
the Old Man. An' did you see the face on him?"

"Who? The captain?"

"For Gawd's sake, you didn't see it? Th' first mate? I tell
ya, there was th' mark on him!"

"The mark?"

"Didn't I say it? Th' mark of a man lookin' death in th'
eyes. Dead scared. And that goes for the second mate too.
Yeller-bellied, them two. Look . . ." The helmsman lowered
his voice. "Me, I've sailed in this ship the las' five trips, but no
more. We make Bombay – if we ever make it, that is – an' I
figure I'll go ashore, an' likely as not forget to come back
aboard.

"There's better mates, mebbe better ships than this. I'll sign
aboard somethin' that ain't got a couple o' walkin' corpses on
her poop callin' themselves mates. These last few days o' dirt
scared th' guts outa both of 'em. There's only the Old Man left
doin' the work of two mates, an' that don't get ships to port,
does it? Like a man sleepwalkin', the Old Man was, when he
tells me, beginnin' of this watch, 'Nor-'east, an' keep 'er steady
there.' With that he walked away, out on his feet. It ain't
human. That's why I'm gettin' out, see?"

The senior apprentice contrived a grin: "Bide your time,"
he counselled. "You're tired, like the rest of us. Once we tie up
in Bombay you'll feel different. Why, you'll –" He stopped in
the middle of the sentence.

"I'll do what?" the helmsman asked.

The apprentice nudged his elbow. "Pipe down. We've a visitor —"

Without so much as by-your-leave, a tall, barrel-chested man pushed past the astonished helmsman and peered into the compass; the binnacle light emphasized in strong relief the ugly weal of a wound that curved across one temple, bisected the cheek, ended just below the grim-set lips. "Steer nor'-nor'-east."

The helmsman was plainly startled by the abrupt order: "Beggin' your pardon, but I ain't takin' no course th' Old Man didn't give me. Nor'east, he said."

The stranger spoke again, this time with an urgent note in his voice: "I said take the ship nor'-nor'east, man, and look lively, for every moment counts!" Then he was gone.

"For God's sake," implored the puzzled helmsman, "what am I to do? Look, you just step out on th' poop an' tell th' second mate I been ordered to change course. I ain't changin' course without th' Old Man's say-so; him or the second mate's."

As puzzled as the senior apprentice, the second mate asked the helmsman, "Who was this man?"

"Ain't no idea, sir. He come in here, ordered me twice to change course, then walked out. So do I take 'er nor-'nor'east or don't I?"

"Best ask the Old Man," suggested the apprentice.

"He's sleeping," objected the second mate, "so he wouldn't thank me for rousing him. You said nor'-nor'east, helmsman — that's what you were told?" The helmsman nodded in reply. The second mate passed a hand across his eyes, then looked at the compass: "All right, man — plenty of searoom around these parts. Take her nor'-nor'east like you were told." And the bark swung slowly on her fresh course . . .

The skipper was just awakening from his first real sleep in a week when excited shouting on deck brought him tumbling to his feet. A pale dawn had broken, splitting the heavy skies with shafts of light, and in that light four lifeboats were coming alongside, oars shipped by men reaching the limit of human endurance. They were helped aboard and their spokesman moved wearily across to the captain.

"Our ship took fire," he explained, like a man waking from a hideous nightmare. "We did our best to quench the flames, but the wind fanned them and there wasn't a chance. She

burned down to her water-line, then went down. You showed
up just in time, for we couldn't have lasted another hour."

"Your captain here?"

"No, sir. He was killed as we lowered our boats. The burning mainmast split two-thirds of its length and he was struck
across the head and knocked overboard. We searched, but
failed to find any trace of him. He was our only fatality. There
are some of us with minor wounds, but nothing serious."

They were taken below to be tended. Shortly after dawn the
lookout called: "Object off th' port bow, sir!" It was the lifeless
body of a man; a tall, barrel-chested man whose face was dis-
figured by a wound running from the left temple to the pain-
twisted mouth, set firm in death . . .

This, then, is the story that was told me during Christmas,
1959; the story of a ghost captain who came aboard the elegant
three-master and changed her course so that his officers and
crew might be spared. I have, with permission, filled in just a
few gaps in the story. Who was my storyteller? A retired
naval commander, a man who chose the sea straight from
school at the age of fourteen. He was the senior apprentice who
attended the skipper while he read ship's articles to the four
tardy seamen, and who sat enjoying himself in the galley while
the cook spun his crazy yarn. He was, also, the youngster who
was with the helmsman when the phantom captain came
aboard and altered ship's course.

I have purposely omitted names of both ships out of consideration for the feelings of any living relatives of the officers and
men concerned. But in every other respect the story is true and
set down as faithfully as it was told to me.

THE HOODOO OF
THE *GREAT EASTERN*

For a dozen years, American and British shipping interests and governments, with what seemed utter contempt for cost, had battled for supremacy on the world's most lucrative trade route, the North Atlantic. Since 1840, two main contestants, Massachusetts-born Edward Knight Collins and Newfoundlander Samuel Cunard, firmly established in London, each with government financial blessing, had planned, built and launched ships capable of clipping off the odd hour or two in crossing from New York to Liverpool, Boston to London. Their ships ranged from the earlier 1,000-tonners of Cunard to the Collins newcomers of around the 3,000-ton mark.

Neither side appeared to be getting anywhere. Meantime, Washington and London glowered at each other across the 3,000-mile expanse of sea.

To a man like Isambard Kingdom Brunel the whole situation was ridiculous. There was no real vision displayed by either contestant, nothing was really accomplished. They just went on battling it out the hard way.

Brunel considered the matter carefully from every angle. It was all so very simple; a really large ship could do the work of two smaller, and cost less to operate, provided of course that the larger vessel was designed and built attractively enough to enjoy a full passenger list, with her holds packed tight with profit-earning freight each voyage. If a shipbuilder constructed a fine liner, an elegant ship, twice the size of those Collins and

Cunard were operating, her money-making capacity would be stepped up not twice but fourfold.

Collins' record makers, the *Pacific* and the *Arctic*, both measured 2,860 tons; Cunard's largest was of the same tonnage, though Cunard had plans to build a 3,300-tonner. However, she would not be ready for two to three years. In that time, with larger, swifter ships, the world would rapidly shrink in size.

Brunel had decided on building a giant liner, the largest in the world – 20,000 tons gross, with a displacement around the 35,000-ton mark. She would make anything the main contestants now possessed, or dreamed of building in the foreseeable future, appear dwarfed.

Successful builder of bridges and railroads, Brunel sketched his rough plans, then visited London's most famous shipbuilder. No time was to be lost. He said: "We will put this new ship of mine on the London–Australia service and there attract so large a portion of the world's traffic on this long haul as to make certain of full freights and passenger lists at highly remunerative rates both outward and homeward." He registered his company, the Great Eastern Steam Navigation, guaranteeing shareholders 40 per cent dividends.

A sceptic queried his ideas about size. Brunel told him, "The *Great Eastern* will be at least twenty-five thousand tons." The questioner raised his eyebrows. "But why stop there? Why not make it one hundred thousand tons?" Brunel grinned. "Maybe I'll take you up on that idea."

Slowly, his monster ship took shape – 608 feet long, 80 feet in the beam; her hull would be divided into ten separate compartments of 60 feet each by using transverse bulkheads, then those ten would be subdivided into thirty-six, and the whole lot would be enclosed in a double hull, so that there would be two ships, one within the other, all constructed of cellular steel framing.

That double hull – two iron "skins" three feet apart, one ship within another – was Brunel's master stroke, revolutionary, something never visualized before in world shipbuilding – a hermetically sealed compartment that would extend from the great keelplate up to the water line.

This enormous hull would provide for ten vast boilers, fed by 112 furnaces; to carry away furnace smoke there would be five tall funnels, towering towards the skies like huge fingers.

The boilers would generate steam power amply sufficient to turn two 58-foot paddle-wheels and, in addition, an auxiliary 24-foot propeller. Working normally, Brunel predicted, those boilers would comfortably produce around 15,000 horse-power.

The average mind was staggered by these facts and figures. A contemporary historian wrote: "We are lost in wonder at the amount of mechanical power which will thus be brought into play in the propulsion of one vessel, and the smoothness and harmony with which that duty will be performed, in a space necessarily confined and limited and amid all the violent turmoil of the ocean. No work of art ever produced furnished more exalted ideas of one man's genius and skill than the unceasing and regular motion of these gigantic engines when once they are set working!"

Just in case this giant should ever suffer temporary engine failure and need to rely on the forces of nature, Brunel rigged her with six towering masts to carry a colossal expanse of sail; and in the very unlikely event of meeting trouble on her voyages, she would carry not two but ten mighty anchors weighing five tons apiece.

For interior furnishings and decorations, Brunel combed the world's luxury markets and installed richly carved walnut, velvet seating, arabesque panelling, elegant cut-glass mirrors, drawing-rooms such as passengers never hoped to see anywhere but in fashionable hotels. She would be born of his genius and could not avoid reflecting his own ideas of beauty.

When the *Great Eastern* was completed she was a staggering achievement; she even had artificial moonlight "all around her" provided by a gas-making plant, claimed to be "the most outstandingly original scheme of all in this superb and revolutionary vessel". On 2 November, 1857, the *Great Eastern* lay on the Thames water-front awaiting launch the following noon.

On account of her immense size, the liner had been built broadside-on to the river, therefore she would slip gently broadside into the water. It would be quite a simple operation.

Her great keel had been constructed across two vast cradles, each around 18 feet square, which she would take with her into mid-river. To overcome any unexpected hitch in launching, Brunel ordered a couple of powerful hydraulic rams, capable of lending a 1,000-ton pressure against her hull; and, to halt her progress once she started moving into the river, there was a series of heavy chains that would hold her back and still let her go carefully, gracefully on her way.

Londoners braved a spell of inclement weather, with a hint of snow, and converged on the water-front to witness the breathtaking event. The guests took their places on the grand-stand built for the occasion, and from the shipyard came the army of men who had laboured so long to complete the *Great Eastern*. Everybody had been invited as Brunel's guests; but not everybody attended. One man – a master shipwright, seldom seen during construction, for his time had been concentrated on fashioning the double hull – was missing, nobody knew where he could be located.

The hands of the shipyard clock moved slowly, the waters of the river lapped gently around the launching cradles; and from some place below the towering hull spectators heard the hollow thud of hammer blows. It was an annoying sound. But it was drowned when the assembled multitude cheered them-selves hoarse as the liner was christened. Her launching gear was set in motion, drums took the strain of the heavy chains, and the ship was away.

She moved a couple of feet, a yard, then those chains brought up taut, sagged, tautened again, fell limp into the river. Slowly, the *Great Eastern* slewed around, her forepart moved exactly three and a half feet, her stern shifted seven feet; then it became obvious, her cradles, not moving in time together, had jammed, holding the ship at an awkward angle.

Experts went into hasty conference, inspected the launching gear, shook their heads in dismay. The only thing to do, they decided, was wait until high water. A dismal silence wrapped itself around the scene . . . a silence broken unexpectedly by the thud of hammer blows from some place near the midships keel.

Lunch-time came and passed; the fabulous banquet became a mockery. The rising wind with its biting chill froze the crowds which began drifting away. The hours dragged by, and then shortly before three o'clock, the launching drums were in-spected again and set moving; the chains tautened, slacked, tautened once more, taking the strain. Nothing happened, nothing, that is, until one of the chains burst its great links and fell into the river. The *Great Eastern* remained motionless. The remaining guests took a last look at her bulk and faded away into the growing darkness.

Days grew into weeks; the hydraulic rams were tried again and again, finally burst away from their moorings, fractured the launching cradles. On the evening of 22 November, Brunel asked a fellow director of his company what he thought of the giant liner and her prospects. He was told that maybe the best thing Brunel could do was to bed her down permanently where she lay and open her to the public as a fun-fair.

Seamen passed her, outward bound in their ships, looked across the river and shook their heads. They said she would still be there next year and the years after. It looked, they told each other, as if the *Great Eastern* would stay there forever. The more superstitious seamen claimed she had a sinister streak and it would be an evil day when she sailed.

On 28 November, Brunel tried once again, using new drums, but they too burst apart. However, while they worked they managed to shift the liner four inches at her forepart, nine inches at her stern. Then she halted and lay undisturbed through December, over Christmas and into the first week of January. With every means available, a fresh attempt was made to get her into the river, and she moved sufficiently until almost eight feet of the Thames lapped at her starboard quarter. Then she brought up to a halt.

A combination of strong easterly winds, an early spring tide and unexpectedly heavy rains did the trick where all the ingenuity of man had failed. Towards mid-March the big ship eased away, took the wrecked cradles with her, and drifted gently into the river. She was afloat. That same evening Brunel faced his fellow directors and told them, "Gentlemen, I estimated that the cost to launch our ship would be in the region of £14,000. Instead, it has now cost our company nearly £120,000."

They offered the liner for sale to the British Government, claiming that in civilian service she could be a money-spinner, in time of war nothing afloat could hope to stand up to her. But the politicians were not impressed; they said they might reconsider the matter if and when Brunel could send this great liner of his into the open seas and maintain twenty knots economical speed. Two weeks later the Great Eastern Steam Navigation folded up, having exhausted its subscribed capital, and a week later the liner was bought for £160,000 by the newly formed Great Ship Company.

It was fine and warm, 15 September, 1859, when the *Great*

Eastern, escorted by four river tugboats as a precautionary step, steamed downriver and into the open sea at thirteen knots. Brunel was not there to watch her go – this product of his genius. He had died. The day his death, the *Great Eastern*'s captain complained to his chief engineer that his rest had been "rudely disturbed by constant hammering from below".

Four hours later, nearing Southampton in the teeth of a stiff breeze, her pilot reported her as "quite at ease at a time when large sailing ships nearby lay under doule-reefed topsails; this magnificent ship is in every respect an excellent sea boat and I can state without any hesitation that, with sufficient sea room, she is even more easily handled and under command than any ordinary ship, either under sail or steam."

Moments later the casing of one of the five tall smoke stacks exploded in a deafening roar, killing six members of the engine-room crew and wrecking the grand saloon.

Fitted out at long last, widely advertised as due to "sail for the Port of New York, 17 June, 1860," the North Atlantic newcomer – her new owners had given up the idea of putting her on the Australian service – lay alongside in Southampton awaiting her passengers. She had accommodation for 800 first-class, 2,000 second-class, 1,206 third-class passengers, with a crew of 400. But when she steamed out on her maiden voyage she carried 36 fare-paying passengers, including two women, a couple of hardy directors of the Great Ship Company and her full crew complement. She reached New York after a totally uneventful crossing on 28 June; she had made a new record of eleven days.

On her second North Atlantic crossing with 100 passengers aboard, she made New York, a distance of 3,093 miles under steam, in 10 days, and her future looked bright indeed. She was clipping off not just hours but days, as Brunel had foretold.

Her third voyage was into Quebec, commissioned as a British Government transport, and she carried 2,079 soldiers, 46 officers, 159 women, 244 children, and 40 fare-paying civilian passengers. It was a splendid triumph, and complete vindication. Something sinister about this superb liner? Just foolish talk . . .

Back in England, though on this occasion switched from Southampton to Liverpool, the *Great Eastern* was released from government requisition and returned to normal passenger service. Her advertised sailing date attracted four hundred people ready to pay for first-class accommodation, besides a number of emigrants. She steamed out of the Mersey on a mild afternoon in autumn, out to the Irish coast, and altered course so that she would pass the Fastnet Lighthouse, off Cape Clear, most south-westerly point of Ireland. With supreme disdain, she steamed serenely past the record-making Black Ball packet *Underwriter*, heading into a vicious sea. Late that night the weather broke unexpectedly, but for all that, and in the teeth of increasing headwinds, the *Great Eastern* was on her way west. Then, in late afternoon, somewhere below the engine-room plating, came the dull thud of hammer blows.

Minutes later, meeting mile-long combers coming at her haphazardly and with monstrous strength, she was caught broadside and almost overturned. Her terrified passengers sought shelter behind anything that looked reasonably secure. Then, moments before an enormous sea took her in its giant grip, those muffled hammer blows were heard again. A split second later one of the 58-foot paddle-wheels was torn from its mountings, her rudder stock was fractured. Four lifeboats went overboard, splintered to matchwood. Indescribable scenes of panic followed as still greater seas struck at her. The second paddle-wheel came unshipped and disappeared to the sea-bed. One by one, her lifeboats were torn from their falls and flung into the raging seas. Furnishings were wrenched away and strewn across wrecked saloons and cabins.

By nightfall passengers were huddled in groups, alternately praying and singing hymns. Shortly before dawn the crew mutinied, broke open the spirit storeroom and began a drunken orgy. Captain Walker mustered every available male passenger, armed as many as he had guns for, set them to patrol the stricken vessel. So it continued all day until, late in the afternoon, the 3,871-ton Cunard *Scotia*, Queenstown to New York, steamed out of the east, circled the *Great Eastern*, then continued on her way. Throughout a long, agonizing night the big liner rolled helplessly. At dawn a Nova Scotian brig appeared out of the west, changed course, came alongside and looked over the scene incredulously. It seemed to one passenger aboard the stricken liner a heaven-sent chance; he hailed the brig's captain, offered £100 for every day the Nova Scotian would stand by. The offer was refused, and immediately increased with a bid to buy brig and her freight outright so that all passengers could be transferred and taken back to an English port. But the brig, taking one more disbelieving turn around the *Great Eastern*, turned on course and sailed away.

Two days later, after unceasing work patching her up as best they could, her engineers rigged a jury rudder stock, got her propeller turning, and worked the big ship painfully back into Queenstown. It was the end; she would never again hope to become a North Atlantic record maker. She was a suicide ship, they said around the coast of Britain . . .

She was stripped of her ornate and elegant furnishings, fitted with new boilers and a new smoke stack. Between 1865 and 1866, she helped lay a section of the first North Atlantic cable; then she returned to port and was offered for sale to the highest bidder. But nobody wanted this "much belauded pet of Brunel's constructive genius"; nobody bid for her; even port authorities around Britain petitioned the Government to pass a law forbidding the laying-up of the ship in waters under their control. In the end she changed hands once again, and her new owners, conceiving the idea that here was a superb floating publicity billboard, hired the *Great Eastern* to a Liverpool store, whose directors had her cliff-like sides plastered with posters offering "Genuine bargains for Discerning Men and Women seeking Elegant Attire and Household Furnishings".

The experiment lasted less than one month, then she lay derelict, deserted, until 1885, when a ship breaker bought her for £16,000 and arranged to have the unwanted giant towed to his yards. And as tugboats hooked their lines to her and began hauling her on her last journey, the lone watchman left aboard ran to the rails and pleaded to be taken off immediately. He had heard the thud of hammer blows, and though he searched the ship from stem to stern, he could find no trace of human agency. The tugboat crews laughed his fears to scorn, but took him aboard and hauled away at their tow. But before they could reach the breaker's yard the helpless giant appeared to slip the towlines and then tried hard to hurl herself on the nearby coast. Only by superhuman efforts was she again taken in tow and thus brought to her journey's end. There, on the slipway, opening up the double hull above the keel amidships, breaker's men found a carpetbag of rusted tools; and alongside, the skeleton of the master shipwright who had been accidentally entombed between the hulls during the final stages of the *Great Eastern*'s construction.

WHAT THE DONKEYMAN SAID

It happened in 1949, when the *Port Pirie*, a 10,500 ton freighter, was alongside the Sydney water front after a fine run out from United Kingdom ports. In such times it usually falls to the unenviable lot of junior engineers to work nights in the engine room, from around the beginning of the middle watch until just before the morning watch takes over, tackling odd jobs the senior second engineer figures need tackling. And on this night Jonesy, the sixth engineer, had been required by the senior second engineer to repack the swing arms of the port main engine, which meant he would work most of the time right inside the engine crankcase. Not a particularly enjoyable space to be confined in on a night like that, for it was unbearably hot and humid. Keeping him company would be the donkeyman, new to the job, whose work was no more strenuous than tending the small, oil-fired Cochrane boiler.

Jonesy and the donkeyman went on watch around 11 p.m. and even then reckoned it seemed a mighty long while before the clock showed seven and released them from duty.

The polished steel handrails felt unusually slippery with a mixture of oil and moisture as they stepped below, and the engine-room atmosphere was in sharp contrast with what little fresh air there was on deck. It was far too warm, too steamy, for in any ship, in port or afloat, some steam always manages to find its way outside the steam pipes and cylinders. Tonight, the place did not echo with the noise of thumping machinery, and that was a blessing, Jonesy thought, though it did seem to create a strangely quiet atmosphere. Maybe too quiet. Only the diesel generator over on the starboard side was working, and then merely with a soft purring sound.

They stepped down to the engine-room plating; right across the way was the fire room and, on a night like this, no place for any man to work in. Away towards the stern was about the quietest place down below, an alleyway in which ran smooth columns of steel which turned around and around when the ship was at sea, without a sound. Those columns, stilled now, were the propeller shafts.

Jonesy paused and gazed around him and aloft; this was a spacious compartment, as lofty, as imposing in its way as a cathedral and nearly as silent. He wondered why deck officers took so little notice of the heart of a ship; not exactly the tactful thing to do, for without an engine room a ship is useless. The engineer makes machinery work, taking a ship across the seven seas and back; but navigating officers ignore the engine room, as a man ignores his stomach until something goes wrong. And when something goes wrong in the engine room, the deck crowd are as helpless as a man with acute dyspepsia and just about as cheerful.

He climbed into the crankcase and climbed out again. A thought had struck him. He called to the donkeyman, "Everything under control?"

The donkeyman nodded.

"Okay," said Jonesy, "then you nip up aloft and grab a couple of hours' sleep. I'll take care of that Cochrane job while you're away. Maybe, according whether I've got these swing arms repacked around three o'clock or thereabouts, we'll change places and you can take over until seven."

The donkeyman grinned. "Suits me, but what would the second say?"

"Plenty – if he knew, but he doesn't and won't."

The donkeyman climbed the long steel stairway and disappeared, and Jonesy went to work inside the port main engine crankcase; as he worked he could hear the generator running, a comforting sound muted by distance. For between that generator and him were the two main engines; and the boiler room, a half-enclosed compartment, was located in the engine room's port forward section, and from inside the crankcase he could hear a slightly louder sound – the sound of the feed pump as it fed water into the boiler.

He had always had his own pet label for the sound that feed pump made. He called it the "engineer's lullaby". For the piston of the pump started on its upstroke with an insidious, sibilant *whee* that started well down the musical scale and worked its way slowly up; then, on the downstroke, the *whee* went into reverse, and each subsequent *whee* ended with an audible click as the shuttle valve moved across and set the whole thing in motion once more. Jonesy always reckoned it was second nature for an engineer to keep an ear tuned to that *whee*, because if it stopped suddenly, that was the signal the boiler was short of water. If a man ignored the cessation of that subtle sound, a boiler could blow up.

The hands of the engine-room clock moved towards twelve; from way up above on deck Jonesy heard the ship's bells as watches changed, the middle watch taking over from a bunch of weary-eyed seamen who needed sleep. And then, as near silence returned to the engine room, in the confined space of the crankcase Jonesy's ears picked up the sound of that feed pump. Its *whee* had suddenly become erratic as it speeded up.

He stopped work for a moment, assured himself it meant nothing, as the rate of pumping was automatically controlled; but when the sound became faster and threatened to trip over itself on down- and upstrokes, he knew he had better take a look at the thing.

He went to the boiler room. The feed pump was working flat out. He glanced over at the boiler gauge, and that indicated that the boiler was pretty near capacity. Jonesy thought it was cockeyed, for if the boiler was almost full, then there was no need or reason for the feed pump to work at pressure. He changed the pump from automatic to hand control, slowed it down, went back to his job and climbed inside the crankcase.

Within a minute the feed pump was working itself into a frenzy of activity. He climbed out again, investigated, found that the gauge still registered capacity load inside the boiler. He stopped the pump completely and went back to his job.

This time, there was barely a few seconds gone when that feed pump went mad, feeding water into the boiler like nobody's business. Yet Jonesy knew he had shut it off. Okay! If a feed pump felt that way, he reckoned he knew what ought to be done; this time, he promised himself as he climbed out from the crankcase, *this* time he would make dead certain it *did* stop. He selected a wheel key from a rack of engine-room tools.

Stripped of technical jargon, this is how a wheel key works: It is a spanner for closing valves, a steel bar forked at one end, with one end of the fork a hook, the other a cup – not unlike the two rests a fisherman places his rod in. By placing a wheel-key hook *over* a valve wheel and the cup *against* it, a valve can be closed hard down.

Jonesy used the wheel key and closed down that valve so tight, two strong men couldn't have opened it by hand. He stepped back and watched the feed pump. It had stopped. He was satisfied it would not work again until he opened it with the wheel key. He went back to the crankcase, climbed inside, and was picking up a tool when the feed pump went completely haywire again.

He stepped across to the pump with purposeful stride; *this* time, he decided, he would do what he ought to have done in the first place. He would test the boiler gauge for accuracy.

Just how long that gauge had been out of action Jonesy had no idea; all he knew was that it did not mean a thing. The boiler was so nearly empty that it made no difference, yet the gauge showed it almost full. Slowly, it dawned on him: Had it not been for the strange behaviour of the shut-down feed pump the boiler would have exploded any moment now and would have destroyed itself, including the engine room and much of the ship herself. His brow was cold with sweat, his legs trembled; his hands were shaking, too, as he made good the fault, started up the feed pump and took the first deep breath in minutes. He reckoned he had a lot to be grateful for. Then he went back to the crankcase, climbed inside, set to work repacking the swing arms, and completed the job just as the morning watch was taking over at four o'clock. It had been a fearful night. He gathered his gear, crawled into his bunk, but sleep eluded him for a very long time.

It was long past noon before Jonesy wakened, shaved and dressed and went along to the engineers' dining saloon. He nodded absent-mindedly at two senior engineers smoking their after-lunch cigarettes; they looked as if they were sitting on top of the world; he wished he felt that way. Last night's affair still puzzled him. He muttered thanks to the steward as a meal was placed before him, picked up knife and fork, paused as the second senior engineer, looking across the table at him with an air of good-humoured indulgence, said: "You look like a man with a bad hangover. You been on the bottle?"

"If I had, I had plenty of reason."

Jonesy put down his knife and fork, pushed the plate away, leaned forward in his chair and gave them the story, punctuating each occasion when he had climbed out of the crankcase with an emphatic square-ended finger on the white tablecloth. He gave his two seniors the bare facts. No frills. And when he stopped speaking, he cocked an inquisitive eye at them and challenged: "None of the crowd tried pulling a fast one on me, maybe? There wasn't another wheel key down there anyway."

"So what?"

"Just an idea that struck me. It wouldn't have been particularly clever if somebody did."

"Don't be silly. Who'd want to?"

"I wouldn't know, and that's for sure. But the way I figure it somebody must have opened that feed-pump valve after I locked it, but who? I used the wheel key. The entire engine-room department couldn't open it after that . . ."

One of his two listeners, a man who had served on the *Port Pirie* since her launching, lighted a fresh cigarette, drew on it thoughtfully. "Look, Jonesy, if that feed pump hadn't gone haywire, even after you locked it with the key, you wouldn't have finally checked the boiler gauge, wouldn't have found it wasn't working and the boiler darned near empty, and then . . ." He paused, blew a thin stream of blue smoke. "And then, before you could do anything more, the boiler, much of the engine room, maybe the ship herself, if there had been fire, could have been destroyed. Yes, you and us, too. No. None of the engine-room boys pulled a fast one. After you locked that valve down it wasn't any human agency opened it up again."

Jonesy stared. "What you're saying is . . . No, you're crazy!"

"Our first donkeyman we signed on shortly after the ship was commissioned. He was killed one night when that boiler blew up. Lack of water. The poor devil lived just long enough to mutter it wouldn't happen a second time, and died. And it hasn't happened again. I'm no believer in the supernatural, but I reckon I'm not wrong in saying he's been aboard *waiting for what happened last night*."

" 'It won't happen again'?" Jonesy was talking quietly, as if to himself.

The steward entered the saloon. "Not feeling like lunch, sir? Like some coffee?"

Jonesy roused himself. "Eh? Oh, coffee? Black and strong. Strong as you can make it." But the coffee remained untouched and went cold.

I have set down this story exactly as it reached me from former sixth engineer Peter Jones. I would not presume to add any personal comment, for that would be unnecessary. I accept it as it stands; whether you will, it is not for me to forecast.

Recovered from the Deep

THE JONAH EXPERIENCE?

"Now the word of the Lord came unto Jonah the son of Amittai, saying 'Arise, go to Nineveh, that great city, and cry against it; for their wickedness is come up before me.' But Jonah rose up to flee unto Tarshish from the presence of the Lord, and went down to Joppa, and he found a ship going to Tarshish; so he paid the fare thereof, and went down into it . . ."

The Prophet Jonah's subsequent adventures are proverbial. According to the Scriptures, as laid down in the Book of Jonah, a mighty tempest blew up, threatening the ship in which he sailed with utter destruction. Panic reigned aboard. All possible ballast was hurled over the sides, as the sailors swore and prayed. Jonah, somewhere under hatches, slept through it all, until the captain shook him awake and asked him, somewhat roughly, no doubt, to add his prayers to theirs.

Sailors are superstitious creatures. Women and priests are, or were, notoriously unlucky people to carry to sea. Neither being present on this particular cruise to Tarshish, they drew lots to find out who was the passenger responsible for attracting bad luck. It was Jonah who drew the short straw, or whatever they used. They questioned him keenly.

"What is the cause of this calamity? What is the reason for it? Who are you? What do you do? From whence do you come?"

"I am Hebrew," he answered. "I fear the Lord, maker of the sea and the land." And then he admitted that his purpose in going to sea had been to fly from the Lord's command. The sailors discussed among themselves what was best to do to calm the wild sea and save their ship. And Jonah, no doubt troubled and confused in his mind, and glad of a way out, however desperate, said to them: "Take me up and cast me forth into the sea; so shall the sea be calm unto you, for I know that for my sake this great tempest is upon you."

It seemed a rather extreme remedy, even to these simple sailors. They did their best to bring the vessel under control and get her to land, but the waves were too strong for them. With a prayer, they did what Jonah had suggested, and threw him into the sea. Immediately the tempest calmed.

Now comes the familiar, but odd, element in the story. "The Lord had prepared a great fish to swallow up Jonah. And Jonah was in the belly of the fish three days and three nights."

The chapter which follows – Jonah's prayer to the Lord "from the belly of hell" – is dramatic enough, told in its matchless Tudor English. Jonah does not actually describe what it was like being inside this great fish. He refers instead to floods, billows and waves, encompassing waters and weeds. Apparently he prayed constantly, until "the Lord spake unto the fish, and it vomited out Jonah upon the dry land".

After that he obediently went to Nineveh, as he had been told to do in the first place. It would have saved him a lot of trouble if he had not changed his destination to Tarshish.

It is a striking story, which has given us the term "Jonah" for anyone who brings bad luck to others. But it is highly improbable, by any criterion, as a basis for the "Jonah and the Whale" legend.

The Old Testament nowhere mentions whales, merely "a great fish"; and whales are mammals. Their digestive systems are not adapted to eating anything nearly so large as a man. The mouths of the Whalebone Whales are enormous, it is true, but their food is plankton, a mass of tiny sea-animals and plants which are taken in by the open mouth and strained through the hairy fringes of the baleen plates lining the mouth (known, very inaccurately, as whalebone; in fact, they are a form of skin). It seems very unlikely that the whale's oesophagus could take in such a large object as a man's body; or that, if taken in, its presence would not kill the creature in a very short time.

So, a great fish? No known fish survives which could take in such a meal. Supposing the Loch Ness Monster to be a reality, however widely accounts of it differ, all agree that it has a very small snake-like head and a long thin neck, certainly not intended for swallowing anything bigger than, say, a plaice or a pike. There were carnivores among the prehistoric monsters that roamed the earth, but they never had a chance to develop a taste for human flesh, dying out before Man evolved.

Bible scholars have dismissed the whole Jonah story as a parable. His cry, in chapter two of the prophet's book, they say has been transferred from somewhere else; hence the lack of reference to his fishy host. Jonah is a mythical figure standing for Israel, which had neglected its duty and was swallowed up by foreign lands in punishment. The Old Testament is full of references to dragons, which sometimes represent Chaos; there is one in the Book of Jeremiah, Bel, the Babylonian dragon, who is made to disgorge what he has swallowed.

So we can forget the story of Jonah as a literal happening. Or can we? For there are curious echoes of it in tales which have got themselves into print in much more recent times. As lately as 1896 a French newspaper published, in good faith apparently, an account of an expedition made by the whaling ship *Star of the East.*

Whaling, perhaps the ugliest of trades, had by this time reached the point when the wonderful and intelligent monsters (who, we know, enjoy and thrive on the company of humans, being only larger versions of the dolphin family) were threatened with extinction. No danger to man, unfitted for combat with him, the huge sperm whales were being murdered in their thousands, for sperm oil and blubber. At one time the hand-held harpoon had been as dangerous to the hunters as to the hunted, for at close quarters the threshing of the wounded whale might, and often did, capsize the boat from which it was being attacked. By the end of the nineteenth century the harpoon gun had been invented. Now the whale could be pierced from a distance. It was denied even the revenge it had been able to wreak in its death-throes.

One James Bartley was coxswain of one of the *Star of the East's* boats. He happened to be nearest to the wounded whale, "insane with pain", when it charged blindly at his boat and tipped him out of it – straight into its open mouth.

The crew rowed hastily back to the *Star*. After all, they reasoned, there was nothing they could do. Their spirits were revived next morning, though, when a shape seen bobbing
among the waves turned out to be a dead whale, of great
size.

It took them two days to strip the corpse of its blubber; a
nasty business, which deterred them not at all so long as they
got their money at the end of the voyage. Just why it should
have occurred to them that the whale might have been the
very one which had swallowed Bartley is not clear, except that
one of them had spotted the mark of a harpoon on it. But they
took the unusual course of examining its stomach. They found
in it a human body, blood-bathed and livid. It was Bartley;
and, quite incredibly, he was not dead.

Strenuous resuscitation brought him back to consciousness.
For a time he was out of his mind; literally "fit to be tied" to
his bunk, so that he should not injure himself or anyone else.
He raved and babbled of fearful heat – the fires of hell. In time
he grew calmer, until he was able to give a remarkably lucid
account of his sojourn in the whale. It was as follows:

"I remember very well from the moment that I fell from the
boat and felt my feet strike some soft substance. I looked up
and saw a big-ribbed canopy of light pink and white descending over me, and the next moment I felt myself drawn down-
ward, feet first, and I realized that I was being swallowed by a
whale. I was drawn lower and lower; a wall of flesh surrounded me and hemmed me in on every side, yet the pressure was
not painful, and the flesh easily gave way like soft india-rubber
before my slightest movement.

"Suddenly I found myself in a sack much larger than my
body, but completely dark. I felt about me; and my hand
came in contact with several fishes, some of which seemed to
be still alive, for they squirmed in my fingers, and slipped back
to my feet. Soon I felt a great pain in my head, and my breathing became more and more difficult. At the same time I felt a
terrible heat; it seemed to consume me, growing hotter and
hotter. My eyes became coals of fire in my head, and I believed every moment that I was condemned to perish in the
belly of a whale. It tormented me beyond all endurance, while
at the same time the awful silence of the terrible prison
weighed me down. I tried to rise, to move my arms and legs, to
cry out. All action was now impossible, but my brain seemed

abnormally clear; and with a full comprehension of my awful fate, I finally lost all consciousness.''

Well, it is a good horror story. There is something plausible in his mention of great heat; a whale's body is hotter than a man's, for it is a warm-blooded mammal, and the temperature within its stomach might well be oven-like. The presence of a man's body there could have killed the whale, causing its temperature to drop and saving him from being boiled alive. But that he could have survived three days and nights (just like Jonah, how odd!) in a compartment where no oxygen could reach his lungs is quite incredible. Yet his story was printed in all seriousness, and reprinted in an American magazine in this century.

An earlier "Jonah" had been himself American. A whaler known as Peleg (could that have been Pegleg?) Nye fell out of a longboat into a sperm whale's jaws. They snapped together, and the whale disappeared under the waves. But Nye's fate was less horrid than the alleged swallowing of Bartley. It was not long before he reappeared, to be pulled aboard by his shipmates. Fortunately for him, he had floated upwards instead of sinking, when the startled whale had released him. Perhaps he was "Pegleg" after all, and his wooden leg was too much for it to accept.

The postscript to this tall tale of 1863 is that another body soon afterwards appeared on the sea's surface. It was the whale, dead from no cause anyone could ascertain.

Perhaps the innocent and amiable whale has often taken the blame for the less well-disposed shark, which, long before *Jaws*, had a reputation for swallowing people, piecemeal if not wholesale.

> *O, Sally dear! it is too true –*
> *The half that you remark*
> *Is come to say my other half*
> *Is bit off by a shark.*
>
> *O, Sally! sharks do things by halves*
> *Yet most completely do.*
> *A bite in one place seems enough,*
> *But I've been bit in two.*
>
> *Alas, Death has a strange divorce*
> *Effected in the sea;*
> *It has divided me from you,*
> *And even me from me!*

And that, in turn, reminds one of an unsolved sea mystery of this century.

On 25 April, 1935, a tiger shark, newly captured at sea and placed in an Australian aquarium pool, had an attack of indigestion. The contents of its stomach which it brought up included a human arm.

It took little time for the police to identify the limb's former owner. There was a tattoo of boxers on it; and a former boxer, James Smith, aged forty, was known to have been missing from the Sydney vicinity for a fortnight. Fingerprints were obtained from the hand and found to be Smith's. Moreover, forensic examination revealed that the arm had not been bitten off, but severed by knife.

Smith's known associate, Patrick Brady, a reputed forger, was promptly arrested. He admitted to forgery, but not murder. A name he mentioned in connection with the former charge was that of Reg Holmes, a Sydney boatbuilder who had employed the missing man. Holmes, too, was questioned, but denied even knowing Brady, let alone being associated with him in forgery.

A few days later, however, Holmes's motorboat was stopped in Sydney Harbour by a police launch. He was found to have a superficial bullet wound in his head. On this occasion he confessed that he did know Brady, who, he asserted, had murdered Smith.

Brady was put up for trial; but before it could take place Holmes had been shot dead in his car. Two men were charged with his murder, but acquitted. Without him, the case against Patrick Brady fell down. He lived for another thirty years, always protesting his innocence. Forensic opinion had it that James Smith's murdered body had been dismembered and the remains disposed of at sea, where the shark had swallowed the tattooed arm whole. But nothing could be proved, and the so-called Shark Arm Case remains unsolved.

THE *VASA* LIVES AGAIN

National heroes have always been a breed apart – Frederick Barbarossa, Joan of Arc, William Tell, Nelson, Churchill, and many others. Beyond the bounds of their actual achievements legend has added something to them, an aura which has made them somewhat more than human, almost saviour figures in a mystical sense.

In Swedish history one of these was Gustav Eriksson Vasa, born in the early sixteenth century to a distinguished family of noblemen. He grew up into a world of turmoil and violence. King Christian of Denmark was attempting to conquer Sweden and under the terms of a patched-up armistice in 1518 Gustav was taken to Denmark as a hostage. There he escaped and, disguised as a cowherd, made his way back home where he became the leader of the country folk against the invaders and ultimately the elected king. As a man of exceptional ability, persuasive power and strength of character he was able, by the end of his reign, to centralize the government, abolish the independence of the nobles, regain independence from Denmark and lay the foundations of modern Sweden, all this in less than forty years.

By the seventeenth century, therefore, "Vasa" was a name as potent in Sweden as King David's had once been in Judaea and Gustav's grandson, Gustavus Adolphus, known as "the Hurricane", who reigned from 1611 to 1632 enhanced it still further by extending Swedish dominance in the eastern Baltic

and in a series of campaigns in Germany thwarting the designs
of the Catholic Habsburg Emperor against his Protestant
homeland.

To achieve these striking successes Gustavus needed not only
men but ships to transport armies and supplies across the Baltic
and the navy was rapidly expanded, culminating in 1625 with
an order for a great galleon or battleship of 1,400 tons, mounting 64 guns, including 48 twenty-four pounders. All the
country's new-found power, the pride of her people, the glory
of the monarchy were to be centred on this huge vessel, to be
known as "the King's Ship", and no other name was possible
or desirable for her than *Vasa*.

The *Vasa* took three years to build and except for decorative
features was made entirely of oak cut from Sweden's great
forests and hauled to the Stockholm shipyard. In those days
master builders, in this case a Dutchman named Henrik
Hybertsson de Groot, did not draw up detailed plans but
worked to simple measurements and to these de Groot had
obtained the king's agreement: length, 162 feet; beam, 39 feet;
three masts, square-rigged.

On Sunday, 10 August, 1628, all was ready for the maiden
voyage and just after Vespers, on a beautiful sunny afternoon
with a gusty wind from the south-west, *Vasa* was warped slowly
forward from a point where she had been fitted out under the
lee of a small island in Stockholm harbour. Warping, which
meant dropping the anchor further and further ahead while
the ship was drawn by hawser towards it, was a tedious business, but at least it gave time for those ashore to feast their
eyes on a scene of unique grace and beauty.

Ten great sails were just being set, topped by pennons 20 feet
long and the flag of Sweden, a gold cross on a blue ground. On
each side of the ship glowered twenty-four gun-ports in two
rows, the barrels pointing menacingly below raised flaps painted red with snarling lion heads carved on them. The high
stern, both sides and back, was thickly encrusted with carvings
covered with gold leaf and on the bow as figure-head was a
magnificent carved lion over ten feet long in the act of springing forward to attack its prey.

Of the men who were in the ship some of the names are
known: Severin Hansson, the captain; Joen Larsson, chief
gunner; Per Bertilsson, chief boatswain; Hans Jonsson, the
dockyard captain. But of the remaining 133 crewmen nothing

is recorded, except that some lived to see the end of that day and some did not. But we can now picture them well enough in their everyday clothes (uniforms were not worn at that time), consisting of a drab-coloured jerkin, breeches of brown or blue, homespun stockings and home-made shoes. Most wore caps to keep their long hair out of their faces and no doubt the younger hands were hearing for the first time what lay ahead of them. They would sleep on the bare lower deck, eat dry bread, groats, salted fish or pork. Sometimes there would be butter and always beer, five pints per man per day. Punishments were severe. For blaspheming, drunk or sober, a man would "die the death without mercy". Disobeying an order meant keel-hauling, for theft a man could have his ears cut off. In a little while, when the ship had cleared the harbour, 300 soldiers would be taken on board from one of the outer islands.

But the *Vasa* never reached that island. She had been warped clear of the land and was heading east under full sail towards the harbour mouth when a sudden strong gust of wind made her heel over alarmingly. She righted herself and sailed on, only to be struck again, this time even more fiercely. The great ship rolled over almost on to her beam ends, water poured in through the open gun ports and she went down like a stone, as a contemporary said, "with sails up and flags flying", only fifteen hundred yards from her fitting-out berth.

For a poor, sparsely inhabited country this was a shattering blow and a court of inquiry was immediately set up to determine the cause. But despite rigorous questioning of the captain and boatswain who had survived and of de Groot's brother (de Groot himself having meanwhile died), negligence could not be proved, not surprisingly for the disaster sprang from an insoluble dilemma facing contemporary shipwrights. Heavy cannon, weighing one and a half tons, were now in use, capable of sinking enemy ships. If they were mounted too high the ship's stability was endangered, if low, peering through gun ports only four feet above the water, there was a grave danger of capsizing when the ship rolled. This fate had overcome the *Vasa* and it had happened to many others, including Henry VIII's *Mary Rose* in 1545.

Almost immediately unsuccessful attempts were made to raise the *Vasa*. Then she lay undisturbed, 115 feet down near the middle of Stockholm's well sheltered harbour, slowly sinking deeper into the mud, until in the 1660s another salvage attempt was made, this time by an ingenious Swede using a dome-shaped object, open at the bottom, closed at the top like a church bell. The diver stood inside with his feet on a platform fixed below the opening, breathed in the trapped air bubble and looking downwards fixed long-shafted grapnels to the *Vasa*'s protruding gun barrels. By this means, incredibly, over fifty of her valuable bronze guns were salvaged.

After this, no further interest was taken in the ship and in the course of three hundred years any record of where she lay was forgotten. Then, in 1956, emerged one of the heroes of this story.

Swedish-born Anders Franzén, then in his mid-thirties, had been obsessed by the mystery of sunken warships ever since childhood and in the last ten years had spent all his spare time from a job with a Swedish oil company plying to and fro in his father's motor-boat, searching the sea-bed in and around Stockholm harbour with sweep wires and grapnels. He knew that several ships were lying there and in fact he found four, but the biggest and finest, the *Vasa*, eluded him. Then, one evening, reading through ancient archives, he came across a letter which the Council of the Realm had sent to Gustavus Adolphus two days after the disaster and one sentence rivetted his attention: "She came to Beckholmsudden where she entirely fell on her side."

So that was where he had to look, off Beckholm island, to the east of the inner harbour! Full of excitement, Franzén spent days puttering about in his launch, testing the sea-bed with a core sampler. This was a heavy cylindrical instrument with a razor-sharp hollow tube at the lower end which would cut into wood below water and return a sample to the surface. Franzén tried in several places and at last at the end of the tube found a small blob of pitch-black oak, half an inch in diameter. Did it come from the *Vasa*? Again he lowered the sampler, and again, and again, and each time up came an identical piece of oak, obviously very old.

It was 10 August, 1956. Convinced he had found the King's Ship at last, Franzén hurried ashore to see the commanding officer of the Royal Naval Diving School, told him of his discovery and persuaded him to hold the next test for trainee divers at the spot where the oak had come from. The chief diver went down first and after agonizing minutes of silence began to give a running commentary over the telephone. There was a big ship down there with towering walls . . . There were square openings in the sides, gun ports . . . pieces of carved wood lying about . . . It could only be the *Vasa*. There and then the diver took possession of the wreck in the name of the Crown.

So began a salvage operation unique in the age of the ship to be rescued and the fact that she was positively identified and dated. Unlike other ancient vessels she was not just an anonymous hulk, badly damaged or burnt up in war, so there was every hope of discovering a mine of information, both inside and outside the hull, about detailed construction and decorative features down to the life of the ordinary sailor on board, his possessions, his clothing, what he ate, where he slept. At that time, very little was known about these aspects of seafaring life in the olden days.

There were other reasons for this optimism. The first diver's report had suggested that the *Vasa* was embedded up to her original waterline in mud, and mud, curiously enough, is an excellent preservative owing to the lack of free oxygen. Secondly, Anders Franzén had made an important discovery. Throughout history enormous damage has been inflicted on underwater timber by the "death-watch beetle of the sea", the ship worm or *teredo navalis* which bores tunnels into wood and undermines the substance from within. But this particular creature cannot thrive in the brackish waters of the Baltic because the salt content is too low. Consequently, sunken ships there are in a better state of preservation than anywhere else in the world.

All the same, the feasibility of raising the *Vasa* was still in doubt, quite apart from the expense, and in 1957 an expert committee was set up to study the question. Here there were interlocking problems of great technical complexity: how to raise the ship intact, how to preserve her when she was raised, where to house her so that the great hull could go on permanent exhibition. One suggestion was to fill her with pingpong balls to give her positive buoyancy; another, to freeze the entire ship into a block of ice which would then rise spontaneously to the surface. These ideas were rejected mainly because in both cases the ship would come to the surface too quickly, with the result that, as the water pressure outside the hull rapidly decreased, the weight of mud inside might break her apart. So it was decided to use the conventional method of lifting pontoons.

These deliberations took over a year, ending with a report favourable to the project in all its aspects. Meanwhile, in anticipation of the lift, divers had started to tunnel in six places, preparatory to passing wires under the wreck. It was a very slow and dangerous job. Dressed in conventional divers' suits, the men had first to clear a passage vertically downwards past the side of the ship, then continue boring at right-angles underneath the hull and past the keel till they tunnelled their way up to the surface on the other side, this through a six-foot bed of mud lying on top of hard blue clay. It was done by means of a "Zetterström" water jet, a version of the fireman's hose made recoilless by some of the water being thrust backwards. This useful gadget was complemented by a large suction pipe which the crouching diver held between his legs to draw the spoil to the surface.

So far, so good. But no one could tell what the effect of this tunnelling would be. The ship was listing to port because her ballast of heavy stones had slipped and she might heel over at any moment. Mud might collapse behind the diver and bury him. And all the time, in turbid water which no light could penetrate for more than three feet he would be working in almost total darkness.

But at last, by August, 1959, after 1,300 dives and 330 feet of tunnelling, the heroic enterprise was completed without mishap and on the 20th all was ready for the first short and cautious lift. On the surface on either side of the wreck two enormous pontoons were waiting, filled with water. The wires were passed under the hull and clamped taut in position. Then very slowly the water was pumped out of the pontoons so that they began to rise. An hour passed, two hours, three hours, then at last bubbles coming up showed that the *Vasa* was beginning to lift from the mud.

A less careful plan might have brought her straight to the surface, but divers' reports showed that the *Vasa* was in no condition to float. Gunport flaps had collapsed or fallen off; in the hull were thousands of holes where iron bolts had rusted away; parts of the bow and stern had gone, probably torn off by ships's anchors dropped unknowingly on the wreck in the past. Before she could surface she would have to be made watertight and that entailed drawing her carefully, with many intervening rests on the bottom, six hundred yards into shallow water.

This tricky operation – six feet at a time in eighteen stages – took a month until the *Vasa* was lying in only 50 feet of water. It would have been easier, of course, for the patching up job to be done in the open air, but that would have meant raising the ship completely and leaving her suspended in the wires for months on end, an impossible proposition.

So the divers got to work again underwater, and spent two years plugging the holes, sealing the gun ports, fixing a temporary bow and stern. Then on 24 April, 1961, it was time for the final lift. The pontoons were brought alongside again, this time to act only as platforms for powerful hydraulic jacks. The *Vasa*'s wires were attached. Close by, large crowds had gathered with people from the world's press, radio and television to watch a unique operation, never before attempted with a ship of that age and weight.

The jacks took the strain. By noon the outline of the *Vasa*'s hull was clearly visible beneath the grey-green water and two hours later it broke surface for the first time in 333 years. At once, powerful pumps were taken on board to clear the interior of water. The mud was a different problem. This had to be sifted, bucket by bucketful, and teams of archaeologists were waiting eagerly to start.

Everything so far had gone according to plan. But more tough work lay ahead. When the ship had been cleared sufficiently for her to float without the wires it was planned to take her into a dry-dock in which a concrete pontoon had already been placed to provide a permanent support. After more cleaning, the *Vasa* would be drawn out of dry-dock on this base and towed to a temporary museum site where a housing of aluminium, glass and concrete would be erected to box her in completely.

Again, these operations went without serious trouble and once the ship was housed the long, delicate job of preserving and restoring her could begin. This involved using a humidifier within the protective shelter to prevent the air becoming too dry and spraying the *Vasa*'s woodwork, all 32,000 cubic feet of it, with a substance called Polyglycol, or PEG. This spraying had to continue at certain intervals round the clock for several years with the aim of soaking the PEG into the

wood cells where it would stabilize them and prevent shrink-
age. Boric acid and borax were added to inhibit rot.

Of course, the cost of the whole project was enormous,
though it was hoped to recover it eventually by putting the
Vasa on exhibition. But what, after all, would there be to exhibit? She was older than Nelson's famous *Victory*, admittedly,
unique among ships of her period, but all the same just a badly
damaged hulk, surely, of scant interest to anyone but naval
historians.

Or was she? The real picture was very different. Around
the hull when they were tunnelling those first divers had made
extraordinary finds, pieces of carved wood by the score that
had obviously fallen off the ship. When brought to the surface
many of these proved to be statues, life-sized, from biblical and
classical sources. Here was a Roman warrior in full armour
with a lion and a dog at his feet, here Hercules on a pedestal
with his club, the Emperor Tiberius, a Bacchanalian figure
with grapes in his mouth, the sea god Nereus. There was a
huge coat of arms, there were cherubs playing musical instruments, caryatids, mermaids, crowns, rampant lions, griffons'
heads, gargoyles, all carved in wood, beautifully wrought by
master craftsmen. It began to seem that the *Vasa* had not only
been a fighting ship but, in modern terms, a floating
museum.

In all, over 700 sculptural and ornamental pieces were
found on the sea-bed, as well as bits of ordinary wood in their
thousands. All were subjected to the same treatment as the
hull. Then came the difficult problem of assigning them to
their original places around the ship. It was clear that, according to contemporary fashion, most of the decoration would
have been on and around the stern castle, the tallest part of the
ship, and nail marks in the damaged wood enabled the re-
storers to match these with like patterns of holes in the statues,
so identifying in some cases their original position.

Thus slowly the stern could be built up as it had been:
above, the Swedish coat of arms, shining with gold leaf, framed
by red-painted imitation curtains upheld by angels, flanked by
gilded figures, topped by winged griffons below an archway,
all gold. Lower down, five gargoyles against a background of
blue, below them the Vasa coat of arms – a sheaf of corn with
cherub supporters – flanked by six knights with shields and
spears, lower still in descending ranks, nineteen figures of war-

riors, tritons, mermaids, and on each side of the stern a rank of eight gilded fighting men in close order, standing on a platform supported by gargoyles, while on the bow, restored to its place, would be the figure-head, the ten-foot springing lion.

In view of this flamboyant splendour so dramatically recovered from the sea can one wonder that the committee was confident of recovering costs, or that people have come from all over the world to see the *Vasa*?

But perhaps, all the same, the most poignant finds were those from inside the ship: eighteen skeletons, remains of clothing still on them, some crushed by gun carriages as the ship heeled over. Vessels for the captain's meals, which he ate off a small refectory-type table, were also found: a pewter tankard, pewter plates, a wine glass, a bronze candlestick, a ceramic bowl and bottle, wooden spoons. Many other items of wood were found, brandy barrels, beer tankards, a pestle and mortar, and a butter keg with the butter still in it, only slightly rancid. Ammunition was plentiful in the form of cannon balls, and shot in wide variety for destroying an enemy's rigging. But personal arms were scarce. Perhaps they were to be brought on board later with the soldiers.

Today we can also see the meagre contents of a sailor's sea chest – two pairs of leather shoes, a shoe last, a piece of leather and, packed separately, a comb, thimble and thread, some bits of cloth, a few coins, in striking contrast with the plentiful content of chests found in the derelict *Mary Celeste* nearly 250 years later.

But perhaps the greatest contrast of all is that between the resplendent exterior of the ship and the scene inside the lower gun deck. Here there is nothing to relieve the mind of grim reality, of the sense that the *Vasa* was above all a fighting ship. Rows of gun carriages are ranged on either side in an oaken cavern with low, oppressive beams above a deck, bare now, where once the sailors were intended to work and sleep, eating their miserable fare, shivering in the icy blasts blowing through open gun ports, and dying, as the records tell us, in their scores of disease and exhaustion. Somehow, irrational though it may seem, it is good to know that those eighteen skeletons now lie peacefully in a Stockholm churchyard, deep in the warm earth.

Lost
Continents

THE RE-EMERGENCE OF ATLANTIS

More than 25,000 books have been written about the sunken continent of Atlantis, and they have been published in virtually every country and language in the world. For more than 2,000 years Atlantis has been regarded as a legend or myth, originating largely in Plato's description of the lost world in his Timaeus and Critais dialogues, part of a trilogy which was never finished.

In the past decade, however, physical evidence of man-made structures on and under the sea-bed in the Bimini area off the south-east coast of the U.S.A. have been discovered and photographed, indicating, though not conclusively, that the western part of the Atlantean continent is rising from its oceanic grave – or, more accurately, that the movement of shifting sea-bed sand and mud is revealing for the first time in millennia proof of an antediluvian civilization located where Atlantis ought to be.

There are certain aspects of recent research concerning Atlantis which are relevant beyond the point of mere coincidence. The first, obviously, is Plato's remarkably detailed description of Atlantis written 2,400 years ago about a continent which vanished, almost overnight, around 11,500 years ago. Second is the destructive force itself: the great flood or deluge which, in one form or another, forms part of international mythology (though the date of the flood varies, as might be expected in any long-term legend). Third is the odd and unexplained

intercontinental spread of particular cultural patterns between
the East, Europe and the Americas in the West. And fourth,
for the present, are visualizations and predictions about Atlantis at psychic level, the most famous, perhaps, being that of
Edgar Cayce, an American clairvoyant and psychic healer
who, in trances, described Atlantis before and after the great
earthquakes and flood that destroyed it, gave details of its culture, technology and civilization, referred (in 1942) to Atlantean use of maser and laser beams, before they had actually
been developed by modern scientists, and, above all, in 1940
predicted that the western part of Atlantis near the Bahamas
(and, incidentally, beneath the zone of the Bermuda Triangle)
would rise from the sea around 1968–69. That, so far as one
can judge, is precisely what has been happening since 1968. It
was discovered mainly as a by-product of underwater research
and aircraft and space-satellite photography during investigation into the mystery of the Bermuda Triangle (which is
covered elsewhere in this book).

By "rise from the sea", Cayce presumably meant "be uncovered by the shifting sea-bed". There is certainly no evidence at the moment that Atlantis is "rising". But beware –
Cayce also predicted sub-oceanic upheavals in the Atlantic
during the next twenty to thirty years that would not only
uncover Atlantis but would also inundate and submerge parts
of existing land masses, including New York plus the surrounding eastern seaboard, and Japan.

Finally it is worth noting that Cayce considered the Atlanteans at least as technically advanced as ourselves today,
and able to develop and deploy fantastically huge energy resources (possibly nuclear, but more likely magnetic) which
ultimately destroyed their continent and themselves, apart
from survivors in South America and the Mediterranean area,
including Egypt.

There we have the legend, the theories, the hypotheses and
the predictions – the latter being uncomfortably accurate so
far. But to form a true picture, one has to be objective. There
are, after all, other allegedly sunken continents, the best known
being Mu and Lemuria. Is Atlantis just a dream, or a disturbing fact?

One must go back to Plato, the Greek philosopher, who was
the first to commit the story of the Atlantis legend to paper
nearly 400 years B.C. Although Plato claimed that his account

was obtained from ancient Egyptian records, no such records have ever been traced, nor did anyone ever write about Atlantis before Plato. All subsequent written work on Atlantis has been largely based on Plato's unfinished trilogy (until the recent Bimini sea-bed discoveries and the psychic or clairvoyant communications of Cayce and a few others).

There are, however, certain basic mysteries and arguments to which the existence at one time of Atlantis provides a possible and plausible solution, though that does not necessarily mean that it is the correct solution. The questions have been asked mainly by scholars, and are concerned principally with the curious similarity of certain cultures, and design and architectural concepts between the East and the West, separated as they are by the vast expanse of the Atlantic Ocean. Common flora and fauna, too, can be found on continents separated by thousands of miles of water.

How did primitive races, thousands of years ago in different lands, develop the basic civil engineering technology, identical in fundamental respects, that enabled them to erect gigantic architectural structures of stone blocks weighing scores of tons each and so precisely cut (without modern tungsten steel tools) that the gap between adjoining blocks can be as small as one-thousandth of an inch? Even a modern engineering consortium would find such a task virtually insuperable. Why do the Mayan pyramids in South America have exactly the same angle of repose on the sloping sides (almost 52 degrees of arc) as the pyramids of Ancient Egypt? Why are there basic similarities between Mayan and Ancient Egyptian hieroglyphics (one could ask "why not?", but then there are no similarities between Chinese–Japanese script, Arabic and Western Roman-based script).

All the indicators point to a "missing link" in the form of a continent, centrally located in the Atlantic Ocean many thousands of years ago, whose inhabitants spread their advanced civilization and technology to both East and West. Quite apart from the pyramids, and similar massive constructions of stone and granite, who built Stonehenge and the giant statues on Easter Island in the Pacific? Certainly not the unsophisticated people of the day.

Plato was quite specific in his description of Atlantis, although one must separate what is presumably fable (the references to the gods) from what could be fact (topography, architecture, etc). Atlantis began, Plato states, when the gods were made responsible for particular parts of our earth. Poseidon, the Greek god of sea and earthquakes, received Atlantis. There Poseidon met and fell in love with a human female named Cleito who lived on a hill in Atlantis. To protect her from other humans, Poseidon surrounded the hill with circles of land and moats of water.

Between them they produced ten male children, among whom Atlantis was to be divided so that it was ruled by a kind of "parliament" of kings. The first-born son was Atlas, after whom Atlantis was named, and he became the chief of the kings.

Atlantis became rich and prosperous, attaining a great civilization founded on advanced technology, engineering and architecture. The main city of Atlantis grew and spread around the foot of Cleito's hill; the city was circular in shape and more than ten miles in diameter. Bridges connected the land rings around the hill, and there were huge tunnels through which ships could sail. The entire city was encircled by a great ring which became a harbour for ships. Atlantis had a large army made up of cavalry and chariots and light and heavy infantry.

The buildings of the city were constructed of locally quarried stone, black, red and white, and the different colours were intermixed in an artistic way. The holy temples were magnificent. Poseidon's temple and palace were lavishly ornamented with gold, silver, bronze, and other decorative metals, and the buildings were surrounded by luxurious gardens with elegant fountains. Inside the temple was an enormous gold statue – so large that it touched the pinnacled roof – of Poseidon driving a chariot drawn by six winged horses and 100 sea nymphs riding on dolphins.

And now for a significant ritual. At intervals of five years the ten kings of Atlantis congregated in Poseidon's temple to debate matters of justice and administration. When these deliberations were over a festival of bull hunting took place, the bulls concerned being allowed to roam freely within the vast temple. When one was caught, the animal was sacrificed on a sacred bronze column, and then followed a banquet.

The point of interest is that the bull played an important part in the rituals of Greek mythology, and one must wonder whether the Minotaur, the Ancient Greek monster, ever existed in the labyrinth of Crete where it was slain by Theseus of Athens; and, further, is there a direct though time-fantasized connection between the symbolic bulls of Greece and Atlantis? Is the legendary Cretan labyrinth a distorted memory of Atlantis?

Another factor of interest is the basic similarity of names used by ancient, geographically separated peoples, for Atlantis. The Greeks and Romans used Atlantis and Atlas respectively, while the Ancient Egyptians used Aalu, which in Babylonian and Sumerian became Arallu. The Welsh Celtic word was Avalon and the Nordic Valhalla. Note the dominance of the A–L combination at the beginning of each name. In Basque the word is Atalaintika, in Aztec is Aztlan, in Mayan is Atlan – the name also used by the tribes of the Americas. All refer to a large island in the Atlantic Ocean, the point of origin of ethnic or tribal ancestors.

The source of most of the material for Plato's Atlantean dialogues appears to have been the Athenian statesman Solon, who visited Egypt around 1000 B.C. Solon obtained his information from a group of Egyptian priests in Sais, a city having close links with Athens. Solon's story was never written down, but was passed by word of mouth to a relative who told it to his son, Critais the Elder, who later recounted it to his grandson, Critais, who features in Plato's dialogues.

A noteworthy feature of Plato's written delineation of Atlantis is that it describes land masses and islands off the east coast of America – a continent at that time quite unknown. This, many believe, was a direct stimulus to Columbus, an avid student of Plato, to cross the Atlantic Ocean in search of such hypothetical land and islands. At the time of which Plato was writing, the Atlantic contained much larger islands and land areas, plus mainland coasts stretching far out into the ocean – but it was also much shallower. After the third ice age the water level rose by about 1,000 feet and much of the land was inundated.

Geological evidence exists in the waters of what is today known as the Bermuda Triangle area. Large underwater caves – "Blue Holes" – extending deep into the submarine banks of the Bahamas and Florida contain stalagmites and stalactites (formed by mineral-containing water dripping from the cave roofs), thus proving that at one time and for a long period they were above sea-level, otherwise such formations could not have occurred. Other geological proofs exist in samples of rock core taken from the sea-bed which indicate that the material could only have been formed above sea-level.

Like all great civilizations and empires, Atlantis ultimately had to come to an end. As an empire at its peak, the Atlanteans, according to ancient Egyptian records (as referred to by Plato), spread outwards into the Americas and eastward into the Mediterranean area, conquering North Africa as far as Egypt and concentrated to strike and subdue Greece. Athens, standing alone, defeated and put to rout the Atlantean army – "but afterward there occurred violent earthquakes and floods; and in a single day and night of destruction all your (Atlantean) warlike men in a body sank into the earth, and the island of Atlantis in a like manner disappeared into the depths of the sea." The dating of that cataclysm was around 9500 B.C.

Legend or fact? Here one might consider the siege and fall of Troy as related by Homer in the *Iliad*, regarded until 1871 as imaginary. In that year the German archaeologist Heinrich Schliemann achieved a life-long ambition when he uncovered the remains of Troy at Hissarlik in northern Turkey. It was an archaeological discovery of major importance but, perhaps even more significant, it proved that at least one Greek myth was based on fact, and raised the possibility, and even the probability, that other aspects of Greek mythology might equally have a foundation of truth – Atlantis being an obvious choice.

It is also worth considering the detailed work of Ignatius Donnelly, an American known as the "Father of Scientific Atlantology", who was born in Philadelphia in 1831 and elected Lieutenant-Governor of Minnesota at the age of twenty-eight. He served for eight years in Congress. His forthright promotion of the Atlantis concept prompted the British Prime Minister, Mr Gladstone, to write to him expressing his appreciation of his work. Donnelly died in 1901, but he had laid the foundation stone of a scientifically acceptable Atlantis, and had written what is possibly the most distinguished book on the subject.

Among Donnelly's conclusions were some that can hardly be faulted without adequate factual evidence. He regarded Plato's description of the lost continent as "veritable history" and not fable. Atlantis was the Garden of Eden, the Gardens of Hesperides, the Elysian Fields, etc. – all representing "a universal memory of a great land where early mankind dwelt for ages in peace and happiness".

Donnelly pronounced that the mythology of Egypt and Peru represented the original religion of Atlantis, namely, sun-worship; further, that the oldest colony formed by the Atlanteans was probably in Egypt. The Atlanteans were the first manufacturers of bronze and iron.

He held that the Phoenician alphabet, parent of all European alphabets, was derived from an Atlantean alphabet (which was also adopted by the Mayas of Central America).

When Atlantis perished and sank into the ocean with nearly all of its inhabitants, a few persons escaped in ships and rafts and spread the news of the catastrophe to other countries. This gave rise to the legends of the Great Flood and the Deluge which are common to most eastern and western countries.

Donnelly claimed that Atlantis was the point of origin of all human civilization. He also argued that the similarity between many species of American flora and fauna are the result of their common source in the mid-way continent of Atlantis, and these are linked with common cultural traits, on both sides of the Atlantic, in the form of pyramids, burial mounds, pillars and specific types of metallurgy. He wrote: "I cannot believe that great inventions were duplicated spontaneously in different countries. If this were so, all savages would have invented the boomerang; all savages would possess pottery, bows and arrows, slings, tents and canoes; in short, all races would have risen to civilization, for certainly the comforts of life are as agreeable to one people as another."

Before leaving the historical aspect of the antediluvian Atlantean empire, it is worth taking a final look at architectural structures. An outstanding site is the city of Teotihuacan (near Mexico City), built by a race connected with the Mayas. The ruins today are dominated by pyramids. One pyramid, dedicated to the sun, has a rectangular base measuring 740 feet by 725 feet precisely the same as that of the great Cheops pyramid near Cairo in Egypt. In Tikal, a Mayan city in Guatemala, are pyramids of incredible height. One, rising to 230 feet, was the highest man-made construction in the Americas before the first New York skyscrapers were built.

The Mayans also erected tall carved stone columns with inscriptions recording important events. At Tikal a series of such columns records the passage of each twenty years between A.D. 629 and 790. But such columns, known as *stelae*, were also used by the Egyptians, the Greeks and the Romans. Perhaps the greatest mystery of the past is how the people of the time, without modern technology, were able to transport massive quarried building stones over hundreds of miles, carve them accurately, and position them in height without mortar so that they have survived for thousands of years without change, other than natural weathering and erosion.

Finally, according to the French historian Raymond Cartier, "in many fields of knowledge the Mayas outclassed the Greeks and Romans. They were expert astronomers and mathematicians, and brought to perfection the science of chronology. They built domed observatories with a more exact orientation than those of seventeenth-century Paris . . . They had a precise calendar based on a solar year of 365 days, a Venusian year of 584 days and a 'sacred year' of 260 days" – making an exact solar year of 365·242 days which is correct to three places of decimals. The Mayans also developed a form of picture writing similar to that used in Egyptian hieroglyphics – the Mayan system antedated the Egyptian.

It was in 1968 that signs of underwater ruins were first observed off the coasts of Bimini and Andros, between the Bahamas and Florida. Apparently formations of stone of deliberate design, they took the form of roads, platforms, walls and the remains of buildings of various sizes. They were revealed, it is assumed, by seismic forces affecting the ocean bed.

At first oceanographers and archaeologists were sceptical. The stone formations were interpreted as the remains of rectangular structures for the cultivation of sponges, lobsters and other forms of crustacean marine life. The long Bimini wall was dismissed as a natural fall of fractured beach rock, deceptively looking like a submarine raised road.

But as marine investigators and divers concentrated their efforts in the area, and aerial photographs through the clear water depicted structures as yet uncovered, it became apparent that the underwater stone complex was much vaster than had been originally supposed – comprising concentric circles of huge rectangular stones which could not have been created naturally, tiled level floors, pyramids, carved pillars, remnants of statues, roads and causeways extending widely across the sea-bed in that particular area. The ruins of a temple were reportedly observed. Fragments of statues were raised from the sea-bed near the Bermuda Islands, where pilots of small submarine craft alleged that they had seen unmistakable underwater cities.

Similar submerged ruins are said to have been sighted near the Canary and Azores islands off the coasts of North Africa and Spain, and also off the north coast of Cuba and the American continental shelf, while sea-bed stone walls have been recorded on the ocean bottom off Yucatan and Venezuela. The depths of these various ruins vary from a mere 30 feet to a mile and a half or more. Certainly sea depths on the Bahama Banks vary considerably, and the Bimini wall rises from 35 to 25 feet of depth along its currently visible length of over 1,000 yards. Much further out from land, at depths of around 500 feet or more, pyramids have been seen and inspected by divers, though the results of these discoveries have been kept fairly secret – possibly because of the danger of looting of gold or other valuable artefacts they may contain. The Bahamas Government has, in fact, introduced legislation to protect underwater finds, and where objects can be raised to the surface they have to be handed over to a special museum in Freeport.

More latterly, underwater expeditions researching the sea-bed walls and ruins have been able to confirm that these structures are not of natural origin. They consist of large, deliberately and carefully shaped rocks, mostly rectangular, laid on the ocean bottom, with many of the rocks still supported by pillars. Today, continuing research is revealing more ruins of walls, pyramids and diverse building structures widely submerged throughout the islands in the area. Eventually, small, specially designed submarines will solve the mystery of the sunken cities beyond dispute.

Atlantis or not Atlantis? All that we know is that these underwater remains were not produced by any civilization or culture recorded in orthodox history, but prehistory is another matter. What we do know is that some 12,000 to 13,000 years ago ocean levels rose, as we have seen, about 1,000 feet – sufficient to inundate the vasts areas where the sea-bed ruins have been located. And, one final significant point, the concentric circles of large stones that have been observed tie in very accurately with Plato's detailed description of the design of the city of Atlantis – a design very likely copied by other cities in the lost continent.

Atlantis and the Bermuda Triangle form two of the Atlantic Ocean's greatest mysteries. The solution to one may well prove to be the solution to the other.

THE MYSTERY OF
MU AND LEMURIA

Atlantis is by no means the only submerged continent to attract the attention of archaeologists, scientists, historians and cultists. Of the remainder the two most important are Mu (on the bed of the Pacific Ocean) and Lemuria, beneath the Indian Ocean. There is also the lost land of Pan below the north Pacific, which antedated Mu by over 20,000 years, while Mu itself existed 50,000 years ago. The origins of Lemuria apparently go back 100,000 years or more. All (as in the case of Atlantis) are claimed to be the original birthplace of man, though this clearly cannot be so.

The name Lemuria is of interest in that it is derived from the lemur, a small mammal that has been described as a cross between a monkey and a squirrel. The lemur's natural home is Madagascar, but it is also found in Africa, India and Malaya. This suggests that the wide migration of the lemur could only have happened if there had once been a large continent occupying what is now the Indian Ocean. (In which case, however, one might reasonably wonder why there are no tigers in Africa.)

The existence of Lemuria was postulated by an English zoologist, Philip L. Sclater, soon after Charles Darwin had published his famous work on evolution, *On the Origin of Species*. The theory of evolution placed geographical constraints on the development of individual species in so far as they would adapt to a particular environment and therefore "stay put". The little lemur (and also a number of other animals) presented a problem, to which the only feasible solution lay in the existence, millennia ago, of a continental land mass linking Africa with India and the Malaysian archipelago. That continent, now submerged, was named Lemuria by Sclater – "in honour of the lemur".

On such slender evidence, the concept of Lemuria was accepted by many eminent people of the day. Alfred Russel Wallace, a contemporary of Darwin, who had developed his own independent theory of evolution, commented: "Lemuria represents what was probably a primary zoological region in some past geological epoch . . . If we are to suppose that it comprised the whole area now inhabited by lemuroid animals, we must make it extend from West Africa to Burmah, South China and Celebes, an area which it did once possibly occupy."

Another keen supporter of Lemuria was Ernst Haeckel, who saw the lost continent as the point of origin of man. He wrote: "Neither Australia nor America nor Europe can have been this primeval home of man, or the so-called 'Paradise' – the cradle of the human race.

"There are a number of circumstances which suggest that the primeval home of man was a continent now sunk below the surface of the Indian Ocean, which extended along the south of Asia . . . towards the east; towards the west as far as Madagascar and the south-eastern shores of Africa. By assuming this Lemuria to have been man's primeval home, we greatly facilitate the explanation of the geographical distribution of the human species by migration."

Today we have far more scientific reasons to account for the migration of man and the lemur across oceans, but Lemuria nevertheless took its place in the annals of mythology and the occult. The famous Madame Blavatsky, founder of Theosophy, wrote about the "seven root races" that inhabited and will inherit the earth. Of these, the Lemurians were the third race – "gigantic brainless ape-like creatures"; they were followed by the fourth race comprising the human Atlanteans "who were destroyed by black magic".

We of today constitute the fifth race, and the sixth race will evolve from us "and return to live on Lemuria". (Presumably by then sunken Lemuria will have resurfaced – hopefully a not impossible seismic event.)

Our ultimate fate, according to Madame Blavatsky, is that after the seventh root race all life will leave the planet earth and start afresh on Mercury (where, according to astronomers and space probes, it is extremely hot as tiny Mercury is the nearest planet to the sun).

Another theosophist, W. Scott-Elliott, amplified Madame Blavatsky's occult vision in more detailed physical terms. The Lemurians, he wrote, were "far from beautiful" – being up to 15 feet tall, brown skinned, with flat faces, no foreheads and an elongated muzzle of a nose. They had a third eye at the back of their heads, which has now receded into the brain and is known as the pineal eye or body (which, according to modern medical science, appears to have no useful function). However, to quote Scott-Elliott, this third eye was very useful to the Lemurians "because their heels stuck out so far at the back that they could walk backward as well as forward".

He added that the Lemurians began as egg-laying hermaphrodites, but later evolved into normal heterosexual "people". Nevertheless, "during their sexual progress they foolishly interbred with beasts, producing the apes that still populate our planet". They were indoctrinated into the ways of human civilization by highly advanced visitors from Venus, and eventually became intelligent and human in appearance. Their descendants today include the Lapps and the Australian Aborigines (according to Scott-Elliott).

What is interesting is that the hypothesis that astronauts from Venus intervened in human evolution many thousands of years ago, currently and recently propounded by many authors, should have been published by Scott-Elliott as long ago as 1896.

In the course of time Lemuria began to break up, and parts of the continent sank into the ocean. One particular peninsula which extended into what is now the Atlantic Ocean was thus isolated and duly became Atlantis.

Another occult philosopher, Rudolf Steiner, an Austrian who left the Theosophists in 1907 to form his own Anthropological Society, confirmed that the Lemurians were feeble-minded, but had "enormous will-power by which they could lift heavy weights". They were slowly developing the basics of true speech. Starting as oviparous hermaphrodites and making do with a single eye "their vision improved along with their discovery of sex". Apparently the Lemurians were not very keen on this evolutionary change because for a long period they regarded sex relations "as a sacred duty rather than a pleasure". That, at least, was Steiner's view based on "astral clairvoyance".

While it would be easy to dismiss "astral clairvoyance" as spurious fantasy, it should be remembered that Plato's detailed description of Atlantis (which could possibly be included under the same heading) is today taking material shape in methodical investigation and underwater photography on the Atlantic sea-bed between the Bahamas and Florida in the area known as Bimini.

Other more material evidence concerning the existence of Lemuria takes the form of many early maps of the world in which a continental land mass is marked in the southern hemisphere. That was long before the name Lemuria was ever devised, and the land mass was known as "the great unknown southern continent" (Terra Australis Incognita). Exploration in the seventeenth century and later disclosed plenty of water but no trace of any continent, but that does not disprove that the early Grecian and other cartographers were necessarily wrong. Their maps were based on historical records passed down over centuries and not on direct observation. Whether the vanished land mass was Lemuria or Mu is open to speculation. Certainly the discovery of Australia, mainly desert, proved to be no substitute.

It may also be significant that a number of geologists have noticed undeniable resemblances between certain types of rock formation in India and South Africa. The only possible explanation, it was concluded, lay in the one-time existence of a "land bridge" connecting India with South Africa by way of the Seychelles and Madagascar. The dating of such a land bridge, however, defies the imagination: it allegedly existed from 180 million to 70 million years ago, when mammals are supposed to have made their appearance on earth.

There also exists fossil evidence which suggests that at one remote period there were land connections between the major continents, both to the east and west. Finally, in 1915 the German astronomer and geophysicist Alfred Wegener put forward the new theory of continental drift, in which the great land masses move slowly, like icebergs, upon the earth's inner crust which in turn floats upon an inner core of hot molten magma. At one time, it is conjectured, there was one single

enormous land mass. Over millions of years it broke up into
massive continental areas. Some continents subsided into the
oceans and others arose.

Recent computer analysis of existing continental shapes
shows that they can be interlocked quite logically into a single
land mass, though one must take into account the continental
shelves under the ocean as part of the drifting boundaries. On
such a basis Lemuria, Atlantis and Mu (the latter to be considered in a moment) could well have existed, and could well
arise again from earth's deep waters, for continental drift is an
on-going process, slow though it may be.

The only doubts concern the natures of the civilizations and
cultures which inhabited the sunken continents, and it is here
that it becomes difficult to separate legend from fact.

One major product of the continental drift is the Pacific
Ocean, on the bed of which, it is believed, lies what is left of the
great continent and culture of Mu, which originally stretched
from north of Hawaii to Polynesia and the strange Easter
Island in the south Pacific. There was also, according to Dr
John Ballou Newbrough, a New York dentist and spiritualist
medium who wrote a book entitled *Oahspe* in 1882, another
continent named Pan in the north Pacific Ocean which sank
catastrophically some 24,000 years ago. Newbrough predicted
that Pan will begin to resurface around 1980, i.e. approximately now, and its cities, civilization and culture will become
available for investigation and study.

Although the book *Oahspe* contained full details of the Panic
alphabet and included a Panic dictionary, the existence of Pan
seems never to have been taken seriously by anybody other
than Newbrough himself, probably because of the author's
involvement with mediumship and clairvoyance – although
with psychic Edgar Cayce and Atlantis the converse was true.

The lost land of Mu is quite another matter. Perhaps the
most definitive work on the subject was the book, *The Lost Continent of Mu,* written by James Churchward and first published
in 1926 – a book, incidentally, which is invariably referred to
by other Mu-minded writers. Churchward, who had served
with the British Army in India, claimed that his main source of
information about Mu came from inscribed "Naacal tablets"
which were shown to him and translated by a Hindu temple
priest. There were only two sets of these tablets (in the shape of
flattened human figures) – the set which he saw in India and

another in Mexico, discovered by a colleague, William Niven, an American engineer to whom Churchward dedicated his book.

Churchward stated categorically that both sets of tablets had the same origin, as both bore extracts from the "Sacred Writings of Mu". The two sets were complementary, inscribed in the alphabet of Mu, and were between 12,000 and 15,000 years old.

The opening paragraphs of Churchward's book are dramatic enough, and certainly uncompromising: "The Garden of Eden was not in Asia but on a now sunken continent in the Pacific Ocean. The Biblical story of creation – the epic of the seven days and seven nights – came first not from the peoples of the Nile or the Euphrates Valley but from this now submerged continent Mu – the Motherland of Man.

"These assertions can be proved by the complex records I discovered upon long-forgotten sacred tablets in India, together with records from other countries. They tell of this strange country of 64 million inhabitants who, 50,000 years ago, had developed a civilization superior in many respects to our own. They described, among other things, the creation of man in the mysterious land of Mu . . .

"I learned that in this beautiful country there had lived a people that colonized the earth, and that the land had been obliterated by terrific earthquakes and submersion 12,000 years ago, and had vanished in a vortex of fire and water."

Mu, it seems, was a beautiful, tropical country of richly grassed plains for grazing, and tilled, cultivated fields. There were no mountains, but rolling wooded hills around which curved broad streams and rivers which irrigated the fertile land. Naturally the flora and fauna were superb, including beautiful butterflies, huge mastodons and elephants, while the human inhabitants (white, olive, yellow, brown and black) enjoyed a "gay and happy life".

The "Muvians" built broad roads of precisely chiselled stone blocks leaving no gap between them for grass to push through. They mastered the oceans and colonized all other continents. On pleasure boats, elegantly dressed and bejewelled men and women enjoyed "an idyllic life".

At the peak of this Utopia, Churchward states, disaster struck. Earthquakes and volcanic eruptions shattered the southern part of the continent. The land was inundated by tidal waves. Volcanic lava reared up into the massive cones that today form the islands of the South Pacific. But it was not yet the end of Mu. Cities were rebuilt, pastures refurbished and the good life duly returned – for a while.

The second disaster, many generations later, was to be the last. Churchward wrote: "The whole continent heaved and rolled like the ocean's waves. With thunderous roarings the doomed land sank. Down, down, down she went, into the mouth of hell – a tank of fire . . ." Finally, 50 million square miles of water poured over the continent, drowning the vast majority of its handsome inhabitants.

Nothing remained but the volcanic cones protruding above the ocean to form chains of small islands. Naturally, they were crowded by survivors from sunken Mu. With no clothing, shelter, tools or food the idyllic Muvians, Churchward wrote, "had to become cannibals in order to survive". The colonies that Mu had founded continued for a while, but without the help of the Motherland they decayed. Atlantis, perhaps the most important colony, was destined to suffer the same terminal fate as Mu about 1,000 years later.

Churchward believed that his thesis solved the mystery of the early inhabitants of the South Sea Islands and ancient local cultures and civilizations – on some of these tiny islands there stand today vestiges of temples and other stone structures that date back to the time of Mu. It was inevitable that one of the islands he mentioned was the famous Easter Island, which is about thirteen miles long and seven miles wide and stands virtually isolated in the Pacific Ocean, roughly 2,000 miles west of Chile in South America and over 1,200 miles east of Pitcairn Island – its nearest inhabited neighbour and home of the descendants of the mutineers of *HMS Bounty*.

Easter Island, with its hundreds of remarkable immense stone statues having elongated heads originally topped by tall cylindrical red stone hats, is the subject of a special chapter in this book, for it is indeed a mystery worthy of consideration in its own right. Much of the archaeology and anthropology dealt with elsewhere is contemporary and to a large extent based upon the researches of Thor Heyerdahl and his Kon-Tiki expedition. Even so, the origin of the statues and their true purpose remain speculative in a legendary sense. The islanders of today cannot satisfactorily explain the weird giant statues and other stone structures, nor can they read the tablets and boards inscribed with what appears to be very early picture or hieroglyphic writing.

Naturally, such an intriguing mystery has been, since the discovery of Easter Island in 1722, a challenge to scholars of all nations. It was not too long before two Frenchmen, the Abbé Charles-Etienne Brasseur de Bourbourg, and later an archaeologist, Auguste le Plongeon, claimed to have found a link between the Mayan alphabet and script and the Easter Island hieroglyphics which seemed to prove a common point of origin in the sunken continent of Mu – and, further, a distinct relationship with Ancient Egypt. According to Le Plongeon's reading of a Mayan "book" known as the *Troano Codex*, the ruler of Mu at one time was Queen Moo. She was deposed by her brother, Prince Coh.

When Mu began to sink into the ocean, the ex-Queen Moo was able to escape to Egypt where, under the name of Isis, she founded the Egyptian civilization. She also built the Sphinx as a memorial to the now dead Prince Coh. Le Plongeon considered that Egyptian hieroglyphics and Mayan picture writing were similar, but this view has not been upheld by linguistic experts.

Again one is confronted by the conflict between myth and fact. Easter Island is undeniably a fact, but it is not an isolated case. Elsewhere in the South Pacific are stone artefacts which can be related to those of Easter Island, though perhaps individually they are not so spectacular.

Remains similar to those on Easter Island exist on Mangaia Island (part of the Cook Group between Tahiti and Fiji). As there are no quarries on the island, one can only assume that the stone was "imported" – though by whom and when is a matter for conjecture. On Raratonga Island is a section of stone road which is actually referred to in the Easter Island tablets and legend.

The coral atoll, Tonga-tabu, has no natural stone whatever, but on it is an immense stone archway comprising two 70-ton upright columns linked across the top by a 25-foot stone slab – not unlike a piece of England's Stonehenge.

A number of islands in the Gilbert and Marshall Groups have tall pyramids built of stone, ornamented by, it is claimed, sacred and royal symbols and insignia of Mu. The Caroline Islands are said to possess some of the most astonishing ruins in the South Seas.

The most important ruin in the South Seas, according to Churchward, is located in the island of Panape. It comprises the ruins of a large stone temple 300 feet long by 60 feet wide, with walls which, when discovered in 1874, were 30 feet high and 5 feet thick at ground level. The walls bear carvings which, apparently, have been identified as "Muvian". The temple, built of basalt, has passages, vaults and platforms, and there is a central chamber of pyramid shape. Panape has other mounds of stone ruins, but none so well defined as the temple, and it could have been the site of one of the cities of Mu.

East of Panape, on Swallow Island, is a stone pyramid and the remains of a large quadrangle mainly covered in soil. On Kusai Island, to the south-east of the group, are ruins similar to those on Panape, though not so extensive, but a special feature is a series of stone-lined canals which intersect at right-angles.

The list continues – roads, channels and canals, pyramids, quadrangles, temples – through numerous islands south of (and including) Hawaii. Churchward comments, in his dramatized style: "At one time in the earth's history there was a great continent of land in the Pacific Ocean which embraced all of the groups of islands where prehistoric remains are to be found. This great continent had an exceedingly high civilization."

One must accept facts, of course, but their interpretation is another matter. Mu and Lemuria remain oceanic mysteries of our planet, as does Atlantis. Perhaps, as time goes by, the ever-shifting bed of the oceans will provide answers to the un-answerable questions, as appears to be happening now with Atlantis west of the Bahamas. All three submerged continents have, in turn, been claimed by scholars to be the original Garden of Eden – the point of origin of mankind. We are deal-ing with prehistory, however, and, in particular, a prehistory coloured by the highly articulate visions, dreams and predic-tions of alleged psychic and clairvoyant historians who have claimed to see both the past and the future.

In the final analysis it will be the scientists who will solve the mystery of the ocean depths, a task which will probably prove more difficult than putting a man on the moon. The Apollo programme was a spectacular success, but is it not now time for a Neptune programme? – for, surely, research and in-vestigation, like charity, should start at home.

Accident or Sabotage?

WHO MINED THE *MAINE*?

A familiar sequel to fatal acts of terrorism nowadays is the telephone call to a newspaper office by a spokesman for an organization anxious to claim responsibility for the crime. Chilling though it is to most people that anyone should want to brag of killing, maiming and wrecking, it has become the perpetrators' view that there is prestige to be gained. It is a warning of intent, a reaffirmation of resolution. It is good for morale, a reminder to waverers within the movement that law and order can still be defied. It is a demand for recognition.

So prized is this triumphant notoriety that there are sometimes several contenders for the publicity. Police and security forces have found it expedient to agree a standing form of code message with the more "recognized" terrorist groups, enabling the genuine boast to be separated from the false ones and the sick hoaxes.

It is all very different from the days when anyone remotely likely to have done a barbarous act would deny it to the last, and would take elaborate pains to shift the suspicion on to someone else. It is a nice point to argue which attitude is the more commendable: to claim or to deny. Neither diminishes the victims' tragedy.

There were no claimants to have caused the explosion which sank a ship and resulted in a war. There were all sorts of denials, though; and there have been many theories, involving people other than the obvious suspects.

The scene of the occurrence was Havana harbour, Cuba, and the date, 15 February, 1898.

Cuba, which is today an ironic spearhead of anti-American action in far-flung parts of the world, was then still a Spanish colony, whose people's hope of freedom lay in American support for their revolutionary struggle against their Spanish rulers. The Spanish Government, determined to crush the insurrection, sent out a tough commander, General Weyler, with a force of young volunteers, eager to obey his ruthless orders. He gave his men free licence to brutality and backed them with concentration camps and torture chambers. Only the determination of the revolutionaries and supplies of American arms and provisions enabled the struggle to go on, while American diplomacy sought to persuade Spain to abandon the policy of repression. Her reply was that if the rebels would lay down their arms they would be fairly treated and negotiations about some form of home rule could begin.

The rebels did not believe such promises. They pinned their hopes on holding out until America would decide to intervene by force. This seemed more than likely, and the Spanish Prime Minister, Cánovas, moved to forestall it by laying before the cortes, the Spanish parliament, a bill for Cuban home rule. It caused much resentment in Spain, the once mighty colonial power whose pride was wounded by the thought that she might be going to cede yet another possession at the insistence of an interfering foreign power. Cánovas was assassinated.

This prompted the United States Government to send a new minister to the court of Madrid, General Woodford, carrying with him a strongly worded protest about the state of affairs in Cuba and demanding that military oppression be ended. The new government took the hint, recalled the hard man, General Weyler, and replaced him with Marshal Blanco, a commander more sympathetic to the Cubans' aspirations. Negotiations for home rule were begun.

The Spanish soldiers who had been dealing enthusiastically with the rebels resented what they saw as a climb-down by their government. Who were the Americans to dictate the destiny of an old-established Spanish possession? Their dissatisfaction infected many of the Spanish settlers in Cuba, who doubtless wondered what their own future would be in an island enjoying self-government after centuries of Spanish rule.

Feelings rose high. In cafés and bars in Havana, where politics were debated nightly, arguments raged and tempers gave way. Boiling-over point was reached on 15 January, 1898. Exceptionally hot and humid conditions that evening exacerbated already overheated sentiments. Somewhere an argument erupted into tables and chairs being overthrown, bottles and glasses smashed; and then the streets were alive with shouts and running footfalls as Spanish soldiers broke loose.

It was a brief demonstration – half an hour or so – and there was nothing more substantial that it could achieve than a token protest. Yet, in that short time, enough happened to lead to the brink of war. Certain banks, business offices and the premises of two newspapers had windows smashed and suffered other slight damage on the strength of their having connections with the United States.

As soon as the news of this reached Washington the U.S. Government reacted in the classic fashion of those days: it sent a warship. A few days after the futile outburst of frustration in Havana the cruiser *Maine* slid into the harbour and anchored.

The implied threat was wrapped up in one of those white lies which play so important a part in diplomacy. The United States minister in Madrid explained that his country was anxious to revive the happier relationship which had formerly existed with Spain by resuming friendly exchanges of naval visits. Spain dutifully played the game by the rules, promptly dispatching a cruiser of her navy to New York. Her captain and officers were formally welcomed by American dignitaries, while the *Maine*'s complement, in their turn, were courteously greeted by Marshal Blanco and the senior Spanish naval officer in Havana.

But while a Spanish warship off New York could represent nothing more than the polite gesture she was claimed to be, the presence of *Maine* at Havana meant something very different. It did not go unnoticed by watchers on shore that when the tide swung her at her mooring it brought her 10-inch guns to bear on the city.

True, they had their own batteries, and a single, moored ship would be a sitting duck in the event of an exchange of fire. What the *Maine* symbolized, though, was the might of the U.S. Navy. The message was unmistakable, and it rankled deeply with the Spanish people in Cuba and back at home in the country whose navy had been one of the world's proudest and most powerful in its time.

Passive protest manifested itself in Havana. The *Maine*'s Captain Sigsbee and his officers, invited to bullfights, noticed the expressions of unconcealed resentment and scorn on many of the faces around them. The sailors found themselves cold-shouldered by men and girls in harbour bars. A ferry boat's passengers, crossing the cruiser's bows, openly jeered.

As well as such spontaneous shows of defiance more active moves were afoot. On makeshift backroom printing-presses leaflets were being turned out. Ardent young men stuffed their pockets with them and distributed them in the cafés and bars, dropping some like litter on the pavements to catch the eyes of the curious and be picked up and read.

"SPANIARDS," they exhorted in a bold heading, "LONG LIVE SPAIN WITH HONOUR."

Their message was: "Why do you allow yourselves to be insulted in this way? If our brave and beloved Weyler had not been recalled he would have finished off the rebellious rabble who are trampling our flag and our honour. And now these Yankee pigs, who meddle in our affairs, humiliate us to the last degree with their man-of-war. Spaniards, the moment for action is come. Do not fall asleep. Let us show these vile traitors that we have not lost all our pride, and that we know how to protest with the vigour worthy of a nation such as our Spain has always been and will always be!

"Death to the Americans!"

On another intensely hot, humid night, when the editors of the leaflets were able to see the inflammatory effect their crude production was having on their readers, arguing fiercely over tables and as they leaned on waterfront railings, they suddenly got their wish.

At one moment the long, low cruiser sat placidly out there, complacently lit. The next, with a thunderous roar and a flash which lit the whole area as bright as midday, the *Maine* exploded.

The gasps of people merely witnessing a horrifying spectacle, and cries of natural compassion, were mingled with the cheers of those to whose desires Fate seemed to have granted miraculous fulfilment.

"Death to the Americans!" indeed.

Captain Sigsbee and his entire complement were aboard when it happened. He was in his cabin, at his writing desk, when he was picked up by an invisible force and tossed from the chair. The explosion deafened him. In his words it was "a bursting rending and crashing sound or roar of immense volume, largely metallic in character . . . followed by a succession of heavy, ominous, metallic sounds, probably caused by the overturning of the central superstructure and falling debris."

At the same time the electric lights failed. Captain Sigsbee picked himself up and crawled up on deck. He saw that the fore part of his ship was alight with towering flames. The after part, seemingly unscathed, was crowded with men of all ranks, dazed and shocked. There was a list to port and the *Maine* was sinking by the head.

Captain Sigsbee shouted commands, rousing officers and crew to grab what few fire appliances remained and use them. He also had presence of mind enough to order men to take up watch all round. Those insolent stares in the Havana bullrings had impressed themselves on his mind. He suspected that the destruction of his ship had been the first crazy blow in a war between Spain and the United States. Though no attack materialized out of the darkness beyond the flames, distant cheering could be heard.

The puny fight against the fire was hopeless. The survivors could only retreat further and further back on the poop, waiting to be rescued by boats from other vessels in the harbour, American and Spanish. Heads were bobbing and lolling in the water, along with clusters of wreckage. Faint cries sounded. It was obvious that many of the crew had been hurled far overboard by the explosion, and others had jumped for their lives.

Captain Sigsbee knew the chief remaining danger. While they huddled there on the poop the conflagration would be nearing the magazines where the ammunition for those once-menacing guns was stored. It could touch off an explosion far greater than the earlier one. He yelled orders to abandon ship by any means.

The cruiser's after part had already settled on the harbour bed. The burning bows reared upward, but sank back again towards the water. By the time everyone had got off they had disappeared, with a mountainous hiss of steam. The further explosion which would have destroyed the rescue boats and perhaps part of the city had not happened.

It was not until morning that an assessment of the loss of life could be made. It was worse than anticipated. Out of the

Maine's complement of some 350 officers and men, more than
two-thirds had perished.

There were conflicting tales to be exchanged. Some said there
had been just the one almighty explosion. Others claimed
to have heard two: a small one followed by the larger.
Some survivors had been asleep at one moment, and threshing
about in the sea the next. One, lying in his hammock, had felt
himself lifted and propelled right through the canvas deck
awning above him, to land, still hammocked and unharmed,
conveniently close to some wreckage which he had grabbed.

One impression was uppermost in the thoughts of the
shocked Americans: their ship had been torpedoed or mined.

Whether the Spanish authorities knew what the truth was has
never been determined. What they did know was that this
same interpretation would certainly be placed upon the incident by an outraged United States. As quickly as possible the
Spanish set up a court of inquiry and ordered divers to investigate the wreck. But they dared not risk waiting for the
outcome of either finding. Less than five days after the disaster,
with nothing more than hearsay evidence to hand, they declared that the sinking of the *Maine* could not have been from
any external cause. The explosion of a mine, they explained,
invariably killed all fish within its vicinity. Havana harbour
abounded with fish, but not one dead one had been found after
the disaster. Therefore, the explosion must have been inside
the ship, and a complete accident.

To the American authorities this was a fishy tale, to say the
least. The Spanish thought it was enough, and took no steps
to enlarge upon it. They had made a formal request to be
allowed to interrogate survivors, but did not follow it up.
Their divers seemed to have nothing to report. There was no
admission forthcoming that there were mines in the harbour,
or even whether they possessed any powerful enough to sink an
armoured vessel. All they would say, after less than a week's
ostensible investigation, was that the cruiser had definitely been
sunk by an internal explosion, probably due to spontaneous
combustion in a coal bunker.

The American Press was quick to retort that the Spanish
story was too glib, and that the disaster was too much of a coincidence, in the light of known resentment at the cruiser's
presence. There must be a full and proper inquiry . . .

America's own court of inquiry was convened in Havana on

21 February, and sat for a month. Survivors' evidence was taken. Divers were questioned. Theories and counter-theories were examined. The court's finding was unequivocal: the *Maine* had been sunk by "the explosion of a submarine mine, which caused the partial explosion of two or more of the forward magazines".

Internal explosion, according to the Spanish. The Americans blamed a mine. On only one point – a major one – did both agree. There had been two explosions, a minor one followed by a cataclysm. Witnesses ashore and American survivors were mostly agreed about this. The obvious conclusion was that something had caused a minor explosion, either in the ship or outside it, which in turn had touched off a magazine.

Spontaneous combustion in a coal bunker, suggested by the Spanish, would not have been enough in itself to blow up a 6,682-ton man-o'-war. It was true that six bunkers adjoined the *Maine*'s magazines; but they were equipped with alarms and safety devices to give warning of any untoward build-up of heat. All these had been in full working order on the evening of the disaster. They were regularly and frequently checked, and written records were kept of temperature readings. Moreover, on that day four of the bunkers were completely empty and had been cleaned out. The fifth was half full and in use, which ruled out conditions favourable to spontaneous combustion. The sixth was well laden, but, the American court accepted, it had been carefully examined by an engineer officer and was constantly checked unofficially by crewmen passing along a companionway beside it: it was their automatic habit to touch the bulkheads as they went by, anxious to notice any undue heat so near to the magazines. There had been no sign of any.

The magazines themselves were so constructed that no steam pipes or electrical wires passed through them. Their lights were housed under double-thickness glass. Men working in these chambers, which were otherwise kept locked, wore rubber-soled shoes to obviate any chance of causing a spark. In any case, the volatile material – high explosive, detonators, primers – was stored aft, in magazines under the officers' ward room. And there had been no explosion in that part of the *Maine.*

The boilers, too, were vindicated. They were well away from the magazines, and with the cruiser at anchor only two had been in use, at low pressure.

Could a bomb have been planted by someone from on

shore? This was ruled out. Well aware of the feelings of the
Spanish, Captain Sigsbee had taken every precaution. Only a
few visitors, authorized by him, had been permitted on to the
Maine, and none of these had been allowed out of sight of an
escorting officer or rating.

In short, the American inquiry concluded that the initial
explosion could not possibly have been due to some misadven-
ture in the ship. It had been caused from outside. That implied
a torpedo or a mine. Either would have been a deliberately
hostile act. And if that were proved, the outcome could be war.

Yet the Americans knew that the Spanish had no wish to
precipitate a war with them. They could not hope to win one
and had everything to lose in defeat. It was inconceivable that
their government would have ordered, or condoned, an attack
on the cruiser. This seemed to dispose of any suspicion of tor-
pedoing by the military. Any idea that irregular anti-Amer-
icans could have set up a torpedo tube, hit the *Maine* with a
single discharge, and dismantled the equipment again so
quickly that nobody had seen it would have been absurd.

This left the question of a mine. Although the American
inquiry had accepted this as the likeliest cause there were
many features about the nature of the explosion to throw
doubt on it. The Spanish assertion about the absence of any
dead fish was quaintly dismissed with the counter-suggestion
that either the fish were in the habit of leaving the harbour at
night; or that they had all been stunned by the blast but
had subsequently recovered, without any fatal casualties.

More importantly, witnesses acquainted with exploding
mines affirmed that the first explosion had not had the characteristic muffled sound. It had been more of a sharp crack.
No column of water, usually thrown up by a mine going off
under the sea, had been seen. And the feel of the impact had
not been consistent with the lifting movement a blast under the
ship would have caused.

An obvious obstacle to the mine theory was that no power in
the world would lay contact mines in a major harbour, used by
ships of all nations, without at least making the danger areas
known. But there was another type of mine, harmless if
bumped against but capable of being detonated electrically
from on shore. There might well have been such devices under
the surface of Havana harbour. But if one had been responsible
for the destruction of the *Maine*, the vital question became that

of who had pressed the button? One of the fanatical patriots among the Spanish forces, with access to the control? Or someone acting under orders?

If the latter were the case, the sinking had been a deliberate act of war. It was most unlikely that the Spanish would have risked it in the hope that a mine explosion would never be suspected. That would have been an almost certainly suicidal gamble.

They knew it, and made haste to state that no mines of any sort lay in the harbour. Yet, shortly afterwards, while speculation about war breaking out was rife, the Spanish newspaper *El Heraldo* published a comment by the Navy Secretary, Admiral Berenger. Either forgetfully, or not recognizing the significance of what he was saying, he boasted that there need be no fears about American warships entering Cuban ports because their waters were defended by electrical mines. He specifically mentioned Havana. The newspaper added that the late premier Cánovas had ordered the laying of the mines – and Cánovas had been dead for half a year before the *Maine* was blown up. The mines must have been in position for months.

It was quite possible that the anchorage allocated to the cruiser had been mined with one of these devices. That would be a natural precaution by authorities with reason to fear that the warship might eventually open fire. It emerged in later inquiries that her mooring buoy had been moved from its usual position when her arrival was expected, most likely with the purpose of placing her over a mine.

Examination of the wreck proved no easy task. It was much tangled and was sinking steadily into the soft mud of the harbour floor. The divers spent hours at work and pooled their opinions afterwards. Their consensus was contained in the findings of the court: only a mine could have caused the damage which they had found at a point on the hull.

The American court's conclusions were declared on 21 March. Spain at once began frantic approaches to the European powers and to the Pope, desperate for mediation that would avert war. Although the powers were by no means convinced that the *Maine* had been mined, let alone deliberately, none went further than to suggest mildly to Washington that the unfortunate and tragic incident did not justify the carnage and destruction of warfare.

On 20 April America's minister in Spain delivered an ultimatum: activity by Spanish occupying forces against the Cuban freedom fighters must cease at once, to be followed by the evacuation of the Spanish army from the island. These demands were considered at a cabinet meeting presided over by Queen Cristina herself. Several major ministers urged compliance with them, pointing out that the country stood no chance in a war with the United States. But Spanish pride was founded of old. They were voted down by the majority. The U.S. ambassador was given his passports, and the war was on.

It was over by August. The Spanish fleet had been annihilated. The mother country was cut off from her colonies, which she surrendered in the peace pact which followed. Cuba, Puerto Rico and the Philippine Islands were Spanish territory no longer. The *Maine* and her dead had been avenged.

The investigation into the mystery of the disaster was not ended, though. In 1909 the wreck was declared a danger to shipping. Half a million dollars was appropriated by Congress for raising her. U.S. Army engineers prepared for a field day exercise.

It proved tougher than expected. The plan was to encase the wreck in a huge metal chamber, from which the water would be pumped, leaving the contents dry and easy to inspect. Twice the sum had been spent before the objective was partially achieved, at the end of 1911. The portion of the ship directly affected by the explosion lay encased at last. Sure enough, the examiners reported, a mine had exploded outside the hull at a spot adjoining a small magazine where black powder, used for firing salutes, was stored. This had ignited and set off the bigger magazine nearby.

It seemed to have been an unfortunate chance. Had the mine gone off against almost any other part of the hull than one enclosing a magazine it would probably have done little more than give the ship, and American complacency, a sharp jolt.

Whether the electrical detonator button was pressed by a Spanish patriot, determined to perpetrate an act of defiance against a meddling superpower, or by a Cuban rebel, desperate to provoke America against his Spanish oppressors and set his country free, we do not know. And there are still theorists who maintain that it was all an accident, and there never was a mine.

A SIGHT
TO FREEZE THE BLOOD

In the First World War British destroyers of the Home Fleet were kept busy on a variety of tasks, contraband control, reconnaissance, keeping the Channel lanes open for troop transports going to France, hunting U-boats and, in the later stages, escorting convoys. Not so the bigger ships. Their job, from bases on the east coast of Scotland and Scapa Flow in the Orkneys, was to block exits from the North Sea so that German raiders could not reach the Atlantic and, if possible, bring the enemy High Seas Fleet to action. Constant training, constant readiness for battle combined with long months and years of waiting placed a heavy strain on crews and this, as a matter of policy, was relieved by generous bouts of shore and home leave, sporting activities and ship entertainments.

One ship to experience this kind of life was H.M.S. *Natal*, the first and last warship ever to receive that name as a tribute to the South African colony that had remained loyal to Britain during the Boer War. She was a first-class armoured cruiser of 13,550 tons mounting six 9·2-inch guns and four 7·5-inch guns, ten years old and last of a type which was replaced some years before the war by the battle cruiser. With her four slightly raking funnels, low bridge structure and slim lines the *Natal* looked both business-like and beautiful; moreover she had the reputation of being highly efficient – her gunnery record was second to none in the fleet – and "a happy ship" which meant that her officers and men worked well together as a team.

In 1911 had come the high point of her career to date when, with three other warships, she had formed the escort for the P & O liner *Medina* carrying King George V and Queen Mary to India for the Coronation Durbar. Now, in the winter of 1915, still awaiting a chance with other units of the Grand Fleet to engage the enemy, she had been sent south as part of a cruiser squadron from Scapa Flow to Cromarty Firth with its main town of Invergordon. Scapa was grim, Cromarty with its lowering hills slightly less grim – that was the best that could be said for the scenery, at least at that time of year. But recreational facilities were more varied there and there was an opportunity for some of the men's wives to come up and live ashore for a while.

Considering wartime needs – boilers always with steam up in case of a sudden order to move, anti-submarine lookouts constantly on watch, some gun crews always closed up – Christmas had been a joyful occasion with naval rations (always good) topped up with delicacies, a canteen well stocked by the Army and Navy Stores (no NAAFI in those days), a makeshift variety show and of course Divine Service at which, as on every day in the fleet since the sixteenth century, that special prayer had been said "to be used at sea": "O Eternal Lord God who alone spreadest out the heavens and rulest the raging of the sea . . . be pleased to receive into thy Almighty and most gracious protection the persons of us thy servants, and the Fleet in which we serve . . ."

Christmas Day had been on a Saturday. By the following Thursday, 30 December, a more normal harbour routine had returned. Almost alone among ships in the Royal Navy the *Natal* possessed a cinematograph projector and that afternoon the captain had invited various people on board to see a show, three officers' wives including his own and two civilians with their three children. At around two o'clock the officer of the watch, Lieutenant Denis Fildes (son of the famous Victorian painter Sir Luke Fildes), had with the captain's permission invited three nursing sisters from a hospital ship to join the party and they duly arrived to swell the number of guests to eleven.

Two football teams plus supporters had already gone ashore in the squadron drifter to play a match between the chief petty officers and the foretopmen, followed by a handful of officers intending to play golf or stretch their legs – a total of 103 men. Those left on board were either enjoying a free afternoon's make-and-mend, waiting to go on duty or already on watch, manning the secondary armament or acting as duty lookouts for submarines and floating mines.

In recent days the weather had been performing in typical Cromarty style with icy squalls and snow showers. Now it was a little warmer with only a light breeze and spells of apologetic sunshine. In monkey jacket and swordbelt, with his telescope under his arm, Fildes paced up and down, listening occasionally to the strains of the Royal Marine band wafted up through the wardroom skylight as it played for the captain's party or chatting to one or two people on deck, including Mr Daunt, the boatswain.

At about 3.20 p.m. one picket boat was alongside taking in coal. The second had just been hoisted out and was waiting to take the captain's guests ashore, according to instructions. Leading Seaman Barkshire, the coxswain of No. 1 boat, was coming aft towards the officer of the watch and Fildes heard him say: "Excuse me, sir, could we have some more coal brought up for the picket boat?"

At that moment, at 3.25 precisely, before Fildes could reply came a terrific explosion.

Barkshire was hurled clean overboard (which incidentally saved his life). Fildes found himself face down on the deck, clothes scorched, cap and telescope gone, feeling the deck planking suddenly hot against his cheek, while more explosions rumbled and roared from somewhere deep in the ship and the acrid stench of cordite fumes seared his throat. Still perfectly lucid, he watched the pitch in the deck seams begin to bubble, then catch light and burn.

The explosions lasted only a few seconds, then huge sheets of flame were roaring up from the wardroom skylight and the upper deck ventilating trunks, licking forward to the mainmast, bursting and swirling from a starboard gun turret. Staggering to his feet, Fildes shouted for the after magazines to be flooded, but no one could get near them through the inferno. Fire hoses were useless, too, as the pumps had gone, so had the dynamos supplying power to signalling lamps which might have called to other ships for help. Within two minutes the *Natal* was listing twenty degrees to port and Fildes could see and hear that she was doomed.

There were new sounds now, the deep rumble of water pouring into the hull mixed with the crash and thud of fixtures
tearing loose below decks as the ship heeled over. Fildes called
on the men, those still alive, to bring up with them from below
anything they could cling to in the sea and get overboard
down the starboard side. When there was nothing more he
could do, he followed them, slithering down to the bilge keel as
it reared up towards him and from there into the icy waters of
Cromarty Firth.

Within five minutes over 350 people had died, officers and
men, all the captain's guests, killed outright by the explosions,
incinerated in the raging fires, trapped and drowned below
decks when bulkheads gave way or steel ladders collapsed, leaving no escape. Survivors in a boat still tied up on the port side
were all crushed when a massive gun turret tore loose from its
mountings and fell on top of them.

But there were some survivors, upwards of three hundred,
though none could say afterwards what exactly had happened
and why. Leading seaman Rust had been dozing uncomfortably with his head on a mess stool when the first explosion
catapulted him on to the deck beneath a table. From that
moment he had no doubt the ship would sink and he ran forward through the stokers' mess deck till he found a ladder still
intact which led him up to the forecastle from where, in less
than a minute, he jumped, still in his sea boots. Another man,
engine-room artificer Steve Mattocks, was also sure of what to
do. He had been in the coppersmith's shop writing a letter to
his girlfriend when the explosions came. The ship shuddered
and all the lights went out. Mattocks groped forward to the
foot of a ladder from where, above him, he could see nothing
but flames and smoke. Desperately he started to climb – and
got through to the upper deck, just how he never afterwards
could explain.

But some ratings could not believe there was anything seriously wrong until too late. The explosions had come from the
after magazines, deep in the ship. Men of the off-duty watch in
the foremost mess deck heard a rumble, felt a vibration,
nothing more. One man roused by his mate even turned over
to sleep again, thinking perhaps it was some kind of joke. He
was never seen again.

Meanwhile on shore the football match was over and one of
the spectators, a rating from the *Natal*, happened to look at his

ship lying at anchor below the playing field. "It was at this moment", he wrote later, "that there occurred a sight that froze the blood in my veins and lives with me today in nightmares . . . A tower of sickly yellow flame had suddenly shot up from the after part of the ship. It leapt above the mastheads, seeming even to dwarf the mountains in the background . . . It was unmistakably the flash of burning cordite. Almost simultaneously there sounded a deep rumbling explosion . . . This was followed by two sharper explosions. The ship trembled violently, then suddenly began to list to port. Over slowly she went. Those of her crew who by then had reached the deck slid into the water like beans from a shovel. Farther over she went until her bilge keel was clear of the surface. For a moment she lay there while a straggling line of survivors floundered on her slimy hull. Then she disappeared."

A mass of boats had already set out from other ships and were picking up survivors. Four officers and 279 ratings were eventually rescued, but some so badly burnt that they did not live. Others were taken to a hospital ship and two poignant photographs are in existence, the first showing a bunch of fifty or so grouped in front of a lifeboat on the morning after the sinking and the second taken some time later, before they were discharged to their depot at Chatham. No one would guess, looking at the first photo, that these men had just suffered a terrible disaster. Many are smiling, almost all look steady and composed, and the reasons seems clear: they are just thankful to be alive. But by the time the second was taken the reaction had set in and expressions had changed to a sadness verging almost on tears.

A court martial on the survivors, which meant in practice a court of inquiry into the loss of the ship, sat in January, 1916, under the presidency of a rear-admiral and reached no conclusions beyond expressing the opinion that ammunition had exploded in the after magazines and that neither officers nor men were in any way to blame. Then why the explosions? Inspection by divers showed that the ship's plates had been blown outwards which excluded a torpedo attack by submarine, so there were two main possibilities: spontaneous combustion in an old batch of cordite that had become unstable, possibly due to excessive heat in the magazines – for which there was no evidence – or the planting of an "infernal machine" by an enemy agent or disaffected dockyard worker, an Irishman perhaps, a Sinn Feiner bent on blasting Britain into conferring Home Rule on Ireland.

The court briefly considered this possibility with visions, apparently, of an infernal machine being large enough to be easily detected. Admittedly, the *Natal* had been at Birkenhead refitting from 22 November to 5 December, with all her ammunition landed. But anti-sabotage precautions were strict there and the ship had been searched before leaving. Moreover twenty-five days had elapsed before the explosions, which made the sabotage theory seem even more unlikely. So the second possibility was dropped and cursorily dismissed in the inquiry's report.

Thus the *Natal* explosion was allowed to sink into oblivion, unexplained, apparently inexplicable, until eighteen months later there was another disaster.

On 9 July, 1917, the Grand Fleet, consisting of 28 capital ships, 9 light cruisers, 57 destroyers, 25 submarines together with fleet auxiliaries, store ships and hospital ships, was lying at Scapa Flow, among them the Dreadnought battleship *Vanguard* of 19,250 tons, eight years old, mounting ten 12-inch and eighteen 4-inch guns. She had had her brief moment of glory at the Battle of Jutland in the summer of 1916 when for eighteen minutes she had engaged Admiral Scheer's scouting cruisers. Then came anti-climax and the long wait for another fleet action which never came.

But in July, 1917, that was still a possibility and at Scapa every ship in the fleet was kept busy with training and exercises, including the *Vanguard*. By mid-afternoon on the 9th she had conpleted her schedule and was anchored among the other ships of her squadron. Later, the watch was changed and those off duty walked the upper deck, chatting and smoking in the warm evening air until around 10 p.m. they turned in, read for a while perhaps and then slept. One of them was Stoker Fred Cox, another, Private John Williams of the Royal Marine Light Infantry.

Apart from officers and ratings on leave or for other reasons not on board, only those two men, and one officer who died within a few days, survived that night. At 11.20, duty lookouts on other ships saw to their horror a brilliant tongue of flame shoot up abaft the *Vanguard*'s mainmast, to be followed instantly by a giant fireball and a shattering explosion. Within seconds this was followed by another and when the smoke cleared nothing visible was left of the battleship. She had disappeared. Then debris began to rain down on the other ships and the surrounding shore, massive chunks of steel, flaming, unidentifiable objects, bits of human bodies, all of which kept the fleet busy all night and for several days with hoses and working parties. In that instant of time over 880 men had died.

Once more a court of inquiry was held and again there was much discussion of temperatures in magazines, of the undoubted fact that for many reasons they were liable to be higher in wartime, of spontaneous combustion of cordite, of safety checks, security precautions, accidental fires. The court moved on to talk of wireless waves. Could they be used by an enemy to ignite cordite? An expert summoned for an opinion said emphatically no.

Still groping in the dark, the court was able to exclude the possibility of U-boat attack and then turned to an interesting discovery. When the *Natal* had been at Birkenhead work had been done on the magazine cooling system by three civilians, a skilled labourer from Chatham, a fitter from Devonport dockyard and a foreman of ordnance fitters from the Naval Ordnance Depot at Chatham. As the work was not finished when the ship sailed for Scotland these three men had stayed with her and left a week before the explosion. But that same foreman had also been on board the *Vanguard* at Scapa on another job and had left the anchorage only two days before she blew up.

The court sent for the foreman, interrogated him closely and was not satisfied with his answers, particularly on one occasion when, incredibly, he claimed ignorance of the general details of ships' magazines. So he was sent for further questioning to the Director of Naval Intelligence, but there is no record that this ever took place. Perhaps he was a lucky man to have been left in his job, dying some years later quietly in bed, and perhaps he was spared a severe grilling because no one in the Admiralty believed that a device small enough to avoid detection with so long a time-fuse could be invented, let alone planted in His Majesty's ships. If so, the Admiralty was wrong.

To people of an older generation the name Kapitänleutnant von Rintelen will still be familiar, the charming, debonair German naval officer who after the First World War created quite a sensation in Britain with his book *The Dark Invader*. It

was one of the earliest Penguins and told of his exploits in
spying and sabotage. On the outbreak of war he had been
serving on the Admiralty staff in Berlin. Then in early 1915 as
a good English speaker he was sent to New York under a false
passport as a Swiss businessman to try and impede the export
of American munitions to Britain. One way was to pass on
information about Allied shipping movements and cargoes to
the German Embassy and thence surreptitiously to Berlin for
the use of U-boats. Another and better way was sabotage.

Here von Rintelen was helped by the presence in American
ports of many dockers of Irish extraction hating Britain and
only too anxious to do her injury, and above all by a certain
compatriot, a Doctor Scheele, who had invented an incendiary
device. This consisted of a hollow lead tube, only four inches
long and one inch in diameter. In the centre of this tube was
sealed a copper disc and the spaces on either side were filled
with sulphuric acid and chlorate of potash. Each end of the
tube was then plugged with wax and a lead cap. When, as
Scheele demonstrated, the acid had eaten through the disc and
mingled with the potash a two-foot sheet of flame giving off
intense heat and lasting several minutes surged out, leaving
behind only a small blob of molten lead.

It was a perfect instrument for sabotage, easily carried
about, easily concealed and delayed action could be adjusted
simply by varying the thickness of the copper disc. Von Rintelen achieved many successes among Allied ships with these
bombs, handing them out in dozens to Irish dockers in ports
along America's eastern seaboard until, as he later claimed,
they become over-enthusiastic to destroy life, whereupon he
ceased to employ them.

Von Rintelen operated for only a few months before the
British got to know of him and captured him by a ruse. But
with heavy traffic crossing the Atlantic every week it is easy to
see how the secret of that little tube could have reached sab-
oteurs in British ports, including Chatham and Birkenhead.
Just as the acid and the potash came together to create fire, so
it only needed the combination of one determined man with
access to British warships and one of Scheele's devices for a
calamitous explosion to be almost certain.

That man may well have been the foreman of ordnance fitters and his achievement may not have been two but three
warships destroyed: the battleship *Bulwark* also blew up at

Sheerness in November, 1914, though that date seems too early for the lead tube to have been used. Her fate was almost identical with the *Vanguard*'s: a sudden streak of yellowish flame from the after magazine – at breakfast time in this case – followed by a thunderous explosion which literally blew the 15,000-ton ship to pieces together with 780 officers and men. At this time, less than four months after the outbreak of war, naval officers on the inquiry were probably not attuned to the scope or intricacies of sabotage and with the innocence of the dove rather than the cunning of the serpent they declared in their report: "It is clear from the evidence produced that the explosion was due to the accidental ignition of ammunition on board. There is no evidence to support a suggestion that the explosion was due either to treachery or to an act of the enemy." No evidence – but there were clues. Workmen from Chatham dockyard, only a few miles away, had been on board the *Bulwark* doing various repair jobs until just before the explosion. But whether it was accident or design that led to her destruction, the fact remains that throughout the war enemy fleets suffered no similar disaster while among the Allies a total of five big ships blew up in mysterious circumstances, an Italian battleship at Taranto in September, 1915, and a Russian Dreadnought in the Black Sea in October, 1916.

In all these disasters probability suggests enemy-inspired sabotage, even outright enemy action. But we cannot be sure. Life is full of coincidences which no novelist would dare to contrive, coincidences so strange that mere chance seems inadequate to explain them. Yet they result from no one's deliberate intent. What would von Rintelen himself have said on this score?

In August, 1915, the British had got hold of a top-secret German code and using this they ordered Rintelen by telegram back to Berlin, took him off a Dutch ship when it stopped at Ramsgate for contraband control and brought him to Admiral Hall, the Director of Naval Intelligence in London. From there, with the British still unaware of Scheele's device, he was extradited to the United States to serve four years' imprisonment for sabotage, returning to Britain in 1921 where he wrote his book.

The book, and a lecture tour he undertook to boost sales established him in the public mind as "the gentleman spy", humane, always careful of human life. But one of those lectures was attended by a man who had reason to think otherwise, a retired naval officer named Denis Fildes.

After the lecture Fildes went up to von Rintelen and congratulated him on the talk. Then he said; "May I congratulate you also on sinking the armoured cruiser *Natal?*" Von Rintelen waxed red in the face and very angry. What an outrageous suggestion! What an appalling accusation that he, von Rintelen, could ever contemplate such a cowardly act! He must ask for an apology at once.

But no apology was forthcoming.

Deadly Effects?

THE ATLANTIC'S
SINISTER TRIANGLE

There is a story, probably apocryphal, that an airline executive, on a flight between Florida and Bermuda, sent as a joke a handwritten note to the captain of the aircraft asking, "Do you know we are in the Bermuda Triangle?" The captain wrote back, "Can't worry about that now – all my instruments are off and my compasses are spinning."

True or not, that joke sums up concisely the fundamental mystery of an area of the western Atlantic Ocean, roughly triangular in shape, between Florida, U.S.A., Bermuda and the Sargasso Sea between 40 and 50 degrees west longitude. It is a zone in which, since 1945, hundreds of ships and aircraft have vanished completely, leaving neither wreckage nor survivors – and not even a trace of oil slick as evidence of explicable disaster. On a smaller scale, between 1974 and 1976 more than 600 yachts and pleasure boats disappeared without trace off the Florida Coast; a large percentage of them had ventured into the zone of the Triangle.

These strange disappearances go back long before 1945, but no serious attempt was made to collate and investigate them until the end of the Second World War, when advancing technology and increasing military intelligence and security rendered such investigation obligatory, particularly in the United States which harbours, if that is the word, the Triangle. Even so, the ordinary people throughout the world were hardly aware of what was happening until Charles Berlitz, author and lecturer, fluent in twenty-seven languages and a well-known researcher into what he calls "natural mysteries", published in 1975 his best-selling book entitled bluntly *The Bermuda Triangle*. The book was translated into twenty languages, and was the focus of many television and radio programmes, quite apart from detailed newspaper and magazine reviews and features. Like UFOs, the mystery of the Bermuda Triangle became an international talking point and guessing game.

On the question of facts, however, Berlitz was not guessing. His list of case histories (dating back in his second book, *Without a Trace*, to the year 1800) is long and impressive. Even if one were to write off cases with an element of doubt as "natural disasters" (but without wreckage or survivors!), the remainder, which is the majority, defy rational explanation.

In the space available here it is only possible to refer to a few of the more significant events which form the present pattern of the Triangle tapestry – but first it is necessary to consider what makes the Bermuda Triangle zone so unusual. There is no doubt that very many people, sailing or flying through that sinister area, have had experiences which on the surface would appear to be unbelievable, but which may, nevertheless, have a logical explanation beyond our current scientific understanding.

Recorded disappearances seem to be invariably associated with a luminous haze or cloud. The weather may be good and the sea calm, but a ship or aircraft entering the luminous fog may never be seen again.

Aberrations and anomalies of various kinds are reported. For example, compasses spin wildly, radio communication is blacked out, gyros, radar, sonar and navigational instruments cease to function. Bright lights are seen in the sky and under the sea (producing the phenomenon known as "white water").

Even more puzzling than the total loss of electrical power is the time anomaly in which the ship or aircraft – particularly aircraft, where time and speed are vital parameters to a flight – may show an inexplicable gain or loss, not as indicated by the aircraft clock but as recorded by ground observers and airfield controllers. A tail wind or a pilot's error in reading wind velocity could possibly account for a number of cases, but ground control and the meteorologists would know the facts, anyway.

For example, Pilot Bruce Gernon, of Boynton Beach, Florida, flew from Andros Island to Palm Beach, Florida, on 4 December, 1970, and was unable to avoid flying through an elliptical cloud in the Triangle, although he increased altitude to overfly it. The centre of the cloud became a tunnel, and towards the end when the wing-tips of his aircraft touched the sides of the tunnel he experienced what he described as "zero gravity".

He emerged into a greenish haze with zero visibility and total malfunction of all instruments. When the haze cleared he was able to make radio contact with ground control and soon afterwards landed at Palm Beach – but the flight had taken only 45 minutes instead of the usual 75 minutes, and the aircraft had travelled 250 miles instead of the normal 200. His maximum cruising speed in that particular aeroplane was 195 m.p.h.

On checking previous fuel records he calculated that the plane ordinarily used about 40 gallons for that particular trip, but on this occasion fuel consumption had been only 28 gallons. According to Gernon, that would account for the half-hour of missing time since the plane would have used a further 10 gallons to fly for the additional half hour. But – during the approach to Palm Beach, Gernon had, it was recorded, over-flown Bimini Keys and Miami, a swift flight of only a few minutes duration and quite impossible for Gernon's small plane.

The final computations were totally unacceptable to authority, unless one could accept the fact that while he was in the cloud tunnel and haze Gernon's small plane had been flying at around 1,180 m.p.h. (nearly Mach 2); alternatively, that the cloud complex itself had been moving at Mach 2, which would account for the saving in fuel.

Coincidentally (or perhaps not coincidentally) during that same December many other aircraft were lost in cloud formations in the same area at roughly the same time – late afternoon.

Variations in clock time on aircraft have been both shorter and longer than Gernon's. In another instance, a U.S. Navy P2 was returning from a training flight over Bahama waters when it suddenly encountered heavy turbulence. While climbing rapidly an engine cylinder failed. The pilot transmitted a Mayday signal but received no reply. Nevertheless, he was able to land successfully at Jacksonville where he was asked if he would take off again to help locate an aircraft from which a Mayday call had been received – that is, to look for himself! In some odd way his Mayday call had been suspended in the ether (or possibly in time?) for a quarter of an hour.

At the other extreme in November, 1970, Air Force pilot Tim Lockley, flying on a NATO mission from Pope, North Carolina to Mildenhall, England, via the Azores, reported a three and a half hours gain in flight time over other planes in the group which were taking off at half-hour intervals. Weather conditions were normal and there was no electrical disturbance. Air speed was as scheduled, but ground speed was several hundred knots faster than it should have been – and there were no strong tail winds. The timing was confirmed by ground control – but there was no explanation. Pilot Lockley commented, "You hear a lot of rumours about things like this – when planes fly into white-outs – where the sky and water look exactly alike. You get disorientated about everything, even about time."

Charles Berlitz muses, but makes no positive statement, on the possibility of a time anomaly operating within the Bermuda Triangle, "as if time at certain moments could project individuals from the present into the past or otherwise bend the continuum of time in a manner blending the past and the present – and perhaps the future as well". Add to that gravitation, energy and mass, and their "anti" opposites, and one is approaching the foundation fringes of Einstein's unified field equation – the final unravelling of the relativity knot – which he sought in his later life but, it is said, never achieved before his death. And, to be truly speculative, one way in which ships and aircraft and all they contain could disappear without trace might take the form of impact with antimatter. Add one to minus one and the result is zero. However, that is still in the realm of science-fiction, although the reality may not be so far away.

The time anomaly would, of course, account for phantom ships, in particular large ships quite void of passengers or crew. There have been many such sightings, especially in the Pacific near Australia and New Zealand, and these phenomena are not exclusive to the Triangle. Indeed, Great Britain's King George V, when as a Prince he was a naval cadet on the H.M.S. *Bacchante* in the Pacific in 1881, wrote a matter-of-fact entry in the ship's log at 4 a.m. on 11 July of that year: "*The*

Flying Dutchman crossed our bows. A strange red light, as of a phantom ship all aglow, in the midst of which the masts, spars and sails of a brig two hundred yards distant stood up in strong relief . . . Thirteen people altogether saw her."

Very much more recently a phantom "old sailing ship" was photographed during an electric storm north-east of Bimini in the Bermuda Triangle. The photographer, using a Pentax camera, was Dr J. Thorne, director of a research and filming expedition on the yacht *New Freedom*. He was taking a series of colour photographs of green and purple lightning flashes, and the sailing ship, which had passed unnoticed in the spectacular pyrotechnics of the storm, was clearly visible in the developed film.

There are many other instances which suggest that "time slips", although discounted by orthodox physicists, are and have been manifest at sea, but the subject of phantoms is covered elsewhere in this book. Also dealt with in other chapters is the subject of sea monsters – including USOs, or Unidentified Submarine Objects – which, it has been suggested, could, if of giant size, offer a possible explanation for the total disappearance of ships (though obviously not aircraft).

In the case of the Bermuda Triangle one is concerned with both ships *and* aircraft, so that it is essential to find a common denominator, if one exists. While the answer could be connected with UFOs, it is hardly likely to embrace USOs – unless there is some obscure interconnection between the two. It is necessary, therefore, to return to documentated evidence plus comment and then project further into possibilities that may at first appear to border on fantasy but may well, in the course of time, prove to be fact.

First a concise and necessarily abridged summary of some of the Triangle incidents listed by researchers, including reports in U.S. and British Commonwealth newspapers and journals. These include:

A Cessna jet business aircraft encountering a "cloud", resulting in total failure of instrumentation and death of the pilot (confirmed by some surviving passengers). An Eastern Airlines flight experiencing a powerful jolt, then loss of altitude and landing at a non-scheduled stop. Crew and passengers find that their watches have all stopped at the moment of the airborne shock, and there are marks of great heat or electrical burning, possibly both, on the fuselage.

Radar loss of a National Airlines 727 for ten minutes while flying through light fog or haze. On landing, the plane's clock and all watches on board show a ten-minute lag despite a time check just half an hour before landing. A Cessna 172 loses radio contact with ground control at Grand Turk Island, Bahamas, but the tower controller can hear the pilot telling a passenger that they must be over the wrong area because "there's nothing down there". The plane flies on and is never seen gain.

On *Queen Elizabeth II* one of the crew sees a plane flying directly at the luxury liner, but suddenly the aircraft plunges into the sea about 100 yards from the ship. The sea opens to receive it, and there is no noise, wreckage or oil.

Ships' logs have contained entries naming other ships that were sighted, but the ships they apparently saw were already listed, and in many cases long listed, as sunk or disappeared without trace.

A large "hill" of water rising up from the ocean is seen and reported by members of the crew of the U.S. *Josephus Daniels*, so the ship changes course, which has to be logged. In port the log is examined by authority but is never returned to the ship. Why?

A cargo ship turns aimlessly in a full circle as a result of failure of all navigational instruments; a few moments later a gigantic "fireball" nearly sweeps the mate on watch from the deck while swooping low over the vessel.

The above selection merely illustrates a few of the curious anomalies of different kinds in the Bermuda Triangle which contravene established science, and possibly indicate the existence of unknown forces affecting ships, aircraft and people. But, naturally, as stated in Newton's second law of motion, "for every action there is an equal and opposite reaction". Critics of the Bermuda Triangle enigma have not been slow in voicing their views, and their overall attitude is not dissimilar to that of the anti-UFO lobby, with possibly parallel motivations.

The critics go through the customary procedure of waving aside substantiated evidence, mainly on the following grounds.

They claim that the Bermuda Triangle does not exist as an identifiable area of potential danger, and that the controversy is merely a ploy to arouse public interest – and, by implication, to ensure a profitable best-seller basis for authors writing on this contentious subject. The same argument could, and has been, used in respect of authors writing on different paranormal subjects.

In fact, the Bermuda Triangle, leaving aside the question of mysterious and dangerous unknown forces, is indicated on the sea and air charts of the British Admiralty as a zone of magnetic aberration, although any connection with authenticated disappearances of ships, aircraft and people is ridiculed. Even the Press is, perhaps under pressure, unimpressed. There have been headlines, somewhat jocular, in various countries, ranging from *Are there Hijackers in Outer Space?* through *How the QE II almost ended up in a Space Museum* and *Your Friends may be in a Martian Zoo* to *Is there a Hole in the Sky?* The attitude of the U.S. authorities is parallel, although there is little doubt, as with UFOs, that much secret investigative work is going on behind the scenes.

Another critical view is that any unexplained disappearance can be called a mystery until the cause is unveiled, and that the lack of visible evidence of disappearances is due to the fact that the Atlantic is a big ocean. Further, to cover up loopholes, ships that have vanished (but presumably not aircraft) might have been lost in unexpected violent storms, been hit and sunk by much larger ships, or been hijacked and "repainted" – and no doubt renamed (which would pose a problem for Lloyd's of London and other marine insurers).

Berlitz, while acknowledging such criticisms of the concept of the Triangle, points out that this would be an expected reaction from airline and shipping companies, whose prime aim is to increase passenger and freight loading to improve profitability. For them the existence of such a potential menace as the Bermuda Triangle would naturally be an anathema. He adds that some of the most articulate critics have "either not had the opportunity to visit it personally, do not deem it necessary to make an on-the-spot investigation, or have discreetly kept away from it".

Oceanographers, and also geologists and meteorologists, who know the area are naturally unwilling to commit themselves to what they regard as nebulous theories, although they will concede that inexplicable disappearances have taken place during freak storms and violent weather conditions. Even so, most disappearances occurred in relatively calm weather, and the ab-

sence of floating wreckage, oil slicks or survivors is blandly
overlooked.

It could be possible, of course, and here authority frowns
severely, that the absence of wreckage of vessels and planes is
due to the fact that they did not go down into the sea, but
went up into the sky. How? Antigravity, quadrature into the
time dimension or some other dimension, or total disintegra-
tion by high-energy ionization fields? But what would pre-
suppose the hypothetical existence of an alien intelligence, and
in this military-security-conscious post-war era no government
could possibly make such an admission. Extraterrestrial space
(and even worse – intelligence) is a highly sensitive subject.
Students of UFOlogy will already know that the CIA was
briefed by the U.S. Government to explain away, whitewash
and play down UFO sightings, and the Condon Report on
Unidentified Flying Objects, commissioned by the U.S.
Government and running to about 1,000 pages, brushes UFOs
aside (though not without courtesy) in an excellent example of
what might be termed negative public relations. With a little
luck the world may be graced in the foreseeable future with a
further sponsored report on USOs.

The essential point is that scientific and governmental estab-
lishments must predictably deny the very existence of the Bermuda Triangle – except as a navigational zone of magnetic
aberration. Meanwhile, according to Berlitz, unexplained total
disappearances in the Triangle are continuing at an average
rate of about one ship per week and one aircraft every two
weeks.

An odd and unexpected side-effect of the Triangle involves,
of all things, orbiting weather satellites which, on a polar orbit
some 800 miles above the earth's surface, frequently fail to
function for a period – but only when passing over the Bermuda Triangle. This has been confirmed by Professor Wayne
Meshejian, a physicist at Longwood College, Virginia, U.S.A.
He attributes the temporary malfunctions to some kind of
powerful energy source under the sea. Although the interference can erase videotapes in orbit 800 miles up, it apparently
does not affect the satellite's orbit, but Meshejian thinks it
should, otherwise "we are talking about a force we know
nothing about".

That is not a mind-blowing idea; there are probably many
forces we know nothing about. Indeed, it has been suggested

by a few irreverent physicists that the Bermuda Triangle (and certain similar zones scattered over the globe) is a point of entry for cosmic forces, delineated by the curvature of space and time. If that means anything at all, at least it encompasses the time anomalies which are characteristic of the Triangle and could conceivably support the contention that vanished ships and planes go up rather than down, but so far there seem to be no mathematics to substantiate the hypothesis. Perhaps the equations will materialize in due course.

Back to a classic case history, as related by Lawrence David Kusche, author of *The Bermuda Triangle Solved*, in a concisely written chapter entitled "The Legend of the Bermuda Triangle". Clearly Lawrence Kusche, a reference librarian at Arizona State University, regards the Triangle as a myth, each disappearance being capable of rational explanation provided sufficient information is accessible. His approach is fair and objective, and largely he leaves the reader to form his own final opinion and judgement. Here, then, is the strange story of Flight 19 on the afternoon of 5 December, 1945, when five U.S. Navy Avenger torpedo-bombers took off from Fort Lauderdale Naval Air Station on a routine patrol that was destined to end in tragedy and the apparent deaths of twenty-seven men.

There was no evidence of bad weather, but the Flight Leader nevertheless radioed that all five planes were lost and unable to find out in which direction they were flying. Shortly afterwards communications ceased and were never restored. A rescue plane was sent to the plotted area of the lost patrol – but it also disappeared. One of the biggest searches in the history of aviation went on for the next five days, but no trace of the six missing aircraft was ever found.

After a long investigation the U.S. Navy found itself more confused than before the inquiry began. It was another, and spectacular, Bermuda Triangle mystery, and one naval officer remarked, "They vanished as completely as if they had flown to Mars".

Lawrence Kusche's own subsequent investigation of the incident is lengthy and must necessarily be summarized since it quotes detailed radio communications verbatim, but his conclusions are clear and terse enough. The flight instructor leader of Flight 19 was Lt. Charles C. Taylor. The most important factor contributing to the loss of the Flight was the failure of

Lt. Taylor's compasses. Why they failed is not explained. Apparently neither Taylor nor his crew had a watch because Taylor kept asking the time over the radio. It is a sure formula for navigational disorientation to fly for an unknown period in an unknown direction, and Taylor had already stated that "I am over land ... I'm sure I'm in the Keys, but I don't know how far down and I don't know how to get to Fort Lauderdale".

Taylor was mistaken. He was not familiar with the Bahamas and he was not over the Keys. In fact, he did not know whether he was over the Atlantic Ocean and east of Florida or over the Gulf of Mexico and west of the peninsula. He changed direction several times, leading the patrol further north of the Bahamas.

Another vital factor was that Taylor declined to switch his radio to the emergency channel, so that he lost contact with the ground stations. Apparently he feared that the other planes in the patrol might fail to turn to the correct frequency and so lose communication with each other. The emergency frequency was 3,000 kHz – a channel free from interference.

Finally the weather closed in. Fair at take-off, it rapidly worsened, with high turbulence, strong winds and, below, a heavy sea. To attempt to ditch in such a sea after dark would have been fatal.

The main trouble, according to Kusche, was not that Taylor or his men did not know the direction in which they were flying, but that they could not decide which was the correct direction to pursue. Completely disorientated, they kept changing direction, but stayed together as a patrol until, after more than four hours, they ran out of fuel and allegedly plunged into the Atlantic north of the Bahamas.

The Martin Mariner rescue plane sent out to find the missing patrol took off into a clear sunlit sky and vanished without trace as it was about to enter the zone where Flight 19 had disappeared. An explosion occurred after 23 minutes of flight. Mariners were known as "flying gas tanks" because of fumes that could easily be ignited by one of the crew lighting a cigarette, or any kind of spark.

The Mariner was not the only rescue plane. Several took off, and ships were also sent to the disaster location.

A later report after the inquiry implied that Lt. Taylor asked to be replaced before the Flight took off, but the request was denied. One account adds, "it is thought that he might have been sick or possibly intoxicated". This matter was dismissed and never pursued further (as it would have been had there been any grounds for such a charge). In fact, the U.S. Navy absolved Lt. Taylor of all blame for the loss, which was fundamentally attributed to "some unexpected and unforeseen development of weather conditions . . ."

Lawrence Kusche concludes that many factors prevented Flight 19 from being saved: the failure of Taylor's compasses; the failure of the one radio channel needed by the senior flight instructor at Fort Lauderdale to continue communicating with the Flight; bad radio reception; nightfall and the sudden onset of bad weather; the failure to locate the Flight promptly with radio bearings and the failure to broadcast the fix data once it had been calculated.

Also the failure of the teletype system at ground control; the icing of the radio antenna of a rescue plane; the discipline that kept the Flight group together even though several of the pilots apparently knew they were flying in the wrong direction; and the fact that Flight 19 was the last flight of the day.

Kusche adds, with irony, that had any one of the above factors not prevailed, the flight might have ended differently. In the event, according to later evidence, Lt. Taylor first reported his navigational problem when he was over the reefs just north of the Bahamas. At that time Flight 19 was almost exactly on course – but it was also "lost".

It is for the reader to form his own judgement, a policy which Lawrence Kusche meticulously maintains. What are the mathematical odds against so many – and there *are* many – coincidental failures occurring simultaneously, or virtually so? Compass failure, radio failure, disorientation, fair weather changing suddenly to foul weather, an unexplained explosion destroying the rescue plane soon after take-off. All are reportedly characteristic of what one might call the Bermuda Triangle syndrome. Would it not be simpler to adopt the principle of Okham's Razor and accept as fact, albeit reluctantly, that within the Triangle zone an unlikely series of navigational failures, disruption of electronic systems and disappearances without trace can, and do, occur from time to time as a result of forces beyond our present knowledge and understanding?

Furthermore, the story of Flight 19 is not an isolated case; it slots into scores, indeed hundreds, of similar incidents.

Kusche's logical argument may be sound vertical thinking, but the broad spectrum of Bermuda Triangle disappearances is lateral. The two lines may intersect and yet prove nothing in one direction or the other. Here again one must draw a parallel with UFO sightings and investigations, where an objective analysis of each incident individually does not change the ever-growing accumulation of such incidents. It is that relentless growth that really demands explanation.

In summing up, and before going on in the next chapter to consider similar phenomena in other parts of the world, various oddities are worthy of mention, although most of these form part of the subject-matter of other chapters. Historically, the peculiar nature of the sea and weather in what is now known as the Bermuda Triangle goes back to earliest times.

Columbus, on his first voyage to America, recorded the luminous waters of the Bahamas and observed a fireball which circled his ship before diving noiselessly into the sea. The ship's compass ran wild and began to spin in complete circles to the alarm of officers and men. Two years later Columbus saw what appeared to be a sea monster near the island of Haiti, and in the same year a powerful whirlwind spun three of his ships round and round until they sunk, and at a time when the sea was calm with no hint of a storm. On later occasions twenty-six out of thirty galleons carrying treasure to Spain sank in a sudden storm – "leaving the smell of burnt powder in the air" – and another treasure fleet of seventeen ships vanished in an unexpected storm.

Violent storms and hurricanes are, of course, common enough off North America's eastern seaboard, and they, together with the activities of pirates, no doubt accounted for most of the losses. There is no direct evidence either way. But there seems little doubt that a number of inexplicable disappearances gave rise to the macabre reputation of the Sargasso Sea in the eastern part of the Triangle zone, where "lost ships" were seen drifting among the massed seaweed in that area of the ocean.

A curious aspect of the sea in the Triangle is the spectacular and often violent activity within the water. Holes and trenches may open up suddenly in the sea, or alternatively the sea may rise into a formidable hill. The latter phenomenon, taking the shape of a massive raised level of sea water half a mile high was seen by the pilot of a Boeing 707 jet on 11 April, 1963, and there have been many other sightings. Conversely in May, 1965, near Key West, Florida, a fisherman named Irwin Brown and his wife were returning from a fishing trip when ahead of them they saw a "trench" in the water. The gulley was about four feet deep and 20 feet wide, running absolutely straight across the boat's path, as if it had been created in some strange way by a gigantic bulldozer.

In September, 1954, a member of the crew of the *Queen Mary* saw an area of the sea in the Triangle change colour from dark to pale green. The surface was quite calm. Suddenly a column of water up to 25 feet wide rose into the air to a height of around 50 feet. Moments later a second column appeared, about half a mile from the first. After the columns had subsided the area of sea returned to its normal dark-green colour.

The normal "logical" explanation of such dramatic activity is seismic explosions in the ocean bed, but the depth of water is such that one would expect the surface effects to cover much larger areas.

The possibility of giant sea monsters or artifacts (Unidentified Submarine Objects) wreaking havoc among ships and perhaps pulling them below the surface into the depths of the ocean has already been mentioned. Smaller vessels have certainly been sunk by whales; for example, *Essex*, a whaling ship, was sunk near the Equator in 1820 by a 90-foot sperm whale. There may well be serpents and monsters of much greater size on the ocean bed, but for such creatures surfacing would pose serious problems of decompression, assuming they have a standard physical structure, physiology and metabolism.

Perhaps the most fascinating Triangle theory is that the zone lies above the lost continent of Atlantis, described by Plato some 2,400 years ago in his *Timaeus* and *Critais* dialogues. Atlantis and other lost continents are dealt with elsewhere in this book. Plato relates how the "great and wonderful" Atlantean empire ended catastrophically: "There occurred violent earthquakes and floods, and in a single day and night of rain . . . the island of Atlantis disappeared and was sunk beneath the sea."

While Atlantis has generally been regarded as legend or myth, recent exploration of and research into the underwater infrastructure of the Bermuda Triangle sea-bed have produced remarkable finds, particularly off the coasts of Bimini and Andros. There, in 1968, first sighted from the air and then

verified by divers, were discovered submerged ruins indicative
of roads, walls and buildings and even a temple. The "rising"
of Atlantis was, strangely enough, predicted by the clairvoyant
Edgar Cayce in 1940 – twenty-eight years before the actual
event.

So far as the Triangle is concerned, with its weird paranormal forces, the significance of Atlantis lies not so much in its
culture and history, but in its technology. Was it a highly advanced civilization in scientific terms? Captain John Alexander, of Scofield Barracks, Honolulu, a well-known lecturer on
pre-cataclysmic civilizations, is on record as saying, "I will go
along with Edgar Cayce and some of the clairvoyants who say
that the second civilization (of Atlantis) was the one that really
reached an advanced state of technology. They certainly had
the capability of heavier-than-air flight, subterranean areas
with self-contained atmospheric conditions and an energy
source far beyond that which we have attained.

"I think our civilization has overlooked some tremendous
source of energy that is basically very simple. A lot of people
tend to agree with this, and they say that the second sinking of
Atlantis was due to runaway energy and a terrific implosion.
Edgar Cayce said the final sinking took place about 10,000
years ago. Dates are extremely hard to get psychically, but that
is what I received, too – about 10,000 to 12,000 years ago."

A noted archaeologist in Miami, Florida, Dr J. Manson
Valentine – very much involved with underwater exploration
and research – confirmed that Edgar Cayce had predicted that
the remains of Atlantis would begin to rise from the sea near
Bimini Islands in 1968 and 1969. By means of air surveys and
diving in the whole area of the Bimini chain, Dr Valentine
found on the sea-bed what he considered to be a valid indication of human habitation and a designed artifactual pattern –
rectilineal arrangements, squares, rectangles, pathways and
roadways – perfectly straight lines on the windward and leeward sides of all the keys down to Orange Key. He located the
remains of a structure identical in shape and size to the Mayan
Temple of Turtles at Uxmal in Yucatan, but considers that the
submerged temple pre-dates that of the Mayans.

When interviewed by author Brad Steiger, Valentine said:
"We have some very amazing sites that look like cities over an
extensive area of the Ocean bottom. We have subsequently
discovered a very important site east of Bimini. There is a sort

of dyke there, a great dam of 24-foot-long blocks, concentric circles, and areas where the blocks are marked.

"In addition we have many ghost patterns (below the sea-bed) all over the Great Banks – rectangular shapes and others that simply cannot be explained as natural formations. We have added to this materially in recent years so that we have discovered at least 50 sites."

When finally asked whether Atlantean technology was comparable with ours today, Dr Valentine commented: "I think it was far beyond us."

This poses the obvious question, namely, are the strange energy fields operating in the Bermuda Triangle derived from a still functioning power source in long dead (or is it?) Atlantis, or is Atlantis being used as a point of entry for extraterrestrial energy manipulation by, presumably, beings not of this world? It is, incidentally, worth noting that in ancient Chinese mythology there are four poles on the planet earth: east and west poles as well as north and south, which could account for magnetic aberrations. Also, directly opposite the Bermuda Triangle on the other side of the globe is the Japanese Devil Sea – an area of similar electromagnetic anomalies.

Finally, a spokesman for the National Environmental Satellites Service in the U.S. once said: "I guarantee it's nothing in the Bermuda Triangle any more than there's a hole in the North Pole – as some people think."

Well, the North Pole normally has cloud cover, but on 23 November, 1968, an American space satellite photographed the North Pole, and there, incredibly, is a black ice-ringed circle unshrouded by cloud which looks remarkably like a hole. And in 1929 Admiral Richard E. Byrd overflew the South Pole and radioed that, on suddenly emerging from a fog he found himself flying over a land free of ice and was able to distinguish vegetation, lakes and what seemed to be animals resembling mammoths . . . and also men in the vicinity of the animals. Although the transmission was broadcast, parts of it were cut out – by what? Electromagnetic or governmental interference?

The Earth is certainly not flat, but could it be hollow, with access vents at the poles, and possibly also the Chinese east and west poles? Certainly Adolf Hitler sent a number of expeditions to discover a possible entrance to the inner world, but without success. He told Hermann Rauschning, the Governor of Danzig, that the hollow centre of the Earth, with its own internal sun, contained a race of supermen. "The new man is living amongst us now. He is here! I will tell you a secret. I have seen the new man. He is intrepid and cruel. I was afraid of him." Well, well!

If the Earth be hollow, is it inhabited by survivors from the Atlantis holocaust? Do UFOs come from outer space or from the interior of the Earth itself? Shall we ever know?

The true solution to the mystery of the Bermuda Triangle may provide the answer to many questions which today are unanswerable.

VILE VORTICES

However one might try to explain or sweep away the strange disappearances of ships, aircraft and people that have occurred in the Bermuda Triangle, it has to be conceded that such incidents have occurred at a rate far exceeding the world average for maritime (and air) disasters. There are, however, other parts of the world on behalf of which similar claims are made.

Immediately opposite the Bermuda Triangle, on the other side of the earth, is the Devil Sea, south-east of Japan, where many boats and ships, small and large, and aircraft have disappeared without trace. It was not until 1950 that the Japanese authorities began to pay attention to the increasing number of incidents in that area. Between 1950 and 1954 nine large freighters, carrying radio and radar and fitted with good engines, vanished during perfectly calm weather conditions. An inquiry showed that one freighter did make a curtailed distress call.

The Japanese sent investigating ships to the Devil Sea, and one of these, the *Kaiyo Maru*, was sunk by the explosion of an underwater volcano. But even volcanic activity could not account for all the losses of ships, and certainly not aeroplanes. Consequently the Japanese Government declared the Devil Sea to be a danger zone. Oddly enough, both the Bermuda Triangle and the Devil Sea are positioned to the south-east of the nearest land mass, though whether that is significant is open to question.

The issue is confused by conflicting statements from Japan. When questions were asked by American writers and resear-chers, the replies were ambivalent. The U.S. Embassy in Tokyo stated on 31 October, 1973: "We have not heard of the Devil Sea. The Japanese Government Maritime Safety Agency informed us they have no knowledge of such a place and that no danger zone appears on their chart of Iwojima and Marcus Island."

A note from Mr Shigeru Kimura, Associate Editor, Science Department, *Asahi Shimbun* (Japan's largest newspaper), dated 30 October, 1973, read: "I inform you that there is no such area called the Devil Sea near Iwojima. But in September, 1952 there was a big eruption of an undersea volcano called Myojinsho ... A research ship, *Kaiyo Maru*, was sunk by the blast of the eruption and the lives of 31 persons on board were lost ..."

However, on 18 November, 1973, Mr Kimura wrote again, adding at the foot of his note: "As for your question – is the area still considered dangerous?, we might say that ever since the declaration of Dangerous Zone was made in 1953 in our Notice to Mariners at the time, the area has remained danger-ous to date. Mariners have been strictly cautioned not to be within ten miles of the Myojinsho Reef due to possible sub-marine volcanic activity."

This inquiry was conducted by the American author and reference librarian Lawrence David Kusche (who was men-tioned in the previous chapter). Not satisfied with the con-tradictory nature of these replies from Japan, he obtained an-other Japanese newspaper which gave a factual account about the nine vessels that were lost, and an article from *Yomiuri Shimbun* dated 14 January, 1955, in which it was stated:

> "In September, 1952, an inspection boat, the *Kaiyo Maru*, dis-appeared. Since then it has been indicated that this area is danger-ous. Since no bodies of the crewmen were found and only a little debris was seen, it was assumed that these missing boats were sunk in deep water by rough seas. Because it was not the monsoon season the reasons for the missing boats are completely unknown, but there is a rumour that it may be because of some unknown power connected with the 'Atomic Age'. The loss of the *Kaiyo Maru* was completely unexpected because it was well equipped to survive any possible difficulties."

An unsigned letter in the *Mainichi Daily News* (26 December,

1973) admitted that the Devil Sea "is a pseudonym for the area about 70 miles off Japan's east coast, named by fishermen ... Also, staffers of the Guard and Rescue Department of the Maritime Safety Agency in Tokyo and Yokohama branch said they don't call the area a Devil Sea nor designate it as a 'special danger zone'. The area is not specially dangerous in comparison with the other areas. In summer it is rather safe, except for typhoons, and in winter the sea is rough . . ."

From all this inconclusive material, Lawrence Kusche decides that the Devil Sea is in no way a smaller replica of the Bermuda Triangle. The lost vessels were not large freighters with good engines and radio, but small fishing boats, and it is doubtful if they all had radios. He forms the opinion that the writers of the Japanese articles felt that wind and rough seas were to blame for the losses, and that, in any case, the Devil Sea is virtually unknown in Japan.

So far as aircraft are concerned, there are reports that planes have regularly disappeared between Guam and Japan, but no specific information has ever been published, he asserts.

The Devil Sea is not, of course, an official geographical name any more than is the Bermuda Triangle. Both are pseudonyms identifying in a colloquial sense a particular zone of interest. The lack of satisfactory information about incidents in the Devil Sea could be a result of governmental policy, especially as Japan, an island highly dependent on maritime imports of raw materials and exports of manufactured goods, could be expected to discourage stories concerning mysterious hazards in the sea (and air) approaches. The Pacific Ocean can be hazardous enough when it feels so inclined.

From the Bermuda Triangle and the Devil Sea to the Vile Vortices. This expression was first used by Ivan T. Sanderson and his Society for the Investigation of the Unexplained (SITU) in the August, 1968 issue of *Argosy*, and has been repeated in four further books or articles since then.

Accepting the Bermuda Triangle as the first vortex, and the Devil Sea as the second, because of unexplained disappearances of ships and aircraft, Sanderson and his researchers began to investigate the possibility of other vortices existing in other parts of the world's seas and oceans where the level of unexplained incidents exceeded the global statistical average. They approached the task sceptically, it is said, but nevertheless were able to locate three such zones in the northern hemisphere where disappearance rates were well above what could be attributed to normal hazards such as the weather and faulty equipment and instruments. The zones were near the Mediterranean Sea, Afghanistan, and Hawaii.

On analysis, a "breakthrough" occurred; the researchers found that all these anomalic zones were the same distance above the Equator, and were evenly distributed around the world – that is, they were 72 degrees of longitude apart. Furthermore, as the precise positions of lost ships were plotted, the zones took on an elliptical or trapezoid shape and all sloped towards the east by roughly the same angle.

So far the southern hemisphere had remained untouched. Research was concentrated below the Equator and, as might have been expected, further anomalic zones were identified – five in all. Again, they were elliptical and all tilted at the same angle towards the east, all the same distance below the Equator as the others were above, and all equally spaced apart.

A final total of ten anomalic areas emerges, including the Bermuda Triangle and the Devil Sea. Of these, eight are sea locations and the remaining two are inland (Afghanistan and Morocco, opposite the Straits of Gibraltar, both in the northern hemisphere). All are at the same latitude, north and south of the Equator, and all are equidistant at 72 degrees of longitude.

It becomes immediately obvious that they could not have been selected strictly on a basis of above-average ship disappearances, since two of them are inland. Aircraft disappearances could shift the balance, but there is no evidence that Afghanistan and Morocco contain areas where aircraft disappear without trace. It does rather look as though Ivan Sanderson and his Society for the Investigation of the Unexplained, acting certainly in enthusiastic good faith, *created* a symmetrical pattern of global anomalies rather than *discovered* one. However, SITU does add a rider that these anomalic areas "are also famous, incidentally, for other strange phenomena, most notably a high incidence of poltergeist manifestations and UFO sightings". Any connection between that observation and ship-aircraft disappearances without trace is anybody's guess, particularly in the case of the two inland zones.

There is, nevertheless, one point which could be significant. According to SITU, all of the anomalic areas are located near well-defined warm ocean currents. The result could take the form of atmospheric and water disturbances located, in general, near to densely populated areas of land. SITU claims that Lloyd's, the U.S. Navy and other maritime agencies continue to be "baffled by the losses".

And SITU adds: "Even the special geographical situations do not explain the large number of complete disappearances in the ten areas, as compared with regular founderings and ditchings."

Apparently scientists have found evidence that the two polar areas of earth can be regarded as anomalic zones. This not unreasonable assertion completes the SITU tapestry. There are now twelve anomalic zones, and if they are connected by intersecting lines, it will be seen that the spheroid surface of earth is divided into a number of equilateral triangles – in other words, earth is a power grid in which power is released, or available for release, at points of intersection.

Strangely enough, this concept corresponds with recent Australian research, with the exception that the Australian plan of a terrestrial power grid is based on the intersection of certain lines of latitude and longitude, i.e. it is a horizontal–vertical grid rather than a triangular one. Both concepts cannot be simultaneously correct.

SITU pleads: "Surely there must be some scientific explanation for nature working in such a manner." To which the reply has to be, as Dr Isaac Asimov, the well known science-fiction author, once said, that everything can be explained if sufficient information is available. Unfortunately, there are today many areas of experience which defy explanation because the necessary explanatory information has yet to be discovered or developed.

While turbulent air and water and temperature differentials in the anomalic zones might well be the reason for many disappearances and disasters (and obviously are), there are nevertheless incidents which cannot be accounted for in physical terms. Such incidents involve loss of electrical power, loss of radio and radar contact, spinning compasses, gyro malfunctions, and, in general, magnetic, electromagnetic (not the same thing) and gravitational anomalies. The evidence that these effects exist in certain locations is beyond dispute, but one can certainly argue that there is no evidence of such phenomena whatever in many of the so-called anomalic zones.

For the record, the twelve anomalic zones are: (1) the

Bermuda Triangle; (2) the Devil Sea; (3) north-west Africa (Morocco); (4) Afghanistan; (5) off the west coast of the U.S.A. beyond Hawaii; (6) near the coast of western Australia; (7) in the Pacific islands east of Australia; (8) off the west coast of South America, almost mid-Pacific; (9) near the east coast of South America, in line with other southern hemisphere zones; (10) near the east coast at the foot of Africa; (11) the North Pole; (12) the South Pole.

A final note from SITU adds: "Until it can be explained where all those lost airplanes, ships, submarines and people have gone, such theories as UFO kidnappings, reverse gravitational fields and time warps must be considered as possible explanations."

Anyone with an analytical turn of mind must necessarily take everything into consideration, but there seems good reason to believe that a number of the listed "vile vortices" are suspect, to say the least. Two are based on the loss (without trace) of some military aircraft and submarines during the Second World War. A vile vortex may well have been responsible, but without substantiation it would seem more reasonable to suppose that the cause was enemy action.

The Devil Sea is certainly a starter, if only because of the complex fabric of denials and admissions which blanket it. In the end, when it comes to undeniable case histories and fact, one is left with the Bermuda Triangle (and its possible connection with sunken Atlantis and, above sea-level, UFOs).

THE TORPEDO CLOUD

It was the only cloud in the sky, that beautiful spring Sunday afternoon, in 1878. In almost every part of south-west England, people turned out for post-prandial walks, feeling their spirits rise as they sniffed the light airs, and thought of the summer to come.

"What a perfect day!" remarked a lady to her husband, as their carriage took them across Brunel's Clifton suspension bridge on their afternoon drive out from Bristol.

"Such air!" exclaimed another, stepping out on to the terrace of her Malvern home.

"Not a cloud in the sky," declared a third, Worcester-way. "Heavenly!"

But there was a cloud; that one cloud.

"What a curious shape. Like a cigar."

" And moving so quickly!"

"Must be miles long," remarked the husband on the suspension bridge "Twenty . . . thirty . . ."

"Brrr!" cried his wife, who had stepped down from their halted carriage, like many others just then passing that way. "It's gone so cold. Do let's go back."

Her wish was shared by all the others. There was no turning on the bridge, so they had to drive across it, turn, and head back towards town. So many were doing it that there developed a minor traffic jam, from which female cries of alarm arose as the sudden chill was followed by a blinding, wind-

whipped deluge of snow and the boom of thunder. The motion
of the bridge was enough to induce a sort of seasickness. People
on foot in those parts flung up collars, clutched at hats, ran for
the cover of trees, cried out with alarm at having been so taken
by surprise; and with wonderment at the spectacle of the cloud,
so oddly shaped, so fast moving, so darkly menacing compared
with the bright sky still prevailing to each side of it – and so
solitary in all that clear heaven.

Wherever the cloud passed there came the same experience:
tearing wind, enough to make people clutch at the nearest support or be bowled over; the overhead sky blackened out and
cascading snow which stung like hail; and that thunderous
roar which seemed to continue without pausing throughout the
half an hour or so it took the torpedo-like cloud to pass.

Then, just as suddenly, everything was bright again, with
the colours of rainbows and jewels, as the sun shone through
the moisture in the air and on the ground. Everything was
heady-freshness once more. People who had been cowering
fearfully minutes earlier were stepping forth cheerfully re-
assured, to tell one another what magic nature could perform.

Some, though, were sharing a different, more awed wonderment. These were families who had been strolling on the cliffs
and shore of the Isle of Wight before having to take shelter.
Before they had had to run for it they had been admiring the
noble sight of a Royal Naval frigate, homeward bound for
Portsmouth from the Caribbean, on a flat-calm sea and in the
most welcoming weather conditions which any travellers returning to green England could have imagined. She was under
plain sail in the light westerly breeze: top-gallants and royals,
lower and topmast studding-sails on the foremast and topmast,
studding-sail on the main; the epitome of the most beautiful
mechanical creation of man.

In stolid contrast with her had been a heavily-laden schooner, wallowing in her wake. Only, now that the watchers on
shore came out to look, and blink, and look again, there remained only one vessel where there had been two. The schooner was still there, plodding phlegmatically on her errand,
carrying coal from Swansea to Poole, in Dorset. Of that proud
frigate, though, there was no longer a sign.

Captain Langworthy Jenkin, the collier's skipper, knew
what had happened. Peering through the dying squall he had
seen what looked like wreckage ahead. He fancied he heard a

man cry out. He immediately ordered one of his hands up into the rigging as lookout. The shout came quickly down that there was a sail flapping in the sea's surface, and a man floating in a cork lifejacket. The skipper ran up the sails he had had to take in so hastily when the storm broke. Then he tacked and lowered boats. Five men in all were got aboard the schooner *Emma*. One of them was dead and two more far gone.

While his crew struggled to restore the half-drowned survivors' breathing, Captain Jenkin circled his vessel slowly, hoping to spot others. All that was seen, however, was the eerie sight of three mast-tops slanting slowly up from the depths. The frigate must have gone down by one side, then slowly righted herself underwater as the pressure of the storm receded. Apart from this sight, and a line of debris streaming away on the offshore surge, there was no movement.

Captain Jenkin stood *Emma* for Ventnor, her colours at half-mast. Two of the survivors died on the way. The remaining two were taken off the *Emma* by the Ventnor coastguard boat, which had come hurrying out to meet the schooner. With her had come a naval officer, who at once recognized one of the dead men as an officer of the Royal Engineers, and the other, personally known to him, a Lieutenant Tabor, R.N., first lieutenant of the training frigate H.M.S. *Eurydice*.

Eurydice, 921 tons, 26 guns, was one of the Navy's best-found, liveliest vessels of her class. In the year before the disaster she had been refitted in John White's Cowes shipyard as one of several training ships able to accommodate well over three hundred officers, sailors and boys. With an efficient crew she had sailed from Portsmouth on 13 November – the sailor's unlucky 13th – for a four-month cruise to the Bermudas. Now she had been almost home again, carrying the best part of four hundred people: time-served civilians and soldiers from the Indies, as well as her own complement of men and boys. Of all that number, only two remained to be carried ashore alive. They were Sydney Fletcher, an ordinary hand aged nineteen, and an able seaman named Cuddiford.

It was plain that Cuddiford, too, would die. Sympathy for his state had to come second to the need to know the circumstances of this appalling tragedy. The two were taken before the Commander-in-Chief, Portsmouth, Admiral Fanshawe, who elicited from them an account of sudden and complete disaster.

On that calm, fresh afternoon, *Eurydice* had been passing quietly past Dunnose Head, Isle of Wight, with scuppers open to air ship. The crew and boys were engaged in the usual Sunday afternoon make-and-mend activities; homesick passengers leaned on the rails, watching the longed-for land. Then that single cloud was noticed.

It was racing out of the north-west, far quicker than the light breeze seemed to be propelling it. The sky on either side of it almost glowed, in contrast to its blackness. At about twenty minutes after seven bells, with the afternoon watch looking forward to their four o'clock relief, the sea changed in an instant from flat calm to ragged torrent. Captain Hare reacted immediately. He ordered the watch up into the shrouds to fetch in the royals – the topmost sails – and the stun'sails below. The bosun called all hands to help them, but there was no time. The stun'sails had been dealt with, but Captain Hare was already bellowing to the men to get down and save themselves. No furling of sails was going to help a ship which was being literally lifted out of the sea, flung down pointing in an entirely different direction, at the same time being swamped with hundreds of tons of foaming water over her decks and through the scuppers, which there had not even been time to order to be closed.

Everyone below decks was battered to death or drowned by the inrush. Those above were either broken against iron or wood, or tossed into the lower rigging to strangle, or flung into the sea. These latter might have been the lucky ones, but for the icy coldness of the water and that sudden squall of blinding snow which the cloud brought. The few who could swim well could not survive these. One by one, the bobbing heads vanished under the waves.

Admiral Fanshawe wanted Cuddiford's explanation of his survival. Speaking weakly, and with difficulty, he stated:

> "I caught hold of the main truss, fell, and caught hold of the weather netting and got on the ship's side. She righted a little before going down, bringing the mizen tops'l out of the water. She then went gradually over from for'rd, the greater part of the hands being at the fore part of the ship outside. I saw the captain standing on the vessel's side near the quarter boat and the two doctors struggling in the water. I swam some distance, keeping over my head a lifebuoy which I had found, and then picked up some piece of wreck, which I gave to some of the men in the water.

"I then came across the copper punt full of water. Five men were in it. The sea capsized the punt, and they all got onto the bottom. They asked me if there were any signs of help. I told them the best thing they could do was to keep their spirits up. I next saw Mr Brewer, the bosun, with a cork lifebelt on. I then saw Fletcher in the water with a cork belt and breaker. I lost sight of him during the snow. About five minutes afterwards the weather cleared up. I saw Fletcher again, and we kept together. Then we saw land, but finding it too rough we turned our back to the land, and saw a schooner. The schooner bore down on us and sent a boat. A rope's end was thrown to me, and I was then picked up. I judged that I was in the water an hour and twenty minutes."

Throughout the day following the disaster Admiral Fanshawe was in constant touch with the Admiralty, in London. Crowds, anxious for details, massed before Portsmouth dockyard gates. An official came out and pinned up a piece of paper for them to surge forward to read. It was addressed to the First Lord of the Admiralty, W. H. Smith, of newsagency and bookshop fame:

"The Queen would ask Mr Smith to make known her grief at the terrible calamity to the *Eurydice* and her heartfelt sympathy with the afflicted friends and relatives."

It was one of hundreds of telegrams from all parts of Britain. Many were also expressions of sympathy and shock; but they were outnumbered tragically by those begging for news of individuals known or believed to have been aboard the stricken ship. There was little news to give. Only five bodies were washed on to the Isle of Wight. A few more drifted as far as France. The rest lay deep in the English Channel, many still inside the wreck.

During following weeks divers and riggers worked to dismantle the spars, sails and rigging from the three masts, whose tops remained visible above the sea's surface. Then attempts were begun to lift *Eurydice* bodily. They failed; she lay in nearly ten fathoms, her keel firmly held by thick mud. The Admiralty ordered that she be stripped of any useful materials where she lay, and her carcass left to rot. But Rear-Admiral Foley, in command of the dockyard, was determined to get her up. He had strong wire ropes made fast to her and to four floating hulls above her. As the tide rose, lifting the hulls, the wires tautened, lifting the wreck clear. Steam tugs towed the whole assemblage to beneath Culver Cliff, on the Isle of Wight, where what was left of *Eurydice* was left to lie on one side, partly visible at low tide.

It took months of work by divers, hampered by bad weather and fierce undercurrents, to get her into a state to be towed into Portsmouth. It was an exercise with little point, except perhaps to give an excuse for a display of public grief. Weeping, bareheaded crowds watched the half-dismantled hulk being brought in, to the mournful accompaniment of ships' whistles, hooters and foghorns. A vast swathe of black crepe had been placed at her bow.

Perhaps it had been useful practice in wreck-raising. To some onlookers, it must have seemed more like a manifestation of man's determination to wreak his futile vengeance upon the vessel which had so inexplicably capitulated to the elements and carried so many innocent youths to their death. Almost as soon as she had reached port she was invaded by an army of workmen who proceeded to tear her to pieces. Within a few days there was nothing more to show of her than piles of battered copper and fouled timber.

With grisly formality, the dying Cuddiford and his sole fellow survivor, Fletcher, had been arrested and put on trial, as the only remaining representatives of a ship's company who might be found to have been responsible for the loss by neglect of their duty. After several days of this fresh ordeal they were both discharged absolutely. The verdict read: "Her Majesty's ship *Eurydice* foundered on the afternoon of Sunday, 24 March, 1878, by pressure of wind upon her sail during a sudden and exceptionally dense snow storm which overtook her when its approach was partially hidden by the proximity of the ship to high land."

Of the cigar-shaped cloud, which had "torpedoed" her to instant doom on a balmy spring day, there was no precise explanation.

Eurydice's figurehead and certain other relics are in the Victory Museum in Portsmouth dockyard. Scattered about the world are grim curios, manufactured from her remains at the time by men who saw a chance to cash in on grief and tragedy. And there must still exist some of those thousand letters which had been accumulating at Portsmouth, awaiting the homecoming ship's arrival, and which were returned to their senders simply marked: SHIP FOUNDERED.

Miscellany

THE GREAT BOMBAY EXPLOSION

Once the ship reached Alexandria heading for the Suez Canal the entire crew from the captain to the youngest seaman breathed a hearty sigh of relief.

The ship was only two years old, built in Canada from Lease–Lend funds made available by the United States, one of twenty-six identical cargo boats all called Fort something, in this case *Fort Stikine*, from a river in British Columbia. But this was wartime and though staunch in every respect the ship was no more than a floating volcano, for she was carrying 1,395 tons of explosives, a cargo which a torpedo, even one bomb from an aircraft could send sky-high, probably with catastrophic effects on other ships sailing with her. So when she left Birkenhead in February, 1944, the *Fort Stikine* was put in the outside lane of a heavily protected convoy, which made her more vulnerable to U-boat attack but less lethal to other ships if, to put it bluntly, she blew up.

If those ships had passed anywhere near the Bay of Biscay in earlier war years they would probably have been decimated. But by this time, with greatly improved radar, depth-charging devices and the so-called Merchant Aircraft Carriers which could fly off scouting planes the U-boats were no longer the hunters but the hunted and this particular convoy reached Gibraltar without a scratch.

Then a grievous ordeal began. At Gibraltar the convoy split up, some ships continuing southwards down the coast of Africa and others, including the *Fort Stikine*, sailing east through the Mediterranean. One evening when they were off Algiers they were attacked by twenty German Focke-Wulf aircraft which dropped bombs haphazardly and sprayed the decks with machine-gun fire. The convoy threw up a terrific barrage and red-hot shell splinters began to shower down on the *Stikine*'s deck plating less than half an inch thick. If just one of those splinters had got into the cargo ... Then the ship's oerlikon guns opened up and the vibration sent a rack containing live shells crashing on to the deck. Near nightfall, with the German planes still hovering around, the convoy commodore ordered the ships to make smoke, whereupon when seamen aboard the *Stikine* tried to light a smoke cannister it burst into flames.

The convoy suffered no serious damage and the *Stikine* survived unscathed. By the time she reached Alexandria the crew thought their troubles were over. But that first brush with disaster was a mere foretaste of things to come.

Meanwhile, as throughout the voyage so far, the subject of the dangerous cargo was banned among the crew. To speak, let alone joke about it was felt to be tempting providence. But from now on the journey was uneventful and on 30 March the *Stikine* docked at Karachi after crossing the Arabian Sea. There some crated gliders and Spitfires were unloaded and the spaces filled with fresh cargo destined together with the explosives for Bombay. And what a cargo! Scrap iron, stinking fish manure and rice were the sort of stuff a ship might have to accept. But the rest was highly inflammable: hundreds of drums of lubricating oil, 8,700 bales of raw cotton, sulphur and resin. Except in wartime a captain would have been within his rights to refuse such a mixture. All he could do now was bow to the inevitable and get one of his officers to search the reference books for details of raw cotton, how to stow it and the dangers to be avoided. Such a cargo was seldom if ever exported from Britain and all he knew was that cotton was tricky, but just why he could not remember.

The officer came up with a note about damp cotton giving off hydrogen. That was bad enough. But if he or the captain had possessed two standard works published in the U.S. they would have found something else. After listing the fire precautions to be taken when loading or unloading raw cotton one of them stated: "Cotton bales which are or have been in contact with oil or grease are very liable to spontaneous combustion."

And the other, under the heading of explosives: "These commodities should never be stowed in the same hatch with cotton but in a properly constructed magazine in the opposite end of the ship from that in which cotton is stowed." In No. 2 hold of the *Fort Stikine* 769 tons of raw cotton were stowed in the bottom with timber and scrap iron above it. Then in the upper compartment drums of lubricating oil, some of which were leaking, were stacked on tarpaulins which covered most but not all of the deck between the upper and lower holds. In this upper compartment there were also 124 gold bars valued at a million pounds, sealed in a steel tank lashed to the bulkhead and consigned to a Bombay bank, and 168 tons of Category A, the most sensitive explosives. Two more of the ship's five holds were also stowed with explosives and cotton.

On 9 April, the *Fort Stikine* sailed from Karachi in convoy with tankers from the Persian Gulf down the west coast of India towards Bombay, arriving three days later in the beautiful harbour lying between the mainland on the east and, to the west, the long tongue of Bombay Island with its docks, warehouses, railway terminus and street upon street of poor wooden houses. The ship tied up in Victoria Dock, flanked by Prince's Dock to the north and Alexandra Dock to the south, all three of them on the east side of the island. Normally, port regulations required that ships carrying explosives should fly a red flag and unload into lighters in the harbour. But in wartime the first requirement would have been an advertisement to enemy agents and the second had to be waived for the sake of rapid turnround. So it was that on that day the *Fort Stikine* found herself at the nerve centre of western India while only a handful of people knew just what she was carrying.

On the 12th, the same day that she docked, unloading began by Indian stevedores – first the fish manure because the stench had plagued the crew ever since Karachi, then sundries such as dynamos and wireless sets, some of the timber and scrap iron. It was not until the following morning that the foreman of stevedores was told about the explosives. The less sensitive categories, B and C, could be unloaded straight on to the dock. Category A would go into lighters. But the lighters did not come alongside until midday just before the lunch break and in the afternoon only half the stevedores worked on the explosives. The result was that by Friday the 14th most of Category A was still in the hold.

Meanwhile, the chief engineer was dismantling part of the engines to replace a faulty slide valve, which meant that in a sudden emergency the ship could not move under her own steam.

During the midday break some stevedores went ashore, others stayed on deck to eat and rest. There was, of course, a strict no smoking rule and this was partly enforced by eight watchmen, two seamen and six civilians divided into two parties, their primary duty being to guard against sabotage. But at this time there was confusion as to which party was supposed to be on duty and so, unbeknown to anyone, no watch was being kept.

Eventually perhaps a stevedore noticed this and slipped down into No. 2 hold for an illicit cigarette, leaving behind a burning stub. More likely, oil was leaking on to raw cotton. At any rate, around 12.30 p.m. smoke was seen drifting lazily from the hold – but not yet by anyone aboard the *Stikine*. The chief officer of another ship in the Victoria Dock saw it spiralling from a ventilator. Someone else on a third ship noticed the same thing. Ashore, an inspector of police watched it curling from a hatchway – but smoke so thin and slight that none of these men thought of raising the alarm.

Fifteen minutes passed before the foreman of stevedores saw and smelt the smoke, but when fire hoses were brought up they proved too short to reach every corner of the hold. Even so, a massive weight of water applied immediately might have quenched the fire. But here came another snag. There was a routine instruction in the docks that if a ship carrying explosives caught fire a special message had to be passed direct to the Bombay Fire Brigade. The man detailed to do this failed to get through, so he sounded off an ordinary street fire alarm – which brought only two fire engines to the scene.

From now on, shortcomings, confusions and failures piled up. Despite sixteen pumps that were eventually pouring water into the hold the smoke and heat kept on increasing. Certain that the ship would blow up, the officer in charge of ordnance at the docks wanted her scuttled. But this could not be done because the sea cocks in the *Fort Stikine* and others of her class were designed to let water out, not in. Someone else wanted her towed out into the harbour and sunk. But as Mr Coombs the fire chief explained, that would involve taking her off shore-based hoses, so letting the fire rage almost unchecked. As for the captain, he believed his ship could still be saved. In the result, she stayed where she was, in the very heart of Bombay's docks, surrounded by 60,000 tons of shipping.

Meanwhile, no general alarm had been given and the busy life of the huge port with its hundreds of warehouses continued. Indeed, no system existed for giving such an alarm. In the previous year, when the Japanese threat had diminished, Bombay had been declared a "white area" for the purposes of air-raid precautions and an organization which might have been used for such a purpose had been largely disbanded, including its ambulance, rescue and auxiliary fire services. Other facilities existed, of course, for work such as this, some of them voluntary, but in a situation of looming disaster and in the absence of the A.R.P. set-up no one was empowered to give overall direction. The naval officer in charge, Bombay, migh have done so, but strictly speaking that was only his job in the event of enemy sea-borne attack.

So the danger grew with no general precautions taken. Just before 3 p.m. the driver of a trailer pump standing on the dock below the port side of the *Fort Stikine* felt heat on his face and, looking up, saw a patch of paint on the plates beginning to bubble, then moments later fly off in hardened flakes. Immediately news was passed to Mr Coombs that the seat of the fire had been located and he ordered up a gas cutter to make a hole in the ship's side so that hoses could be passed through. But when the gas cutter arrived and a match was applied to the jet only black smoke emerged and no one could rectify the fault. Still, another cutter was on its way or should have been but for another twist of fate. Minutes previously, before it was realized that the Fire Chief had one at hand, someone had put through a call to the works department at the docks asking urgently for a cutter, then, when the first cutter was brought up but before it proved faulty, the request was cancelled.

By now thirty-two hoses had poured 900 tons of water into No. 2 hold, but still the smoke was increasing and the deck itself was so hot that planks of wood had to be laid down, then soaked with water for the heroic Indian fire fighters to stand on. But many people were wondering why with that weight of water in the hold the fire was not extinguished. The only possible explanation was – not realized till later – that the water had hardly touched the fire and had actually helped to bring about the final cataclysm. As the water level rose burning cotton bales must have floated up with it, nearer every minute to the Category A explosives in the upper hold until at a certain moment the fires reached the strips of wood used as packing around boxes of ammunition.

That moment arrived around 3.40 p.m. and within minutes some of the ammunition exploded. There was a sudden belch of yellowish black smoke and flames started to lick round the hatch coaming. The fire fighters fell back, then with great courage surged forward, grabbed their hoses again and played the jets towards the ammunition boxes. But it was too late.

The flames rose and fell for a while longer then suddenly without warning roared up mast-high, carrying with them wisps and streamers of burning cotton that floated down and started fires on surrounding ships. Coombs yelled to his men to get clear and they made a rush for the gangplank. The captain ordered "Abandon Ship". Meanwhile, crowds of sightseers were gathering at the dockside in blissful ignorance that at any moment the ship might blow up. There was still no red flag at the mast that might have warned them.

Having checked that everyone on board had left, the captain went ashore – and was still there, helplessly watching his stricken ship, when at 4.06 p.m. No. 2 hold exploded.

In that split second the Bombay docks up to a mile away and almost everything in them were devastated. Flaming oil drums and blazing cotton bales shot up as though fired from guns, then fell on ships, sheds and houses to start yet more fires. Of twenty-four ships in or near the Victoria Dock eleven were set on fire and four sunk or badly damaged, while the 3,935-ton, 400-foot British-owned steamer *Jalapadma*, lying behind the *Fort Stikine*, was wrenched through a right-angle and ended up with her back broken, her bow in the water and the stern perched 60 feet high on top of a dockside shed. People were seized by the shock wave and flung high in the air, to land in some cases hundreds of yards away, dead or still breathing. White-hot metal splinters came humming down, tearing off arms and legs, inflicting terrible injuries. As for the *Fort Stikine*, the bow section sheered off and sank immediately, leaving the stern with forward bulkheads intact still afloat. Her captain was never seen again.

The explosion produced many freak effects. Fire Chief Coombs was standing on cotton bales piled on the quay when it came. When he looked down he found he had lost his trousers, all but the waistband and the two side pockets. A captain of ordnance was flung from his motor-cycle on to a heap of rubbish. Staggering to his feet he made for an abandoned car, to find the ignition key still in place but the engine blown clean away. Mr Motiwala, a Parsee civil engineer who lived in a flat some way behind the docks, heard something smash through the corrugated iron roof, bounce through his living-room and end up with a clang against the balcony. When he picked it up he found it was a gold bar.

But mostly the aftermath was a grim struggle to save ships, warehouses, goods, homes and human lives, a struggle impeded by lack of organization. The consequences in a disaster of that magnitude were serious. Immediate action was necessary to stop fires reaching residential areas, shift dangerous explosives piled high in warehouses along the quays and salvage goods worth millions of pounds. But no strict priorities were observed because no one was in charge. Instead, thousands of volunteers, service and civilian, helped as best they could with whatever lay to hand amid a confusion that grew worse as the day wore on. Stevedores were sent home while 40,000 boxes of ammunition still lay in sheds, waiting to be moved. Then soldiers came to do the job – and were stopped by harbour police who demanded to see their passes. Initially the volunteers were also prevented from entering Prince's and Victoria docks. When the soldiers were at last let through some brought with them pumps requisitioned from fire stations which in their ignorance they thought were faulty because, after pumping for a few minutes, the water pressure fell off. But this was simply due to the filters becoming clogged with cotton floating in the docks. No one thought of that. The consequence was that sixty-five experienced firemen were robbed of their pumps to no purpose.

But the greatest error of all was made by three people, two naval captains and a colonel, the Deputy Director of Ordnance Services. After the explosion each separately tried to assess the situations in Victoria and Prince's docks and each came to the same conclusion: that the fierce fires raging made them inpenetrable. This assessment, passed to subordinates, prevented many fire-fighters and volunteers from going in. But in fact heroic individuals had been there all the time and almost single-handed one man was in process of saving his ship, the Norwegian motor vessel *Belray* in Prince's dock.

Twenty-year-old Able Seaman Roy Hayward, R. N., had been drafted as gunlayer to the armed cargo ship which was lying three hundred yards from the *Fort Stikine* with a broad quay between them. When the explosion came several Indian workers on board the *Belray* were gruesomely injured and Hayward spent some time carrying them one by one to the quay from where transport took them to hospital. Then he helped to put out some fires on the boat deck, after which he noticed a big warehouse ablaze on the north side of the dock near a Burmah Shell oil storage depot. Some firemen were already working there and he joined them until, looking back, he saw the *Belray* was burning again.

By now the threat to the oil storage depot was over, so some of the men came back with him, with their pumps. First they had to hose a passage through some burning sheds that lay between them and the ship, then Hayward climbed a crane, dragging a hose pipe with him, so that he could direct it straight into a hold where timber was on fire. That done, he got down to the quay again – and saw that the stern close to the 4-inch magazine was aflame. A moment later, ninety-eight rockets stored on deck for a rocket-firing weapon exploded. Meanwhile the bow had broken loose and was out in midstream and now the stern was inaccessible so, determined to get aboard, Hayward borrowed a fire ladder and climbed up over the side, to find he was the only man on the ship. From there, as the decks were too hot to walk on, he worked his way aft step by step outside the ship's rail and was finally able to direct the quayside hoses into the magazine.

By that one man the *Belray* was saved to sail again, and many other people, British, Indian and American, from Army, Navy or Air Force as well as civilians performed staggering feats of heroism on that fateful Friday and on into the following night, without official help or organization, plunging into the inferno of the docks to rescue men calling for help from burning ships or clinging to anything that would float, up to their necks in water hot from incandescent debris, so covered with wreckage that at a casual glance it looked like a rubbish tip on dry land. And this in spite of the fact that at 4.40 p.m. the after part of the *Fort Stikine* containing 790 tons of explosives and still afloat had blown up with a shattering roar, raining down fragments as in a volcanic eruption.

Cold statistics tell of the loss and destruction: 1,376 known deaths (but many more unknown), thousands injured, 34,639 tons of shipping destroyed, 55,000 tons of grain intended for human consumption, likewise thousands of tons of other foods, ammunition, war equipment, textiles, timber and machinery. Fifty thousand people from 6,000 firms thrown out of work, 3,000 made destitute. Upwards of a million tons of rubble and debris.

When it came to restoring the shambles, organization came belatedly into its own. Acetylene torches sliced up wrecked warehouses. Bulldozers cleared rubble. Tugs trailing huge nets towed accumulated rubbish from the docks. Some ships, damaged beyond repair, were dragged out and sunk in the harbour, others were patched up till they could be properly repaired.

Next, with great ingenuity the forward end of the *Jalapadma* was sealed and made watertight, then cut free from the stern so that it too could be sunk in open water. After that, the stern was sliced up into manageable pieces and taken away. Finally, the walls of Victoria Dock were repaired, which involved draining out the water completely. Eight thousand men worked on this job, apart from thousands more in the residential and industrial areas, and within seven months the docks were in operation again.

A marvellous recovery. But when we think back to the events of that terrible day the whole disaster and the scope of the aftermath seem to have depended on factors apparently disconnected but brought rather than coming together to produce a fatal result. The captain of the *Fort Stikine* who did not know what happens when oil meets cotton – the wartime abandonment of safety precautions for ships carrying explosives – the delay in discharging Category A – the ship unable to move under her own steam – confusion over watch-keeping duties – delay in spotting smoke from the hold – fire hoses too short – fire brigade not properly informed – scuttling impossible – no general alarm – gas cutter not working – substitute cancelled – fire hoses float burning cotton towards explosives – sightseers not warned of danger – stevedores sent home – soldiers stopped by harbour police – "faulty" pumps – false appreciation by senior officers – no plan for such a disaster – no overall authority.

Nor were these the only factors. A principal water main in the residential area was cut through by a piece of jagged steel. Over 200 fire pumps owned by private firms were never used because no one asked for them – and at an early stage the general manager of the docks and two of his deputies, experienced men badly needed to give orders, were killed.

Might it not be, as some intelligent people believe, that in a mysterious way life can produce clustering effects, whether for good or ill, independently of human volition or any ascertainable cause, and that what we call "coincidence" is sometimes not due to chance at all?

THE STATUES OF
EASTER ISLAND

Many centuries ago there were people living on a small island
whose existence was dogged by fear. The island was inhospitable, formed of grey-black solidified lava from a dozen extinct
volcanoes which in pre-history had exploded upwards from the
sea-bed. The vegetation was sparse offering no protection from
the wind, in some places sheer thousand-foot cliffs ringed the
circumference and there were no safe anchorages. Worse still
from the islanders' point of view, they were utterly alone. On
all sides, right up to the horizon, stretched nothing but bare
blue sea, a vast expanse where no ships sailed, which no mariner crossed to bring news of the outside world.

As the years passed with only that blank unchanging vista
the inhabitants began to wonder whether that world existed at
all, or whether they were the only creatures apart from birds
and fish in the entire material universe, fighting to survive in
the face of treacherous nature, accident, illness, disease.

To win that fight they felt they had to cultivate a sense of
continuity with something more enduring than themselves.
They needed a myth, a story, and they had one, or rather they
built up a series of stories, strange, fascinating and some – as
has only recently been discovered – almost certainly true. They
believed they were descended from a great king named Hoto
Matua who long ago had crossed the ocean with many companions in boats made of reeds tied together in bundles. The
boats were very large and shaped like the crescent moon with

three masts from which hung square sails also made of reeds, strung together horizontally one above the other. Hoto Matua, his men and women, settled in an area on the north side of the triangular island and they, according to legend, were the first discoverers of that tiny blob in the ocean.

So was forged the first link in a chain connecting the lonely inhabitants to mankind and the gods, for Hoto Matua was deified and through him his progeny. But though legend uplifted, physical isolation still oppressed and to get round this the islanders performed an extraordinary mental switch. Far from being isolated and cut off, they convinced themselves that their little home was the centre of everything that existed and they call it *Te Pito o te Henua*, "The Navel of the World". That, to the present-day inhabitants, is still its name though long ago in 1722, when the Dutch Admiral Roggeveen rediscovered it on the most sacred day in the Christian calendar, it was re-named Easter Island.

But if Roggeveen hoped that the people would thereby become christianized he was mistaken. The tiny island with its forty-five square miles still remained cut off from the cultures of its nearest neighbours, from Chile 2,300 miles to the east and Pitcairn Island 1,200 miles westward, a navel without a body, a test-tube in which for over a thousand years human chemistry worked unaffected by civilization.

The results were astonishing and presented many mysteries which have only been solved in recent times in relation to the origins of those first inhabitants. For many years it was thought that they came from Polynesia or even further westward, but thanks largely to Thor Heyerdahl who proved by his Kon-Tiki expedition that a primitive raft could sail west across the Pacific and later spent a year on Easter Island researching into its customs and history, it now seems certain that the first people reached the island from Peru around the year A.D. 400. In other words, they came from the east, not the west.

A number of facts support this theory, and the theory also explains the facts. The insistence of legend, for example, that Hoto Matua and his followers were bearded white men with red hair: these people, of unknown racial origin, were already present in Peru at the time of the Incas and in the Easter Island story they became the "long-ears" because of their custom of attaching weights to the lobes. They it was who must have built the walls and platforms on the island, consisting of

massive blocks cunningly fitted together without mortar, after
the exact pattern of Peruvian remains. And there are other
connections: the sweet potato, found in Peru, cultivated on
Easter Island, but not indigenous in Polynesia; the *totora* fresh-
water reed from which boats were made, growing to this day
on the shores of Bolivian Lake Titicaca and in the island's
volcano craters; finally, the most famous product of Easter
Island, familiar on the eastern shores of the Pacific from
Mexico down through Colombia, Ecuador and Peru, and also
found on four islands in Eastern Polynesia but nowhere else —
the statues.

Popular imagination about Easter Island begins and usually
ends with those massive, legless, greyish-yellow monoliths,
weighing anything between fifteen and eighty tons, that brood
inscrutably, like petrified visitors from another planet, above
the grassy, rock-strewn landscape. Some, as though in process
of rising from an underground cavern, show only the head and
neck, others lean back as if in sleep, others are tipped forward,
their faces hidden in the dust. All have been carefully carved
from a single prototype, with sharp, up-tilted noses, long pen-
dulous ears, short pointed beards, tightly compressed lips,
heavy protruding foreheads below which the eyes, if marked in
at all, are lost in shadow.

These enormous busts seem to portray Man rather than a
man, and Man at rest, with arms hanging loose and face relaxed, as though in contemplation. Even today, to people of a
totally different culture, they are awe-inspiring, and not only
because of their size. But what did they mean to the people
who made them? The answer to this should tell us why they
were made and why, as we shall see, such colossal effort was
spent on carving, transporting and setting them up on sites
around the island.

Here an extraordinary story unfolds. There are no less than
six hundred statues on Easter Island totalling tens of thousands
of tons of carved stone, and this in an area one-third the size of
the Isle of Wight. Why so many? It is thought they were
connected with the cult of sun-worship, but their chief virtue
was surely to possess protective power, over the temple sites
round which they were clustered and over the population as a
whole, even over the island itself, scoured and fretted by the
remorseless sea. So there could not be too many of them. One
statue was good, ten statues were better, a hundred better still.

But the signs are that in their fear and loneliness the people never felt they had enough, and thus for centuries they chipped and toiled and strained to build themselves an ever stronger ring of security, not against earthly enemies, for they saw none, but against evil spirits which they sensed but could not identify and the malevolence of fate.

Fear, in short, seems to have been the whip that drove the people on and its power to galvanize energies is everywhere apparent on the island. Towards the eastern end there is an extinct volcano called Rano Raraku which the stone-carvers used as their workshop. Inside the crater and around its steep inner walls they hacked out and shaped the statues with primitive stone cutters, then hauled them up the slope, lowered them down the outside and set them upright in deep holes for the final task of scrubbing and polishing. When that was finished they still had to be transported to their sites around the island, sometimes as much as eight miles away, and here is indeed a baffling mystery. How was it done by people to whom the wheel was unknown?

In some cases a single statue weighed as much as two railway trucks, twelve horses and five elephants put together. The workmen might have shaped wooden levers and even sledges, though the island was practically treeless, and they had manpower, perhaps thousands of men to help them, but that was all. Yet, as Heyerdahl discovered, after their journey over rough, stony ground the statues arrived at their destination without a scratch or a scar. When he asked the natives how this could be, they replied patiently, as though to a simple child, that of course the statues had walked there.

By that time Heyerdahl was almost ready to believe anything, for he had visited Rano Raraku. All around lay thousands of the cutters that had been used to carve the images and these were everywhere. In his own words:

> The whole mountain massif has been reshaped, the volcano has been greedily cut up as if it were pastry . . . And in the midst of the mountain's gaping wound lie more than a hundred and fifty gigantic stone men, in all stages from the just begun to the just completed . . . We had them above us, beneath us and on both sides. We clambered over noses and chins and trod on mouths and gigantic fists, while huge bodies lay leaning over us on the ledges higher up. As our eyes gradually became trained to distinguish art from nature, we perceived that the whole mountain was one single

swarm of bodies and heads ... The cavalcade of stiff hard-bitten stone men, standing and lying, finished and unfinished, went right down to the lush green reed-bed on the margin of the crater lake, like a people of robots petrified by thirst in a blind search for the water of life.*

All this was strange enough, but there was a mystery within a mystery. The scattered tools, the unfinished statues, some complete except for a ridge down the back which still held them to the rock, some standing below the outer slope for the final polishing, showed that the work had been abandoned suddenly, from one day to the next. Had the people tired of their obsession and turned to new gods? Had a tidal wave from some remote volcanic eruption shown that the statues were after all powerless to protect? The islanders told Heyerdahl this was not so: there had been a battle.

In distant times, they said, brown-skinned men had come from islands in the west, people they called the "short-ears". The long-ears had put them to work moving statues and clearing the ground of rubble so that it could be cultivated. But the short-ears were indolent and there soon came rumblings of revolt.

On the eastern tip of the island the long-ears then barricaded themselves behind a man-made ditch over two miles long and filled it with brushwood so that, if the short-ears attacked, they could set light to it and protect themselves behind a wall of flame. But one defender's wife, who was a short-ear, betrayed the secret of how to get round the ditch and one night the attackers rushed through, outflanked the long-ears and drove them into the flames so that they all perished except for a few women and one man.

That man's descendents, so the natives told Heyerdahl, were still living on the island and it was they, and they alone who could show him how to carve and erect a statue. So they got to work and from experiments he conducted with them it emerged that it would take 6 men a year to carve a 15-foot statue and 12 men could raise a 25-ton statue from the horizontal to the vertical in 18 days, levering it up inch by inch with poles and propping it at each stage with stones. As for transport, 180 natives were needed to drag even a small statue across the

*Aku-Aku, The Secret of Easter Island (Allen and Unwin).

bumpy island plain, chipping and scarring it on the way, so that clearly was not the method the ancients had used.

These facts highlighted the immense task the early long-ears had set themselves, but even this was not all. When they reached the temple sites they had to set up the statues on walls sometimes 12 feet above the ground, and when that was done there came a final incredible feat. On the heads of the monoliths as high as four-storey buildings they placed a top-knot to represent bunched human hair consisting of a cylinder carved out of red rock from another volcano crater in the south-west of the island. The cylinder weighed ten tons.

All this work stopped after the short-ears arrived around the middle of the seventeenth century. When they had all but annihilated the long-ears they set about destroying their temples and their statues so that today not a single one stands in its original place. Those that we see in photographs are usually the ones that stood at the foot of Rano Raraku to await the final polishing, too deeply embedded for the short-ears to overturn. Time has gradually silted them up till only the head and neck are visible.

So the cultural life of the island fell into decay. Cannibalism had arrived with the strangers and, to make matters worse, the island so peacefully named by Roggeveen was continually disturbed in the following centuries by intruders from overseas. In 1769 a French ship paid a brief visit. In the following year, fearful perhaps that the French might take over the island, the Spaniards came with two ships, two priests and a large number of soldiers. Surrounded by cheering natives they marched up to a patch of rising ground, planted three crosses there and persuaded some inhabitants to sign away their island to Spain – which they did, it was said, "with every sign of joy and happiness", making their marks on a document held out to them with pictures of birds and other strange creatures. After teaching their new subjects to chant "Ave Maria, long live King Charles III of Spain", the Spaniards trudged contentedly back to their ships and sailed away, never to return.

In 1774, Captain Cook landed briefly, found only a few hundred men in a miserable condition and wondered – an odd thought – whether the rest of the population with the women and children might not be hiding somewhere underground. If so, the Spaniards may have made the people cautious for, three years after Cook's peaceable visit when the Frenchman

La Pérouse came ashore, they seem to have plucked up courage and he was met by two thousand people with swarms of children who even showed him some narrow tunnels where they had previously been hiding.

Alas for the trustful islanders! The next visitation was anything but peaceful. In 1805 an American schooner, the *Nancy*, brought armed men ashore to capture colonists for an intended sealing station on Juan Fernandez, off the coast of Chile. After a fierce struggle twelve men and ten women were taken on board, and after three days' sailing they were allowed up on deck, whereupon they immediately jumped into the sea and started swimming back to their island home. Without paying the slightest attention to them, the captain then calmly put about and returned to make another raid.

From that time on, further visitors, French, Russian or American, were greeted with a hail of stones or sometimes amicably, depending on the islanders' whim, and unfortunately they were in their carefree mood when, in December, 1862, a flotilla of seven Peruvian ships arrived. Some of the natives swam happily out to the ships where to their pleasure they were invited to draw bird pictures on a piece of paper – thereby agreeing to work as labourers on the guano islands off Peru. When they unsuspectingly tried to swim ashore again, they were tied up and taken below. Meanwhile, on the coast, a boatload of armed men had brought brightly coloured gifts which the natives were examining when they were set upon, bound and taken off to the ships. In all, a thousand islanders were kidnapped in this way and not released until, many months later, the Bishop of Tahiti had lodged a strong protest. By that time 900 of them had died and of the hundred who were brought back all but fifteen perished *en route*. As a final calamity, these few brought smallpox with them which ravaged the island until the entire population was reduced to 111 persons.

After that, the figure began to climb again until in the 1960s it was back to one thousand. In the interval, the island had been annexed by Chile in 1888 and turned into a huge sheep farm, missionaries had arrived and the Chilean Navy had taken over the administration, backed by the once-yearly visit of a warship.

But a way of life is not changed so easily. The people had cheerfully allowed themselves to be christianized, but those massive statues still stared inscrutably over the landscape and there were mysteries which even the most zealous priest did not dare to explore. His flock was living on two levels. There was the Christian plane, typified by Sunday services which all would eagerly attend, singing hymns to Spanish words and Polynesian tunes, and there was something else which to them was *otra cosa aparte*, another thing apart. This was their underground life, metaphorically and literally, the life of their pre-Christian unconscious, centred on caves originally formed from cooling bubbles of lava which abounded in the island.

Heyerdahl encountered this and has a strange tale to tell. The natives, with whom he got on very well, kept bringing him gifts, not only wooden figures which they themselves had carved, but small stone ones, some obviously very old, representing animals, human faces, skulls, boats, reptiles, bird-men and monsters with glowering eyes and wide, fish-like mouths. There was no end to the variety of objects produced and they came, it was explained, from family caves with hidden entrances which no stranger could detect. These caves were in fact cult-centres where the carved stones were supposed to possess protective magic and the bones of ancestors were laid up, as in an open tomb. They were holy places, only to be approached after certain rituals had been carried out, otherwise bad luck, even death would ensue. To judge from the ancient carvings, they had been revered since long before the short-ears' time.

But now the taboos connected with them were loosening and the natives seemed almost glad to entrust the secret to a visitor from the Western world, not to any visitor but to the white-skinned, reddish-haired "Señor Kon-Tiki" who some insisted was a direct descendant of the long-eared race and as such possessed something supremely powerful. That was, in Polynesian, his "Aku-Aku".

Every long-ear has an Aku-Aku, a familiar spirit who advises, informs, warns, protects and sometimes, if not respectfully treated, punishes. The best families had several such spirits, some guarding the sacred cave, other accompanying individuals. The Aku-Aku was both tyrant and friend and the surest way to placate him was to let him scent the aroma of baked chicken, for he had a nose but no mouth.

The long-eared supremacy, physically abolished by the short-ears, continued on in ritual and tradition, and was supported by other cults. Periodically, right into modern times, young girls would be shut up in a cave until their skins turned white, when they would be brought out for religious festivals. This practice was matched by an all-male event when the strongest of the men would sit up for months on the highest point in the island, awaiting the arrival of the first sooty terns on a small island a thousand feet below. The first man to swim out and find a newly laid egg would have his head shaved and painted red and be then immured for a whole year in a hut at the foot of Rano Raraku as "the sacred bird-man of the year".

So the natives built a wall of protection for themselves, with the statues, the ancestor worship going back to King Hoto Matua, with the Aku-Aku, the spirit of wisdom, and the bird-man symbolizing freedom. But still, as we have seen, it was not enough. The outside world kept breaking in, sometimes with calamitous results and Easter Island, despite its isolated position, proved to be no more than an outpost of a troubled world.

Today, still under Chilean administration, the island has an airport linking South America with Australia and a tourist hotel. Guided tours will no doubt be arranged to the sacred caves, now lit with electricity. Parents will snap their children sitting on the stomachs of fallen giants and the inhabitants will be wage-earners, serving the new amenities, drinking the imported alcohol, succumbing to the visitors' diseases.

But though the island may soon be swallowed up in the world's collectivism, there will always be some people, surely, who, perched on that little dot between sea and sun, amid the vast expanses of the Pacific, will sense its mystery and feel a kinship with the statues that have watched there for centuries, silent, absorbed, and in some curious way at peace with all creation.

THE *GROSVENOR*

More than six weeks out from Ceylon and the *Grosvenor* East Indiaman had not yet rounded the Cape of Good Hope. She had been unusually late in the year leaving Madras, laden with passengers and merchandise, and thus it was not until early August, 1782 that she began to approach the coast of south-east Africa – and in those latitudes it was winter. Seaman Thomas Lewis was glad to leave the helm at the end of the second dog-watch and go below for his Saturday night grog ration, for the evening was cold and the wind freshening.

At midnight Lewis was back on deck with Habberley, Haynes and other men of his watch under the command of second mate William Shaw. The ship was running under close-reefed topsails and foresail only, and as time went on the wind increased yet further and veered to the south-west. Men went aloft to shorten sail yet further and saw lights which they presently decided must be fires on the shore, at which the second mate prudently began to bring the ship on to the other tack to avoid the land. But the captain, John Coxon, below in his cabin, noticed the change and came on deck. Brushing argument aside, he stated that land was 300 miles off and ordered Shaw to put her back once more upon her westerly course towards the African continent.

While the captain returned to his cabin Lewis gloomily watched the strengthening wind and the labouring ship, awaiting the inevitable order to climb the ratlines to the swaying yards and struggle with the recalcitrant canvas. The order came at 3.30 a.m., and Lewis had no sooner reached the yard than he saw quite distinctly a dark mass on the horizon which could be nothing but land. Hastily he regained the deck and reported to Shaw – but he was not believed; the captain had said land was 300 miles off; what Lewis had seen was a cloud-bank or some trick of light.

He was ordered aloft once more and there, as he hauled canvas in and clung to the pitching yards and lines, Lewis kept an eye on the dark smudge on the horizon; more clearly with each passing minute it resolved itself into land.

At 4.30 Lewis's job was done. The watch had changed and was now under the command of third mate Beale. (Logie, the first mate, who should have had the watch lay ill in his berth, tended by the young wife he had married in India.) But Lewis did not go below; concerned by his confident belief that land was not far off, he told his shipmates what he had seen and they also began to keep a lookout. Soon a number of them thought they too could see land, and this from the fo'c's'le. One man ran to the officer but the latter, although he had been warned by Shaw of the strange lights and told to keep a sharp lookout, refused to listen or even to cross the deck to see for himself. After some hesitation, for it was a serious matter to go over the head of the officer of the watch, the seaman ran to wake the captain who at once came on deck.

Captain Coxon took one look from the fo'c's'le and at once ordered the ship put about: but it was too late. As the *Grosvenor* came round the port bow struck with a jarring crash and the ship shuddered to a halt, her bows facing what appeared to be huge rocks. While the seamen fought to bring down the sails the passengers rushed terrified on to deck, their cries of alarm mingling with the shouted orders of the officers who themselves hardly knew what to do. Eventually some kind of calm was restored. The passengers, nine men, three women, six children aged from twenty-two months to eight years, and four native servants, were herded on to the quarter-deck out of the way while the captain took stock of the situation. The wind had shifted again, and he determined to try to refloat the ship which was lying broadside on to the shore. It was a fatal mistake for, as the *Grosvenor* turned, her stern was found to be fast on the rocks and she immediately started to make water by her bows.

Dawn was now breaking but daylight brought little comfort. The shore was so near – only some 400 yards – but the rocks were precipitous and the sea high. A boat which was lowered was immediately dashed to pieces; a raft suffered the same fate. Eventually five men, two Italians and three lascar seamen, volunteered to swim ashore with a light rope. One man drowned in the attempt, but the others reach safety and contrived to pull in a line and then a hawser attached to the rope and make it fast to the rocks. By now crowds of woolly-headed Kaffirs had gathered on the shore to watch, but not one of them made any attempt to help in any way.

During the day a number of men from the ship managed to make their way ashore by way of the hawser; others drowned in the attempt, snatched away by the waves. Yet others succeeded in swimming ashore. Those left aboard the ship, whose courage failed them, gave themselves up for lost as the ship began to break up.

It was now late afternoon. As the stern gradually disintegrated many of the people still remaining on the Indiaman huddled on to her starboard quarter where the hawser, secured to the mizzen mast, provided the last tenuous link with land. It was a lucky chance, for the great waves now began to drive this part of the ship towards the shore until finally it was deposited upon a sandy beach and the wretched survivors could climb on to dry land virtually unharmed. Others, on the fore part of the ship, were also washed ashore; some survived by clinging to pieces of wreckage. From a total complement of 138 persons only 15 were lost and none of the survivors had very serious injuries.

Once ashore the seamen hastily set about collecting up anything beached from the wreck which could be of use to them. The natives, still surly and aloof, had the same idea and started to burn spars and other wreckage in order to obtain the copper fittings. They were not interested in the bales of cotton and silk goods which were washed ashore, but they were prepared to contend with the castaways for any metal items. Thus while the seamen were not hampered in their attempts to erect tents, make fires and salvage foodstuffs in order to feed themselves, such useful items as saucepans and carpenter's tools were forcibly taken from them by the natives who had now armed themselves with assegais. Captain Coxon did all he could to keep the atmosphere peaceful. Open friction could be fatal, for the survivors had virtually no weapons with which to defend themselves. Everything they found must therefore be hidden; even so the natives became more daring, entering the makeshift tents to steal what they could.

Originally it had been decided that the survivors should remain beside the wreck until the chief mate, Mr Logie, and others who had been injured during the wreck should have recovered, but after three days captain Coxon deemed it wiser to move on. The natives were becoming more and more rapacious and daring, and provisions were short. The captain estimated it should take them about sixteen days to reach the nearest Dutch settlement.

It was agreed that they should proceed in one large party, for mutual aid and to ward off the attacks of the Africans. The survivors made what preparations they could for the journey, dividing between them the loads of useful goods. Two men were to be left behind. John Bryan was a discharged soldier who had suffered an injury to the knee during the wreck and who, knowing he could not keep up with the others, elected to stay behind in the hope of ingratiating himself with the natives by making them trinkets from metals salvaged from the wreck and thus eventually getting away; and Joshua Glover, who was said to be "of unsound mind". The latter had gone off with the Africans the day after the ship was wrecked and not been seen again. He seems to have been sane enough when he left England and it is not known whether he was really deranged or whether he had suffered a head injury during the wreck.

At any rate the rest of the company set off, divided into three groups. The first group, led by Mr Shaw, consisted of seamen; the second of women, children and the sick, carried by sailors; and the third of officers and the rest of the crew members led by Captain Coxon. They carried with them what foodstuffs they had managed to salvage, but even so they knew they would have to rely on finding food or bartering with the natives to keep alive. And their progress was pitifully slow. While their safest plan was to keep to the shore, this meant no easy stroll along sandy beaches. Great rivers ran down into the sea and must often be followed inland for some distance before they could be forded. Rocky headlands had to be climbed and crossed, deep gulleys negotiated, forests and swamplands skirted. The women, children and injured slowed the speed of the party down to a crawl.

To add to their problems the natives became even more troublesome and before long had stolen from the virtually helpless castaways almost everything they possessed. They snatched bags of flour, slashed them with their spears and threw their contents on the ground. They cut buttons from clothing and, not knowing how to get at the articles they could feel inside, cut off the women's pockets. They also entertained themselves by throwing stones at the Europeans, although the latter made every effort to demonstrate their peaceable intentions. Finally the exasperated sailors became involved in a number of scuffles with the Africans, by whom they were hopelessly outnumbered, while any attempt to barter for food merely resulted in the Kaffirs stealing the goods the sailors had to offer.

Eventually, after four days of snail-like progress, Captain Coxon was forced to agree to the party splitting up. The sailors were becoming increasingly impatient at the delay caused by the sick and the children and it was obviously useless to try to detain them. By now the party had been robbed of almost everything it possessed and was even short of water. The strong could do little more to help the weak than to try to reach civilization and send help for the others who might yet be saved.

So a number of seamen, both European and Indian, set off, led by second mate Shaw. With them went one of the children, a seven-year-old boy called Thomas Law, who had become so attached to the ship's steward that he cried on the threat of being separated from him. The other passengers remained behind. Logie was still ill, and a passenger from India, Mr Nixon, had injured himself in a fall. But two other passengers, Mr Hosea – father of the twenty-two-month-old girl – and Colonel James, both wealthy men, managed to persuade some of the ship's company to remain behind to help with the sick and the children and to carry what little food and blankets they had left.

So, on 11 August, one week after the wreck, about half the ship's complement set out under the command of the second mate. Among them were seaman Lewis, whose unheeded warning might have saved many lives, and Shaw's servant William Habberley, who later wrote an amazingly accurate and detailed account of their journey. This party struggled along some 400 miles of coastline, encountering on the way every kind of privation and difficulty. Injuries, hunger, accidents and sickness gradually took their toll, and although the natives they encountered were not all as antagonistic as those of Pondoland where the ship had been wrecked, few helped them and many actively hindered and hurt them. Again and again the men were forced to turn inland in order to cross rivers or skirt forests and on one of these occasions a difference of opinion arose between the members of the party as to whether to journey inland or to try to keep near the coast. Accordingly about half the members of the party, led by the ship's carpenter, left the second mate and his men and moved inland.

Less than four weeks after they had set out from the wreck there were no more than ten men remaining with Mr Shaw. One by one they had died of weakness, hunger, disease or wounds. The party continued to dwindle and Shaw himself died. Eventually Habberley was the sole survivor. By the end of fourteen weeks he himself was reduced almost to a skeleton, but he was eventually found by friendly natives and given food and shelter. Later he learned that two other castaways were also being cared for in neighbouring villages. Eventually, on 14 January, 1783 some five and a half months after they had set out from the wreck, these men were found by a rescue party sent out by order of the Governor of the Cape.

The carpenter's party fared little better. Several of his men wandered off in small groups and the child, Thomas Law, died despite all the sailors could do for him. Six of the men, however, including a cabin boy of fourteen, survived to be found by a group from a Dutch settlement who were out searching for stray cattle.

The fate of the captain's party is largely unknown; only one of its forty-seven members was ever seen again. This one, a lascar seaman, came up with Habberley and others in the second mate's party early in September and gave them the astonishing information that Captain Coxon, with several of his officers and seamen and one of the passengers, had left Mr and Mrs Logie, Mr and Mrs Hosea, "and others who were unable to get forward" on the very same day that the second mate had left with half the survivors. The captain and his party had passed Colonel and Mrs James, with four seamen, and the Colonel was unable to move without help.

It seems, then, that the main body of lascars and sailors had barely departed when the rest of the survivors also began to break up into small groups. None of the reports of the captain's party mentions any of the five children which remained with it. Mary Hosea, however, would hardly have abandoned her twenty-two-month-old daughter, nor the little boy who was being sent to England to be educated and who had been entrusted to her care. There were also three other children, a boy of about eight and two girls whose age is unknown but who had probably been put aboard the *Grosvenor* in the care of the captain – a common practice of the time.

Nobody knows what happened to these women and children. First mate Logie was reported (by his wife's servant who abandoned them and was later rescued) as being "near to death" and so was Colonel James. What happened to their wives? One woman did, apparently, travel some considerable distance for the leader of a rescue expedition sent out later found a woman's torn clothing lying upon a beach many miles south. But nobody knows who she was. The natives would probably not have harmed Mary Hosea and her child in arms, nor Lydia Logie who was pregnant.

A tragic-sounding clue has come from an account published some years later by a Lieutenant Farewell who reported finding the wreck of the *Grosvenor* when travelling along the coast and said that "a carpenter and an armourer" had lived near the spot until recently. There were also, he had been told, two women who had lived on the spot for some time, "but upon an irruption of the natives from the westward, all the tribes that then inhabited that part of the coast were killed, when these women fled, hid themselves in the bush and were then starved to death". One may assume that these two were the men left behind by the rest of the castaways when they set off upon their journey, the "armourer" being the sailor who had relied on his skill in making metal objects to ingratiate himself with the natives. Who the two women were nobody knows: they may have been the two girls who had been among the child passengers, for it seems that the married women had left the area. Speculation has continued to this day whether the women were forcibly taken by the natives to be their wives, but there is no evidence for this.

Two rescue expeditions which set out to search for survivors found plenty of evidence and heard tales from the tribesmen of castaways who had travelled some distance but who had all eventually died. In all, of the 115 people who came safely ashore and set out to find safety, only nine seamen, one of them Italian, reached civilization; seven lascars and two Indian maidservants were later found by the first relief expedition. These people were finally returned to their own countries and for the first time many details of the story became known. The wreck of the *Grosvenor* achieved a kind of glamour; novels, stories, poems and even a spectacle, performed at the Royalty Theatre and accompanied by other attractions such as "Juan Bellinck on the flying rope", appeared. For years the story of the shipwreck was the inspiration of many dramatic tales.

However it was not until a hundred years had passed that there was any suggestion that the *Grosvenor* had been a "treasure ship". When she was wrecked the East India Company had valued her cargo at some £300,000, which was certainly a tidy sum but was largely represented by perishable goods. The two rescue expeditions which were sent out had been ordered to look for survivors, not to try to salvage any cargo which would have been a comparatively simple task in the early years. The second rescue expedition did indeed meet natives who had gold and silver coins found near the site of the wreck, but this did not represent a major hoard. It was not until 1880 that a report in the *Natal Mercantile Advertiser* described how two travellers had passed the spot where the *Grosvenor* was wrecked and had picked up some coins on the beach which, said the report, "shows that there must have been large quantities of bullion on board".

Thus, with such comments and the use of the word "bullion", legends are born. One of the two travellers later returned to the spot with a friend to search for treasure and found more coins and odd items such as a silver spoon, some jewellery, a massive seal and a turquoise. The explorers also found nine of the *Grosvenor*'s guns, which they removed but, unfortunately, during their search they not only blasted many of the rocks on the shore but failed to make a map of the exact location of their finds. Soon, although other treasure-seekers set out to try their luck, nobody could tell for certain where the wreck lay. Over the years odd items were found, but none to support the theory of a great treasure ship. Nevertheless the rumours grew and soon regular treasure-hunting companies were set up, properly backed by investors.

One of the most dramatic stories which arose was that of the "Peacock Throne". This tale was first put about no less than

150 years after the wreck, in 1921, soon after the prospectus
designed to interest investors in the first organized hunt for the
Grosvenor's treasure was published. This Peacock Throne of the
great Moguls was first described by a traveller to Delhi in the
1660s. Despite the fact that there is excellent documentary evidence to the effect that the throne was looted, among other
treasures, in 1738 and taken to Persia, a legend grew that it
had been hidden after the Persian raid on Delhi and later put
aboard the *Grosvenor* to be taken to England. How this story
arose, and how it continues to be given credence (unless deliberately fostered to attract the money of investors) is a mystery, for it has no foundation in fact. Nevertheless this, and
other equally unfounded stories of treasure carried upon the
ship continue to be repeated as fact to this day. Several expeditions set out to search for this mythical treasure during the
early part of this century, without any success beyond the discovery of the sort of items any ship of its kind might have
carried.

However one mystery connected with treasure can quite
reasonably be ascribed to the *Grosvenor* wreck. In 1925 an
elderly man who had retired to a plot of land on the Great Kei
river, some seventy miles from the site of the wreck, found
diamonds upon his land. Having acquired the mineral rights
on his property, he pretended a diamond "strike". Eventually
it was proved that the gems he had found were not indigenous
to South Africa. It was well established that Captain Coxon
had been entrusted with several bundles of diamonds to bring
back to England for various people, and it is more than likely
that he would have brought them with him from the wreck. It
seems reasonable to suppose that either the captain himself, or
perhaps a seaman to whom he had entrusted them, had buried
them in order to lighten the burden of what was proving to be
a more difficult journey to safety than any of them had supposed.

The origin of the diamonds has never been established, but
there seems no other explanation for their presence. And this is
the only one of the many *Grosvenor* treasure stories which seems
to have any truth in it. And yet the *Grosvenor* wreck is now
regarded as a tale of lost treasure, and the saga of the tragic
and ill-fated castaways has been overshadowed by legends
created by man's own gullibility and cupidity.

THE FLOOD THAT
CHANGED THE WORLD

"And God said unto Noah, The end of all flesh is come before me;
for the earth is filled with violence through them; and, behold, I
will destroy them with the earth... And it came to pass after
seven days, that the waters of the flood were upon the earth. In the
six hundredth year of Noah's life . . . were all the fountains of the
great deep broken up, and the windows of heaven were opened.
And the rain was upon the earth forty days and forty nights. And
the waters returned off the earth continually; and after the end of
the hundred and fifty days the waters were abated . . ."

The above brief excerpts from the Book of Genesis in the
Holy Bible, leaving aside the Ark and the animals and other
fauna that went in two by two, is, to Christians and many
others, the Flood. It was not, in the simple poetic language of
the Bible, a geological, meteorological or seismic event, but
was a manifestation of the wrath of God, who saw "that the
wickedness of man was great in the earth, and that every imagination of the thoughts of his heart was only evil continually".

Some might feel that times have not changed very much
since The Flood, but in this chapter we are not concerned with
human morality, frailty and punishment – though it is interesting to note that the great catastrophic flood which is recorded
in the mythology of other races throughout the world is attributed to punishment by a deity of one form or another for the
sins of mankind. Theologically, The Flood is polytheistic and
transcends the frontiers of different religions.

A world-destroying flood ("world" in those days being loca-
lized rather than planetary) is a common legend in the ancient
history of many races apart from the Hebrews; for example,
the Americans, Babylonians, Indians, Persians, Polynesians
and Syrians. The Babylonian legend has remarkable similarities with the Hebrew biblical version. There is also the classic
Deucalion myth: Deucalion (the Greek Noah) was the son of
Prometheus and King of Pythia. Zeus flooded the earth, but
Deucalion and his wife Pyrrha escaped in a chest which he had
already made on the advice and instructions of his father (the
Greek "ark"). After floating upon the flood for nine days the
chest finally settled on Mount Parnassus. There is also a Boeo-
tian version of the same story in which Noah is Ogyges, King
of Thebes, and an Arcadian version where Noah is Dardanus.
The biblical Mount Ararat on which the ark grounded is replaced in the Greek legends by the mountains Parnassus, Ger-
ania and Othrys.

Archaeologists in Mesopotamia have discovered evidence of
severe flooding at various levels – in particular a stratum of
clay eight feet deep, excavated by Sir Leonard Woolley at Ur,
which he identified with the biblical flood.

In complete contrast, let us consider for a moment the terrestrial "flood" theory of Dr William Whiston, a scholar and
clergyman who succeeded Sir Isaac Newton as Lucasian professor of mathematics at Cambridge in 1710. In his book, *A
New Theory of the Earth*, he suggests that originally this planet
was a comet which was eventually trapped into orbit round
the sun and duly cooled down and solidified. The sins of the
first men were so heinous that a small comet was sent to by-
pass the earth, causing an enormous tide to wash over and
inundate the continents and resulting in a violent rainstorm
that lasted for forty days and forty nights – in fact, the biblical
flood. The date of this event, according to Dr Whiston, was 28
November, 2349 B.C., or 2 December 2926 B.C. (he could not
decide which). Ominously he predicted that the flood-raising
comet will one day return and cause even greater havoc. We
can only wait and see.

It was pointed out by Sir James Frazer in his book, *Folklore
in the Old Testament* (published in 1918), that most flood legends
occur among the races surrounding the Mediterranean,
beyond which they thin out and are virtually non-existent in
Australia and China. This, he suggested, indicated a point of

origin in mid-Atlantic, which is the location of the legendary sunken continent of Atlantis . . . but more about that later.

First we must return to the Bible in which there are many allusions (perhaps metaphorical) to world disasters and floods. The following are some brief quotations from the Psalms. "Then the earth shook and trembled; the foundations also of the hills moved and were shaken . . . His pavilion round about him were dark waters and thick clouds of the skies. At the brightness that was before him his thick clouds passed, hail stones and coals of fire . . . Then the channels of the waters were seen, and the foundations of the world were discovered . . ." (Psalm 18); "Though the waters thereof roar and be troubled, though the mountains shake with the welling thereof . . . though the earth be removed and the mountains be carried into the midst of the sea . . ." (Psalm 46); "The clouds poured out water; the skies sent out a sound . . . the lightnings lightened the world; the earth trembled and shook." (Psalm 77).

But the Bible is not the only source of information and allegory about a world cataclysm. Legends of many other races and nations repeat the same story, though with variation in detail, as might be expected. Roy Stemman in his book, *Atlantis and the Lost Lands*, quotes a poem from Iceland contained in a volume of ancient Scandinavian poems of great but undated antiquity. It reads:

Mountains dash together,
Heroes go the way to Hel,
And the heaven is rent in twain . . .
The sun grows dark, the earth sinks into the sea,
The bright stars from the heaven vanish.
Fire rages, heat blazes,
And high flames play 'gainst heaven itself.

Stemman writes: "The sky grew dark and a fearful rain fell upon the earth . . . Nothing escaped this global holocaust. Men and animals were engulfed. Forests were crushed. Even those who reached the caves were not safe. Darkness gripped the earth and tremendous quakes convulsed the planet. Mountains were thrown up to the heavens and continents were sucked beneath the seas as the stricken earth rolled and tilted. Hurricane winds lashed the planet's wretched surface and tidal waves swept across the vast stretches of land . . . A catastrophe of such proportions would account for the sinking of a huge continent such as Atlantis – but did such an event ever take place?" The chapter on Atlantis in this book will probably show that such an event did take place, and that Atlantis is now being uncovered by the shifting sands of the ocean bed.

The Babylonian legend repeats the formula. Records some 4,000 years old refer to a "dark cloud" that encompassed the planet and intense fire that scorched the land – "all that was bright was turned into darkness. For six days a deluge of water driven by hurricane winds swept over earth, destroying all forms of life and changing the face of the planet." At this point one must seriously consider the possibility of such a disaster being caused by the long tail of a passing comet.

Hesiod, an eighth-century Greek poet, wrote about an "aerial monster" that descended upon earth with a thunderous noise that even made Mount Olympus shake. Lightning, winds, fire and floods destroyed both land and life.

In Oklahoma, U.S.A., the Indians have a legend about a time when earth was cloaked in darkness. After a long time a light appeared in the north, but it was from "mountain-high waves rapidly coming nearer". And the aborigines of Brazil tell of a similar catastrophe when "the lightnings flashed and the thunders roared terribly . . . and fragments fell down and killed everything and everybody – nothing that had life was left upon the earth."

On the opposite side of the planet the Samoans of the South Pacific have a parallel myth about smoke which became clouds, and "the sea too arose, and in a stupendous catastrophe of nature the land sank into the sea. The new earth arose out of the womb of the last earth."

Hindu legend tells of the appearance in the sky of a rapidly expanding dark shape in the form of a boar, which suddenly broke into loud thunder. The shape hurtled into the water which, convulsed by the motion, rose in enormous waves.

The same basic story is related in the mythology of other races and countries, including even the Celts of Britain and the Maoris of New Zealand.

A single coincidence is one thing, but multiple coincidence involves astronomical odds. An American lawyer and Congressman, Ignatius Donnelly, published in 1892 a well-considered book on Atlantis, of which only three points are relevant in this chapter. Atlantis, he stated, was the original focal point of the Aryan or Indo-European family of nations, the Semitic peoples, and also possibly the Turanian races. The continent was totally destroyed in a terrifying natural convulsion of the planet and sank into the Atlantic Ocean with nearly all of its inhabitants. A few survivors escaped, possibly on rafts or small boats, and spread the news of the disaster – and that news has survived in the form of legends of fire, flood and deluge in many nations of both the eastern and western hemispheres. It is very difficult to fault the logic of such a conclusion in view of the mass of mythological evidence which appears to have its origin in a common source.

As to the explanation – well, the most sensational theory is that advanced by Immanuel Velikovsky, a Russian-Israeli doctor, who in 1950 published a book entitled *Worlds in Collision*. Part of his work is concerned with Atlantis, whose existence he clearly accepts. To some extent he agrees with Ignatius Donnelly that the earth was shaken and engulfed by a comet that passed too close for comfort, but he goes much further into space. What happened, according to Velikovsky, was that the planet Jupiter collided with another planet and produced a comet which went into elliptical orbit round the sun. Jupiter is still with us, but what happened to the other planet? Oddly enough, between Jupiter and Mars there is the asteroid belt, an orbiting ring of small and massive rocks which most astronomers now accept as the shattered remains of a planet (often known by the name of Maldek).

The comet in question came very close to earth around 1500 B.C. and caused global catastrophe. The comet's tail would produce smoke, incandescent fire and storms; it would drag the waters of the earth into an immense tidal wave and create seismic quakes and eruptions. Apparently the comet returned again to earth some fifty-two years later and again caused chaotic damage and immeasurable loss of life. So far, the theory is not unacceptable.

The remaining history of the comet is more debatable. Having lost most of its tail due to the pull of earth's gravitation, and after a "close encounter" with Mars (which must have shaken the Red Planet up a bit), the comet settled down, solidified and took up an orbit round the sun as a planet in its own right – namely, the planet Venus.

This latter part of the theory has not impressed the orthodox scientists. American science writer, L. Sprague de Camp, points out that the Babylonians left records of observations of

Venus 5,000 years ago . . . "Comets are not planets and do not evolve into planets; instead they are loose aggregates of meteors with total masses less than a millionth of that of the earth . . . And the gas of which a comet's tail is composed is so attenuated that if the tail of a good-sized comet were compressed to the density of iron, I could put the whole thing in my brief case!"

One must bear in mind, however, that nobody has yet ever closely examined a comet, and the question of density and mass is a matter of computation based on solar orbit and gravitational mathematics. Until fairly recently it was commonly believed that there was a network of canals on Mars, but now that space probes have photographed Mars from close orbit and made soft landings on its bleak surface, we know better. Also, Venus probes have shown that the planet has an atmosphere of hydrocarbon gases and dust, which is what one would expect from a condensed comet – and that in turn would be a function of the actual size of the comet, which nobody knows. Finally, Venus rotates in the opposite direction from other planets in the solar system, which could imply a major disturbance or a non-indigenous evolution.

Velikovsky suggests, of course, that the destruction of Atlantis and its submersion resulted from the first approach of the comet. This same event was responsible for The Flood and all the other legendary floods throughout the world. The dates may not link up, but there is much guesswork in dating in matters of great antiquity, and a few thousand years here or there is not too significant.

The destruction of Atlantis by a comet is not a new concept. It was put forward in 1785 by Gian Rinaldo Carli, an Italian scholar (his chosen date was 4000 B.C.) and also in the 1920s by Karl Zschaetzch, a German writer whose purpose was to prove that the Aryan race came originally from Atlantis, the cradle of all culture and civilization. The late thirties and early forties in Germany rather put paid to that particular philosophy.

An Austrian engineer, Hanns Hörbiger, proposed that the earth had had a number of moons before the present one. They all shattered in turn and fell upon earth, causing immense havoc. But it was the capture of our present moon by the earth's gravitation that caused The Flood, and the sinking of Atlantis, Lemuria and Mu. Hörbiger has predicted that the break up of our moon will in due course erase all life on earth, but he does not say when this is likely to happen. His theory and prediction were published in 1913.

Orthodox scientists are, of course, sceptical of all such theories. They regard the several floods, earthquakes and disasters as separate events spaced over a long period – centuries and possibly millennia. Folklore and legend have integrated on the basis of a common denominator, and of course the legends were enhanced and embroidered as they were handed down through generations. It sounds reasonable, but scientists are not always right.

What does seem acceptable is the localization of various catastrophes with some separation in time (though there is no actual proof of this). The biblical flood is thought to have been a real flood that inundated some 40,000 square miles of the Euphrates Valley around 5000 B.C. Similar great floods have occurred in China (though rarely) and Bengal (more frequently). The Zuider Zee in the Netherlands was created within one day in 1282 when the dykes around that area of land below sea-level collapsed during a tremendous storm.

An ocean-bed earthquake can create a tidal wave, hardly noticeable at first, which will grow to a tremendous height as the pressure wave rises on the continental shelf of a land mass – tidal waves of 200 feet or more have been recorded, especially in the Pacific, a "hot" seismic area. But a tidal wave cannot sink a continent.

There is little doubt that continental drift is involved in the slow geophysical evolution of our planet. The continents are moving millimetre by millimetre on the molten fluid core of the world. There are existing fault and fracture lines that will open, and gaps that will close. The American clairvoyant, Edgar Cayce (referred to in the chapter on Atlantis), predicted the submersion of the American east coast and the Japanese islands before the end of this century, and the emergence of new lands from the great oceans. That may or may not be, but it is doubtful whether the local betting shop would give better odds than evens. The bookmaker, if he knew his geological form, would probably offer odds-on to a bet on the further fracturing and widening of the famous San Andreas fault line running down the west coast of the U.S.A. – the cause of the tragic San Fransisco earthquake. The Americans are reportedly pumping billions of gallons of water into the fault line to smooth any sudden movement and displacement of bedrock. The water will not stop the movement when it happens, but it will act as a kind of lubricant to reduce a potential Force 8 earthquake to, say, Force 2 or 3 on the Richter scale. And if it should fail, then the west coast of North America might conceivably plunge into the depths of the Pacific Ocean. It is no more incredible than the reality of man setting foot on the surface of the moon.

A final word of consolation, however, and here we return to our starting point, the Book of Genesis in the Bible (Chap. 8, v. 20): "And the Lord said in his heart, I will not again curse the ground any more for man's sake; for the imagination of man's heart is evil from his youth; neither will I again smite any more everything living, as I have done."

AN END OF TRAITORS

"Lo, my masters, what this fellow hath done! God will have all his treachery known."

Sir Francis Drake's short beard seemed to bristle more in the heat of his fury. His countenance was "cholerick". As prosecutor, he demanded that the jury of forty of his officers and men pronounce the traitor in their midst guilty. When they had done so, as judge, too, he imposed the death sentence.

Yet, when the condemned man came to take his last Holy Communion, Drake knelt beside him to share it with him; and afterwards, he entertained the traitor in his cabin, where they "dined at the same table together as cheerfully in sobriety as ever in their lives, each cheering up the other and taking their leave by drinking to each other as if some journey only had been at hand". A few hours later, Drake nodded his satisfaction as one stroke of a sword sliced Thomas Doughty's head from his body.

It is not known when these two very different men had first met. Most likely, it was during that period of Drake's tactful absence from England, in his early thirties, serving as a volunteer under Walter, Earl of Essex, commander of the English forces in Ireland. Doughty was Essex's friend, serving him as an aide-de-camp. He was a gentleman, well-born and educated, with a smooth, ingratiating manner. Francis Drake, by contrast, was a thoroughgoing "tarpaulin", a yeoman's son who had been apprenticed on a coastal vessel as a boy and had swiftly made a reputation in his twenties by "playing the seaman and the pirate" under a privateering commission from Queen Elizabeth. He was blunt, strongly-spoken, fiery-tempered, notoriously strict with his crews; yet, for an Elizabethan seadog, he was enlightened, deeply religious, popular with his underlings, and remarkably humane towards prisoners, even the Spanish, with their own reputation for inhumanity and their bitter hatred of England.

Each was the sort of man who would have admired certain qualities in the other which he himself did not possess. If Drake knew of the mischief-making between the Earl of Essex in Ireland and the Earl of Leicester at Elizabeth's court which lost Doughty Essex's favour, it didn't prevent him trusting the man enough to invite him to join the great enterprise which Drake proposed to Elizabeth on his return to England. He suggested an expedition to the South Seas, where lay an uncharted country named Terra Australis Incognita. Drake's plan, shared by some of the Queen's principal courtiers, was to reach this land and establish relations with its natives before there could be any possibility of the Spanish doing so. Whatever trade there was to be gained would go to the first country to make its influence felt there. Drake's intended route was through the Straits of Magellan, between Tierra del Fuego and the South American mainland. It was a passage never yet attempted by Englishmen.

The Queen was enthusiastic. She had been seeking some way of undermining Spain's trade without provoking actual war, and it had been at her initiative that Drake was invited to put forward some proposal. He knew how great a secret it must represent; so much so, that he refused to proffer it in writing, but did so verbally to the Queen.

He had an additional suggestion to make. In order that the expedition should be certain of paying its way, he would like, during the voyage, to make another of his raids in Spanish waters, taking a few ships and their rich cargoes.

The Queen agreed again, but stressed that this made the enterprise even more secret. If even her most trusted minister, Lord Treasurer Burghley, came to hear of it he would oppose it and probably expose it, for his policy towards Spain was "peace at any price". Burghley knew that if English ships returned to plundering Spanish treasure-vessels, King Philip would certainly renew the war. That could damage severely

England's vital trade and might even culminate in national defeat.

Queen Elizabeth gave Drake the means to furnish a small fleet. He assembled an innocuous-looking one of only five small vessels, putting abroad the impression that it was to sail for the Indies or the Mediterranean. His personal fame and respect attracted a crew numbering overall 166 men. Among the "gentlemen" of that company was Thomas Doughty.

The fleet sailed from Falmouth on 13 December, 1577. Drake's charts were marked up with his intended course: by the west coast of Morocco and the Cape Verde Islands, making for Brazil. They were well at sea, though, before he let any of this be known to those under him. The news was not well received; the dangerous reputation of the untried Magellan Strait was feared, and the sailors recalled that theirs had been a 13th-day departure.

Apart from some initial bad weather, however, things went well. Two Portuguese ships were captured. Into one of them, re-named the *Mary*, Drake put Thomas Doughty as captain. With him went Drake's young brother Thomas, and the admiral's personal trumpeter, Brewer. It was this Brewer who, at an island port of call, told Drake that Doughty had been found stealing from the cargo of his captured ship.

In his volatile fashion, Drake confronted Doughty, raging and swearing at him. Doughty blandly begged him to calm down. Yes, he had in his possession a few articles which had belonged to the Portuguese; but all had been given him as presents, out of gratitude for his good treatment of them. The admiral knew this to be a lie, and said so, growing monumentally fierce. Tougher men than Doughty had wilted before this brand of fury. He changed his story: Thomas Drake had stolen the goods.

A hint of mystery is plain at this point. Instead of boiling over completely at the accusation against his young brother, Drake did nothing more than deprive Doughty of his command of the *Mary*, which he gave to Thomas. He himself transferred his admiral's flag to that ship and stayed aboard her; but he appointed Thomas Doughty to a position of authority in his former flagship, the *Pelican*: Doughty, the man who had dipped his fingers into official plunder, and, upon being given the lie to his explanation, had sought to implicate the admiral's brother. Doughty, moreover, who by this time was

known to have been encouraging the seamen in their com-
plaints about the true nature of an expedition for which they
would most likely not have volunteered had they known it.

The voyage continued, long and boringly. The men's discontentment grew; and once again, in a manner that any thinking man must have known would be seen as deliberate, Thomas
Doughty affronted his admiral.

The trumpeter, Brewer, was now back at Drake's side. One
day he sent him by small boat to Doughty's ship to deliver an
innocuous message. The greeting he got was a de-bagging and
a painful caning, carried out by a party led by Doughty himself. This "cobbey", as the practice was known in the navy,
would have been ruefully accepted by an ordinary seaman. To
the admiral's personal messenger, it was a hurtful insult, in
more ways than one. He reported back to Drake, who at once
summoned Doughty to row over. Instead of calling him
aboard for a tongue-lashing, though, the admiral called down
to Doughty in his boat, "Stay there, Thomas Doughty, for I
must send you to another place."

That place proved to be the fleet's store-ship, the *Swan*, in
which Doughty was ordered to remain, without authority,
under the charge of her captain, John Chester. It suggests that
Francis Drake had come to regard Doughty as something more
than a gentlemanly rogue. A pernicious influence, perhaps,
who would be better isolated from the already discontented
sailors?

This discontentment grew to positive fear as they at length
came in sight of the Brazilian coast. Fires were springing up on
shore, with dancing figures about them and the sounds of
chanting reaching the ships. If the sailors were frightened, so
were the natives, at the sight of this small armada. They had
fallen to propitiating the local devils, and chanting incanta-
tions designed to raise storms and wreck the ships. Whether by
mystical or purely natural means, their wishes were granted.
Dense mists sprang up, then storms, then mists again. The
ships were scattered. Yet, tiny though they were, all survived,
to reassemble and plough on to the port of St Julian, north of
the Strait of Magellan.

Magellan himself had paused here, in 1520, before hazard-
ing the dangerous passage since called after him. There had
been mutiny among his men, and he had hanged the ring-
leaders. There was evidence of it for Drake's near-mutinous

crews to see: a rotting mast, once a gallows, and, buried in the ground at its foot, the bones of men. The men stared down at these, full of morbid superstition. Thomas Doughty saw them, and chose that time to let it be known that he was a wizard, able to raise the devil "and make him to meet any man in the likeness of a bear, a lion, or a man in harness".

This was at the least wild, hysterical talk. Those were times when witches, male or female, were hunted, tortured or burned, if enough evidence could be gathered against them. Doughty was running a great risk of this kind of treatment. But was the risk calculated? Was he playing on the super-stitiousness of the seamen to persuade them that he would prove a safer leader for them than Francis Drake? Was he, in fact, inciting that mutiny which he had been quietly fostering throughout the voyage? And if so, to what purpose?

If his purpose was to terrify Drake himself, it certainly did not succeed. The admiral was not a man to be frightened. The discovery of Magellan's mutineers' bones did not move him; and when a band of Patagonian natives, armed with bows and arrows, came attacking, Drake snatched up a gun, charged it, and fired at their leader, "and, striking him in the paunch with hail shot, sent his guts abroad with great torment, as it seemed by his cry, which was so hideous and terrible a roar as if ten bulls had joined in roaring."

Wizard or no, Thomas Doughty was put on trial, the admi-ral constituting himself prosecutor and judge, but appointing a quarter of his force jurors. The charge, in Drake's words, was: "Thomas Doughty, you have here sought by divers means, inasmuch as you may, to discredit me to the great hindrance and overthrow of this voyage, besides other great matters where I have to charge you withal."

Doughty impudently answered that he had no objection to standing trial, provided the admiral had the authority to try him. Drake quickly disabused him about that.

Just how deep Drake's suspicion of Doughty had been is not known. If he merely believed that he had been trying to incite mutiny for some personal advantage, he was quickly to learn that it was more sinister than that. Evidence was given that Doughty had told someone, "Burghley has a plot of the voyage."

Drake himself interrupted: "No, that he hath not!"

Doughty returned him a supercilious smile.

"My Lord Burghley has all along known the purpose of the voyage."

"How?"

"He had it from me."

It was at this point that Drake's outburst about treachery came. It ended, "Her Majesty gave me special commandment that of all men my Lord Treasurer should not know it. But see how this man's own mouth hath betrayed him!"

It does not seem to have occurred to Drake to ask Doughty why he had so glibly made the admission which would undoubtedly bring about his execution. He could just as easily have denied it. He did not, either, ask Doughty how he had learned of the purpose of the voyage, enabling him to report it to Burghley. Perhaps Drake knew the answer to that: had he himself confided it to Doughty, in the naïve belief that he was dealing with a gentleman of integrity?

Of course, the answer may be the straightforward one that Lord Treasurer Burghley, who had plenty of spies in his employ, had learned of the nature of the expedition when it was too late to stop it, and had succeeded in recruiting Doughty to try at least to sabotage it and remove the risk of a confrontation with Spain. If that were so, then Doughty's crime was treachery to his commander, yet hardly to his country, if Burghley's fears were well founded.

And there remains the question of Drake's odd behaviour towards him. He put up with the man's intransigence until he could do so no longer. Having heard him confess his guilt in the open, he sentenced him to swift death. Doughty's request that he might be put ashore in South America was rejected, as was a proposal that he be placed in confinement and taken back eventually to England, to stand proper trial. Drake seems to have wanted him dispatched before he could cause any more trouble.

Yet, on the eve of execution, he dined with the traitor and shared Holy Communion with him; and heard him, during that solemn service, affirm to the chaplain that he was an innocent man. Such a declaration as this, coming on top of a confession of guilt, should surely have shocked the deeply religious Francis Drake into reconsideration of the matter. It did not. As he watched Thomas Doughty's head being severed, he declared, "Lo! This is the end of traitors."

Drake's voyage continued, to last almost three years and

become the first circumnavigation of the globe by an English-man. It was a triumph, which brought him his knighthood. As Queen Elizabeth's sword touched him on each shoulder as he knelt before her on his deck at Deptford, did he spare a thought for the blade which had conveniently ended Thomas Doughty's life, ensuring that the Queen would never learn that it had been Drake himself who had carelessly given her secret away?

DID IRISH MONKS
DISCOVER AMERICA?

In the so-called Dark Ages when war, invasion and rapine were endemic in Western Europe certain Irish monks resolved to cut themselves off from an evil world and withdraw into solitude to lead a life of prayer and contemplation. Along the west coast of Ireland and up into the Scottish isles, even as far as the Faroes and Iceland they sought out the most inaccessible places, a battered crag on some sea-girt promontory or a wind-torn hilltop site, built themselves primitive stone shelters and, casting themselves on the mercy of God, settled down to live in poverty and asceticism.

But these monks were by no means inactive. As their settlements grew into well-ordered monastic communities some felt the urge to study or explore. Irish monks became known as the learned men of Europe, highly valued even at the court of Charlemagne himself. As for exploration, the motive was in essence simple. The ancient Celts had believed in something they called The Other World that lay beyond the ocean towards the sunset, a place of strange delights where departed souls lived in bliss, but not unattainable to men of flesh and blood. It could be reached and visited, and it was possible to return.

This dream was converted by Christian influence into the idea of a Promised Land, equally attainable, equally delectable but no longer in a worldly sense. It was now a place of spiritual contentment which men of particular holiness might reach as a reward for virtue. This motive for exploration – and of course there were others – proved strong enough for men to brave the unknown, surviving if they could, if not, certain of a heavenly reward.

Early poems and records contain many references to the long sea voyages of the Irish monks and one in particular, the *Navigatio Sancti Brendani Abbatis* (The Voyage of Saint Brendan the Abbot), is of special interest as it raises the question whether, nearly a thousand years before Columbus and hundreds of years before the Vikings, America was first discovered by Irish monks. Written around A.D. 800 the *Navigatio* seems to some scholars to be a random collection of seafaring stories stretching back over centuries and brought together under the name of one man. But St Brendan is no mythical figure; he was born in County Kerry about A.D. 489 and he is known to have been a great traveller, founding monasteries in western Ireland, voyaging to the Scottish islands, even perhaps to Brittany and the Faroes. It is possible, therefore, that the *Navigatio* recounts his adventures and his alone, and for a special reason he was being celebrated as a hero.

But there is a difficulty. The account is written as a fabulous adventure story and seems at first glance to contain more fantasy than fact. For instance, St Brendan, voyaging north with his companions, is said to have come upon a small island where the men disembarked and lit a fire to cook their dinner. Much to their surprise the island turned out to be a sea creature and swam off with the fire still alight on its back. Another time, they came to an island where the inhabitants pelted them with burning rocks. Elsewhere they meet choirs chanting hymns – this in a most desolate region – dressed in purple, white and blue. Again, inside a pillar of crystal floating on the sea they find a Christian chalice and paten on a shelf. No doubt this is the symbolic language beloved of early writers. But where, if anywhere, is the basis of fact?

All this is important because the *Navigatio* records that St Brendan actually found the "Promised Land" and some students have inclined to the view that this Land was in fact North America. In the early 1970s one of them was a young Englishman by the name of Tim Severin, an Oxford graduate, a former Harkness Fellow at Harvard and, with several adventurous journeys behind him, already a recognized expert on exploration and its history. He noticed three things about the

Navigatio. The descriptions in it corresponded quite closely to a journey by what is known as the Stepping Stone Route to North America, that is, starting from Ireland, by way of the Hebrides, the Faroes, Iceland, Southern Greenland to Newfoundland or Labrador. Secondly, unlike other medieval texts the *Navigatio* gave many practical details of times, distances and so on. Thirdly and most important, the account stated that St Brendan set off in a boat covered with oxhide tanned in oak bark.

This detail had struck many experts as final proof that the entire *Navigatio* was a fabrication. Wet leather deteriorates rapidly, everyone knew that. A man had only to stand outside his front door in the rain and see what happened to his shoes. Sailing across 3,000 miles of sea in a leather boat was therefore an impossibility – just another fanciful touch, they said, in an account riddled with fantasy.

But Severin thought differently. Suppose he could build such a boat and reach North America from Ireland in it, that would surely banish a major obstacle to accepting the *Navigatio*'s account. Then it could be studied with new attention and a serious attempt made to sort out fable from fact. It might turn out that even the fabulous bits had a basis of truth in them. And then . . .

But Severin was above all a practical man and he did not let his imagination run too far. A clear intention was necessary and this was to build and test out a leather boat in an attempted crossing to America – nothing more or less. Certainly it would be a test for the crew and whatever equipment they took with them. But that was not the object. The object was simply to see whether leather properly prepared would stand up to the Atlantic.

In his book, *The Brendan Voyage*, Severin describes the long process of having the boat designed, getting the wooden framework constructed, then, a more difficult job, finding suitable oxhides and arranging for them to be tanned in oak bark. Nothing not authentically medieval was to be used on the vessel, down to the leather thongs tying the frame members together, the flax cord for double-stitching the forty-nine hides on to the frame, more flax for the sheets and halliards and several hundredweight of grease from sheep's wool to be plastered over the hides and allowed to sink in to preserve and waterproof them.

The work went slowly. Leatherwork was a diminishing trade in Britain and to find experts with the experience to help took time. And then, sixteen hundred joints in the frame had to be lashed with two miles of greasy leather thong. As for the stitching between the hides, it had to be done with the utmost care; shoddy work at any point could lead to a fatal leak at sea.

But at last, after three years, in the summer of 1976 all was ready for the start. Early in May the square-rigged, black-brown medieval boat, tipping up at both ends so that it looked like an overripe banana, performed its sea trials and although it would sail no closer to the wind that ninety degrees it did at least prove to be watertight. As it lay in Brandon Creek, southwest Ireland, the traditional starting-point of St Brendan himself, Kerry fishermen watched it with undisguised scepticism. The hides, they were told, were only one-quarter inch thick. There was no keel. The sails were made of flax, not in their opinion a good material. Steering would be done by a paddle lashed to an H-shaped frame at the stern. The boat was 38 feet long and 8 feet in the beam. Less than a quarter of the space was under cover, with a tarpaulin-roofed "cabin" abaft the mainmast and a shelter in the bow hardly bigger than a dog kennel. And yet, with stores aboard as well – kit-bags, food, fresh water, cooker, hurricane lamp, radio telephone, carpentering tools, spare hides, wool grease, sheepskins and what-have-you, the skipper was proposing to take four men with him, all strong experienced sailors admittedly, but all blissfully ignorant of just what the North Atlantic had in store for them. It was just as well they had a life-raft lashed to the cabin roof.

But the sceptics knew nothing of the qualities of a leather boat – none had been in existence for over a thousand years – nor of this particular crew. They were certainly not out to make fools of themselves and in token of that the boat had been called *Brendan* and on the sails was the same sign under which he had embarked, in this case the fifteenth-century Irish ringed cross known as the Cross of Saint Martin, picked out in scarlet.

In the evening of 17 May, 1976, *Brendan* was rowed out of the Creek against an Atlantic swell and set sail, watched by curious crowds on a nearby headland. The seas were slight, the wind was fair from the south-west, pushing the boat northwards up the Irish coast. For the time being the crew had no

problems apart from sorting out the gear and arranging watch-
keeping duties. But Severin was under no illusions about the
difficulties ahead. With its shallow draught of less than one
foot the boat tended to slip sideways unless the wind was dead
astern and the steering paddle (another medieval touch) would
be incapable of keeping it strictly on course. This meant that
sailing near a lee coast would always be dangerous where rocks
could so easily split the leather skin. With the gunwale only
eighteen inches above the water there would also be a risk of
swamping in the high seas that sooner or later would certainly
be encountered. In all it was best, Severin decided, to take a
leaf out of St Brendan's book, watch the weather and seek a
sheltered harbour whenever it threatened to turn really foul.
There was no hurry. This was not a non-stop race and it was
comforting to read in the *Navigatio* that St Brendan himself had
taken no less than seven seasons to reach his Promised Land.

So, further up the coast *Brendan* put in for two days of bad
weather at Inishmore in the Aran Islands, where the crew
were royally entertained. When a fresh breeze sprang up from
the south Severin put to sea again and made good progress
until a sudden storm swept the boat a hundred miles out into
the Atlantic, to be replaced at the limit of the bend by westerlies which blew the boat in again to Ballyhoorisky on the north
point of Northern Ireland.

After a short stay to replenish provisions the men set off
again for the Hebrides. By now, after the storm which the leather hull had splendidly survived, they were gaining confidence
in the boat and their power to handle it. In good conditions it
could make up to twelve knots or more and by a combination
of trimming the sails and using the paddle could be manoeuvred quite well. Even the shallow draught proved a blessing when, driven in towards a bay, *Brendan* managed to slither
over weed-covered rocks without hurt.

From the Hebrides, where more riotous entertainment had
been enjoyed, to the Faroes was another two hundred miles and
this was the next leg in the journey, *Brendan*'s first taste of the
open Atlantic. It was now mid-June and for the first few days
all went well, apart from the boat being driven for twenty-
four hours in a wide westerly loop. But nearer to the sheer,
cloud-capped mountains of the Faroe Islands a vicious storm
broke from the south and though headed east *Brendan* was swept
helplessly northwards towards a tide race between two islands.

She shot through the gap at twenty knots with the main-mast threatening to collapse, then lurched on towards another island where for a full hour, despite a strong wind from astern, the boat was held stationary as in a vice by contrary tide rips. A passing trawler offered a tow so that by evening the boat, still intact though with masthead stay gone and broken halliards, found itself resting at Torshavn, the capital, where Severin and his friends felt quite at home: not far off there is a spot called Brandarsvik – Brendan's Creek.

After restocking supplies and enjoying more splendid hospitality at the Faroes, Severin and his crew sailed, this time for Reykjavik in Iceland, 700 miles away. They had examined the boat carefully meanwhile. The wooden frame, lashed with leather thongs which allowed movement, did not thump in the seas as a rigid hull, say of fibreglass, would have done but adapted itself to the waves. Under the stresses the oxhides had crinkled in places but the leather seemed as strong as ever. The covering of wool grease was intact, probably because the cold northern waters had not allowed it to soften, and the stitching between hides seemed to have been strengthened by absorbing some of the tannin from the leather. Only a small amount of water seeped through the leather itself, not through the joins, producing an inch or two of water in the bilges.

The weather this time was kind. Wind from the east – just what was wanted. Fast going – fifty miles and more a day. Everyone aboard felt snug and contented. The only danger was that *Brendan* might be carried clean past Iceland to the west. But conveniently, when the boat was off the south-west corner, the wind began to blow from the north and Severin was able to claw in to Reykjavik.

There had been one curious and distinctly perilous incident, however. It had started enjoyably enough with a visit from pilot whales, literally scores of them, weaving about under the boat, surfacing, fifteen or so at a time, sighing and blowing, then plunging again in extraordinary aquatic ballets, each lasting a good half hour. By now there was a man from the Faroe Islands on board as crew-member with long experience of whales. He had never seen anything like it and concluded that there must be something about *Brendan* that attracted the whales, probably the smell of the grease or the leather that made them think she was another animal.

The pilot whales were harmless, but one day a killer whale

arrived to inspect, surging up as leader of a troop spread out like a wolf pack. Alone of the cetaceans the killer whale is carnivorous and the danger was that this one might mistake *Brendan*'s leather hull for a meal. Striped black and white, 30 feet long, all of eight tons, the monster came up to within twenty yards, his enormous six-foot fin wobbling sideways like soft india-rubber, then when closer still, so close that the men could smell his stale breath, he dived right under the boat, came up the other side and began to move slowly away . . .

There were plenty of Irish connections with Iceland. Early Icelandic literature spoke of the Norsemen finding "Christian men" when they arrived on the island, men who "must have come over the sea from the west", for when the invaders drove them out "there were found left by them books, bells and croziers". Other records told of Christian priests fleeing before the pagan invaders. But most interesting to Severin was a reference in the *Navigatio* to St Brendan's arrival at what was called "The Island of Smiths" and the description of his crew being pelted with burning rocks. The passage told of the whole island being on fire, of the sea seeming to boil, smoke rising from the sea, a great noise, a terrible stench – clearly a portrayal of a volcanic eruption, with anthropomorphic touches. According to a leading Icelandic volcanologist this description closely resembled a submarine eruption he himself had observed when, in 1963, the small island of Surtsey had been thrust up from the ocean floor off Iceland.

At Reykjavik *Brendan* was taken completely out of the water and examined. The stitches were still perfect, so was the hull apart from a few slight gashes near the bow, due probably to sharp-edged flotsam. The leather was then painted again with hot wool grease, fresh stores were brought on board and all was ready for the passage to Greenland.

Severin had wanted to put in there, but a trip in a coast-guard plane convinced him that heavy pack ice around the southern tip would make it impossible and even dangerous to attempt the next section of the journey at this time of year. Moreover the season of gales was approaching which might well sink the boat. Meanwhile for weeks a strong wind had been blowing persistently from the west, the direction in which he wanted to go. After much thought, and perhaps remembering St Brendan and his "seven seasons", he decided to call off the trip for 1976 and resume in the following year. Would his companions go with him then? With one accord George Molony (Cockney), Arthur Magan (Irish), Trondur Patursson (Faroese) and Edan Kenneil (Scottish) said yes.

Brendan was laid up at Reykjavik for the winter and, none the worse, was ready to sail again at the beginning of May, 1977, for the last, potentially most dangerous leg of the journey. Edan Kenneil had been forced to drop out for business reasons, so there were now four men to manage the boat. The previous season had taught them interesting lessons. In an open boat the old materials such as St Brendan would have used were best. Modern ones like steel or plastic tended to spoil rapidly. Dehydrated foods were unsatisfactory also and instead Severin had acquired smoked sausage, smoked beef, salt pork, hazelnuts, oat cereal and cheese. Again, these were what the medieval monks would have eaten and they proved much more sustaining.

On 7 May, 1977, *Brendan* sailed from Reykjavik and for the first week sauntered along in light airs and calm seas. There was time for fishing and photography and many hours cocooned, as Severin has expressed it, in the leather boat, away from the world's troubles and with the happy feeling that *Brendan* was moving steadily towards her goal.

Then strong winds began to blow from the south-west and with a heavy swell from the south-east the only possible choice was to let *Brendan* run before the rising gale that the radio had reported would shortly be at Force 9 or forty-five miles an hour. On the chart of her course the line of *Brendan*'s progress began to look like a child's erratic doodle, north-east for a day, then as the wind changed south-west for two days, then north-west and south-west. Meanwhile the swell had also changed direction and following seas began to engulf the stern and flood forward throughout the length of the boat. The bilges filled, *Brendan* began to wallow and it was clear that one more sea might sink her. To a man pitched into those waters, Severin had been told, death would come within five minutes.

While the helmsman struggled desperately to prevent the boat broaching-to as it slid down the waves, the other three jumped to the bilge pumps and started pumping for dear life. Compared with the weight of water in the boat, the miserable squirts from the pipes seemed to mock their efforts, but at last, with no more seas breaking over, they managed to give *Brendan* the buoyancy to survive. By now everything on board from

sleeping-bags to salt pork was sopping wet or actually floating.

Tired after pumping continuously for over an hour, the
men were just beginning to sort out the mess when another
huge wave came over the stern and the whole process had to
be started again. Pump, pump, pump, with no time for a let-
up, no time to take breath. Again the water level sank far
enough to save the boat, but total exhaustion was near and
something had to be done. Heaving-to with a sea anchor
would probably smash the bow. But what else was there?
Then Severin remembered the spare oxhides they had brought
with them. It might be possible to stretch a cover aft so that
the seas no longer broke into the cockpit but slithered off
harmlessly. In fifteen minutes the work was done and the
answer had been found. As Severin watched the next sea wash
past over the leather perhaps he thought again of St Brendan.
Had he known the answer to that one, too? Or in his day, as
was probable, was the weather in those northern latitudes
calmer and warmer?

Having survived danger from the sea, Severin now faced
problems with the wind. The gale abated, to be replaced by a
strong wind from the south and this was driving *Brendan* up
towards the pack ice around southern Greenland, huge crunch-
ing blocks spelling mortal danger to the boat. It was possible
the wind might change, on the other hand it often occurred
that local winds blew parallel to the edge of the pack ice, in
which case *Brendan* might find a north-easter closer in. Severin
took this gamble and it paid off. For nearly a week *Brendan*
surged down on her intended course with this following wind,
clocking up a record run on 26 May of 115 miles in twenty-
four hours and heading for the Davis Strait between Greenland and Canada.

Several days later, almost becalmed, the crew were peering
into fog, followed by rain and sleet, a situation doubly frustrating
as by now they were only a few hundred miles from Newfoundland. Then the boat picked up speed again and on the
evening of 13 June they saw ice close at hand for the first time,
great chunks of it bobbing to and fro in the current. There had
been a radio report that the pack ice off Canada's eastern coast
was moving north, so Severin took these pieces to be part of an
isolated ice raft. But in fact the pack ice had not moved completely. The size and extent of the "raft" grew steadily larger

and Severin was wondering how to get round it when a passing steamer offered to tow him clear, an offer gratefully accepted. What he did not know was that disintegrating pack ice awaited him further south, only two hundred miles from his goal.

Brendan hit the edge of the ice at 3 a.m. on 19 June, and there was a new sound, a high-pitched crackling from chunks colliding as the boat brushed over them at speed. This was so unexpected that for a moment Severin did not think of ice at all. Then instantly the sail was dropped and torches were brought out to inspect the surroundings. They showed a frightening scene. On all sides *Brendan* was boxed in by jagged lumps of ice, shifting in the swell with water channels opening and closing between them. And there was no end to the vista, consequently no action could be planned except to try and survive by steering very slowly between one ice floe and the next.

With one man at the bow shining his torch ahead, one at the helm, two at the sails to raise or lower them as needed, *Brendan* went squirming between the floes, bumping heavily into some, grazing past others, with now and again that ominous chink-chink from ice scraping past the hull. All that night in bitter cold and on towards dusk the following day the awful game went on. Some floes were rounded, others razor-sharp, some had underwater ledges deep green in colour that might slice into the leather hull at any moment.

But *Brendan* survived and was nearing the edge of the ice pack, the crew believed themselves almost out of danger when disaster struck. So far, despite the continual movement of the floes, edging towards one another, colliding sometimes, then parting again, they had managed to weave a way between them. Now, as the boat was between two floes, they closed in and pinched the hull sharply before moving away. A moment later Severin saw water rising under the floorboards and realized that *Brendan* had sprung a leak.

In the dark it was impossible to locate the site, and to survive the only possibility was to go on pumping until daylight. Fortunately the inflow of water was not unmanageable, though it took two thousand pump strokes an hour to keep it under control. At 6 a.m., when dawn was breaking, Severin had a brainwave. He had been wondering all night how the leak could be found and if found whether it could be mended. Now he suddenly remembered a curious thing. At night when he was pumping there had been green phosphorescence outside the boat along the gunwale and each pump stroke had brought phosphorescence up into the tube. Were those outer and inner gleams connected? Did they show the site of the leak?

Leaning over the gunwale amidships on the port side at the site of the pump, Severin found a dent about the size of a grapefruit in the leather between two ribs of the hull. Clearing a space to inspect the inside, he then found a tear about four inches long. Greatly relieved, he called to the others: "I found the leak. And it's in a place where we can mend it."

So began the work of patching, one of the most extraordinary events of the voyage. A leather patch was cut. George Molony leant over the gunwale holding it in place below water while Trondur Patursson, with awl, nine-inch needle and flax, pushed through the first thread from inside. The awl was handed over, Molony made a hole, pushed the needle and thread back to the inside, then the process began again. The temperature of the water was zero Centigrade and every time a sea came Molony was drenched. But plastered with grease the patch held – and *Brendan* was saved.

There were only a few more miles to cover now, a few more days to go, and in this time nature seemed to relent and there were light airs, calm, barely ruffled seas. *Brendan*, the boat that wiseacres had said would sink the moment she touched the water, moved slowly towards the shores of Newfoundland after travelling 4,500 miles. On the night of 25 June lights were visible ahead; next morning came the scent of pine trees and at 8 p.m. that evening *Brendan* came ashore where the winds chose to put her, at Peckford Island in the Outer Wadham Group, some 150 miles north-west of St Johns.

So twentieth-century men had proved that St Brendan, the sixth-century monk, could have reached the New World. And if he did, he may not have been the first. The *Navigatio* tells that other men met him there and spoke to him, presumably in his own language.

Is that a fabulous touch, like others in that early account? Or will archaeological discoveries somewhere along Canada's east coast, the remains of typical Irish beehive huts for instance or inscriptions carved on stone, prove that even further back than St Brendan some of those intrepid monks reached their Promised Land, and that the Promised Land was indeed America?

"THOSE COWARDLY CAPTAINS"

"SIR –
I had little hopes, on Monday last, but to have supped in your cabin: but it pleased God to order it otherwise; I am thankful for it. As for those cowardly captains who deserted you, hang them up; for, by God, they deserve it.

Yours,
DUCASSE."

The mystery of six days in August, 1702, is not what – but why? That Admiral John Benbow's last action lives in naval history as one of the most disgraceful débâcles of all time is beyond doubt. Reasons were assigned at the time and men punished with the utmost rigour of the law. By all accounts they deserved what they got; yet no account tells us precisely why "those cowardly captains" deliberately followed a course of action which they must have known could only have the direst consequences. Cowardice is not explanation enough.

In 1701, England faced one of her many conflicts with France, this time allied with Spain, over her interests in the West Indies. The Spanish had been first in the West Indies, explored by Columbus in several expeditions, and had established settlements on many of the islands, whose people they had promptly proceeded to enslave and oppress. The English had followed, early in the seventeenth century, staking claims first on the tiny island of St Christopher (later called St Kitts), then quickly expanding to more and bigger islands, basing

their occupation on that sound agricultural planning which
has remained the West Indies' principal benefit to this day.

The British had shortly been followed by the French, and by
the end of the century all three countries had substantial
interests in the sunny isles. But with the succession to the
Spanish throne in dispute, and Louis XIV of France with his
boundless territorial ambitions backing one of the candidates,
a Franco-Spanish squeeze upon England's West Indian
settlements seemed highly likely.

Accordingly, in September, 1701, John Benbow, Vice-
Admiral of the Blue, serving in the Grand Fleet under Sir
George Rooke, was invited to command a squadron sailing for
the West Indies to safeguard British lives and property. King
William III was reluctant to let him go: he liked men of
Benbow's kind about him and often consulted and confided in
him. Other candidates were suggested. They hastened to ask to
be excused: at that time the West Indies was a station looked
upon – and rightly – more as a fever-trap than a paradise.

"Well then," sighed the king, consoling himself with a jest,
"I find we must spare our beaux and send honest Benbow."

The pun, if it was ever made, was an apt one: there was
every difference in the world between "honest Benbow" and his
courtier-colleagues. Benbow was a "tarpaulin", and proud of it
– a self-made man who had raised himself from nothing to high
rank in a service in which wealth and favour so often counted
for more than ability and courage. A courtier or gentleman
with enough money and the right connections could get himself an officer's appointment in a favoured ship, no matter how
little he knew about working her or handling men, a disgraceful state of affairs which was to persist, in decreasing degree,
until the post-Trafalgar years. For an ordinary seaman to
achieve the right to walk the quarter-deck, though not unknown, was exceedingly rare. Even down to our own time
argument has continued as to whether gentlemen or ex-rankers
make the best officers: there is, of course, no answer. Everything depends on the man.

> Bill Benbow, the tanner, at Shrewsbury did dwell,
> He taught his son Johnny and thrashed him as well;
> He 'prenticed him early a butcher to be,
> But John loved adventure and ran off to sea.

Benbow was of the type which constituted the cream of

naval seamen: as tough as they came, "with every hair a rope-yarn, every tooth a marlin-spike, every finger a fish-hook, and his blood right good Stockhollum tar". He had been born in 1653, son of a Shropshire tanner, and had served since a boy in the Merchant Marine, from where the Navy found those experienced, no-nonsense officers who could hand, reef, steer and, if need be, do any other task aboard those complicated marvels of ingenuity and beauty, the great wooden ships. He had entered the Navy, aged twenty-five, as a Master's Mate in the *Rupert* under Captain Philip Herbert, later Earl of Torrington. Pepys had written of Herbert, "Of all the worst men living he is the only man I do not know to have any one virtue to compound for all his vices." And he must have been just the commander to appreciate Benbow's rough-and-ready nature, for he himself was even rougher and readier with a number of extra, singularly nasty traits thrown in. A weakness shared by many "tarpaulins" was that of overdoing their natural coarseness and boasting of it as a virtue, a habit which tended to disgust more moderate professional officers every bit as much as it offended – as it was intended to – foppish amateurs. Benbow was guilty of this weakness, and his manner combined with the favour shown to him by someone of Herbert's stamp must have told against him in many decent men's minds. Among those he most despised, it must have kindled actual hatred.

> *So John was a sailor and lived merrily,*
> *A-hunting the Frenchman all over the sea,*
> *He caught twelve black pirates a-raiding the main,*
> *And had their heads pickled and sold them to Spain.*

Herbert gave him a command, and he distinguished himself in a minor way in a couple of Mediterranean engagements against Algerian pirates. But his ship was then paid off and he found himself back in the Merchant Service, this time as master and part owner of a frigate in the Levant trade. It was during this time that there is said to have occurred one of the most famous incidents associated with his name. His ship, the *Benbow*, was attacked and boarded by a Sallee rover. The native pirates swarmed everywhere, fighting with their usual ferocity, but Benbow's men stood firm and drove them off. Thirteen native corpses lay in their blood on his deck. He ordered their heads to be sliced off and tossed into a tub of pork-pickle and the bodies thrown over the side. This was no mere gesture of contempt. Pirates' heads were worth money, if produced to the Spanish authorities, and Benbow was making for Cadiz.

As they entered the port he ordered his negro servant to decant the pickled heads into a sack, throw it over his shoulder and follow his master ashore. As the two men stepped on land, revenue officers came up, asking to know what was in the sack. Benbow, not a man to tolerate petty officialdom, refused to tell them. Still polite, they insisted upon knowing. Provisions, he grudgingly admitted. Might they take a look, just to make sure? This was too much for the fiery Englishman who bellowed that he was hanged if he was going to have his word questioned in a port where he was so well known. Very well, replied the customs officers, who evidently knew their man: he could complain to the magistrates who happened just then to be in session in a building nearby. If they would take his word, then there would be nothing more to say.

Benbow must have known what was coming and we can imagine his wink to his man Caesar as they were shown into the court-room. The matter was explained to the magistrates who in their turn courteously asked for the sack to be opened. Benbow still pretended reluctance and indignation, until, having been assured that there was no question of victimization, and that even the highest Spanish nobleman would have to submit to customs examination, he allowed himself to be persuaded. Turning with a sigh to his servant, he ordered his "salt provisions" to be turned out on to the table, adding that if the magistrates wanted them they could keep them.

When the Spaniards had got over their astonishment and horror at the sight of thirteen pickled human heads, they abandoned the dignity of the court and crowded round Benbow, congratulating him on being a jolly fellow and hero enough to have overcome so many Moorish marauders. The story, which even if not true is not uncharacteristic of Benbow, goes on to say that the magistrates reported the affair to the King of Spain, who invited Benbow to court to tell him about the adventure in his own words. (It is not recorded whether he was required to take the heads along.) The king wrote to James II of England, singing Benbow's praises and recommending him as a fitting leader of men, and thus it was that Benbow was invited to rejoin the Royal Navy with every implied prospect of rapid promotion.

So more and more famous John Benbow he grew;
They made him a captain, and admiral too;
In battle and tempest for years he was tossed,
Yet never a battle he fought but he lost.

Whatever the truth of this, he certainly got on quickly – from Third Lieutenant to Captain in four months. A few months later he was Master of Chatham Dockyard; a little later Master of Deptford Dockyard; and, within a few more weeks, Master of the Fleet at the Battle of Beachy Head, in 1690, when his admiral was his old soul-mate, Philip Herbert, now Earl of Torrington.

The battle was not the Royal Navy's brightest encounter, the superior French force driving the Anglo-Dutch warships all the way back to the Thames, where they hastily took refuge and pulled up the buoys after them to prevent being followed and burned where they lay. Torrington was peremptorily dismissed the Service and imprisoned in the Tower of London, but was soon court-martialled and acquitted, partly, without doubt, because of Benbow's evidence on his behalf. The trial had a partial echo a few years later, though. Torrington's defence was that he had chosen to run from the French rather than fight them because "most men were in fear that the French would invade; but I was always of another opinion, for I always said that, whilst we had a fleet in being, they would not dare to make an attempt." Something of this philosophy, though less artfully expressed, can be detected in the defence offered by Benbow's "cowardly captains" after the disgrace of August, 1702.

Benbow emerged from the Beachy Head disgrace without a stain on his record. By now he was becoming a popular figure, termed "the famous Captain Benbow" in print, and generally admired as the very model of an outspoken sea-dog. That his name and fame, such as it was, have endured at all is perhaps due more to the colour of his personality and the quality of his courage than to his actual deeds. He won no outstanding battles. He went on to play his part at the Battle of Barfleur and in sorties against French ports before being sent to the West Indies as Rear-Admiral in command of a squadron charged with defending British interests and hounding down such piratical embarrassments as Captain Kidd. He acquired more enemies on his own side during this time by throwing his

weight about unnecessarily, insulting officials, pressing crew
members – regulations did not permit this in colonial ports –
and seeming to care more for the welfare and health of his
sailors who were dying like flies than for the feelings of officials
and his own senior officers.

There was no little relief felt when he was ordered home in
1700 and no less dismay when he returned to the West Indies
the following year. He soon began pressing men into his ships
despite the commands, protests and pleas of the islands' admi-
nistrators. "Necessity has no law," he replied gruffly when
taxed about it by the Secretary to the Admiralty.

The war over the Spanish succession at last broke out in
May, 1702, and it was not long before news reached Benbow
that a small French naval force was approaching the West
Indies under the command of an enterprising admiral named
Ducasse, a man of courage, eager to rid the Caribbean of all
interests other than French. On this occasion, however,
Ducasse was not looking for a fight. He was escorting three
transports carrying troops to garrison Cartagene, the French-
owned Colombian port and city which was to be used as a war
base, and was only thinking about getting them there safely
when on 19 August he ran into Benbow. Ducasse was not far
from his destination, and Benbow wasted no time. It was one
o'clock in the afternoon, with plenty of daylight left. Within a
few minutes his flagship, the *Breda*, 70 guns, was flying the
signal to attack. And now began six days of frustration and
humiliation for Benbow, and of disgrace for England.

> *His captains were cravens and would not obey;*
> *He swore, and they swore, and Du Casse got away.*
> *A cannon-ball knocked off his leg with a bump –*
> *John merely said " – " and fought on with the stump.*

In order to form line of battle as laid down in the fighting
instructions which commanders were strictly bound to obey,
Benbow had to wait for his other ships to come up from several
miles astern. To his surprise (or perhaps he was not altogether
surprised: it is part of the mystery) several of his captains
showed no haste to comply. It took all of three hours for the
line to form and bear down on Ducasse's reluctant little fleet.
Then, after the exchange of a few broadsides, the Admiral
found himself and one other ship, the *Ruby* of 48 guns, left
alone in the combat. The rest had either turned away or

simply kept their distance, making no effort to close with the enemy.

It was the same next day, *Breda* and *Ruby* doing all the chasing and firing, the others standing several miles off, ignoring every order to come into line and fight. By the following day *Ruby* was showing the effects of the close-quarters action and, her rigging in tatters, had to be towed out of range of the French guns by *Breda*'s boats. She was too badly damaged to rejoin the action and was ordered back to Jamaica. Yet still the other Enlish ships, fresh and unharmed, looked on and did nothing.

On the fourth day Benbow received the welcome support of one of the waverers, *Falmouth*, 48 guns, whose captain sent his lieutenant to the flagship to ask whether he might leave his station in the line and assist, a doubly significant question as would later transpire. Benbow accepted, and what had been the *Breda*'s and the *Ruby*'s fight now became the *Breda*'s and the *Falmouth*'s, the remaining ships confining themselves to quick tip-and-run sorties, coming close enough to fire an occasional token broadside, then retiring again to a safe distance for the rest of the day.

After five days of this remarkable exhibition which astonished the French and disgusted Ducasse – as he later made plain in a letter to Benbow quoted at the beginning of this chapter – Benbow scored what seemed to be a tangible success, taking the *Anne*, a former English ship, and so battering the rearmost ship in the French line during the night that it seemed certain she would become an English prize by daylight. But before then Benbow had suffered the wound which the song records.

The leg was shattered, not severed, but the pain he suffered was none the less for that. Yet, refusing to be kept below, he ordered his cot to be brought up to the quarter-deck and himself placed in it so that he could continue to watch the enemy and direct the battle. He had the added humiliation of watching the French ships coolly cluster round their damaged countryman and tow it away, while the English ships let them get on with it virtually unmolested. Roused to fury, Benbow sent a message by hand to his captains, ordering them to behave "like Englishmen". Far from having the effect he hoped for, it brought on board the flagship one of them, Richard Kirby (or Kirkby) of the *Defiance*, 64 guns, to protest that any further attempt to engage the French would be disastrous for the English ships which did not possess the strength to over-come such dangerous opposition.

This rejoinder must have come near to finishing Benbow off, agonized as he was from his wound and mortified by what he had witnessed during the past six days. He straightway called his other captains aboard the flagship for consultation, only to see, to his added chagrin, Kirby produce a document which every captain signed, even including Vincent, who had fought his *Falmouth* resolutely, and Fogg, captain of Benbow's own flagship. The paper ran:

> At a consultation held on board her Ma[tys.] ship *Bredah*, 24 August 1702, off Cartagena on the Maine Continent of America, it is the opinion of us, who's names are undermention'd, vizt:
>
> First – Of the great want of men, in Number, Quality and the Weakness of those they have.
>
> 2ly – The Generall want of Ammunition of most Sorts.
>
> 3ly – Each Ships Masts, Yards, Sailes, Rigging and Guns being all in a great measure disabled.
>
> 4ly – The Winds are so small and variable that the Ships cannot be Governed by any Strength each Ship has.
>
> 5thly – Having experienced the Enemyes force in Six dayes Battle following. The Squadron consisting of Five Men of Warr and a Fireship under the Command of Moun:[r] du Cass, their Equipage consisting in Gunns from Sixty to Eighty and having a great Number of Seamen and Soldiers on board for the Service of Spaine.

For which reasons abovementioned Wee think it not fitt to Ingage the Enemye at this time; but to keep them Company this night and ob-serve their motion, and if a fair oppertunity shall happen (of Wind and Weather) once more to trye our Strength with them

> Richard Kirkby
> Sam:[ell] Vincent
> John Constable
> Chr. ffogge
> Coop:[r] Wade
> Thos:[s] Hudson

At best, it was an echo of Torrington's defence, based on the value of a "Fleet in Being" – or, if one prefers it in rhyme, of Goldsmith's

> *For he who fights and runs away*
> *May live to fight another day;*
> *But he who is in battle slain*
> *Can never rise and fight again.*

"THOSE COWARDLY CAPTAINS" 453

a sentiment which, we can rejoice, has held no appeal for the
majority of those who have served in our Navy down its history.

At worst the declaration was an admission of cowardice, for
it was simply not true that the French force was stronger than
the English or that the English had suffered the greater
damage and, in any case, the captains' reluctance to fight
dated from the very outset of the engagement, before a single
shot had been fired at them.

Benbow warned them that the paper would spell their ruin.
They disregarded the threat. Faced with their determination
to fight no more, he was compelled to break off contact with
the enemy and turn away towards Jamaica.

Benbow's leg was amputated soon after his arrival in
Jamaica. After several weeks' suffering, during which he nearly
died of fever, he was thought strong enough for a court martial
to be convened to try five of his captains for their conduct.
They were Kirby and Wade, accused of cowardice and other
crimes; Constable, charged with breach of orders and neglect
of duty; and Vincent and Fogg, who, though they had done
their duty, had nevertheless signed the paper advocating the
abandonment of the action and had to answer for it. The only
captains not tried were Walton, who had fought his *Ruby* so
bravely and had retired to Jamaica before the incident of the
paper, and Hudson of the *Pendennis* who had signed, but had
died from an illness after returning to port.

Public feeling ran high at the trial, and, for all his unpopularity in the islands, Benbow had everyone's sympathy, so
markedly did his personal conduct and courage contrast with
the apparent cowardice of his captains.

To a packed court-room, Kirby seemed to be almost off his
head. His defence, though insistent, was confused, at times
almost hysterical, and his witnesses were unconvincing. The
one argument by which he might have persuaded the court
that there were some grounds for the action to be broken off as
he had urged, that is, the lack of a fair wind, was demolished
quite simply by Benbow who showed that no more favourable
conditions could ever have obtained:

"for we then had the wether gage, a fine gale of wind, six ships to
four, and one of them quite disabled, all our ships in as good a
posture for fighting as could be expected and not 8 men killed in all
our ships (except the *Bredah*) and to defer this to a fitter opper-

tunity to the Adm:[ll] seemed a perfect deniall who having seen the
cowardly behaviour of some of them before had reason to believe
that either they had a designe against him, or to be traytors to their
country if an oppertunity happen'd that the French could have
destroyed the Admirall."

Evidence was also brought that Kirby had behaved with
personal cowardice during the action, ducking into cover whenever a shot was heard. He was found guilty and sentenced to
death by shooting. The same verdict and sentence were passed
on Wade who was shown to have kept his *Greenwich* deliberately out of range, but had fired from time to time with the
remark that the Admiral must be led to believe that he was in
the fight.

Constable, who was said by some witnesses to have been
drunk while the action was on and had made no effort to
engage, was dismissed the Service. Fogg and Vincent, on both
of whose behalf Benbow testified, declared that they had
signed Kirby's paper only because they suspected some form of
treachery by their colleagues which would lead to the capture
or destruction of the English ships if the action were not
broken off. They were found guilty of signing, but were not
punished.

The mystery of the Benbow affair lies in the motives of
Kirby, Wade, and perhaps one or two others. Either they were
cowards or they acted as they did out of personal spite against
their Admiral: in which case they must surely have realized
that they were running their heads into a noose. Benbow seems
to have been convinced that they held a grudge against him or
hoped he might be killed so that they could surrender their
ships. It is known that he had had trouble with them earlier
and had not spared his language, yet it seems incredible that
naval officers, in time of war especially, should hazard their
ships, their country's honour, and their own lives simply to pay
a man back for an insult.

The answer to the enigma, which no one has ever found for
certain, may lie in the difference between "tarpaulin" and
"gentleman". Benbow had heaped abuse on his inferiors in
rank and superiors by birth. They sailed burning with resentment, and found in this an excuse for indulging their natural
cowardice. That Kirby at least was a superior sort of being
there is little doubt. Someone approached Queen Anne on his,

Wade's and Constable's behalf, but she coldly refused to inter-
fere with their sentences.

Kirby and Wade were shot on board H.M.S. *Bristol* at Plymouth on 16 April, 1703. But they outlived the man they had
set out to ruin. He had died on 4 November of the previous
year, only three weeks after the court martial of the cowardly
captains had immortalized his name.

> *So here's to John Benbow, who loved the salt sea,*
> *Was never a seadog more merry than he.*
> *So gallantly fought he, so roundly he swore,*
> *The like of John Benbow we'll never see more.*

THE HORSE THAT SWAM TO THE GRAND NATIONAL

There are many ways of getting a horse to a race: road, rail, air. Moifaa was different. His celebrated sire had been Natator, which means swimmer. Appropriately, Moifaa "swam" to the Grand National – and won it!

He was born in Hawke's Bay, New Zealand, in 1895, out of the mare Denbigh, winner in her day of the Hawke's Bay and Wellington Steeplechases, by Natator, who also sired the Grand National winners Waterbury and Gobo. As he watched the offspring develop, Denbigh's owner and former rider, Mr W. Ellingham, must have wondered what on earth he had bred. Moifaa wore an almost perpetual sneer, as if to say, "I'll show you just how ugly a horse can become."

He grew and grew until he measured seventeen hands. His shoulders and quarters were burly, his legs long and rough, with clodhopping hooves. Where his vast frame did not bulge out it narrowed inordinately, to show his bones. When the English owner Lord Marcus Beresford first saw him he termed him "a starved elephant; the ugliest devil you ever saw". Moifaa merely sneered. It was his destiny to alter his lordship's opinion dramatically.

Mr Ellingham raced him to his first win in a hack race at Waipawa. Then he won a similar class event at Napier Park. He came to wider notice by beating an open field at a Hawke's Bay summer meeting, and then another. He pulled off a double at the Wanganui Cup meeting. Despite all appearances, Moifaa began to be canvassed as a possibility for the Grand National.

A connoisseur of horseflesh named Spencer Gollan put his money where his opinion was, bought the ungainly animal, and took him into his own notable racing stables. Gollan, an all-round athlete who had been a Diamond Sculls winner at Henley, recognized the developing power in those massively-muscled limbs. He decided to ship the animal to England without delay and work him up for the coveted National.

Most of the voyage are uneventful, with Moifaa carefully protected from the more violent motions of the ship. Liverpool had almost been reached when, one cold grey morning, there whipped up one of those storms which the Irish Sea can produce without warning. The ship was quickly engulfed. It was soon obvious that she must sink. The boats were run out and the crew prepared to enter them. Then someone remembered Moifaa.

There was no question of getting him into a boat; they were tossing too violently for that, and the ship was going fast. At least, though, he shouldn't be left to drown imprisoned. They released him from his stall and left him free on deck. As they rowed desperately away they glimpsed him standing there, seeming to be sneering defiance at the sea whose level was rising swiftly to the level of those great shoulders. His expression seemed to defy death . . .

Another vessel caught by that storm was a small fishing boat, manned by a few Englishmen. They succeeded in riding it out. When it had subsided almost as quickly as it had arisen, they went on their way towards a tiny, uninhabited island near the coast of England where they would fish the shallows by casting their nets from its shore.

They had no sooner done this than they lifted their heads to stare at one another. Nearby, on that island which they knew to be deserted, a horse had whinneyed.

Along the shingle they went, until they found Moifaa, exhausted but uninjured. The combination of power and courage which made up for all that he lacked in appearance and grace had enabled him somehow to swim to that tiny hump of land and scramble ashore. Even then, he would certainly have died of exposure and hunger if those fishermen had not come there.

They got a rope round his neck and, with difficulty, coaxed

him into their little boat. They drew in their nets and made for home, abandoning conventional fishing in favour of the queerest catch of all time.

Inevitably, their return caused a sensation, which quickly reached the ears of a local newspaper reporter. He sent off a bizarre-sounding story to the national Press about the incident. Who the horse was, and how he had come to be on that island at all, he couldn't even guess. Spencer Gollan knew, though. As soon as he read the report, with its mention of the animal's massive size, he knew that a seeming miracle had happened. He hastened to claim the nine-year-old survivor from the sea as his property, expressing his hope that Moifaa's ability to run had not been affected by his ordeal.

It seemed, however, that this might have happened. When Moifaa was fit again to race he failed in three successive steeple-chases. Experts who watched him gave him credit for his courage, and acknowledged his New Zealand achievements, but prophesied unanimously that he would never succeed in England, where fences were higher and could not be got over by a mount so big and clumsy-looking.

With his lips drawn back in that challenging smirk of his, Moifaa went out for a practice run over the Grand National course at Aintree. He soared over every fence with little apparent effort. Lord Beresford admitted how wrong he had been about him: "Moifa is a great machine at high pressure over fences," he declared. Even this praise was not enough to gain him high favour for the 1904 Grand National. An unimpressive outing at Sandown just previously had seen him finish in fourth place. The bookies at the National rated him 25–1, and took a lot of money from punters willing to gamble on the unexpected. The favourite, King Edward VII's Ambush II, was at 7–2.

The King was there with Lord Derby to watch the line-up. Moifaa was carrying only 10 st 7 lb, compared with the 12 st on the veteran Manifesto, who had run in the National seven times and won it twice. Even so, the bookies smiled. That awkward nag would never make it.

Their belief seemed confirmed from the very start of the race. With his jockey, Birch, helpless to do anything but stay on his back, Moifaa catapulted into the lead. The only question seemed to be whether he would come down at a jump or drop back exhausted after so reckless an early dash. Yet, at the end of the first circuit of the $4\frac{1}{2}$-mile course, he was still in front, not having been passed even momentarily.

Kirkland managed at last to draw level, but could not get ahead. Ambush II hit the top rail of a fence. Benvenir broke down lame. Detail was knocked over; Loch Lomond killed. Patlander, Inquisitor, Comfit, The Pride of Mabestown, Kiora, Knight of St Patrick and Deerslayer all fell. Only nine horses out of twenty-six finished – and Moifaa was the first of them, by eight lengths from Kirkland, followed by a neck by The Gunner.

King Edward made a bid for Moifaa on the spot, and soon became his new owner. The odds at next year's National were narrowed to 4–1.

But Moifaa was now ten years old. His wind was no longer up to sustaining his great weight over that most punishing course. As the second circuit began he was beginning to flag. He cleared two more fences. Then came the notorious Beecher's Brook, at which many younger, more agile horses have come to grief. Full of courage still, the old boy sneered and rose. He could not get high enough. He hit, and crashed to the ground, leaving Kirkland, whom he had beaten the year before, to go on to win. Moifaa's career, even more remarkable off the race-course than on it, was ended, and he was led off into retirement.

There is another, earlier, recorded instance of a fishing-boat "catching" a horse. It happened in the 1850s, in the Florida Strait of Miami.

The fishermen had crossed from a group of islands named the Biminis to another one, Great Isaac, for a day's trawling. They were packing up for the day when they, too, heard a horse whinneying. They found a pure white stallion, apparently terrified, staggering about the beach. Even before they could reach it it collapsed, writhed, then lay still. They found it dead, its neck broken.

Further along the beach, at a place previously out of their sight, they came upon the wreckage of a four-masted ship. The disaster must have been very recent; bodies floated in the sea and lay sprawled on shore. In the arms of one, a young woman, the incredulous fishermen found a baby still breathing. They threw up a rough stone enclosure round the body before taking the child away with them. When they returned next day, intending to bury the mother, her body was gone, swept away by the night's high tide.

This was a time when the Victorian lighthouse, one of the attractions of the 1851 Great Exhibition in London, was being re-erected on Great Isaac for the more practical service of guiding shipping in the Florida Straits. Several times, the men doing this work saw the figure of a young woman wandering forlornly on Great Isaac's shore, as if looking for something. More than half a century later, in 1913, a lighthouse man met her on the spiral staircase. So did his successor in the post, who contrived a form of exorcism. The distraught young mother has never been reported seen since.

At least one more sea mystery involves land animals. In 1911 the steamer *Tottenham* was wrecked on a reef off the island of Juan de Nova in the Mozambique Channel. Her crew got safely ashore, to be met by a silent reception committee – of dogs.

They were of all sorts and sizes and colours, brown, yellow, white, black. The only things they had in common was that none of them uttered a single bark, and every one's tail hung motionless between its legs. A shot was fired in the air by one seaman. The dogs silently turned and fled. They were heard whining in the night, but never seen again.

BIBLIOGRAPHY

DISAPPEARANCES
Famous Mysteries of the Sea,
                    Bryan Breed, Arthur Barker, 1965
Frogman Extraordinary,
                    J. B. Hutton, Spearman, 1960
The World's Most Intriguing Mysteries,
                    Rupert Furneaux, Odhams, 1965
The Strange Voyage of Donald Crowhurst,
                    Nicholas Tomalin and Ron Hall,
                    Hodder and Stoughton, 1970
When Ships Go Down,
                    David Masters,
                    Eyre and Spottiswoode, 1964
Peter Freuchen's Book of the Seven Seas,
                    Cape, 1958
Ships that Did not Return,
                    Robert de la Croix,
                    Frederick Muller, 1959
Mysteries of the Sea,
                    Robert de la Croix,
                    Frederick Muller, 1956
Last Voyage,
                    Warren Armstrong, Frederick
                    Muller, 1956
Mysteries of the North Pole,
                    Robert de la Croix,
                    Frederick Muller, 1954
The Book of Polar Exploration,
                    E. L. Elias, Harrap, 1928

DERELICTS
The Joyita Mystery,
                    Robin Maugham, Parrish, 1962
Famous Mysteries of the Sea,
                    Bryan Breed, Arthur Barker, 1965

Mary Celeste,
                    Macdonald Hastings, Michael
                    Joseph, 1972
What Happened on the Mary Celeste,
                    Robert Furneaux, Parrish, 1964

SUNKEN AND BURIED TREASURE
  Sunken Treasure, Latil and Rivoire,
                    Rupert Hart Davis, 1962
  Treasures of the Armada,
                    Robert Sténuit,
                    David and Charles, 1972
  Pieces of Eight,
                    Kip Wagner and L. B. Taylor Jr.,
                    Longmans, 1967
  Full Fathom Five,
                    Colin Martin,
                    Chatto and Windus, 1975
  The Treasure Diver's Guide,
                    John S. Potter, Robert Hale, 1973
  Far From Humdrum,
                    Sir William Charles Crocker,
                    Hutchinson, 1967
  The Egypt's Gold,
                    David Scott, Faber and Faber, 1933
  Diving for Treasure,
                    Peter Throckmorton,
                    Thames and Hudson, 1977

MONSTERS
  Ancient Mysteries,
                    Peter Haining,
                    Sidgwick and Jackson, 1977
  The Leviathans,
                    Tim Dinsdale, Futura Books, 1976
  In Search of Lake Monsters,
                    Peter Costello,
                    Panther Books, 1975
  "The Missing Link",
                    Ivan T. Sanderson,
                    Argosy Magazine, May, 1969

SPECTRES OF THE SEA
Their Secret Purposes,
Hector C. Bywater, Constable, 1932
Admirals in Collision,
Richard Hough,
Hamish Hamilton, 1959
Famous Mysteries of the Sea,
Bryan Breed, Arthur Barker, 1965
The Phanton Ship,
Robert L. Hadfield, Bles, 1937

RECOVERED FROM THE DEEP
The Raising of the Vasa,
Roy Saunders, Oldbourne, 1962
Vasa, the King's Ship,
Bengt Ohrelius, Cassell, 1962
The Warship Vasa,
Anders Franzen, Norstedt and
Soners Forlag, Stockholm
A History of Sweden,
Ingvar Anderson, Weidenfeld, 1955

LOST CONTINENTS
Atlantis and the Lost Lands,
Roy Stenman, Aldus Books, 1976
Voyage to Atlantis,
James W. Mavor, Jr.,
Souvenir Press, 1969
Mysteries of Time and Space,
Brad Steiger, Sphere Books, 1977
Without a Trace,
Charles Berlitz,
Souvenir Press, 1977
The Lost Continent of Mu,
James Churchward,
Futura Publications, 1974
Can you Speak Venusian?
Patrick Moore, Star Books, 1976
Citadels of Mystery,
L. Sprague de Camp and
Catherine C. de Camp, Fontana,
1974

Ancient Mysteries,

Peter Haining,
Sidgwick and Jackson, 1977

ACCIDENT OR SABOTAGE?
They Called it Accident,

A. Cecil Hampshire, Kimber, 1961
Strange Mysteries of the Sea,

Len Ortzen, Arthur Barker, 1976

DEADLY EFFECTS?
The Bermuda Triangle,

Charles Berlitz,
Souvenir Press, 1975
Without a Trace,

Charles Berlitz,
Souvenir Press, 1977
The Bermuda Triangle Mystery Solved,

Lawrence David Kusche,
New English Library, 1975
Mysteries of Time and Space,

Brad Steiger, Sphere Books, 1977
Ancient Mysteries,

Peter Haining,
Sidgwick and Jackson, 1977

MISCELLANY
The Great Bombay Explosion,

John Ennis,
Duell, Sloane and Pearce, 1959
Aku-Aku,

Thor Heyerdahl,
Allen and Unwin, 1958
The True Story of the Grosvenor East Indiaman,

Percival R. Kirby, O.U.P., 1960
Drake,

Ernle Bradford,
Hodder and Stoughton, 1965
The Sea,

F. Whymper, Cassell c. 1885
The Brendan Voyage,

Tim Severin, Hutchinson, 1978
Of Ships and Men,

Alan Villiers, Newnes, 1962

Index